I0588876

The United States of America

Dear Reader: This story takes place in Central California – shown by the small box below on the map of the United States – from the Napa Valley in the north, to the Monterey Penninsula in the south, where I go to boarding school.

This area of California contains some of the most beautiful countryside in America – from San Francisco, to the magically beautiful Napa Valley, to the Monterey Pennisula to the south. It is about 175 miles from Pebble Beach (the location of my boarding school) to St. Helena. From Twin Oaks Pony Farm in Rutherford to Grandma Hattie's house in San Francisco is 62 miles and takes a little over an hour by car. The ferry boat from Vallejo to the Ferry Building in San Francisco only takes an hour.

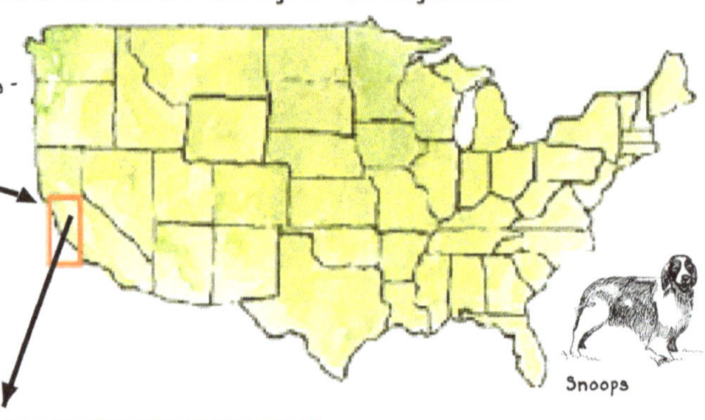

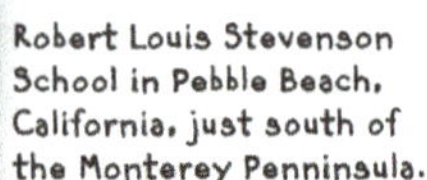

Snoops

Central California

Grandma Hattie's San Francisco house.

View of San Francisco Bay from Grandma Hattie's house in Pacific Heights, San Francisco.

Robert Louis Stevenson School campus.

At the southernmost end of the Napa Valley, the city of Napa is the county seat and has a population of nearly 80,000 people. Heading north, the towns and cities are much smaller: Yountville has 2933 residents, Oakville has only 71, Rutherford 164, St. Helena 5814, and Calistoga, 5155. The valley has always been primarily agricultural. In 1967, the year this story takes place, the main crops were walnuts, grapes, prunes, and cattle. Today, the valley is devoted almost exclusively to the growing of grapes and wine-making and is a very popular tourist destination. The climate is considered to be "Meditteranean," which means summers are warm and dry and winters are wet and mild. On rare years, the summit of Mt. St. Helena is dusted with snow. Visitors to the Valley are often surprised at how dry and golden the foothills are in the summer and how green they are in the winter. It is considered by many to be one of the most beautiful small valleys in the world.

Robert Louis Stevenson School in Pebble Beach, California, just south of the Monterey Penninsula.

The Napa Valley

The Napa Valley is a small valley in Northern California. It is only 30 miles long and from one to five miles wide. Mt. St. Helena lies at the northernmost end of the valley and, at 4,344 feet, is the second tallest mountain in the Bay Area. The famous Scottish author, Robert Louis Stevenson (author of *Treasure Island*, *Kidnapped*, and *The Strange Case of Dr. Jekyll and Mr. Hyde*), spent the summer of 1880 in an abandoned silver mine, along with his new wife, Fanny Osbourne, on the side of Mt. St. Helena. The site is now Robert Louis Stevenson State Park.

Mt. St. Helena at sunset.

The sign on Highway 29, near the top of Mt. St. Helena, showing the location of Robert Louis Stevenson State Park.

Robert Louis Stevenson

Bothe State Park

St. Helena Library

The winery

My 10-speed bicycle

Grandma Hattie's Summer House

Twin Oaks Pony Farm

Napa County Sheriff's Department

Quicksilver

The
Silverado Trail

The
Silverado Trail

Written and Illustrated by
A. Cort Sinnes

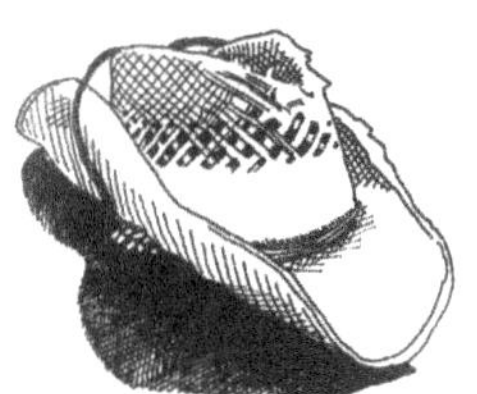

For Nels, my Finnish sea captain grandfather,
who gave me his ship's log with the mysterious missing page and
excited this grandson's imagination for a lifetime

Preface

Many of the places and events in this book are real: Napa Valley, California is one of the most important wine-producing regions in the world (and some say one of the most beautiful small valleys to be found anywhere). There really is a school, located in the California coastal town of Pebble Beach, named after the great Scottish writer Robert Louis Stevenson. Stevenson himself spent part of the summer of 1880 on the slopes of Mount St. Helena, living in an abandoned mining camp named Silverado. And Gustave Niebaum, a Finnish sea captain did, indeed, found a famous winery in the heart of the Napa Valley in 1879. The theft that starts Nick Sinclair on his search actually happened the year I started writing this book. As to the thieves—well, they too are well documented—although not everyone will care to believe the information that comes to light in this book. As for me, I believe it all.

A.C. S.
Napa 2021

Table of Contents

Prologue

Sunday, August 11, 1958
Somewhere on—or more precisely, in—Mt. St. Helena
Calistoga, California

Outside the king's private chambers it was just getting dark, signaling the beginning of another day. As the fog of sleep lifted, King Gob remembered he had been working on a problem when he went to bed a few hours ago. Normally he liked working on solutions to problems – he *was* king, after all, and he considered it his duty to come up with solutions and and then telling his men how to put them into action. This problem, however, was getting the best of him. As hard as he tried, he kept coming back to the same solution, namely "get Dagywn to solve it – when in fact, Dagywn *was* the problem. It hurt King Gob's head trying to understand how something could be both the solution *and* the problem at the same time.

It had all started 79 years ago, when the king and seventeen of his men had stowed away on Capt. Niebaum's schooner – the sailing ship *St. Peter* – surreptitiously boarding it while it was anchored in Helsinki, Finland. After calling on ports in Portugal, Mauritania, and Sumatra, there was a very long, uninterrupted leg of the journey from New South Wales, Australia to the small port of Nawiliwili, Kauai in the Hawaiian Islands. That leg of the voyage was not only long – over 60 days – but it was marked by bad weather and rough seas, resulting in near constant seasickness for some of king's men. Discontent ran so high that five of the sickest men simply couldn't take any more and jumped ship, disappearing into the dense Kauaiian jungle. One of the five escapees was arguably the most important member of the tribe (other than the king, of course), namely Dagywn the Wizard, Possessor of All Magic.

The king may not have been able to come up with a solution to his probem – *yet* – but he was almost certain whatever it eventually was would require help from the Uplanders – the humans – and that irked him. The king had an instinctual dislike of going outside his tribe for anything. From his experience, the Uplanders were, were unpredictable, unreliable, unimaginative and largely unintelligble. But because of the amulet King Gob had given Captain Niebaum – and the friendship and trust it signified – he knew for certain that the Uplander who would ultimately help solve his problem would have to be someone with a direct link to Capt. Niebaum. And as far as the king was able to determine, there were only four of them left – a number that was about to be reduced dramatically.

The king was still lying in bed, pondering his options when a crow fluttered onto his windowsill and began to chatter excitedly. According to the crow (and crows were notoriously accurate in what they reported), Witbeck, his chamberlain, and the king's son, Prince G were, just moments ago, exploring the east side of the mountain. Witbeck was supposed to be keeping his eye on the prince – who at 130 years old was just a youngster – but Witbeck lost track of him. It seemed that the prince had caught sight of a young buck deer and decided to chase it. The next thing the crow heard was a loud crash and the prince whistling frantically for Witbeck somewhere off in the distance.

The crow continued, saying Witbeck followed the sound of the whistle and found the prince on a rise overlooking the road that ran over the mountain. The prince was wide-eyed, pointing to the wreck of an automobile and a bleeding deer lying in front of it. Witbeck went to the automobile and quickly determined that the older woman and man were dead, along with the older boy child. The younger boy child in the back seat of the automobile was still alive, but barely. Witbeck instructed Prince G to use his special powers of levitation to lift the young boy out and transport him to the side of the road, placing him on a thick bed of leaves. It wasn't long before another vehicle approached, this one with flashing red lights and a bunch of adult humans dressed in white. The crow saw the humans in white gather the boy child up and put him in the back of the vehicle with the flashing lights. In an instant, they were gone.

"And?" the king asked, dreading what he was about to hear.

"The dead family is the one you've been having us watch."

"No!" the king said, angrily. "It's not possible."

"Prince G frightened the deer straight into the path of the oncoming car," the crow said. "It was very much possible. It happened. Do you want me to dive-bomb the prince? Peck his ears til they bleed? Crap on his head?"

"No. But if he were here right now I'd… I don't know what I'd do," the king said sadly. "What a disaster. Off with you, Crow. I need to be alone."

With that the crow flew away, cawing heartily as he went, spreading the bad news.

"So now it comes down to just one," the king thought, shaking his head. "You're it, young Nick, you're it."

The studio-workshop at Grandpa Nick's house. He usually paints while I figure out how to use his tools. Grandpa took this photograph.

Chapter I

The Story Begins (Again)

August 2014
Rutherford, California

"How was your day?"

Talk about a lame question... I wanted to take it back the minute I asked it.

But not such a lame answer.

"Interesting."

"Like how?"

"Darren said someone stole a barrel of wine from his father's winery last night."

"Really?"

"Yeah. And he said they found a leather pouch filled with gold nuggets on the floor where the barrel used to be."

That got my attention. I laid down the paintbrush I was using and looked directly at my 14-year-old grandson, Joaquin.

"*What?*" I said with more alarm than I intended.

The tone of my voice made Joaquin look up from the two wires he was in the process of soldering.

"Yeah. I even saw it. Darren got his dad to show it to me. It was a lot of gold."

"They always did overpay for things," I said more to myself than out loud, the words echoing across time.

"What did you say?" Joaquin asked.

"Nothing." But it was hardly nothing. I couldn't believe it had started again.

To this day I'm not exactly sure why I did what I did next: I motioned to Joaquin to follow me. We left the old barn that now served as a combination workshop/studio, and walked across the lawn to the main house. We climbed up the three flights of stairs to the top floor and pulled down the ladder from the hatch in the hall ceiling and climbed up into the dusky, dusty attic. There was a lot of stuff stored up there – generations of stuff, but I made my way straight to the shelf built next to the chimney that held what I was looking for.

I found a rag and wiped off most of the dust that covered a small travel trunk, about the size of a large toolbox. I had just turned 62 years old; I hadn't looked inside the trunk since I put the last journal in there when I was 18 years old. There were three journals in all, one for each of those summers – 1967, 1968 and 1969. Forty-four years is a long time, but still… that I was breaking a promise was not lost on me. What was I doing? I looked at Joaquin. His face was a big question mark.

I took the trunk over to a table and opened it. The three, nearly identical journals were still there just where I had put them so long ago, stacked on top of each other, along with several cardboard file folders tied with ribbon, a small, cube-shaped red velvet box, and various envelopes. The first journal (the one from 1967, when it all started) was on the bottom of the stack. I handed it to Joaquin.

"Here. Read this," I said.

"What is it?"

"You'll see."

•　　•　　•

I may not have looked at those journals for some 40-plus years, but the memories they contained were as clear as yesterday. In all truthfulness, I thought about the whole, big, three-year saga they chronicled more often than I cared to admit. It was with a twinge of guilt that I handed the first journal over to Joaquin – I had no idea what might happen because of the broken promise – the promise I made not to have the journals published, or let anyone read them, for 45 years after I had finished writing the last one. I rationalized my decision, thinking Joaquin would be the only one to read the journals and, after all, he *was* my grandson. Surely Prince G would understand – that is, if he ever even found out, which I sincerely doubted he would. And, if what Joaquin had just reported about the missing wine at his friend Darren's place was correct – not to mention the pouch of gold – it looked like another chapter was being added to the story and he should know as much about the situation as possible, right? At least that's what I told myself.

Speaking of the "situation," it had taken me a long time to admit to myself just how clueless I'd been the day that I arrived at Walter and Ma-D's pony farm – June 14th, 1967. Looking back, I can see now how in so many ways, "the game was already afoot," as Sherlock Holmes would say. Little did I know then that Witbeck had already made plans to steal Quicksilver, in an effort to get back into the king's good graces after the infamous "Hummingbird Affair." And I certainly had no way of knowing that that rat-bag Nigel Stayne was already winging his way from London, England to the Napa Valley with the express purpose of making my life miserable. But the weirdest thing of all – which I wasn't able to wrap my head around for the longest time – was that from the time I was five years old, I had been watched… watched by a group of individuals who had their own agenda and for whom I was only a means to an end. Had I been played like a chess piece on a board? I still don't know how I feel about that, but I can say that the whole idea of being watched without my knowing it still creeps me out. For all I know, I'm still being watched.

Chapter II

The First Journal

August 2014
Grandpa Nick's house
Rutherford, California

I was used to Grandpa Nick's unpredictable behavior – he's an artist, after all – but this journal thing was something new. When I pushed him as to what it was I was holding in my hands, he simply said "something I wrote a long time ago."

"What? Like a story?"

"Well, it kind of turned out that way," he said.

"Is it true?"

"Why do you ask?" he replied.

"I'd just like to know what I'm reading – a made-up story or a true story."

"You're going to have to make up your own mind on that one," he said as he headed back down the ladder.

I stayed behind and looked at the book – a good-sized, hardback book, covered in some kind of faded blue fabric, with triangular maroon leather patches on the corners. The word "Journal" was stamped in gold on the spine. It looked old. It even smelled old. I carried it downstairs and went out to the front porch and sat in one of the Adirondack chairs there, overlooking the surrounding vineyards. I opened the journal and here's what I found on the front page:

Private Journal
Stay Out!

Under that, someone, presumably Grandpa Nick, had drawn a hand with its finger pointing directly at me. And under that:

This means you!
An Account of the Fantastic Events of the Summer of 1967

Private Journal

Keep Out !

This means you!

QUICKSILVER

*An Account of the Fantastic Events of
the Summer of 1967*

Written and Illustrated by

Nick Sinclair

It was a little intimidating, that pointing finger.

Right inside the front cover I found a folded map that looked handmade. It was of central California and the Napa Valley, with a lot of photographs glued onto it, with arrows pointing to where the subjects of the photographs were located. I recognized most of the places in the photographs, including the house where I was now sitting, which was identified as "Grandma Hattie's summer house." I knew Grandma Hattie was my great-great-grandmother, but she died long before I was born; other places I didn't recognize. I flipped through the journal and recognized my grandfather's meticulous printing – he still printed that way. It looked like each chapter began with a watercolor illustration, held in place with those little black triangle holders I'd seen in some of our old photo albums. He'd even included small pen-and-ink sketches in his journal entries. Whatever it was I was holding in my hands, my grandfather had put a lot of work into it. I decided not to go to the last page to find out how the story ends (like I usually do), but start from the beginning instead.

Walter and M-D's house at the Pony Farm. Inset: The bunkhouse where I stayed, behind the main house.

Chapter III

Summer 1967 Begins

Saturday, June 24, 1967
The Twin Oaks Pony Farm
St. Helena, California

I arrived at Walter and Ma-D's on June 14th, just ten days ago — the first day of summer vacation — my favorite words in the English language. Ten days? No way that's all it was. Seems more like ten years! I'm back at the farm now after what could only be called a Very Big Adventure — although that doesn't come close to doing it justice. It all just happened and I was a participant every step of the way, but it seems more like a dream than real. Sorry to destroy the suspense of whether or not I made it out alive, but I'm happy to report, I did.

Even though it's not going to be easy getting anyone to believe me, I've got to get this adventure down in my journal while it's still fresh in my mind. I guess I should start with me, seeing as how I'm the one telling the story, right? My name is Nick Sinclair. I'm 14 years old, and I just finished my first year of boarding school at the Robert Louis Stevenson School in Pebble Beach, California, about 200 miles south of where I am now, in the Napa Valley. More specifically, I'm at the Twin Oaks Pony Farm, run by Walter and Mary Dobson — who everyone calls Ma-D. I've lived with Walter and Ma-D for almost ten years, ever since my mother and father and older brother were killed in a car accident on Mt. St. Helena. I was in the accident too, but somehow got thrown from the car and survived, more or less intact. Sometimes more. Sometimes less.

Technically, Grandma Hattie is my legal guardian. From the little I've been able to put together, after the accident Grandma Hattie had a full-on breakdown and was in no shape to take care of a five-year-old like me. That's when she came up with the idea of having Walter and Ma-D — who had never had children of their own — take care of me. I don't remember having much of a say in it one way or the other, but I liked Walter and Ma-D and their pony farm, which specialized in breeding all kinds of ponies and miniature horses. So Doyle, Grandma Hattie's houseman, packed me up from her summer house, just a few miles away from here, and delivered me to Walter and Ma-D's. Years later I would learn that Grandma Hattie "didn't do good-byes." Once I was out of the house, she set off on a world tour which ended up lasting more than three years. It was during this period I knew my grandmother only by her postcards from one exotic locale to the next. Which isn't to say I wasn't happy; I was, sort of. It may have been a strange set-up — made even stranger by the abruptness with which it all happened — but it didn't take long to fall into the daily rhythm and routines of the pony farm and the consistency of having two caring adults watching over me.

There was only one other house on the lane where Walter and Ma-D lived. It belonged to the Martinez family. It was set way back in the vineyards, right next to the Napa River, which flows through the middle of the valley from north to south. This far up the valley, it's more like a big creek than a river, but most summers you can swim in it, just about. The Martinez's had a son, Jesus, who was my age. Jesus and I met when the bus picked us up at the end of the lane on the first day of school when we started kindergarten. We've been best friends ever since. He's known to everyone by his nickname "Chuy," (pronounced "Chewy").

Chuy and I had gone straight through grammar school together in St. Helena, right up through the 6th grade. When it came time to enroll in junior high school, Grandma Hattie realized that Walter and Ma-D weren't getting any younger and that maybe it would be better if I went to boarding school. I wasn't opposed to the idea and, as things turned out, it was a good choice. Robert Louis Stevenson is a really cool school. I like it there a lot.

If I'm going to tell you what's happened in the last ten days, I think I better back up a bit, like right when I got to the pony farm. So here goes. The last time I'd been back to the farm was for spring break in March. Fast forward to June, and it wasn't hard to see the seasons had changed from early spring to early summer. Everything looked different — especially the seemingly endless rows of grapevines with their new, light green foliage. The surrounding foothills had dried out from the winter rains and had turned gold, a color they would wear for the entire summer. The ancient oaks — with their dark-green, shiny new

foliage — looked as fresh as the tall grassy weeds that lined the culverts next to lanes, buzzing and clicking with the sound of insects busy at whatever it is insects do. The whole valley felt very much alive.

After I got my stuff unpacked, I ran down to Chuy's house to at least see him before he left. I didn't tell you, did I? Chuy wasn't going to be around for most of the summer which was going to be weird. He was going to his grandparents' in San Tadeo, Mexico. His grandma and grandpa had a guava grove there and not enough hands to help run it, so Chuy was going down to help them out. He wasn't so sure about the trip to Mexico — his first ever — but said he'd write and let me know how things were going. He'd be back in a couple of months. We figured we'd do an official catch-up then and, boy, did we.

It had only been a few months since I'd seen him, but apparently we both had gone through some kind of growth spurt or something. He seemed okay and had grown about as much as I had, so we're still even on that score. Chuy and I were pretty competitive: he always won anything that involved running, but I was faster on my bike. Chuy usually won at arm wrestling; I usually won at chess. All in all, it sort of evened out.

I followed Chuy to his room where he was finishing packing. His open suitcase was on his bed and it looked like he was trying to put ten pounds of stuff into a five-pound bag. When he tried to close it, the top and the bottom were like six inches apart. I suggested we move it somewhere solid, like the floor, and both sit on and try to latch the latches. That probably would have worked if the suitcase hadn't been so slippery — so much so that we both slid off onto the floor and started laughing hard. Chuy's dad stuck his head in the room, wondering what the commotion was and basically gave us the stink eye — which I took as a sign that it was probably a good time to exit, stage left.

Quicksilver

Walking back to the farm, I tried not to think about what it was going to be like without anyone to hang out with for the next ten weeks. An empty feeling kind of bubbled up and I felt sad — so much so that I had to make myself think about something else — and fast. Those feelings usually only happened when I thought about my mom and dad and brother. I concentrated on the rhythm of my feet hitting the dirt road and I forced myself to think back to a few days ago when my favorite teacher, Mr. Hayes, had taken me and some of my friends out to a farewell dinner at a Chinese restaurant in Santa Cruz, just a few miles up the coast from our school. Aside from the welcome change from dorm food, I received what I felt was a sign that this summer was going to be special somehow. At the end of the dinner the message in my fortune cookie read "A legacy, however obscure, will soon be yours."

"That's a mysterious one," Mr. Hayes remarked after I'd read it out loud. "What do you think it means?"

"I have no idea," I said, "but if it's anything good, I'll let you know when summer's over," I said, tucking the strange fortune safely away in my wallet, completely oblivious to just how accurate it was in describing what was about to happen next — but, honestly, who actually thinks about things like "obscure legacies?"

Snapping back to reality, I told myself to look on the bright side. "Chuy or no Chuy, it was still summer vacation and that's definitely a good thing." It's true that I like school, but I've always loved summer vacations more. And whether or not this summer turned out to be "special," well, I'd just have to wait and see.

.   .   .

There are just a couple of other things you should know about before I start telling you what's happened over the last ten days. One is a little about ponies; the other is to tell you about Henry and Snoops, which I'll get to. If you're like most people, you probably think that a pony is just a young horse, but that's not the whole story. Yes, ponies can be young horses, but there are also all kinds of ponies who stay small (and in some cases, very small) their entire lives. Permanently small ponies are literally a breed apart from full-size horses — most are under 58 inches tall at the withers (the point between the top of the horse's shoulders and the base of his neck). There are over 100 different small horse breeds, from the American Walking Pony to the Zemaitukas pony from Lithuania.

Over the years, Uncle Walter had raised different breeds, but finally settled on Shetland po-

Snoops

nies, an ancient breed from the Shetland Islands. They are known to be intelligent, long-lived (up to 30 years or more), and are the strongest of all horse or pony breeds, able to pull twice their weight (most full-size horses can only pull half their weight).

Uncle Walter's pride and joy was his prize-winning pony named Quicksilver. To qualify as a Shetland, the pony must be between 28 and 42 inches tall. Heightwise, Quicksilver was right in the middle at 36 inches tall, had beautiful conformation and was pure white. Not that many people will tell you, but some Shetland ponies are known to be cranky and, occasionally, have some bad habits. For as good looking as Quicksilver was, everyone who knew him knew to stand back when it looked like he was going to sneeze — except it wasn't really a sneeze — more like a lot of snorting and blowing which, unfortunately, if you were standing within range, resulted in being sprayed with horse snot. The worse part — although there's no way to prove it — was that it was like he did it on purpose. And then there was the farting. What can I say? It was bad. Even though it was outside, when Quicksilver let one of those rip, he could clear the immediate area in no time at all. All of us that knew him hoped that neither of his bad habits would surface while he was being judged at some show. So far we'd been lucky.

When I got back to the farm from Chuy's house, I saw that Ma-D had left some carrots (with the green tops still on them) on the front porch of the bunk house to feed to the horses. I was still getting reacquainted with them when Henry — Walter and Ma-D's longtime hired hand — drove up the lane in a cloud of dust. He rolled his truck to a stop when he saw me and leaned out the window. "There's a guy I used to know that looked like you, but he was a lot shorter. What's your name, fella? I laughed and put out my hand "How's it goin', Henry?"

"I'm surprised you recognized me, 'cause I think I'm shrinking. Can barely see over the steering wheel anymore."

Henry was a pretty cool guy. Always joking. I put him at about 65 years old, a little younger than Uncle Walter. According to Henry and Walter, they had been friends forever, starting with being in the navy together during World War II, but it was a little hard to know where the truth ended and the lies began with the two of them. "Ma-D just yelled from the back porch and said dinner's ready. We'd better get in there or we'll catch you-know-what," I said. With that, Henry gave me a knowing nod and drove off toward the barn.

A few years ago I decided I wanted to sleep in the bunkhouse instead of the main house. Henry slept in one of bedrooms out there, but there was another unused one, that I liked. Ma-D said it was okay and that's where I've been staying ever since. The bunkhouse consisted of a big living room in the middle with a stone fireplace, and two bedrooms at opposite ends, each with its own small bathroom. Once inside, I stopped for a minute and breathed in the familiar smell of the room. It was part smoky fireplace, part horse smell, part what? I wasn't sure, but it was familiar and felt like home — or at least the only home that kind of felt like it was mine. I washed my face and put on a clean t-shirt and ran back over to the main house, followed by a barking Snoops, loping along, right behind me. Snoops was a big Irish Setter-Springer Spaniel mix who had been around forever. Truth be told, he was probably more good-natured than smart, and he had the bad habit of jumping up on me and putting his front paws on my shoulders and trying to lick my face. That said, he was a great pal and my constant shadow whenever I was at the farm.

•   •   •

So enough about me. Here's what else I found out about the few days leading up to the day I arrived back at the farm and, please note, I'm making some of it up — bits of conversation and other people's inner thoughts I have no way of knowing, but knowing what I *do* know now, I think I'm being pretty accurate.

First off, it was Witbeck who came up with the idea of stealing the pony. Well, according to them, not *stealing*, really. They never thought of anything they took as stealing. More like procuring. They always paid for what they took. They just didn't ask first. It was the way they did things, for as long as any of them could remember. Not only did they not ask whether they could buy something, the gnomes had no idea what anything cost. There was no rhyme or reason for the prices they came up with when they left payment for something so they tended to over-compensate for their lack of knowledge. They always left a lot of gold so no one could say the gnomes were cheats by paying too little — it was quite the opposite — often embarrassingly so.

I know I'm right about Witbeck's motives because he later told me about his troubles with the king. It all lead back to the catastrophe with the hummingbirds, but that's another story best left until later. He figured his one chance to set things right was with the white pony — Quicksilver — the one he had seen on one of his many reconnaissance missions, scouting the area for things the king and his men might find useful. And the pony was definitely going to be useful. As one of the king's chamberlains — not to mention the third-once-removed-in-line as king of the gnomes — it was his duty to make things "right."

Witbeck had gone over the plan many times. The fact that there would be no moon the night he had chosed for his mission, made it ideal. He was certain the cover of darkness would make procuring the white horse from the farm in the valley below and riding it back to gnome's home on the big mountain at the head of the valley known as "Mt. St. Helena," would go off without a hitch. At least it always did when he praticed it in his head. For some time, the king had been complaining about not being able to get around as he used to, owing, no doubt, to his rather astounding girth. Whitbeck was sure that presenting King Gob with the pony would not only make the king ambulatory again, but would get him — Whitbeck — back in the King's good graces; he was sure of that, too.

Witbeck reassured himself that he was just the man for the job. And indeed he was. Not unlike the Uplanders with their individual traits and strengths, every gnome possessed one unique magical power they could practice with great ability. Witbeck's particular magic was being able to appear and disappear at will, traveling great distances in the process. Sometimes a gnome possessed more than one bit of magic, but it was rare. Of course, the Wizard was different: he (although sometimes it was a she) possessed all the magical abilities of the gnomes combined — and then some. But the tribe had been without the services of their Wizard for some time now, a fact that everyone in the tribe was made painfully aware of on a regular basis, especially King Gob.

Earlier in the evening Witbeck had paid a visit to his friend, Wycoff, the king's chancellor of the exchequer, whose job it was to control and keep track of the tribe's gold and other valuables. Because of his position as chamberlain to the king, Witbeck was authorized to make withdrawals from the gnome's horde of gold with just his signature. Witbeck confided to Wycoff his plan to procure the pony for the king, which resulted in a long discussion of how much the pony was worth, neither of them having the slightest idea of what they were talking about, but taking it all very seriously anyway. Once they came to an agreement, Wycoff headed deep into the cave and came back with a leather pouch filled with gold nuggets and handed it over to Witbeck with an *umpf*, adding "you better hope this works — the king's none too pleased with you right now."

"You needn't remind me," Witbeck said, embarrassed and blushing as he signed his name in the big ledger, noting the amount he had taken. "But this is going to make it right, you'll see," he said, tying the pouch of gold to his new polka dot sash. "You'll see," he said again as he waved good-bye and headed out of the cave.

The view across the valley from the front porch of Walter and Ma-D's.

Chapter IV

First Night at the Farm, or
The Calm Before the Storm

Wednesday, June 14, 1967
Twin Oaks Pony Farm
St. Helena, California

"What took you so long? Dinner's on the table getting all cold," Ma-D scolded when I walked in the kitchen. Before we go any further, I have to tell you that Ma-D lives to cook and, truth be told, she's really good at it. I think it's her mission in life to make sure everyone is fed.

"Henry just drove in. He'll be here in a minute," I said.

"Well, his dinner's getting cold, too. Put Snoops out on the back porch, Nick, or he'll be begging from the table."

I ushered Snoops out to the back porch and pulled myself up to the kitchen table with its familiar red-checked tablecloth and green glass-shaded lamp hanging low in the middle. I nodded to Walter, who already had his napkin tucked under his chin. Nothing much ever changed in Ma-D's kitchen. It was at the back of the house and faced east. The big multi-paned window over the sink was covered with sweet potato vines trained on strings. A dome-shaped, red birdcage hung high up, over the sink, home to Buttercup the canary, who sometimes sang so loud it made your ears hurt. The windowsill was lined with small, colored pots filled with African violets, blooming in all shades of purple, lavender, and pink. On sunny mornings, the sun flooded through the window, making the leaves of the sweet potato vines look like a stained glass window and the African violet flowers sparkle. In amongst the leaves, Ma-D had hung a bunch of cut glass crystals, which shot rainbow-colored glints dancing on the kitchen walls and ceiling. It was my favorite room in the house.

The plate in front of me was filled with fanned-out slices of pot roast topped with gravy, a mashed potato volcano with melted butter "lava" flowing down the sides, and steaming, bright green sugar snap peas straight from the garden. Ma-D saw me staring at my plate and said "Don't just sit there, dig in." At the same time Henry came through the back door, letting Snoops back in. "Looks like I'd better git to gittin' if I want anything to eat tonight," he said as he took off his cowboy hat and pulled up his chair. "Sit down Henry," Ma-D said, "and don't forget it's your night to do the dishes. Who let that dog in? Snoops, under the stove!" she commanded. With that Snoops slunk off and curled up on his special rug under the old stove that stood up off the floor on skinny metal legs. In a cooler tone she turned to Henry and said "thank you for remembering to take your hat off."

After dinner, Henry cleared the plates, while Ma-D cut slices of her famous devil's food chocolate cake, which I washed down with about a half-gallon of milk. When I had finished, I could barely get up from the table, I was so stuffed.

The four of us, including Snoops, moved out onto the west-facing front porch of the main house, which over the years had become a kind of after-dinner tradition. It also gave Walter a chance to smoke his pipe since Ma-D had banned him from smoking indoors a few years back.

Walter asked Henry, who was cleaning his fingernails with his pocketknife, what chores he had lined up for me. "Let's see, there's the vegetable garden," Henry said slowly, "we could start with a little plantin,' I reckon. I got some seed potatoes that are almost too far gone, but if I — I mean, we — that's you and me, Nick — get 'em in the ground tomorrow, they should do okay. There's no moon tonight — perfect for planting root crops."

I figured Henry had picked up that bit of wisdom from *The Old Farmer's Almanac*, which was about the only book I had ever seen him read. "But before we plant, I was thinkin' that Nick could move that pile of finished compost from the bin to the garden and spade it in. That compost's well-aged, just the thing to make those taters practically jump out of the ground."

Uncle Walter puffed on his pipe, producing a cloud of bluish-white aromatic smoke. "Yeah, you could say that compost was well-aged, just like a fine wine," Walter snorted. "Seems to me you've been saving it since last fall when Nick went off to school."

Henry pushed his hat back, scratching his head. "I reckon you're just about right about that, Mr. D.," he said, failing completely to catch the gentle complaint. "Well, I guess I'm going to hit the hay. Venus twinkling over there in the western sky is my signal to head to the Land of Nod. You still staying in the bunkhouse, Nick?"

"Yessir," I replied. "I'll see you out there in a little bit."

"Ain't no moon to light the way, so don't get lost," said Henry trailing off with a chuckle as he rounded the back of the house.

Walter, Ma-D and I continued to sit on the porch, watching twilight overtake the western hills, getting caught up with small talk. At school there was always something to do, right up until lights out. It had been a long time since I had just sat and talked, with no homework or anything else to do. I learned Walter was going to enter Quicksilver in the State Championship competition at the California State Fair in Sacramento in August.

"That's a big deal, right?"

"You bet. If he shows like I think he's going to, it's on to the Nationals next year. And if that goes well, breeders from all over the country will be clamoring for Quicksilver to sire their mares. We're talking about some serious stud fees for that little guy," Walter said.

"Now don't go counting the money before there's any to count," countered Ma-D. "I think Quicksilver's a winner, too, but there's many a drip, 'twixt the cup and the lip, Walter. It's a darned good thing we've got Nick to help out. Those shows are no cakewalks. Speaking of which, you better put checking out the Winnebago on your list of chores, Walter. We haven't used it, since when? I can't even remember," said Ma-D.

"Yeah, yeah, I know," Walter said with a note of resignation.

"Whenever it was, I just don't want to be breaking down on Highway 80, somewhere between here and Sacramento," Ma-D said. In an attempt to change the subject, Walter looked at his watch and said, "Nick, it's almost nine. You better go in and give Hattie a call and let her know you're here. She'll worry if she doesn't hear from you. As I remember, she turns in at nine on the nose, so get in there and let her know you're okay."

Walter and Ma-D hadn't progressed very far into the world of electronic marvels; they still had a black wall phone in the kitchen, with a rotary dial, no less. The one improvement was that Ma-D had outfitted the phone with an extra-long cord, so she could talk and manage what was on the stove at the same time. I rang my grandmother's number in San Francisco and got Doyle, her houseman (his main jobs were butler and chauffeur, but he had a lot of other duties). I liked Doyle, with his sense of humor and odd sayings, most of which I didn't understand (partly due to his strong Irish accent), but laughed at anyway.

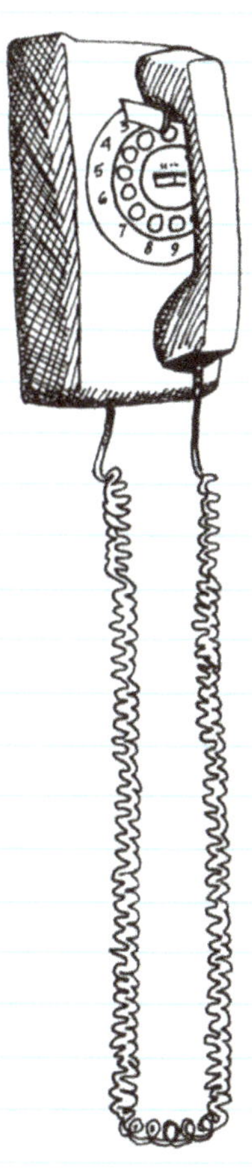

The wall phone with the extra-long cord.

"Sinclair residence, Doyle speaking."

"Doyle, it's Nick. How are you?"

"Excellent, thank you for asking. And how would you be, Master Sinclair?"

"I'm just fine. Is my grandmother around?"

"She's right here in the kitchen, waiting for her toddy. Hold the phone while I put her on."

I tried to picture what was going on at the other end of the line and shook my head.

"Is that you, Nick?" Grandma Hattie yelled into the phone.

"Yes, it's me Grandma. I'm right here. I can hear you just fine, you don't have to shout."

"Oh yes, I'm sure," she said a little more quietly. "How are you my dear?"

"I'm great, Grandma. I got to Ma-D's and Walter's a few hours ago. Everybody's fine."

"I'm so glad to hear that. You know I won't be up to St. Helena until July, but you must come and see me before then. I want to know everything about how you made out in school. Are you okay?"

"I'm just fine, Grandma. I'll call in a few days. This is my first night here and Walter and Henry have a bunch of stuff they want me to do, so I'm not sure when, but I'll come down soon, I promise."

"Bless your cotton socks, Nick. I'll look forward to it. I'll send Doyle to fetch you in the car. Just call and tell me when."

I flinched a little when I thought about "the car." The car was a black Cadillac limousine. And Doyle always showed up in his chauffeur's uniform, all of which was a bit much for me.

"Maybe you can give Doyle the day off and I'll just take the ferry to see you, Grandma. I know how to do it."

"Well, whatever you want. I just want to see you."

"Okay, Grandma. I'll call you. See you soon."

"Goodnight Nick. I'm glad you're back in the valley."

I walked back to the front porch. As I walked out the front door, Walter said "don't let the screen door slam!" just as it slammed shut with a bang.

"Sorry," I said, sheepishly.

"Boy, you'll wake the dead and loosen the hinges while you're at it. Be mindful next time!" said Walter shaking his head.

"Okay, okay, Uncle Walter," I said, thinking that Walter was grumpier than I remembered. "Grandma Hattie says 'hey' to you both. She sounded just fine."

"Grandma Hattie said 'hey' to us?" Walter chided.

"Sit on it, Walter," said Ma-D. "So she's okay?"

"Yeah, she's okay.

"Well, alright. I'm calling it a night. And I think you boys should call it a night, too. Did you hear me, Walter? Nick, you've had a long day. Why don't you hit the sack and we'll call it a new day tomorrow. Breakfast at 7:30, just like always. Now get on."

With that Ma-D got up from her chair and kissed me on the forehead. I went over to Walter and shook his hand and said good night. I heard a bit of a grunt, saw a puff of smoke from his pipe and took that for his sign-off.

I walked back through the front door, Snoops following close behind, through the kitchen and out to the back porch. I looked up, surprised at how dark it really was, and said to Snoops, "Henry was right, "no moon tonight." Snoops and I found our way to the bunkhouse, entered as quietly as we could, and headed to my bedroom. I turned on the light next to my bed.

I'd had gotten so used to my dorm room at boarding school, I'd forgotten how much I liked this place. For one, it was completely paneled in knotty pine, which made it very cozy. I took my Dopp kit into the bathroom and smiled. Somehow, the claw-footed Victorian bathtub always surprised me. Someone, a long time ago, had painted the feet to look like real chicken feet. Definitely not like the big, shared, all-white, brightly lit modern bathroom back at school.

Everything in my room looked just as I remembered it: two twin beds in old iron bedsteads on opposite sides of the window, a honey-colored oak table between the two beds with the window right above it and a green-shaded reading lamp on it. The table was bare except for the lamp and a black and white, formal photograph of my family taken when I was four years old. My mother and father were seated on a couch; my older brother, Lucas, stood behind my mom, leaning into her. I was sitting on my father's lap, looking up to him rather than facing the camera. I glanced at the photo, but I couldn't look at it for long. I knew the familiar sadness would creep over me and I didn't want that feeling right now.

I opened the walk-in closet and pulled the chain to turn on the bare bulb that hung from the ceiling. *Ah, there you are,* I thought to myself, looking up to the straw cowboy hat hanging on a peg. *My lucky hat.* Truth was, it was pretty beat up, having been blown off my head a few dozen times, run over by a tractor, chewed on by a goat and sat on I don't know how many times. But it was still my lucky hat and it felt great to have it on again. Inside the closet was an old chest with drawers that always stuck, except for the top one. I unpacked my bag. In

My beat-up, lucky hat.

the bottom lay my new journal — a large, hardback book, with lined pages, bound in some kind of blue fabric, with triangular maroon leather patches on the corners. The word "Journal" was stamped in gold on the spine. *Very impressive looking,* I thought, *even if what's between the covers isn't going to be.* Just before leaving school for the summer, I'd gone to three office supply stores in Carmel before I finally found what I was looking for in a small, cluttered old stationary store. I'd seen similar journals and logs in my grandmother's library that had belonged to her adoptive father, a sea captain named Gustave Niebaum. I'd always liked the way they looked and their musty smell and admired the captain's neat, formal handwriting inside, page after page. The old man who owned the stationery store looked at the yellowed price tag on the journal when I brought it to the counter. "Haven't sold one of these in years. What're you going to do with it, son?"

"I want to keep a journal. Make some notes, maybe write a story or two for school," I just blurted out. I could feel myself blushing and my ears getting hot.

"A worthy endeavor" said the old man, handing me the journal. "In that case, it's yours. And keep the words alive, my boy, keep 'em alive."

Taken aback, I protested several times, but the old man insisted on giving it to me. Finally I said "thank you" twice and raced back to school on my 10-speed bike, the cool, fog-dampened air whistling past my ears. I felt more than a little strange being given something so valuable by someone I didn't even know. Now, holding the blank journal in my hands, I thought about the old man in the store, wondering what kind of job I'd do *keeping the words alive?*

Last year I bought myself a simple, spiral-bound notebook to use as my first journal — nothing as cool the one I'd just been given. Once I started writing in it every day, I decided it would be a good idea to start a new one on the first day of summer vacation every year, as a kind of ritual. Last year, my new English teacher, Mr. Hayes, had suggested that anyone interested in pursuing a career in writing should keep a journal. The fact that I'd started one on my own, about four months before Mr. Hayes suggested it, made me feel like I was destined to become a writer — a feeling I didn't exactly advertise.

I brushed my teeth and climbed into bed, pushing Snoops off and telling him to get on the other bed, which he reluctantly did. I knew from experience that some time during the night, Snoops would sneak over to my bed and we'd spend the rest of the night fighting over the meager real estate offered by the narrow twin bed. Even though Henry's room was at the other end of the bunkhouse and his door was closed, I could hear him snoring away. *Oh man,* I thought to myself, *it's even worse than last year.* I reached for my new copy of *Ellery Queen's Mystery Magazine* from the table next to the bed. I had started reading it on the train earlier and was in the middle of a new Agatha Christie story about Hercule Poirot that was good — good enough to take my mind off of Henry's snoring. I read for about an hour and then turned off the light and got myself comfortable. I tossed around for a while and realized I was still kind of keyed up. And it was impossible to ignore Henry's walrus-like sounds which seemed to echo even more loudly through the dark. I decided to get up and go outside to see if I could make my brain slow down and catch up with myself. I slipped on my tennis shoes without tying them and silently went out the front door. I headed for the old porch swing but remembered that it made big squeaking sounds when anyone sat in it. So I sat on the porch steps instead, looking across the lawn to where the corral was, practically invisible now, all but lost in the darkness. It was equally dark over at Walter and Ma-D's, except for a faint light in the kitchen windows, lit by the small light over the stove Ma-D always left on.

My mind was wandering, thinking about tomorrow and going down to see Chuy, quickly remembering that, of course, Chuy wouldn't be there. I walked out onto the lawn and looked up at the sky. Without the interference of moonlight, it looked liked there might be a trillion stars, all of them blinking and twinkling to their own rhythm. From the corner of my eye, I caught the sight of a big shooting star, so bright it almost looked like a streak of lightning, racing across the night sky. *Whoa,* I said under my breath, *if I'd been in bed, I'd never have seen that.* Just then I thought I heard a bumping sound over near the corral. One of the ponies let out a whinny and stamped its hooves. I thought it might be Quicksilver, but I wasn't sure why. I looked at my watch — it had numbers that glowed in the dark. *10:13, I better hit the hay.* I crept back into the dark bunkhouse, found my way to bed and collapsed between the cool, clean sheets.

The new journal.

pulling the blankets practically to my nose. This time sleep came in an instant.

●   ●   ●

Wednesday, June 14, 1967, 10:12 p.m.
Somewhere between the town of St. Helena and Mt. St. Helena

Witbeck had transported himself to the Twin Oaks Pony Farm at a little after eleven, figuring that the Uplanders who lived there would all be asleep by then. He slipped into the corral and immediately started reassuring and calming the horses whispering a song he had learned as a boy back in the Old Country. He sidled up to the all-white pony, easing the rope around its neck and started leading him to the gate. Holding the lead in one hand, Witbeck untied the leather pouch from his sash with his other. He had intended to tie the gold-filled pouch to one of the fence posts where the Uplanders couldn't miss it, but Witbeck became momentarily confused when the horse let out a very loud, smelly fart. Whitbeck hadn't been expecting it and with his surprise, he somehow managed to drop the leather pouch into the water trough, which, in turn, startled the horse and caused it to whinny and then sneeze all over Whitbeck's face. Panic ran through Witbeck; this was exactly how things could go very wrong, very quickly. He thought for a moment and decided to leave the leather pouch in the water trough, figuring the Uplanders would eventually find it. He got the horse out of the corral as quickly as he could, closing the gate behind him, and took off down the lane. It wasn't until he reached the river that his heart stopped pounding and he started to breathe normally again.

He carefully led the pony across the shallow part of the river using the harness he had made earlier in the day. Witbeck wished his ability to instantly transport himself at will extended to an animal he happened to be sitting on, but it didn't. "We'll just take it nice and easy," he told the horse, patting its forelock which, for some reason caused the pony to fart again even more loudly than before. Whitbeck chose to ignore it, figuring both he and the horse were probably nervous. He figured it would take them about five hours to travel the nearly twenty miles back to the gnome's cave on Mt. St. Helena. Hopefully he'd arrive before sun-up, when all the gnomes would just be going to bed. He was anxious to get back in the king's good graces and couldn't wait to see the look on his face when he presented him with the horse. Witbeck was sure the king would be pleased.

I put the journal down and looked across the vineyards. I felt like I'd been transported somewhere far away from the porch where I was sitting. The last rays of the setting sun were lighting up the tops of eastern hills and I realized I'd been reading for more than an hour. I heard pots being banged around in the kitchen, so I went into the house and found Grandpa and his helper, Doyle, getting ready to fry chicken in a very large cast iron pan.

Before I go any further, let me explain a few things. Grandpa Nick had inherited the house and property where we all lived from his Grandma Hattie a long time ago. The main house is this big old Victorian, three-story place. My parents and I live in a smaller place a ways down the lane. All the houses are surrounded by vineyards, as it's all part of Eagle's Nook Winery, a business Grandpa Nick had hired other people to run for him. Grandpa is an artist and also a writer. He converted the barn next to the big house into a painting studio that also serves as a workshop. I like it out there because of all the cool, old tools he has. Most days after school I hang there and experiment with this and that while he paints.

This last week I'd been learning to solder; Grandpa said he'd teach me to weld once I figure out basics of soldering. He knows how to do a lot of stuff. It's all pretty old school, but he kind of hinted that maybe we could figure out a way to buy a MakerBoy Digitizer Desktop 3D scanner if I learned all the old-fashioned stuff first. Grandpa calls me a "gearhead" – says I was born one. I just like to figure out how things work and how to fix them. He even ordered all the old episodes of *MacGyver* – a t.v. show from when he was a kid about this cool guy who can get out of any jam using his Swiss Army knife, a can of hair spray, some dental floss and a box of matches – or other random stuff like that. We've watched all of the episodes about a hundred times.

Anyway, when my folks are out of town, like they are this weekend, I stay over at his house. Grandpa and Doyle are pretty funny – not like any of my friends' parents. They usually let me invite Darren or one of my other friends over when I stay there. Doyle was born in Ireland and even though he'd been here for a long time, still speaks with a Irish accent that I'm just now beginning to understand. His first job in America was working as Grandma Hattie's houseman, way back when. After Grandma Hattie died, he moved up here and went to work with Grandpa. He's as much a part of the family as anyone else around here.

I walked into the kitchen just as grandpa was putting the chicken into the hot oil, snapping and popping.

"Hey."

"There you are. What's the haps?"

Yes, my grandfather says stuff like that, even though he's like 60 something.

"I've been reading. On the front porch."

"And?"

"I don't know. How old were you when you wrote it?"

"14. Almost 15."

"14?"

"Yeah. Why do you ask?"

"I don't know. It just doesn't sound like something a 14-year-old would write."

"Well, I might have been a couple of years ahead of myself – I remember thinking so then," he said, sliding more chicken into the pan. "I was a pretty serious kid. I spent a lot of time with my nose in one book or another."

"What happened?"

"Whaddaya' mean, 'what happened?'"

"You don't seem all that serious now."

"Let's just say I learned the benefits of humor. How far have you gotten?"

"To page 32."

"You ain't seen nothin' yet."

"I still want to know if it's true or not."

"Wait until you're finished. You can decide then. You wanna' invite Darren for dinner? It's pan-fried chicken, mashed potatoes and gravy and green beans."

"Sure."

"Give him a call. Tell him if he makes it over here on the double, we'll have time for a couple of games of dominoes before dinner."

•   •   •

We played dominoes at the big table in the middle of the kitchen. Grandpa told Darren that it was okay to use swear words while the game was in play, because you couldn't play dominoes without swearing. Darren wasn't used to playing double nines (he'd only played double sixes at his house); Grandpa told him he'd better learn fast because double sixes were for "wussies." Anyway, dinner was good, as usual. Darren decided to spend the night because we played dominoes for such a long time. And, as usual, Grandpa won.

The next morning Darren had to leave early to do something with his parents. I went back to sleep after he left; by the time I wandered into the kitchen around 10, no one was there. Grandpa left a note on the table (addressed to "Sleeping Beauty") saying he and Doyle had gone into town and that I could make my own breakfast, but there was some bacon in the oven if I wanted some.

I scrambled some eggs, snatched the bacon from the oven and took the journal back out onto the front porch to eat and read. By the time Grandpa and Doyle got back from town a couple of hours later, I had read the next three chapters and was thoroughly confused.

Ponies at the rail, looking for attention (or carrots).

Chapter V

Quicksilver is Missing!

Thursday, June 15, 1967
Twin Oaks Pony Farm
St. Helena, California

I was in the middle of a strange dream in which the old man from the stationery store in Carmel was showing Quicksilver at the California State Fair, when I was awakened by a wet tongue in my face. "Hey there. What's up Snoops?" I said looking sleepily over at the clock. "It's only 6 o'clock. Why are you up so early?" Snoops hopped down and sat next to the bed, slapping his tail loudly on the floor, whining at the same time. "You want out?" I asked as I pulled on my jeans and t-shirt and grabbed my hat. "I get it. I forgot to leave the front door open a little so you could go out on your own, didn't I?" I said as I let Snoops out. I stood on the front porch and waited for him to come back. Light was just beginning to break. Wisps of fog rose lazily off the neighboring grapevines and floated through the towering eucalyptus trees that dotted the vineyards here and there. It was noticeably quiet except for a single bird in some treetop, chirping the arrival of another day. I stretched and yawned as Snoops reappeared around the corner of the barn. I walked across the wet lawn in my bare feet over to the corral. "Morning, guys and gals," I said, leaning against the fence. The horses whinnied as they jockeyed to get as close to me as possible. "Sorry, no carrots yet. It's too early." I absentmindedly scratched one of the horses between her ears. "Where's Quicksilver?" I heard myself say. At that moment I was suddenly completely awake, thinking "where *is* Quicksilver?" I found myself counting the horses over and over, finally accepting the fact that Quicksilver simply wasn't there. I set off on a tear to check out the stalls in the barn, and then ran back to the bunkhouse, barging into Henry's room, Snoops right behind me.

"Wake up, Henry," I said catching my breath, "we've got trouble."

"Trouble? Like what trouble?" Henry sputtered, trying to wake himself up.

"I don't know. Maybe big trouble. I was just out at the corral and Quicksilver isn't there."

"Holy moly. How'd he get out?" Henry asked.

"I don't know. The gate's closed and locked," I said seriously. "I think... I'm not sure what I think."

"Whaddaya' mean?" Henry asked quizzically, pulling on his boots.

"All I know is, we'd better get over there and figure out what happened. Walter isn't up yet and we better have some answers before the you-know-what hits the fan."

"You're right about that," Henry said, grabbing for his hat. Sensing the excitement, Snoops starting barking, causing both of us to turn and "shush" him at the same time.

Keeping one eye on the main house, Henry and I, followed by Snoops, made our way to the corral. I looked around and counted the horses again even though it was plain that Quicksilver wasn't there. With a sick feeling in my stomach, I ran to the stable and looked again in all the stalls. Henry whispered hoarsely, "Nah, he ain't in here; I left all of them in the corral last night."

"I was just looking to make sure," I said, feeling helpless.

"Look," Henry said, pointing to the gate, "it's like you said, the gate's closed and latched. Now how in hell is a horse goin' to open a gate and then close it and latch it behind him, huh? That horse is smart but he's not that smart."

Henry and I went behind the stable to the large fenced pasture and looked around; not a horse in sight. We walked down to the river, Snoops leading the way. On the rare occasion when someone had accidentally left the corral gate open, the horses almost instinctively headed down to the river. Henry and I trudged down the road in silence. I didn't hold out much hope of finding Quicksilver there; it was plain to see there wasn't a hoof print in sight on the dirt road. The sun was peeking over the eastern hills between layers of fog, lighting up the edges of the massive oaks that shaded the riverbank. It was bluish cool and shadowy under the trees. Henry and I skidded down the bank; the slow moving water was almost black. No Quicksilver or any other horse anywhere, only the hushed calls of quail and mourning doves on the other side of the river and a bunch of crows cawing from the top of a huge oak tree; it sounded like they were laughing at us.

I absent-mindedly picked up a flat rock and skipped it across the river, causing Snoops to jump in the water and try to retrieve it. "I can't believe this," I said to no one in particular.

Discouraged, Henry whistled for Snoops and said to me, "come on, let's get outta' here. Might as well get back to the house and break the news. Mr. D's going to bust a gut."

Just like Henry predicted, it wasn't pretty. When we reached the house we left Snoops on the back porch to dry off. Pretty much knowing what was going to happen next, we entered the kitchen as quietly as possible. Uncle Walter was sitting at the table pouring himself a cup of coffee, the morning paper carefully folded in front of him. Ma-D was standing at the stove, flipping pancakes, listening to the morning news on the radio. When Ma-D noticed us, she looked at her watch and said, "You're early."

Unable to contain himself, Henry blurted out "Somebody stole Quicksilver. He ain't nowhere to be found — ask Nick."

I couldn't believe it. Neither I nor Henry had said anything about anyone stealing anything. Uncle Walter had just put his coffee cup to his lips when Henry blurted out the news. Walter spit coffee all over the breakfast table as he jumped out of the chair, knocking it backwards in the process, catching the edge of the table at the same time, tipping over the coffee pot, the pitcher of orange juice and the maple syrup, spilling everything all over the kitchen floor. Ma-D screamed when she saw everything she'd just put on the table heading for the floor. The heavy pottery bowl full of pancake batter slipped out of her hands, landing on the floor with a crash, making her scream again. Shocked by the uproar, Henry started backing up to the back door when Walter yelled, "Hold on Henry, where the hell you think you're going?" Henry muttered something about getting to his chores and kept backing up, right through the screen door, slamming it hard as he hoofed it back to the barn.

"Walter, get over here and give me a hand," Ma-D demanded.

Walter helped her sit down in the wooden chair next to the stove. "What's this nonsense about someone stealing Quicksilver?" Ma-D asked as Walter helped her out of her batter-soaked shoes.

"Hell if I know," Walter said. "What's going on, Nick?"

"I don't know, Uncle Walter. I woke up early this morning to let Snoops out. I went over to the corral and Quicksilver wasn't there. I went and woke Henry up and told him Quicksilver was missing. We checked everywhere — even down by the river — and he's not around. I guess Henry thinks someone stole him because the corral gate was latched and locked."

"Go and find Henry and bring him back up here," Walter told me. "I've got to help Ma-D clean up this mess."

I found Henry in the barn, not actually hiding, but doing a pretty good job of making himself invisible while he swept the floor behind a stack of hay bales.

"I've got to teach you a few things about timing," I said, half to myself and half to Henry.

"What's that?" Henry asked, pretending not to hear.

"Uh-oh. Never mind. Here comes Uncle Walter now. He looks like he's on the war path."

"Did you find him?" Walter asked me gruffly as he stepped into the barn.

"Who?" asked I without thinking.

"Henry!" said Uncle Walter, practically shouting.

"Oh, yeah, Henry. He's right here," I said, motioning to the stack of hay bales.

Henry slunk around the corner of the bales, Snoops hanging back behind him, ears down, tail between his legs. Henry just stood there, staring at the floor. I didn't want Walter to start in on him — all Henry had done was deliver the bad news, even if he had embellished it a bit, so I spoke first and fast.

"Like I said, Uncle Walter, we've already checked everywhere and there's no sign of him. And I know Quicksilver was in the corral last night, because I heard him, late. And this morning he was gone and the gate was closed and latched."

"Now how's that possible?" Walter demanded, clouds of tobacco smoke coming from his pipe. I hoped that maybe some of his anger was going up in smoke.

"I... I... I don't know, but take a look for yourself," Henry stuttered, motioning to the corral.

The three of us walked solemnly to the corral and examined the gate. The other ponies clustered around, hoping for a treat.

"Guess I'd better call the Sheriff," Walter said. Without saying so, apparently he'd come to the same conclusion as Henry — that Quicksilver had been stolen.

Henry shuffled away, headed to the barn. I followed Walter back to the house, deciding about the only constructive thing I could do to help was to clean up the mess in the kitchen.

Down on my hands and knees with a wet towel, I sopped up the pancake batter off the linoleum floor. Ma-D was sweeping up pieces of broken plates and mugs from under the table. I could hear Walter talking on the phone; he had pulled the long cord into the living room.

"Yes, that's right. I'm reporting the theft of a horse — a Shetland pony, 36 inches tall and pure white." He paused, listening to the other end. "No, he doesn't look like a dog! He looks like an Arabian stallion, only smaller." Walter had started to raise his voice. He gave his name and address, hung up the phone with a bang and said a word that made Ma-D yell at him to "Watch it, Walter."

I had to mop the floor three times to get the last of the batter and syrup up. Walter and Ma-D had gone upstairs, Ma-D presumably to change her clothes; I had no idea why Uncle Walter was up there.

I was putting the broom and the mop away when I remembered I hadn't had any breakfast and my stomach was starting to growl. I opened the refrigerator and quickly retrieved the makings of a sandwich: slices of last night's pot roast, a couple of slices of bread, the jar of mayonnaise and the milk carton. I assembled the sandwich and had it just to my mouth when Ma-D came back down into the kitchen. "And what are you doing?" she asked.

"I'm starved," I said, stuffing part of the sandwich into my mouth.

"Here, let me get you something... I can make some more batter and you can have pancakes."

"No, Ma-D, this is just fine," I said with my mouth half full.

Walter came into the kitchen, smelling of Old Spice aftershave and wearing a clean white shirt, just as we all heard the sound of tires crunching on the gravel driveway. Ma-D pulled back the kitchen curtains and announced that the sheriff was here. She shooed me and Walter out the back door, saying she had work to do.

Walter and I got to the sheriff just as he was getting out of his car, patting Snoops on the head as he did.

"Howdy, Gene," said Walter, "thanks for coming out so quickly."

Gene Lyman, the new sheriff, had lived in the valley all his life. His family knew all the other old families, and all their families knew his. I often thought that half the people in the valley were blood relatives, and the other half were married to each other, and everyone knew everything about each other's business or, as Walter had once said, "you can't fart in this valley without someone else smelling it."

"No problem, Mr. D.," said Sheriff Lyman, holding out his hand to Walter. He turned to me, saying "What in the hell are they feeding you down at that boarding school, Nick? Fertilizer? You look about twice the size since the last time I saw you." I knew I was probably blushing because my ears felt hot as I shook the sheriff's hand, "Nah, just a growth spurt or something," I said.

"So what's going on here, Walter?" the sheriff asked.

"Damned if I know. Henry came in to breakfast this morning and claimed someone had stolen Quicksilver, you know, my prize pony." As Uncle Walter was talking, Henry appeared, creeping up like a shadow.

"Howdy, Henry, how's it going?" Sheriff Lyman asked, holding out his hand in Henry's direction.

"I've had better days, if you want to know the truth," Henry replied.

"What makes you think the horse was stolen?" asked the sheriff.

"Well, for one thing, he's gone."

"Yeah, we got that much, Henry. Why don't you start from the beginning and tell me what happened this morning."

Since I was the one who found Quicksilver missing, I started in: "Snoops woke me up at 6 o'clock, wanting to go outside. I walked over to the corral for no particular reason, and I suddenly realized that Quicksilver wasn't there. I ran over to the bunkhouse and woke Henry up. We looked everywhere, even down by the river."

"I take it the gate to the corral wasn't open?" Sheriff Lyman asked.

"No sir," I answered, "it was just like it is now."

The four of us walked over to the corral gate and examined the latch. It was a sturdy thing, designed to be opened from the outside only.

"When was the last time any of you saw Quicksilver?" asked the sheriff.

Walter, Henry and I all looked at each other. "Well, I guess it was probably me," I said. "I fed the ponies a few carrots last night, right after I got here, and they were all in the corral then. And I could swear he was in there when I walked to the bunkhouse last night."

"What time was that?" the sheriff asked.

"Probably a little after 9," I answered.

"Did any of you hear anything unusual last night?

Walter scratched his head. "No, not me."

"What about you, Henry?"

"Nope. I slept like a log, just like I always do," Henry replied.

"The only thing I heard last night was Henry's snoring," I said. "He was snoring so loud I couldn't go to sleep, so I went outside for a few minutes."

"And you're sure you didn't see or hear anything unusual?" asked the sheriff, writing in a small notebook.

"Just a shooting star."

"A shooting star?"

"Yeah, a big one. With no moon last night, the stars were really bright and..." my voice trailed off. "Wait a minute," I said. "There was something. At the same time I saw the shooting star I heard something bump in the corral and Quicksilver gave that funny whinny of his.

"Do you know what time that was?" asked the sheriff.

My glow-in-the-dark watch.

"Yeah, I do," I answered. "It was 10:13 exactly, because I looked at my watch and decided it was time to go bed."

"You could see your watch in the dark?"

"Yeah, the numbers on the dial glow in the dark," I said, holding my wrist up so the sheriff could see.

The sheriff looked perplexed. "Let's take a look around."

We walked around the corral and stood next to the old galvanized water trough, about the size of a big bathtub. "Not much to go on," the sheriff said, shaking his head. "Sure a lot of footprints around here in the mud," he said, pointing to the area around the trough. "Have there been any kids here recently?"

"As a matter of fact," Walter said. "The kindergarten class was down here on the last day of school a couple of days ago. They always come for a visit as an end-of-school treat and bring a picnic. When Ma-D used to teach there, she'd always bring her students here and, since she retired, the new teacher's done the same thing. Kind of a tradition."

Surprised, the sheriff asked: "You let kids inside the corral?"

"Hell no," replied Walter. "They'd have those ponies so worked up we'd never get 'em calmed down. Wouldn't be safe. Not at all."

"Then what are all those little footprints around the trough?" asked the sheriff.

Walter leaned over the fence and looked carefully. "Well, I'll be damned. One of those school kids must have gotten in when no one was lookin'."

Sitting on the corral fence, I noticed the sheriff writing something in his notebook that he underlined three times; I wondered what Walter had said that was so important. The sheriff closed his notebook and we all started walking back towards the house. I was about to jump down from the fence when something in the trough caught my eye. "What the...?" I thought to myself as I leaned in close to the surface of the water. Sure enough, there was something in the bottom of the trough that glinted through the murky water. I was about to reach in the trough when Walter called, "Nick! Get on over here. I need you to do something."

As I walked over to where they were all standing, I decided not to say anything until I knew for sure what was at the bottom of the trough.

"Take the sheriff down to the river and show him where the ponies like to go. I'm goin' in to check on Ma-D. After that, I guess I'm going to have to go down to Napa and fill out a bunch of forms for the sheriff. I'll see you later, Gene. Thanks again for coming so quickly," he said, shaking the sheriff's hand once again.

"What a day!" he said shaking his head, walking back to the house.

The sheriff and I rode down to the river in his cruiser. Normally I would have asked about a dozen questions, like how fast did the it go, what kind of rifle was sitting next to his knee, had he ever arrested any dangerous criminals, and on and on. But just now, all I could think about was what I thought I'd seen in the bottom of the trough.

.   .   .

Thursday, June 15, 1967, 4:30 a.m.
Somewhere on Mt. St. Helena

Witbeck waited until the king was finished with the last meal of the night and in a right, jolly frame of mind, having his second-to-last goblet of wine. He leaned over, close to the king's ear. "Ahem," he started in.

The king was a little startled. "What is it, Witbeck?" he said testily. "Why are you always sneaking up on me from behind? Stand in front of me."

Witbeck dutifully moved in front of the king and was about to make his presentation when the king said "What's that?"

"What's what?" Witbeck responded.

"That thing around your waist?"

"It's my sash, Your Highness."

"I can see that, Witbeck," he said with exasperation. "What does it have on it?"

"They're called polka dots, Your Highness."

"Well, take it off. Whatever they are, they make me nervous. Couldn't you have found a sash in a nice, soothing plaid?"

"Of course, Your Highness. I'll find a plaid sash right away. Plaid is my favorite color," Witbeck said, stashing the polka dot sash into one of his many pockets.

"Good. Now what is it, Witbeck?"

"I have something for you, Your Highness. Would you like to see it?"

"Well, what is it?"

"Allow me," Witbeck said, turning to the doors of the chamber and clapping his hands. With that, the doors opened and in walked Prince G holding a rope with the white pony at the other end.

"What in the world?" the king exclaimed.

"It's called a Shetland pony, Your Highness. Perfectly suited, I believe, for your ambulatory needs. And he'll never get any bigger in size. Shetland ponies are like the gnomes of the horse world — they're just naturally small."

"Bring him here, G. Let me see him."

The prince led the horse over to his father, who pulled himself up in his chair and started scratching the horse's ears.

"I want to ride him."

Witbeck quickly interjected. He knew this was not the right time for the king's first ride on the horse. And he wasn't about to suffer another disaster like the hummingbird affair. "I think it's in Your Highness's best interests if you waited until Tuomo can fashion a saddle and a bit for the horse. We wouldn't want an accident, would we?"

"You're such a party-pooper, Witbeck. But I suppose you're right. Have Tuomo get right on it. I want to ride this horse tomorrow!"

"Very well, Your Highness," Witbeck said, wiping his forehead absentmindedly with his polka dot sash, thinking he'd just barely avoided another catastrophe. He signaled to the prince to get the horse out of the chamber before the king changed his mind. Or before the horse farted, something it did with alarming regularity on the trip up the mountain. Witbeck wasn't sure the king would even notice, but he wasn't in a position to take any chances.

It could have been worse, Witbeck thought as he watched the king stumble off to bed. *Much worse. And at least he liked the horse. Tomorrow will be a better day.* He was certain of it.

The kitchen at the Walter and Ma-D's house — my favorite room.

Chapter VI

Treasure in the Trough

Thursday, June 15,1967, continued
Twin Oaks Pony Farm
St. Helena, California

After Sheriff Lyman and I got back from the river, the sheriff took off back to Napa. As soon as he left, I went off looking for Henry. Yeah, I know it's a little weird, but something made me think it was a good idea to have a witness for what I was about to do — even if it turned out to be nothing.

I found Henry still sweeping the barn with an old push broom.

"Ma-D said the Greyhound office down in Napa just called and said they've got a big crate for you. What'd you order?" Henry asked.

"It's my bicycle. There wasn't any room for it yesterday, so they sent it up on a later bus." I hesitated and then asked, "Will you come over to the corral with me for a minute?"

"Sure. What's up?"

"I'm not sure, but I think it's better if we both took a look. You mind?"

"Nah, I don't mind. But what's the big deal?"

"I think there's something in the trough, that's all." *Something that glinted like gold,* I thought to myself.

"Like what?"

"Like I said, I'm not sure," I replied not altogether truthfully.

Henry, Snoops and I marched out into the bright sunlight, over to the trough. I pushed the sleeve of my t-shirt up and reached deep into the cold water. Snoops was right next to me with his front paws on the edge of the trough. I touched something soft and slimy. Henry was hunched over my shoulder, literally breathing down my neck. "Well... is there something down there or not?" he hissed.

"Yeah, there's something, all right." I said, as I pulled a dark brown leather pouch out of the water. I held the pouch up by its leather drawstrings, letting it twirl around like something out of a hypnotist's show. We both stood there, mesmerized, watching the spinning pouch drip sparkling drops of water back into the trough. Snoops started barking.

"Well, whaddaya' waitin' for? Open it up!" Henry finally said, louder than necessary.

"Shhhhh!" I said, glaring at both Henry and Snoops.

I could feel my heart beating hard. I held the pouch in my hands and started to pull the drawstrings apart. Instinctively, Henry cupped his hands and I slowly emptied the contents.

"Holy mother of god," Henry whispered.

I felt faint. The pouch was filled with gold nuggets, some as big as quail's eggs, glinting in the morning sun.

Henry recovered first. "Where'd ya' suppose that came from?"

I just stared at the gold, not saying anything.

"How'd ya' know it was in there?" Henry asked.

"Some of the nuggets must have fallen out of the pouch. I saw something shining in there this morning when Sheriff Lyman was here," I said as I reached back into the trough and picked up two more pieces of gold from the bottom.

Henry whistled under his breath. "Better make sure that's all."

"That's it," I said, peering into the water.

"Why didn't you say something when the sheriff was here?" Henry asked.

"I'm not sure," I replied. "I guess maybe I thought I was just seeing things."

"Do ya' think it has anything to do with Quicksilver?"

"I don't know," I said, secretly hoping — practically knowing for sure — there had to be a connection.

"Well, we're showin' this to Mr. D., aren't we?"

"Yeah. Of course," I said, thinking to myself that Walter would probably have some practical explanation for it all.

We hustled to the main house, stumbling over each other and Snoops as we all tried to get through the back door at the same time. Uncle Walter was sitting at the kitchen table as we burst in. "Don't let the screen door..." Walter said angrily, just as it slammed with a bang.

Before Uncle Walter could say anything, I held up the pouch; "Look what we found in the trough!"

Uncle Walter looked skeptically over the top of his reading glasses.

"And take a look at what's inside," I said, handing the wet pouch to Walter.

"What's goin' on in there?" Ma-D yelled from the laundry room.

"Wait'll you see, Ma-D," I yelled back.

Uncle Walter whistled as the gold nuggets spilled onto the tablecloth.

"What is it?" demanded Ma-D. When she saw the gold spread out on the table her eyes got as big as saucers. "Is it... is that gold... *real* gold?"

"Sure as hell looks real to me," huffed Uncle Walter.

"Where'd it come from?" asked Ma-D.

"The bottom of the horse trough," I said.

"The bottom of the trough?" Ma-D asked incredulously, pointing to the gold. "Our trough?"

"Yeah, our trough. Nick and I just found it there... ah, I mean, Nick saw it first, but we found it together," Henry blurted out.

The four of us must have sat around the kitchen table for almost an hour, each speculating about how the gold could have gotten there (never even coming close to the truth) and wondering how much it might be worth. Uncle Walter put an end to that question by weighing the gold on Ma-D's kitchen scale and looking up the current price of gold in the business section of the newspaper.

"Looks like we've got somewhere between five and six thousand dollars worth of gold here," Uncle Walter said with some satisfaction. Ma-D, Henry, and I looked on with even more astonishment. Suddenly Uncle Walter looked at his watch like he'd forgotten something and jumped up from the table. "I've got to get down to the Sheriff's Department to file that report," he said. He looked down at the gold on the table and finally said "I guess I should take this with me. Someone must have lost it... it's not ours." A collective groan went out from Ma-D, Henry and me.

"No. It's the right thing — the only thing — to do," said Walter resolutely.

"You want someone to come along and ride shotgun... you know, like a guard?" Henry said with considerably more enthusiasm than normal.

"No, I don't think that'll be necessary, Henry," said Walter, "but thanks for the offer."

"Can I go with you?" I asked, thinking quickly. "I need to pick my bicycle up at the bus station; they called and said it was there."

"I wondered what that call was about," Uncle Walter said. "Too damn much going on around here. You can come, but let's get a move on."

Uncle Walter and I got in the pickup truck, drove out the gravel driveway onto Highway 29 and headed to Napa, about twenty miles south of the farm. We didn't talk much in the truck, each of us thinking about the morning's events. Uncle Walter made the turn off the highway onto First Street in Napa, which headed downtown. The bus depot wasn't much more than a small, one room office next to a wide driveway, just off of Main Street. I jumped out, spotted the bicycle crate leaned up against the wall, and went into the office to show them my identification. The clerk at the desk was nice enough to give me a hand getting the bike in the back of Walter's truck. "Just couldn't be without it, eh?" Uncle Walter asked, chiding me as I got back in the truck.

"No sir. I got this bicycle with the money I saved from picking prunes last year and I bet I've ridden it every day since. It's an 10-speed."

"I thought a bicycle was a bicycle — at least they were when I was a kid," Walter responded, half to himself. Sensing Walter's sour mood, I decided to sit in silence while we drove the few blocks to the Sheriff's Department.

Walter found a place to park and we walked the rest of the way to the rather imposing, big, white building. It wasn't even noon and it was already getting hot. Walter and I both wiped our brows as we stood at the reception desk on the second floor of the Sheriff's Department. The air conditioning inside the building made it feel almost cold.

"Is Gene... ah, I mean, is Sheriff Lyman in?" Uncle Walter asked the receptionist.

"Do you have an appointment?" she asked.

"Well, I guess we do. He was up at our place earlier today. We've got a bit of a problem... actually a couple of problems, now."

With a puzzled expression on her face, the receptionist asked our names and told us to have a seat and she'd let the sheriff know we were there.

"Must be new in town," Walter mumbled, motioning with his head to the receptionist's desk.

The receptionist was back in a minute and told us to go on back to the sheriff's office, which was down the cool, dark hall at the far corner of the courthouse. Walter knocked on the door and Sheriff Lyman said to come in. It was a pleasant, high-ceilinged, bright room, with lots of framed stuff on the walls and big windows on two sides of the room. "Have a seat," Sheriff Lyman said, pointing to a couple of chairs in front of his desk. Before anyone could say much of anything, Walter had the leather pouch dangling in front of the sheriff's face saying "Nick here found this at the bottom of the horse trough, just after you left our place this morning." The sheriff didn't take his eyes off the pouch. "May I?" he asked. "Sure, go ahead," said Walter. The sheriff uncinched the pouch and peered inside. "Looks like a fair amount of gold in there," he said, pretty much unfazed.

"You don't seem surprised, Gene," Walter said. "You get people comin' in here every day carrying bags of gold?"

"No, of course we don't. I just hoped this wouldn't be one of those cases," he said with resignation.

"One of what cases?" Walter asked pointedly.

The sheriff hesitated, scratching his chin. "Another complicated one," he said with exasperation.

"Whaddaya' suggest we do with the gold?" Walter asked.

"We'll run an item in the Police Log section of the *St. Helena Star* — something like 'Leather pouch found on the premises of Twin Oaks Pony Farm. Describe contents to claim ownership,' something like that. We'll keep the pouch in our safe here until we've run the ad for two weeks. After that, if nobody's claimed it, it's yours."

"Well, I'll be," mused Walter. "If I lost something like that, you can bet I'd be able to describe it — and it wouldn't take any two weeks to figure out I'd lost it, either."

"It's what we have to do, Walter," the sheriff said firmly, "is that all right with you?"

"Yeah, yeah. That's okay with me. But whaddaya' goin' to do about Quicksilver?"

"I've sent our best investigator out to the farm. You probably passed him on the highway coming into town. He'll take a look around and see if he can turn up anything. And we'll put a report of the theft in the newspaper, asking anyone who might know anything about it to contact us. For the moment, that's about all we can do," the sheriff concluded tiredly.

"Harumpf!" Walter snorted indignantly, recognizing that we'd been more or less dismissed. "Guess there's nothing else to do but fill out your damn forms."

"Take your uncle on home and see if you can't get him to cool down a little," Sheriff Lyman said to me. "You can fill out the forms later, Walter, if you want."

"I don't need anybody to help me cool down. I need someone who can help me find my best horse! Now where do I go to fill out those forms? I want to get this done now," Walter said, hot under the collar.

"Right down there, Walter," said the sheriff, pointing to a small office next to the reception desk. Our new intern, Cindy Ruffino, will help you fill them out."

"Harumpf!" again.

We walked back to the front of the office, Walter muttering under his breath about a "waste of tax dollars." I had never seen him this upset before. Once we got back out to the reception desk, I decided to sit in a small waiting room next to a couple of vending machines, leaving Uncle Walter to fill out the forms on his own. It seemed like it was taking forever and I realized I had to use the bathroom, which was right next to the waiting room. I'd just closed the door of the stall when I heard the bathroom door open again.

"Did I just see old man Dobson in here?"

"Yeah, that was him."

I recognized the second voice as Sheriff Lyman's; I didn't know who the other person was. I'm not sure why I did it, but I lifted up my feet quietly so no one would be able to tell I was there.

"What's up?"

"Seems as if one of his ponies has gone missing."

"Like 'missing' how?" the other voice asked.

"Probably stolen. Look, Charlie, you're one of the only officers who's been here long enough to know how this fits with the other cases — Dobson came in with a leather pouch filled with gold nuggets that boy of his found in the bottom of their horse trough this morning."

"Jeez," said the other voice, "not again."

"I'm afraid so. Looks like another one for the Eagle's Nook file." When I heard the name "Eagle's Nook" my heart jumped; Eagle's Nook was Grandma Hattie's winery! I held my breath as Sheriff Lyman continued: "And there were those weird little footprints all around the trough. You could see them clearly in the mud. I just checked and they match the ones in the file perfectly."

"That doesn't surprise me," said the voice belonging to Charlie — whoever "Charlie" was.

"I can't believe it." Sheriff Lyman said, almost to himself. "I really thought Sheriff Billings was pulling my leg when he told me about the Eagle's Nook file. Now it's happening to me and I haven't even been on the job three months. Great way to start out — with a crime that can't be solved — and Dobson's the kind of guy who's gonna' ride my rear until I give him some satisfaction. Damnit!"

The two men were silent for a moment. Then the sheriff continued: "You kept this Eagle's Nook stuff under your hat the whole time you worked for Billings, didn't you?

"Sure did," Charlie said.

"Well, I'd appreciate it if you'd do the same for me — not a word about it to anyone, understand?"

"Of course," Charlie said seriously.

I could hardly believe what I was hearing: *A crime that can't be solved? The Eagle's Nook file? Those weird little footprints that matched those already in the file?* What in the world were they talking about? I heard the men washing their hands and the door finally closing as they left the bathroom. I figured I'd better stay in the john for awhile longer or else I might run into the sheriff or the other guy in the hall and they'd know I'd overheard the conversation. As soon as I thought it was safe, I snuck back into the waiting room. Uncle Walter was talking to the sheriff: "Be honest with me, Gene. You think there's any chance you're going to find him? I've got him entered in a competition at the State Fair in August."

"I don't know, Walter, there's not much to go on right now, but we'll give it our best," the Sheriff said, shaking his head.

Without thinking I butted in, "Hey, what about the foot...?" but caught my-self quickly and shut my mouth. I wasn't supposed to know anything about the footprints matching the others in the file — the mysterious Eagle's Nook file. Uncle Walter and the Sheriff swung around and stared at me. I felt my ears turn hot like they always do when I'm embarrassed and knew my face was probably bright red. "Never mind..." I trailed off.

Walter turned his attention back to the Sheriff: "Somehow I knew you'd say something like that," he said with disgust. He turned to me and said, "Come on, Nick. Let's get outta' here. This whole thing's been a waste of time."

Walter and I rode back to the farm in silence. Only once, when we were pulling away from the Sheriff's Department, did Walter say anything. "There's something fishy goin' on here," he said more to himself than to me. But I couldn't have agreed more. And what's more, I told myself, I was going to do something about it.

The old Carneige Library in St. Helena.

Chapter VII

Clues at the Library

Thursday, June 15, 1967, continued
Twin Oaks Pony Farm
St. Helena, California

As soon as we got back to the farm, I found Henry and asked him to give me a hand getting my bicycle off the back of the truck. We took the crate apart and stowed the pieces in the barn so I could re-use it when it was time to send the bike back to school. Henry wanted to know all about what had happened at the Sheriff's Department, but I put him off with a quick "not much," which was definitely not true, considering what I'd overheard in the bathroom. I couldn't sort it all out right then and just didn't feel like talking. I hoped I wasn't catching Uncle Walter's bad mood.

I didn't waste any time jumping on my bike and taking off down the lane to the river. I wanted to make sure the bike was okay, but I also needed some time by myself to think. I've found that I'm better at working things out while I'm in motion, rather than just sitting around, so once I reached the river, I turned around and rode back to farm and then back to the river again. I kept riding up and down the lane for about a half an hour, so many times that Snoops finally stopped chasing me. On my last leg back from the river, the idea I was looking for finally uncovered itself and I said out loud, "That's it!" It felt good to figure out the next step — one that made some kind of sense — at least it did to me.

I stowed the bike on the front porch of the bunkhouse and walked over to the barn to find Henry. After some initial foot-dragging, I convinced him to help me spade the compost into the vegetable garden, a job that took us the rest of the afternoon. Normally it was a job for the cool of the morning, but I knew I was going to need all the free time I could get tomorrow, and that I wouldn't get it if my chores weren't done. While we were working together, I gave Henry the broad strokes of what I was up to. I told him if I was right, I'd fill him in on the details but for now I just said that I didn't think this was the first time something like this had happened in the valley and I thought I had a way of proving it had happened before. Needless to say, he was intrigued.

After cleaning up, I ran over to the main house and into the kitchen just in time for dinner. Walter was already at the table, his napkin stuck under his chin as usual. Ma-D was busy serving up oven-fried chicken, macaroni and cheese, and broccoli. "Where's Henry?" she asked.

"He's right behind me," I said.

I sat at the table, resisting the urge to dig into the hot macaroni and cheese until everyone was seated at the table.

"Hey, Ma-D..."

"There's no need to 'hey' me, Nick, I'm right here."

"Yes ma'am," I said, "I was just wondering if the library was still open late, like it was last year?"

"Some nights it is, but they changed the schedule. It's hanging up there on the bulletin board next to phone. I cut it out of the paper because I can never remember when they're open and when they're not."

I pushed myself away from the table just as Henry came into the kitchen. "Evening everyone," he said.

A chorus of three "evenings" rang out without anyone actually looking up at Henry.

"Cool!"

"What's cool?" asked Ma-D.

"It's open until nine tonight."

"And why is that *cool?*"

I hadn't completely thought out my story so I had to think fast.

"Ah, I... well, Mr. Hayes actually assigned us some extra credit reading for the summer and I'd like to go see if the library has any of the books he asked us to read."

"After dinner?"

"Yeah, if that's all right. I can ride my bike."

Uncle Walter issued what sounded like one of his "harumpfs" but it was hard to tell because his mouth was full. Ma-D didn't say anything but I knew her well enough to know that she didn't think much of the idea.

"It's no problem, really. I ride all over the place when I'm at school — into town and everything. And I've got a light and reflectors and all that stuff. But I'll be back before dark so you don't have to worry."

"I don't know," said Ma-D, "that high-

My trusty 10-speed.

way's a busy place."

"I know. But there's the shoulder next to the road that's kind'a like a bike lane and I'll be careful. I promise."

"Walter, what do you think?" Ma-D asked across the table.

"I was just thinking."

"I can see that, Walter. The point is *what* are you thinking?" Ma-D asked with an edge to her voice.

"Well, I was thinking that a couple of years from now, Nick'll be able to drive wherever he wants and, quite frankly, that scares me a lot more than him riding his bicycle into town. And like he says, he does it when he's away at school."

I could have jumped up and hugged Uncle Walter but I knew better than to embarrass him that way.

"Thanks Uncle Walter!"

"I'm not sure I approve," Ma-D sighed. "I could always drive you there."

"Now, now, Ma-D, let the boy go on his own."

Henry wisely stayed out of the conversation as I wolfed down my dinner. "It's okay, Ma-D. I'll be all right. If I leave now, I'm sure I can be home before dark."

"Oh, all right. Just leave your dishes in the sink and get going. And be sure and check in with me when you get home."

"Thanks Ma-D, I will. See you in little while," I said as I ran out the screen door, holding it just so, so it wouldn't slam shut. I stopped short on the back porch, turned around, and stuck my head back in the kitchen.

"Thanks Ma-D. Dinner was really delicious."

"Oh, go on," she said from the table, pretending like she didn't care. I grabbed my bike off the front porch of the bunkhouse. Snoops was asleep right next to it and looked up when I moved it, as if to ask me if I wanted him to come. I told him to stay put and I think he was relieved after all the exercise he had earlier, following me back and forth to the river. I took off down the driveway, gravel crunching under my bike's skinny tires, and turned right onto the highway towards town, some four miles north.

As soon as I hit the two-lane highway, I began to have doubts about the idea I had had back at the farm. In an effort to keep me up to date with what was going on at home, Ma-D had ordered a subscription to the *St. Helena Star* — the local weekly newspaper — and had it sent to me at school. It was filled with local news, most of which didn't interest me that much, but the Police Log column was a different story: It was filled with all the calls the St. Helena Police Department had received during the week, and it was the one thing I always read, mostly because of the crazy stuff it contained — the usual cats stuck up trees, a guy who was so drunk he went to bed in a stranger's house, mysterious loud music coming from the middle of a vineyard and a lot of lost-and-found items.

I remembered Sheriff Lyman saying that he would put a notice in the Police Log section of the *St. Helena Star* about the pouch I'd found in the trough. I also remembered what Charlie, the guy Sheriff Lyman was talking to in the bathroom, had said — that the gold-filled pouch "was another one for the Eagle's Nook file." I figured if there were other similar cases in the past, there should be other notices in the Police Log, right? Notices of other leather pouches found somewhere in the valley? Made sense to me. But the more I thought about it, the shakier my idea seemed. I wasn't even sure the library kept back issues of the *Star*. And if they didn't, then where would I be?

Once the highway reached the outskirts of St. Helena, it turned into Main Street — about a three-block-long, tree-lined street containing old, two- and three-story commercial buildings, most of them built in the late 1800s. I sped through town and turned left at the north end of town, to the old library, just a block off of Main Street.

I left my bike, not bothering to lock it, in the bike stand outside the library. Once inside, I recognized Mrs. Fly — it was a hard name to forget — behind the check-out counter. She had been a librarian there for as long as I could remember and used to be the person who came to our school to read stories to us kids.

"Hi Mrs. Fly. How are you?" I asked quietly, standing in front of the counter.

"Is that you, Nick Sinclair? My, you've certainly grown."

"Yeah, well, you know…" I said, looking at my shoes.

"As a matter of fact, I do know. Time! What's it all about? Do you want to hear a story?"

"Yeah, sure," I said, remembering that, for an adult, Mrs. Fly could be pretty funny.

Leaning over the counter, speaking like she was telling me some secret, Mrs. Fly whispered: "There's an old lady who lives in my bathroom."

"Really?" I said, interested.

"Yes. And she's really fast."

"What do you mean?"

"Well, every morning I go in there, and I can see her in the mirror and I turn around as fast as I can and she's gone!"

I thought about it for a minute, got the joke, and laughed, even though I wasn't sure I should have.

"What brings you in here so late in the day? It looks like you're on some kind of a mission."

"I am, kind of," I said. "Do you have old copies of the *St. Helena Star* here?"

"Old copies? Like how old?"

"I'm not sure..." I said, trailing off. I had the sinking feeling that my mission was about to turn into a wild goose chase.

"Well, we keep the last couple of months of them in the periodical section."

"I think I'm going to have to look further back than that."

"If you don't mind me asking, what are you looking for?"

"I'm not exactly sure, but if it's there, it'll be in the Police Log section."

"Hmmmmm... in that case we'll have to check in the microfiche section. We have copies of the *Star* all the way back to when it started in 1874."

"Really?"

"Yep. Do you know how to work a microfiche reader?"

"No," I said, not even knowing what microfiche was.

"There's nothing to it. Come on over here."

I followed her over to a desk in middle of the library. I noticed I was the only person there, which was just fine by me. There was a machine on the desk that looked a little like a small television.

"So where do you want to start?" Mrs. Fly asked.

"What do you mean?" I said, feeling like I was already in over my head.

"What issue do you want to start with?"

"How about this time a year ago?" I said, not being able to think of a better answer.

"Okay" Mrs. Fly said and went over to a storage case and pulled out a smallish black box filled with what looked like sheets of black-and-white negative film. "So here's what you do. First you have to turn the thing on," she said, flipping a switch at the back of the machine, causing the screen to light up. "Each one of these sheets contains a year's worth of the *Star*. You insert the film – this one's from last year – into this slot and then you use these little levers to position the lens over the top left-hand corner. Just like a book, the images are in order, left to right, top to bottom. It doesn't take much pressure to move around on the page. You'll get the hang of it. Here, give it a try."

The microfiche machine.

Mrs. Fly had left the lens centered on the image of the front page of the *Star* from exactly a year earlier. I operated the levers and pages of the newspaper whizzed by. Sure enough, it didn't take me long to figure out how to get from page to page. Each issue of the *Star* was only six or so pages, and the Police Log was always on the same page in each issue. In a few minutes I was running through the issues quickly, scanning the Police Log for any mention of a leather pouch — so quickly it had a dizzying, almost hypnotic effect. After about an hour, I felt like I was in a trance. I stood up to stretch and Mrs. Fly called over to me, "Find what you're looking for?"

"Not yet."

"Well, we're open for another couple of hours."

"I don't know if my eyes can take another couple of hours of this, but thanks," I said and sat back down. I'd reached the point where I was almost certain I wasn't going to find what I was looking for. I had gone through nine years of the *Star* when I saw it — a headline on the front page: "Upvalley Family Killed in Crash on Mt. St. Helena." Of course I knew the facts; I don't know how, but I knew them all. But somehow I'd never seen the newspaper before. After all these years, it made it even more real. My eyes spontaneously filled with tears as I read the first lines of the article. About how we hit a deer and went off the road, hitting a massive pine tree. About how we had been returning from a dinner with my mom's family in Middletown. I had only the vaguest memories of the accident. About all I remembered was lying on a pile of leaves after the accident and the way they smelled and being taken to the hospital in an ambulance with the siren going.

I sat just staring at the screen, not reading any more of the article. A huge wave of sadness came over me and I thought I was going to be sick. I got up and went to the bathroom. I went into one of the stalls, closed the door and sat on the toilet and held my head in hands. Suddenly I was crying as more memories came flooding in. The way my mother's pearl necklace felt on my face when she bent over me and the way she smelled, kissing me good night in my bed. The scratchiness of my father's chin when he held my head next to his, telling me how much he loved me. The way my brother, Lucas, and I would wrestle on the grass, Lucas always winning and how he taught me to climb the big fig tree in our backyard. One huge wave of blurred images and feelings.

I've always known these memories were there, but I learned to hold them in check. They were too much. Too sad. Sometimes I hated the fact that I was here and they weren't. Other times, even with Ma-D and Walter, even with

Grandma Hattie, I felt very alone. The strength of these feelings was so strong I didn't know what would happen if I let them out of where I kept them walled up and hidden. I knew I couldn't do anything to help my mom, my dad, my brother. And they couldn't do anything to help me. So whenever the memories came creeping in I'd do something, anything — ride my bike as far and as fast as I could, run through the vineyards and down to the river — anything to replace the feelings with motion, with movement taking me away from the hurt.

I sat on the toilet for a few more minutes and finally stopped crying. I forced myself to come around. It didn't take long to realize that I was sitting in library bathroom, crying my eyes out and that I really didn't want to be there. I got up and splashed cold water in my face at the sink. I dried my face with a wad of paper towels and avoided looking at myself in the mirror. I needed to get back to what I was doing — back to the here and now. I went back to where I had been sitting in front of the microfiche reader. In a couple of minutes I was back speeding through year after year of the Police Logs. All of a sudden it was there. I wasn't sure if I could believe my eyes. I reread the entry and cried out "yes!" forgetting for the moment where I was.

"Yes *what?*" Mrs. Fly asked.

"I, ummm, I may have found something."

"I'm sure you've found a lot of things, but is it what you were looking for?"

"I think so."

I reread the entry for the third time: "Found at Black's Nursery: Small leather, drawstring pouch. If you are the owner, please contact Sheriff Billings at the Napa Country Sheriff's Department to describe contents and verify ownership."

"Wow," I said under my breath.

I walked over to where Mrs. Fly was sitting just as the telephone on her desk rang. "Hold on a minute, Nick," she said as she picked up the receiver. "St. Helena Public Library. Oh hi, Mary, nice to hear your voice. Yes, he's here. Yes. Yes. I'll tell him. Okay. Talk to you later."

"That was your aunt, Nick. She's says to get your... she says it's time for you to be home."

"Okay. Thanks, Mrs. Fly." I said, embarrassed that Ma-D had called. "I was just wondering. Is there any way to make a copy of what's on the screen?"

"Sure," said Mrs. Fly, "let me show you."

"You can just tell me how, I can do it."

"There's a small red print button on the right hand side of the screen. Just make sure the screen is displaying what you want printed and then push the

button. The copy will come out the back of the machine."

"Thanks Mrs. Fly. Thanks for your help."

"That's what I'm here for."

I made the copy, folded it, and put it safely in my front shirt pocket, not really believing I had actually found it. I thanked Mrs. Fly again and was halfway out the door when I suddenly remembered why I supposedly had to go to the library. It wouldn't look good to show up back at the farm without a book.

"Oh, Mrs. Fly, you don't happen to have a copy of *Silverado Squatters*, do you? By Robert Louis Stevenson?"

"Of course we do. Several copies. Do you want one?"

"Yes. My English teacher back at school thought I should read it this summer, seeing as how I was here in the valley and everything."

"You *should* read it. And you should hike up Mt. St. Helena to see where it took place. You know what the book's about don't you?"

"Kind of."

"It's an account of Robert Louis Stevenson's stay here in the valley back in 1880. He had just gotten married to Fanny Osbourne and didn't have any money, so he came up here and spent his honeymoon camped out in an abandoned mine called Silverado up on Mt. St. Helena. Great stuff. You'll like it. And while you're at it, take this one, too," she said as she handed me another book.

"What is it?" I asked.

"It's *Stevenson at Silverado*, written by a local author. It helps explain some of the things Stevenson wrote about in *Silverado Squatters*. We'll make you an expert on the subject."

"I doubt that, but thanks."

I checked the books out, said goodbye to Mrs. Fly and ran to get my bike out of the rack. I got back to the farm just as it was beginning to get dark. Getting off my bike, I realized I didn't remember anything about the ride back; my brain was racing way faster than I was.

Ma-D was waiting for me on the back porch.

"It's about time," she said.

"I told you I'd be back before dark."

"Barely... Did you find what you were looking for?"

Proving that I had what I went to the library to get, I waved the two books in the air and said "I think so, Ma-D. I think so."

•   •   •

I heard Grandpa's truck coming up the drive and jumped off the front porch and reached Grandpa and Doyle as they were unloading the truck.

"How'd you know that?" I said, holding the journal in air.

"Know what?"

"About the leather pouch filled with gold."

"Well, for one, you told me yesterday about what happened at Darren's place."

"No. That's not what I mean. How'd you know about it… what… like 40 some years ago? You wrote about, right here," I said, still waving the journal around.

"Because that's what happened, Joaquin."

"You didn't say the story was true."

"I didn't say one way or another. I said you'd have to make up your mind about it."

"I just talked with Darren and he said his dad did the same thing – he took the pouch to the Sheriff's Department and they said they'd do the same thing."

"What?"

"Put a notice in the Police Blotter section of the *Star* and see if anyone claims it."

"Well, there you have it."

"Yeah, well, it's kind of weirding me out."

"Good."

"What?"

"Just keep reading, Joaquin. You'll see."

So that's what I did. All afternoon.

About the same time as I was arriving at the pony farm, Nigel was flying from London to California, ready to make my life miserable.

Chapter VIII

The Badger

Friday, June 16, 1967
San Francisco International Airport

Nigel Stayne stood in the customs line at the San Francisco International Airport. He had just arrived on an overnight flight from London. After a lifetime of traveling the world, he never got used to waiting in lines. If anything, the older he got, the more impatient he had become. "Maybe," he thought to himself, "if this job works out, I won't have to travel anymore." Trying to put himself in a better mood, he fantasized about what retirement might be like in the Scottish countryside, with nothing but his fishing pole and his two Jack Russell terriers to distract him. "That's more than enough for me," he thought as he inched his way forward in the line.

"That's quite the passport you've got there, Mr. Stayne," the customs officer said, looking for an empty space to stamp with a visa.

"Goes with the territory," Nigel said wearily.

"And what territory would that be?" the official asked.

Nigel didn't like being chatted up by people he didn't know, but knew enough to be friendly with customs officers. "I'm a photojournalist," he said.

"Really?" the officer said, looking interested. "Is this your first trip to California?"

"Yes."

"Business or pleasure?"

"Pleasure, I hope."

"And where will you be staying during your trip, Mr. Stayne?"

"The Napa Valley."

The customs officer's eyes lit up again. "Lucky you. It's a beautiful place."

"So I'm told," Nigel said as the official handed him his passport back.

"Enjoy your stay."

"I intend to," Nigel responded.

Nigel walked to the parking lot to where he had been told he'd find a late model, slightly beat-up, white Jeep Wagoneer, the keys in one of those magnetic holders placed under the front bumper. If there was one thing he had learned over the years it was that it didn't pay to stand out in a new town, especially a small town. When he spied the Wagoneer, he said "perfect" under his breath.

He opened the back, threw his satchel in and thought about the fact that it was just yesterday that he had been summoned to Lord Higgenbotham's office for the first time — not to mention the first time he'd heard the fantastic story Higgenbotham told him — which had led him to where he was right now, all with head-spinning speed. "Rich people are like that," thought Nigel, "everything 'now, now, now.'" And Higgenbotham was certainly rich; he owned the world's largest media conglomerate — comprised of hundreds of newspapers, magazines, and television stations around the world.

Nigel ran through the events of the last 24 hours. He had never had an assignment from Lord Higgenbotham's International News Agency before; they usually used people from their own in-house team to get the stories they wanted. When he received the letter from Lord Higgenbotham, Nigel puzzled over why he would want to use an outsider for an assignment and, more intriguing, why had he been asked to meet with the big man himself? Perhaps it was a personal assignment, Nigel thought to himself, something that Lord Higgenbotham didn't want to reveal to any of his staff. As he sat in the posh offices of the International News Agency on Fleet Street, pondering the possible reasons for the meeting, the receptionist looked at Nigel over the top of her glasses and said: "Lord Higgenbotham will see you now," nodding to the huge wooden doors which led to his office.

Nigel got up and entered the inner sanctum of the lord himself. If anything, it was even grander and more impressive than the room Nigel had just left. At the end of the long room sat the man who owned the world's largest publishing empire. Lord Higgenbotham was a very large man, both tall and very fat, but he looked almost small sitting behind a wood desk that was as big as a boat.

As Nigel walked toward him, Lord Higgenbotham boomed out "so you're the one they call the Badger, eh? You don't look like one."

Nigel didn't wasn't sure how to respond, so he simply sat in one of the chairs in front of the massive desk.

"Your reputation has proceeded you, Badger. I've got a job for someone with your, shall we say, 'determination'."

"Yes?" Nigel responded.

"A private matter of great importance to me."

"I see," Nigel said, thinking he had guessed right.

"Here, read this," Lord Higgenbotham said, shoving a worn sheet of paper in Nigel's direction.

The desk was so wide that Nigel had to lean over on one leg and even then could barely grab the paper. He sat back down and quickly read through it. The writing appeared to be copied from a ship's log — an entry made by the captain of the ship about discovering stowaways and the trouble that ensued after their discovery. Nigel finished reading and looked up blankly.

"My great uncle, Thom Higgenbotham, was a sailor aboard that ship, close to a hundred years ago. He copied that page directly from the captain's log so he'd have proof of what he saw."

"What did he see exactly," Nigel asked.

"What did he see? Gnomes!" Lord Higgenbotham bellowed.

"Gnomes?" Nigel responded, thinking maybe Higgenbotham must be kidding.

"Yes, dammit. Gnomes. You heard me. And what's more, after the ship docked in San Francisco, he saw the gnomes being loaded into crates and being taken away by the captain's own wagon. He found out from the driver that they were going to the captain's farm. Uncle Thom also said they were carrying a ton of gold with them — he'd seen it himself when the gnomes were still on the ship. He went to his grave swearing the story was true. There are still people around who know about him and his story and they all think Thom Higgenbotham was a lunatic. Casts a shadow on the family name is what it does. Came up again just the other day when I was playing cards at the club. Some cheeky S.O.B. suggested the way I played cards was related to my Uncle Thom's lunacy. It's time to prove them all wrong. Big time. Rub their noses in what's going to be one of the biggest stories of all time."

"What exactly do you want me to do?" Nigel said, completely confused as to why he was there.

"Find the gnomes, dammit!" Higgenbotham yelled. "Find them, photograph them, do whatever it is you do."

"But, sir, you just said yourself, it's been almost a hundred years — we're a little late to the game."

"Don't you know anything, Badger? Don't you remember the stories you read as a kid? The little buggers live practically forever."

"Do you have any, ah, any other information?" Nigel asked, thinking this was going to be the biggest, stupidest assignment he'd ever taken — if, indeed, he decided to take it.

SHIP'S LOG

S. S.   Lindesfarne, Voyage #19

From: Glasgow, Scotland   towards   Reykjavik, Iceland

Date: 28 February 1879

Major disturbance onboard just after eight bells this evening. Under full sail, heading SW in the Firth of Henry. First mate Nyquist at the helm. Cold night, good wind. Third mate Higgenbotham, in a very agitated state, summons me from my cabin to go below decks. We were met by Second mate Syrjala standing next to one of the large crates we took on board in Glasgow. Syrjala explained that he and Higgenbotham were in the hold inspecting the lashings on the cargo when he thought he heard faint voices inside the wooden crates. Fearing stowaways, he immediately dispatched Higgenbotham to bring me belowdecks. After some deliberation it was decided to open the crate. There were indeed stowaways in the crate (and in other crates, as well). After several hours and considerable confusion (along with some minor injuries), the situation was resolved. Higgenbotham produced a firearm but, thankfully, no shots were fired. A most unusual evening, indeed.

Signed,
Gustave Niebaum
Master
1st Mate: P. Nyquist
2nd Mate: L. Syrjala
3rd Mate: T. Higgenbotham

**The copied page from the ship's log
(see page 311 for a printed version).**

"Only that the captain's name was Gustave Niebaum — famous bloke in his time — and that the winery he founded is still there — Eagle's Nook — somewhere there in what they call the Napa Valley. I want you to leave immediately, drop whatever else you're doing. Leave tonight. I've already booked your tickets."

"But..." Nigel started to say.

"But nothing," Lord Higgenbotham blurted out, "if it's money you're worried about, don't. I'll double whatever it is you usually charge. I'll even triple it if you come back with the goods. Hell, I'll even split their hoard of gold with you."

Lord Higgenbotham may have been one of the most powerful men in the world, Nigel thought to himself, but he was clearly off his rocker. But if the old fool wanted to throw his money away, Nigel was more than happy to catch it.

•   •   •

As he spread out the map that had been left for him on the front seat of the Wagoneer, Nigel quelled a flutter of excitement in the pit of his stomach. He was well aware that this was potentially the biggest story he had ever been assigned to cover — that is, if it were true, and Nigel definitely had his doubts about that, but Lord Higgenbotham had been insistent. But really? Gnomes? Nigel didn't think so.

Nigel checked the route from the airport to the Napa Valley; it looked straightforward enough. He'd found his way around far more exotic places than California many times in the course of his career. Even though he was just 46 years old, he had been at this business for twenty-five years — a mix of everything from the most sensational stories (like the series he did on the Loch Ness monster), to stories of real substance: hurricanes, tsunamis, earthquakes, you name it. If it was unusual or dangerous, Nigel had covered it with his camera and typewriter. The one thing you could say for him was that his stories sold newspapers, and lots of them, even if the methods he used to get them were often as unconventional as they were brutal.

Nigel took off from the airport and headed north on Highway 101. He found a local classical radio station and turned it on low, just some pleasant background music for his daydreams of retirement — of catching salmon on the River Tweed, and mostly, the pots of money he might just take away from this job.

Snoops and I walked down to the river to try and figure things out.

Chapter IX

Hattie Holds the Key?

Friday, June 16, 1967
Twin Oaks Pony Farm
St. Helena, California

I woke up earlier than usual the next morning. It wasn't even 6:30 when Snoops and I quietly left the bunkhouse to walk down to the river. The morning sky was gray, overcast, and subdued, with only the occasional "coo-coo-coo" of the mourning doves and the sound of Snoops tearing through the vineyards looking for quail.

I needed some quiet time to figure out what to do next. It made me uncomfortable that all my ideas either involved doing something I'd never done before or telling a lie — a white lie I guess, but a lie all the same. But the more I thought about the leather pouch found at Black's Nursery some twelve years ago, the more I knew I'd have to go there to see if I could dig up any more of the story. I wondered if old Mr. Black, who owned the nursery, was even still alive?

Once I got to the river, I absentmindedly threw a few rocks into the water, convinced Snoops not to go after them, and then headed back to the house. As I passed Chuy's house, I thought about how much easier it would be to come up with a plan if Chuy were around — he was good at making plans. Right now, I definitely wasn't working on some big plan. All I could figure out was take it one step at a time and see where it led me. When I had problems writing a paper at school, Mr. Hayes would tell me to "just move from the known to the unknown; if you try to tackle it all at once, you'll get overwhelmed and not be able to do anything."

"Move from the known to the unknown," I repeated to myself as Snoops and I got back to the farm. Well, all that was known to me right now was that something happened twelve years ago at Black's Nursery that caused someone to put that notice in the *St. Helena Star*. If I was going to figure out who stole Quicksilver, I was going to have to see if there was anything I could learn there. A plant nursery seemed like an unlikely place to hold the key to solving a mystery, but that's what I had to work with. *It's the only thing I can do,* I thought to myself.

. . .

I looked at my watch and there was still some time before breakfast, so I decided to get started on planting those potatoes Uncle Walter wanted me to get in the ground. I was about halfway through the job when Ma-D called from the back porch to "come and get it." As I straightened up I saw Henry coming out of the bunkhouse and waited for him by the vegetable garden.

"You're up early, Nick. What? You already got those potatoes planted?"

"Just about. I wanted to get to it before it gets too hot. Hey, Henry, I noticed that Ma-D doesn't have any cucumbers planted. What's up with that?" Every year Ma-D made a big deal out of putting up twenty-four quarts of her famous dill pickles, about half of which she gave away as Christmas presents.

"I hadn't noticed. You'll have to ask her."

The morning overcast was beginning to burn off as Henry and I approached the back door. Snoops had found his favorite spot on the porch in a patch of sun up against the wall of the house. He was on his back with all four paws in the air, rubbing his back, back and forth. It must have felt good because he was letting out little moans of pleasure. Henry and I entered the kitchen to the smell of cooking bacon and Buttercup singing loudly from his cage over the sink.

"Morning, boys," Ma-D said, standing in front of the stove flipping French toast in a large, black cast-iron frying pan. "Everyone feeling fine this morning?"

"Fine as frog hair," Henry said.

"Morning Uncle Walter," I said as I sat at the table.

"Morning," Walter replied from behind his newspaper.

Ma-D started setting plates filled with triangular pieces of golden-brown French toast on the table. "There's melted butter and hot maple syrup in the pitchers. Help yourself. And there's plenty of bacon, so don't be shy," she said as she landed a platter full of crisp bacon in the middle of the table.

"This is really good, Ma-D," I said.

"Don't talk with your mouth full," Ma-D said.

"You going to get those pota-

Snoops sunning himself.

toes planted today, Nick?" Uncle Walter asked.

"I already did. Or at least most of them. I'll plant the rest of them after breakfast."

Walter looked at me with a surprised expression.

"Yeah. I woke up early this morning and decided to get an early start on it."

"Well, I'll be," Walter said, attacking the French toast like it was something alive.

"Ma-D, I noticed there aren't any cucumbers in the garden. Aren't you going to make pickles this year?" I asked.

"Of course I'm going to make pickles this year. The nursery was out of the variety I like when I planted the garden, so now I'm going to have to plant them from plants instead of seeds. Which reminds me, they're supposed to be in at the nursery this week. I'll have to go by and pick them up."

"I'll go and get them for you," I said.

"How're you going to get there? Oh, that's right, you've got that bicycle."

"Yeah, no problem, Ma-D. How many do you want?"

"A dozen... no, make it sixteen, just in case any of 'em turn up their toes on me. And look at the label before you buy them. Make sure they're all the 'County Fair' variety. That's what I ordered."

"Sixteen 'County Fair' cucumbers. Will do," I said wiping up the last of the syrup with a piece of French toast.

"Henry, you have time for givin' me a hand putting up the cucumber teepees?" Ma-D asked.

"Sure, if you show me where you want 'em."

"I want to get them up before Nick gets back with the plants. It's already so late in the planting season."

With that, everyone except Walter pushed their chairs from the table and stacked their plates in the sink. "Just leave those there, Nick, Henry. You've both got work to do. Go on. Shoo!" Ma-D insisted. "Before you go, put this out for Sammy," Ma-D said, handing me a left-over piece of French toast from her plate. She swore her "pet" blackbird had shown up the same day Doyle had delivered me to the farm almost ten years ago, and she'd been feeding him ever since. Somewhere along the way, she had nailed

'County Fair' cucumber plants.

a metal pie plate to the back porch railing and whenever she put some food in it, it was only a matter of a minute or two before Sammy the crow showed up and ate it, usually making a lot of noise as he did. Ma-D was well aware of all the bad things crows were supposed to represent, but she figured as long as she fed it, maybe Sammy would be a positive, friendly force in her world. Walter thought she was crazy.

I put the French toast on the pie plate and Snoops followed me off the porch, back to the vegetable garden. "That wasn't so hard, was it, Snoops?" I said, pleased that I'd been able to take advantage of the cucumber situation and parlay it into a solo fact-finding trip. Feeling like I was "Nick, Ace of Spies," I ran over to the bunkhouse and put on a clean t-shirt and my lucky hat and then ran over to the house to tell Ma-D I was leaving.

"Don't forget we have an account at the nursery, Nick. It's under my name."

"No problem, Ma-D."

"And make sure they're 'County Fairs'!"

"Will do," I said as I attached a basket to the rear rack of my bicycle with a bungee cord.

•   •   •

Black's Nursery was about halfway between the farm and the town of St. Helena. It only took me about fifteen minutes to get to there, long enough for me to try and figure out how I was going to get the information I wanted from Mr. Black, assuming he was still around. Not coming up with much of a plan, I decided to just wing it.

I rode through the parking lot at the nursery and leaned my bicycle next to the small, one-story building that served as a combination office and greenhouse. There didn't seem to be anyone around, so I rang the bell on the counter, marked with a small sign that read "For Assistance."

"Be right with you," came a disembodied voice from a small room behind the counter. A few seconds later Mr. Black — a stooped man with a shock of white hair, wearing a pair of blue overalls and plaid shirt — ambled up to the counter, holding on to anything he could find along the way to steady himself. "And what can I do for you, young man?"

"Hi, Mr. Black. You probably don't remember me, but I'm Nick Sinclair. I'm here to pick up some cucumber plants my aunt, Ma... ah, Mary Dobson ordered."

"Well, well. I can't say I would have recognized you, Nick, but sure I remember you. Good to see you. I was just going to give Mary a jingle to let her know they were in."

"That's great. She's anxious to get them planted."

"I'll bet she is. There's a bunch of six-packs of them right out there on the corner of the first table in the lath house. I'm sure you can find them. It'd take me half an hour to walk over there..." Mr. Black said, laughing to himself.

"No problem," I replied, "they're 'County Fairs,' aren't they?"

"Absolutely. Your aunt was very clear about that."

"Good. I'll be right back."

I returned to the check-out counter with the cucumber plants in the bottom of a cut-off cardboard box.

"Ma-D asked me to put them on her account."

"That's fine," Mr. Black said as he pulled out a receipt book, filling in the information with a slightly shaky hand.

I decided it was now or never. "Ah, Mr. Black, I was wondering something."

"What's that?" Mr. Black said, looking up from the tablet, his smudged glasses low on his nose.

"Well, I was doing some research at the library the other night and I ran across an old item in the Police Log of the *Star* that said something about a leather pouch being found here at the nursery."

Mr. Black looked a little blank, but finally said, "that was a long time ago."

"Twelve years ago, actually. I was wondering if anyone ever claimed it?"

"Well, as a matter of fact, no one ever did. What's your interest in it? That pouch wasn't yours was it? Although, come to think of it, you wouldn't have been much more than a toddler back then."

"No, no," I stumbled, "it wasn't mine." I wanted to ask him what was in the pouch but I doubted he would tell me. "Just out of curiosity, I was wondering if anything was stolen from your nursery around the same time as the pouch showed up?"

"You're an inquisitive one, aren't you? This have anything to do with that horse of your uncle's that's gone missing?"

"You know about that?" I responded, genuinely surprised.

"Sure. Everyone knows about it. You know you can't fart in this town without..."

"Yeah, I know. That's what my uncle says," I said. I thought for a minute, glad of the fact that there wasn't anybody else in the store. "As a matter of fact it does."

"Figures. To answer your question, there *was* a robbery here."

"Can you tell me what was taken?"

"Can't see that it hurts. Forty-eight one-gallon fuchsia plants. Damnedest thing. Wiped me out. And who in their right mind would pay over a thousand... " Mr. Black said, stopping himself in the middle of the sentence.

Fuchsia flower.

"You mean someone stole the plants and then paid you for them?"

"Not exactly. Now listen, Nick, like I said, that was a long time ago and I've never been exactly clear about what happened or why. To tell you the truth, it was all mighty strange. The only person who might know something more is Ed Billings — you know, the old sheriff. He was the one in charge of the case. Go talk to him. He lives right over there across the vineyard. You can practically see his house from here."

Sensing I had learned as much as I was going to, I signed the receipt and gathered up the cucumbers. "Thanks for your help, Mr. Black. I didn't mean to bother you."

"No bother. I just can't tell you any more about what I don't know, if you know what I mean."

"I understand. You wouldn't happen to have Sheriff Billings's address would you?"

"Sure, he's got an account here. Let me look it up. "Here it is: Ed Billings. 1516 Sulphur Springs Lane. You won't have any problem finding it."

"Thanks again for your help, Mr. Black."

"I don't know how much help I was. Maybe you'll have better luck with Ed."

"We'll see," I said, waving goodbye as I walked out to the parking lot.

"That was interesting," I thought to myself as I put the cucumber plants in the basket on the back of my bicycle. "Now what?"

I thought about "now what" as I started to ride back to the farm and decided to take a detour to see if Sheriff Billings was home. "What the heck," I thought, "I'm going to pass right by his place on the way home anyway." And with that I turned up Sulphur Springs Lane and, just as Mr. Black had said, didn't have any problem finding it — a large brownish, one-story ranch house, with a huge front lawn, surrounded by vineyards.

I tried to compose myself as I walked up the path through the lawn. I knocked on the door and heard the sound of steps inside. I was expecting Sheriff Billings to answer the door and was surprised when a woman I assumed was Mrs. Billings opened the door.

"Mrs. Billings?"

"Yes."

"I'm Nick Sinclair and I was wondering if Sheriff Billings was in?"

"Why yes, he is. Would you like to see him?"

"If it's not a bother."

"No bother at all. He's out in his workshop, doing whatever it is he does out there. Come on in. His workshop is in the backyard. Tell me your name again."

"Nick Sinclair."

"That's what I thought you said. You're Mark and Elaine's son, aren't you?

"Yes, ma'am."

"Oh my. I knew your mother and father well, Nick. Such a tragedy. I'm so sorry."

I was somewhat taken aback and wasn't quite sure what to say, other than "thank you."

"Well, I must say you bear a striking resemblance to your father."

"Yes, I've heard that." In truth, I hadn't heard that as very few of the people I met brought up the subject of my parents, let alone their deaths.

"You'll find him out there," Mrs. Billings said, opening the sliding glass door that led from the kitchen to the backyard.

"Thanks," I said as I walked across the back lawn to the small workshop. Before I reached the open door, I could hear some kind of power equipment running. When I reached the doorway, I saw Sheriff Billings leaning over a lathe, wearing protective glasses and noise protectors that looked like big earmuffs. I knocked on the doorjamb and then tried yelling "hello" a couple of times, but couldn't get his attention. Finally I resorted to flapping my arms around and succeeded in catching Sheriff Billings's eye. The lathe whined to a stop and the Sheriff took off his glasses and ear protectors.

"Well, hello there. I know I know you, but I can't remember your name."

"Ah, it's Nick Sinclair, Sheriff, from over at Twin Oaks Pony Farm."

"Oh, sure. Walter and Mary Dobson's place. How you doing, Nick?"

"Okay, sir. Am I interrupting you?"

"To tell you the truth, it's hard to interrupt a man who's retired. I was just working on a salad bowl here," he said, motioning to the large chunk of wood on the lathe. "It's black walnut. Hard as all get out. But like I said, I've got plenty of time. So tell me, son, what brings you here?"

"I was just at Black's Nursery and Mr. Black suggested I come and talk with you."

"Let me guess: this have anything to do with your uncle's missing horse?"

"So you know about it, too?"

"Oh sure. Gene — Sheriff Lyman — called me right after he saw your uncle the other day."

I was uncertain what to say next. I didn't think it was a good idea to admit that I'd eavesdropped on Sheriff Lyman in the bathroom and learned about the "Eagle's Nook file." I hesitated for a minute and said, "Well, then I guess you know all about the leather pouch and the gold, too?"

"Sure I do."

"Well, I was going through some old copies of the *Star* the other night and found out that a similar pouch had been found at Black's Nursery twelve years ago."

"Is that how you spend your evenings, Nick? Going through old copies of the *Star*? That's kind of a strange pastime for a young man like yourself isn't it?"

Embarrassed, I said "no, it's not something I do every evening. But like I said, I was just over talking to Mr. Black at the nursery. He said some plants were stolen, but wouldn't say much more than that."

"Something tells me you're further down this road than you're letting on, Nick. But you need to know that if you're talking about what I think you are, officially it's still an open case. And even though I'm retired, I can't discuss it. Don't get me wrong, Nick. You're old enough to hear the facts. The whole business — and I'm guessing you know what business I'm talking about — was always a little too weird for me. Still is. But weird or not, I can't talk to you about it. If you came for advice, I'd say go talk to your grandmother. She's the one who can give it to you straight."

"Grandma Hattie?"

"Do you have another one?"

"No."

"Well, that's the one I mean then."

"*Grandma Hattie?*" I asked again, not believing what I'd heard.

"Grandma Hattie," Sheriff Billings insisted. "Sorry not to have been more help, Nick, but trust me, I'm steering you in the right direction."

I thanked Sheriff Billings and walked back across the lawn and let myself out to the front yard through a gate by the garage. It was probably rude, but I just didn't want to have to talk to Mrs. Billings again.

I rode away from the Billings's house, more confused than when I arrived. Not only had he given me more information than I thought he would, it was information that didn't entirely make sense to me. And his advice to ask Grandma Hattie made absolutely no sense at all. I wondered if he was just pulling my leg and having a good laugh about it about with Sheriff Lyman. Or Mr. Black, for that matter. I circled back to Grandma Hattie, wondering what she could possibly know about all this, when I noticed I was pedaling harder than normal. I looked back at my rear tire and saw it was low. *I wonder if I've got a leak?* I thought to myself. Luckily there was a gas station on the highway, just up ahead. I stopped in and filled my tire and then went to use the water fountain. At the counter I noticed a stack of new *St. Helena Star* newspapers and bought one, knowing that the notice Sheriff Lyman had written should be in the Police Log. Uncle Walter, of course, subscribed to the *Star* but, for some reason, I wanted a copy of my own. I leafed through the paper, found the Police Log and, sure enough, the notice was there, along with a front page story about Quicksilver's disappearance. I wondered what, if anything, it would turn up. I didn't get my hopes up.

When I got back to the farm, no one was around except for Snoops, who barked excitedly when I showed up.

I noticed that Henry and Ma-D had set up the bamboo teepees in the garden, so I grabbed the cucumber plants, which had begun to wilt from the heat and wind, and decided to plant them right away. After I had them in the ground, I gave them all a drink of water from the hose, hoping they'd revive sooner rather than later.

It wasn't long before Walter and Ma-D drove up in the truck, explaining they'd gone to town to pick up the mail and go to the grocery store. I noticed a copy of the *Star* in Uncle Walter's hand, along with the rest of the day's mail.

"Did you see the notice?" I asked him.

"What notice?" he replied grumpily. He'd been in one long bad mood ever since Quicksilver had gone missing.

"The one in the Police Log."

"Yeah, I saw it. For all the good it'll do," he said walking toward the back porch. Ma-D, who was following Walter with a bag of groceries in her arms, rolled her eyes at Nick.

"I see you got the cucumbers in," Ma-D said, glancing over to the garden. "That's great. No problems at Black's?"

I hesitated, thinking there were plenty of problems at Black's and even more at Sheriff Billings' place, but simply said, "No problems, Ma-D."

"Where's Henry?" I asked.

"Said he was going to get his hair cut," Ma-D answered.

"Okay. I'll be in the bunkhouse reading if you need me," I said, knowing I had to come up with a plan to see Grandma Hattie, as soon as possible.

•　　•　　•

I took off my shoes and lay on the bed, staring at the ceiling. Maybe I was over-thinking this. After all, the last time I talked with Grandma Hattie, just the day before yesterday, she had wanted to see me right away. I decided the direct route was best: I'd just call her and ask if I could come for a visit.

I walked into the living room of the bunkhouse. There was another black wall phone behind the front door, just like the one in Ma-D's kitchen, only this one had a short cord. I dialed my grandmother's number and got Doyle on the third ring.

"Sinclair household, Doyle speaking."

"Doyle, it's Nick. How are you?"

"I'm fine, Master Sinclair. What can I do for you?"

If any of my friends knew someone called me "Master Sinclair," they'd never let me forget it, I thought, cringing.

"Is my grandmother in?"

"She's right here, as a matter of fact. We're playing a very heated game of cribbage."

"I don't want to interrupt."

"She'll be pleased to hear from you. Let me put her on."

"Hello. Is that you, Nick?"

"Yes, Grandma, it's me.

"Well, how are you?"

"I'm just fine, Grandma. How are you?"

"I'd be doing better if I were winning. I think Doyle may be cheating."

I could hear sounds of protest in the background. "I was wondering if I might come and visit you, Grandma?"

"Of course, of course. Any time you want."

"I know it's short notice, but I was thinking..." Right then another voice broke onto the line. It was Ma-D.

"Hello, hello? Who's there?"

I'd had forgotten that the phone in the house and the phone in the bunkhouse were on the same line.

"It's me, Ma-D. I'm on the line with Grandma."

"Nick? Are you there? Who are you talking to?" Grandma Hattie asked.

This was getting confusing. "Ma-D's on the other phone, Grandma."

"Oh, hello Mary. How are you?"

"I'm fine, Hattie. Are you well?"

"Very, now that I know Nick's coming for a visit."

"Nick's coming for a visit? Is that right, Nick?"

"I was just trying to work it out with Grandma."

"When?" Ma-D asked.

"I was hoping I could see her tomorrow."

"Tomorrow?" Ma-D asked, sounding surprised.

"Tomorrow will be fine," Grandma Hattie said. "I'll have Doyle come for you."

"No, no, Grandma, I'll take the ferry. Like I did last year. Really."

"Are you sure?"

"It's not a problem."

"The least I can do is have Doyle pick you up at the Ferry Building. What time will you arrive?"

"I'm not sure yet. I'll call Doyle when I know."

"Oh, that's wonderful. I'll see you tomorrow Nick. Good-bye, Mary. Take care."

And with that Grandma Hattie hung up.

"I didn't know you were going to visit your grandmother, Nick," Ma-D said, sounding perplexed.

It seemed weird to be talking Ma-D on the telephone when she was in the kitchen right across the lawn. "I didn't really know either, Ma-D. I just decided to go a few minutes ago."

"Of course it's all right that you go. I just wish you'd let me know ahead of time."

"I'm sorry, Ma-D. I, I..."

"Don't worry about it, Nick. I just like to know what's going on."

"I know you do, Ma-D. I'll be over in a minute. I've got to call the ferry service and find out the schedule." We said good-bye to each other and I sat down on my bed feeling like I'd done something wrong. Sometimes it's confusing having three adults for parents, none of whom are actually your parents. Not to mention not having any parents at all, but I couldn't think about that again. This may sound strange, but I've found there is one part about being an orphan that works for me — namely freedom — freedom to do what I want to do. Not having any real parents is tough, but it also means no one is looking that closely all the time, or any of the time, really. As long as I do what I'm supposed to do (like get good grades) and not cause any problems, I'm free to do pretty much what I want. Not having a mom or dad — or for that matter, a sibling — is a very, very high price to pay for that freedom. Much too high. But it's a fact of my life, just like all the other stuff.

Bernie, the stuffed bear, guarding Grandma Hattie's house in San Francisco.

Chapter X

A Trip Back in Time

Saturday, June 17, 1967
Grandma Hattie's house
San Francisco, California

It was last summer that I discovered there was regular ferry service that went between Vallejo and San Francisco. Vallejo is about thirty miles south of St. Helena, a historic ship-building city on San Pablo Bay which, in turn, flows into San Francisco Bay. Arriving San Francisco by water appealed to me, especially when the city was hidden by fog, rising from the bay like some kind of gray, wispy dream. The fact that there was a bus that went from the post office in St. Helena directly to the ferry terminal in Vallejo made it an easy trip.

I told Ma-D the night before that I needed to be at the bus stop at 8 o'clock and sure enough, she was over at the bunkhouse at twenty minutes to eight the next morning, asking me if I was ready to go.

"You look all spiffed up," she said to me, handing me a small brown paper sack.

"Well, you know. San Francisco, Grandma and all that."

"Yes, there is 'all that'," Ma-D replied with some amusement.

"What's this?" I asked, holding up the sack.

"Just a little something in case you get hungry along the way."

I was wearing what I called my "city uniform:" white button-down shirt, khakis, my blue blazer and penny loafers. It would never have occurred to me to wear my usual clothes — jeans, sneakers and a t-shirt — to visit my grandmother. I wasn't sure where I had learned what to wear, but by now it was second nature, even so far as to know to leave my lucky hat behind. Grandma Hattie lived in her own world and she had her own way of doing things. Visiting her was like going back in time.

A few quick "Family Facts:"

In the late 1800s, Captain Niebaum became a partner in the Alaska Commercial Company in San Francisco, a world leader in the fur-trading business. Eventually he became the company's president and one of the wealthiest men in America. He and his wife, Susan, visited the Napa Valley in 1879, fell in love with it and bought a piece of property known as Eagle's Nook. It wasn't long before they started a winery known by the same name. A few years later they built their dream home – a Victorian mansion surrounded by a huge front porch which was, in turn, surrounded by the new vineyards and ancient oak trees.

So Hattie wound up inheriting two very grand houses – the first one was in the Pacific Heights neighborhood in San Franciso which became hers when her mother and father died in the deadly flu pandemic of 1918. Her other house was in the Napa Valley, the Victorian mansion that was part of the Eagle's Nook estate and winery. She inherited both the house and the winery from her adoptive father, Captain Gustav Niebaum after becoming an orphan at 14.

Hattie became part of Captain Niebaum's family when Niebaum and his wife, Susan, adopted her. Susan was Hattie's mother's sister, so it was natural that the childless couple adopt their niece after both Hattie's parents died. Later, as a young woman, Hattie met and married a young banker from San Francisco, Erik Sinclair, and whisked him off to her family's winery where he left banking behind and taught himself to become a farmer and, ultimately, a well-respected winemaker.

Along the way, Hattie and Erick had one son, Mark, my father, who married Elaine Simpson from Middletown, a small town on the other side of Mt. St. Helena, in Lake County. They had a son, Lucas, and a couple of years later in 1951, I came along. We were, by all accounts, a happy, hard-working family, my dad continuing in the wine-making tradition, like his father before him. In the months after the accident, I didn't remember much, except that it was a very sad and seemingly silent time. Hattie's husband, Erik, died a year later from a heart attack. Hattie, devastated by so much loss, eventually gave up running the winery and took to a period of restless and almost constant traveling. That's when I went to live with Uncle Walter and Ma-D and, gradually, a little more light and laughter became part of my life.

· · ·

I started reading *Silverado Squatters* on the bus down to the ferry. Once I was on the ferry, however, I put the book in my backpack; there was simply too much to see on the short, one-hour trip across the bay to spend the time with my nose in a book. I liked the steady thrum of the diesel engines and the way the ferry cut smoothly across the water. When the ferry was about 15 minutes from arriving at the Ferry Building in San Francisco, I went outside to sit on the bow of the boat. It was windy and fairly cold out there, but this was my favorite

The Ferry Building in San Francisco.

part of the trip: one minute all I could see was a blank, gray canvas of fog and the next I could just make out the barest outlines of the city's skyscrapers. Bit by bit they would take shape and then, all of a sudden, the Ferry Building would be right in front of me, as the ferry slid its way to the dock.

Once we had tied up, I slung my backpack over my shoulder and ran my hand through my hair, trying to get it to lay down. Sure enough, Doyle was waiting for me at the end of the dock, looking very official in his black chauffeur's uniform, complete with hat. He was a young guy, probably in his early 20s, built like a rugby player which, in fact, he was.

"Master Sinclair, is that you?" Doyle said, extending his hand.

"It's me, Doyle," I said, shaking Doyle's hand heartily.

"I'm surprised I recognized you. What? You've grown a foot, at least."

"Not that much. But, yeah, I've grown."

"Your grandmother is going to be surprised."

"I suppose so."

"Anywhere you need to go, or is it straight home?" Doyle asked, holding the door to the back seat of the limousine open for me.

I hesitated. I wasn't sure Grandma Hattie's place was home or not, but I didn't want to think about that right now. For the time being, it was easiest just to answer Doyle with a cheerful, "Home it is."

"Then we're off in a cloud of heifer dust."

Another of Doyle's strange sayings, which I didn't understand, but laughed at anyway.

After a short ride through the city, Doyle parked the limousine in front of the huge, three-story house, explaining that he had to take Hattie out later in the afternoon for her hair appointment or, as she put it, "out to get my hair dipped."

Doyle and I walked up the front stairs to a pair of massive oak doors, each with its own lion's head knocker in the center. Doyle pushed one of the doors open and I entered the mahogany-paneled entry hall, complete with marble fireplace and crackling fire in its grate.

"Is that you, Nicky?" said a voice from somewhere in the house. I grimaced. I didn't know which one embarrassed me more, "Master Sinclair" or "Nicky."

"It's me, Grandma. Where are you?"

"Right here," she said, suddenly appearing in the hall. "Oh, my," she gasped, "you're a young man! How did that happen?"

I felt my face get hot. What can I say? It was a problem for me — it didn't take much for me to blush. "Grandma! Good to see you," I said leaning over to hug her. I may have grown, but Grandma had shrunk. I stood back and took a look at her. If she weighed more than a hundred pounds, I'd be surprised. And she wasn't much over five feet tall, at least not any more. She was turned out in a camel-colored pantsuit with a leopard-patterned turban and was leaning on a thin bamboo cane.

Grandma put her hands to her head and asked "Like my turban?"

"It's very... um... exotic."

"Yes. Exotic. That's it," Hattie mused. "Actually I'm just wearing it because my hair's a mess."

"The cane's new. Are you okay?"

"Just some arthritis... or bursitis... or some other 'itis' coming back to haunt me from when I broke my leg."

"You broke your leg?"

"Didn't I ever tell you? It was back in '33. Your grandfather, Erik, and I were on the maiden voyage of the *Lurline* between here and Honolulu. Those were the days! I was feeling frisky one night and started showing off how I could walk on my hands — which I could, mind you — just not down the gangplank... oh well, that was a long time ago. Enough about me; let me take a look at you. What are they feeding you down there at school? Growth hormones?"

"No grandma. No growth hormones. It's just my time to grow, I guess."

"Well, I guess so," Hattie said, adding a low whistle at the end of her comment. "Go make yourself comfortable. You know your way around."

"Sure thing, Grandma."

"I had Katia make up your room."

"I wasn't sure if I was going to spend the night."

"Don't be ridiculous. Of course you are. Now go upstairs and stow your stuff. And then let's have lunch in the conservatory. Katia's made your favorite."

"Sounds good," I said, taking off up the stairs and then suddenly said "Wow, where'd he come from?" I was just about eye-to-eye with a huge, stuffed brown bear, front paws outstretched, standing on its hind legs, apparently real at one time.

"I was wondering when you'd notice Bernie," Hattie said. "I found him in a crate in one of the barns at Eagle's Nook. Apparently Gustave shot him in Alaska and had him stuffed. He never quite made it into the house up there. Susan probably wouldn't let it in. I like him. His job is to scare off burglars."

"He should be able to do that," I said. "Nice to meet you, Bernie," I said, nodding to him. "Tell Katia I'll be down in a minute."

Katia was a niece of Hattie's, originally from Germany, who had been living with Hattie as her companion and helper for the last ten years or so. Katia was somewhere in her 50s and still spoke with a heavy German accent. She was fiercely protective of Hattie, so much so that I often felt some hostility from her, as if she thought me too much of a drain on Hattie's energy or something. I tried to be nice to her although, truthfully, she could be a pain.

I could hardly wait to see what Hattie thought my favorite lunch was, and how Katia would interpret it, but I was hungry, having forgotten to eat the fried egg sandwich and banana Ma-D had given me. I went off up the stairs to my "room," if you could call it that. Years ago, I had taken an interest in all things nautical and had discovered a space under the servants' staircase on the third floor, almost big enough to be called a room. When I discovered it, I was surprised to see that it was empty. I asked Grandma if I could use it as my bedroom.

"What? The spandrel on the third floor?" she asked.

"The what?"

"The spandrel. That's what it's called. Look it up in the dictionary."

I'd made a point of looking it up in the big dictionary that stood on its own stand in Hattie's library. Sure enough, the definition read: "Also included is the space under a flight of stairs, if it is not occupied by another flight of stairs. This is a common location to find storage space in residential structures." I wondered how Grandma knew these things.

Once I knew what the space was called, I told Grandma that I'd like it to look like a ship's cabin. In Hattie's typical fashion, she went all out, having the walls covered with shiny mahogany paneling, like on an old yacht, a real ship's bunk with built-in drawers underneath with brass corners and recessed handles, a brass reading lamp and, best of all, because the space was at the corner of the house, she had two brass portholes installed on the two walls which faced outside. She even bought an old spyglass which, to my surprise, worked great. There were a couple of small, recessed bookshelves and a so-called desk, which folded down from the wall, suspended by small brass chains. I loved the room. It was one of the few places in the house where I felt comfortable, the rest of it being so big that it made me feel like I was in a hotel.

The old spyglass.

Once I got up the third floor, I threw my backpack on the bunk, cracked open the portholes to let some fresh air in, and went to the bathroom that had been designated as mine to wash up.

When I got back down to the kitchen, Katia was busy at the stove, Grandma was carrying silverware to the conservatory, and Doyle was putting food from several grocery bags into the refrigerator. I shook my head slightly, thinking to myself that it was quite a collection of individuals rattling around this huge place.

"Hi Katia," I said cheerily.

"Oh, Nick, it's you. It's good to see you again," she said, turning around from the stove.

"Good to see you too. What's for lunch?"

"I'm not quite sure. Your grandmother said it was your favorite."

"Can I help?"

"Ja, sure. Bring me those bowls there."

I placed the bowls on the big table in the middle of the kitchen. Katia began ladling tomato soup into bowls. *So far, so good,* I thought to myself.

"Take these into the conservatory. Your grandmother wants to lunch there."

I found my grandmother fussing over a square, linen-covered dining table in one corner of the glass conservatory. The place was like a jungle with vines growing everywhere, a couple of huge palms rising to the domed ceiling, almost touching a collection of Chinese paper lanterns hanging from the top of the conservatory. A fountain trickled from somewhere in the foliage, while several cages of love birds twittered away. But the warm, humid room was mostly filled with every manner of flowering plants which, I had learned a couple of years ago, were all members of the geranium family. "Over 200 species in the family," Hattie had told me, adding that she intended to collect them all. "Anyone can collect orchids," Hattie had said with a sniff, viewing her geraniums with pride.

"Oh, good," Hattie said when she saw me arriving with the soup. "Are those Tater-Tots ready, Katia?" she yelled in the direction of the kitchen.

"Tater-Tots and tomato bisque soup," I thought to myself. It had, in fact, been one of my favorite meals — back when I was in the first grade. I wondered what made my grandmother remember such an odd thing.

"Here you are," Katia said as she put a napkin-lined basket filled with steaming Tater-Tots in the middle of the table.

"Thank you, Katia," Hattie said from her chair.

As she left the table, I heard Katia say *"merkwürdiger junge,"* under her breath. I was in my second year of German and knew *junge* meant "boy." I repeated *"merkwürdiger,"* to myself a couple of times, vowing to remember it until I had a chance to look it up.

I sat in the chair opposite Grandma, adjusting to the steamy atmosphere of the conservatory.

"As I remember, you liked to dunk the tots in the soup," Hattie said. "Bon appetit!" lifting her soup spoon in one hand and a Tater-Tot in the other with a flourish. "Umm, these tots are good. We ought to have them more often," grandma said, licking her fingers.

Everything was slightly surreal at Grandma's, and this meal in her own private jungle was no exception. As I started to eat, I noticed what was on the cloth-covered table: a small vase of flowers, a radio turned on low to the local news station, a toaster, a small aquarium with two goldfish darting back and forth, a pencil cup holding at least a dozen Ticonderoga pencils and several intense orange, small Rhodia writing tablets. I knew that this was where my grandmother had breakfast every morning. She had it set up exactly as she wanted — a private world within a private world, not unlike the aquarium in which the goldfish swam contentedly, I thought.

I felt a little odd dipping the Tater-Tots in the soup, but somehow knew I'd be disappointing Grandma if I didn't. I was crunching away when I noticed a hanging pot over her shoulder filled with a plant that cascaded nearly to the floor, covered with hundreds of tiny lavender blue flowers.

"Wow. What's that one?"

"Which one?"

"The plant over your shoulder with all the flowers."

"Oh, that's *Geranium ibericum.* It's from the Caucasus Mountains in Azerbaijan. I nipped a cutting from the prime minister's garden there and brought it home in the toe of my left hiking boot. Back in my traveling days. Customs never noticed it, thank goodness."

"Have you collected them all yet?"

"No, there's still a few I'm trying to put my hands on. I just wrote a collector in Kashmir the other day. Trying to see if I can get him to send me a cutting of *Geranium clarkei*. It grows wild there. Beautiful thing with white flowers and pale pink veins. I wonder if I'll ever see it? Oh there you are, Clarence. I was wondering where you were," she said looking at the floor. I looked too and there, next to her feet, was a turtle about the size of a football.

"Where'd he come from?" I exclaimed.

"From the fountain, probably" Hattie said nonchalantly while feeding him a Tater-Tot.

"No, I mean where did you find him?"

"At the winery a couple of months ago. Doyle and I stopped as he was walking across the driveway. I got out and watched him and then he disappeared in the ditch. Then, a couple of days later, there he was again, this time on the lawn. I decided he was trying to tell me something."

"Like what?" I asked.

"Like maybe he was old and wanted a more comfortable place to live. So I put him in a box and brought him back here. He seems to like it. I think he's probably older than I am," Hattie mused, "and that's something of a comfort."

I shook my head, thinking to myself that if my grandmother could name a stuffed Kodiak bear, a tortoise named Clarence in the conservatory wasn't such a stretch. We both returned to our soup without talking for a minute or two then Hattie broke the silence: "Now surely Nick, you didn't come all the way here to talk to your old grandmother about geraniums and turtles did you?"

"No. Not really."

"Well then, out with it. I've known you all your life, Nick, and I could tell something was on your mind yesterday when we talked on the telephone."

"Have you talked with Ma-D lately?" I asked.

"No, just when she broke into our conversation yesterday."

"Then you haven't heard that Quicksilver is missing?"

"Who?"

"Quicksilver."

"Who's Quicksilver?"

"He's a horse, Grandma. Uncle Walter's best Shetland pony."

"Really," she said, with genuine surprise. "I suppose I should have known that. When did it happen?"

"The first night I arrived."

"Oh my! Walter must be beside himself."

"He is. But that's not all of it."

"Somehow I didn't think it was."

"Well, I'm not quite sure how to say this."

"Then just say it."

"I found something in the bottom of the horse trough — it was a... ah... a leather pouch filled with gold. Quite a bit of gold, actually. More than five thousand dollars' worth."

Hattie leaned forward, about to say something, then stopped and just looked up to the ceiling of the conservatory, obviously lost in thought. I sat there waiting. Finally she said: "They always did seem to overpay for things."

When I asked her what she meant, she said we'd better continue our talk in the library, which was at the other end of the house. I finished my lunch and we walked to the library without talking. I pushed open the pocket door just off the entry hall and followed Grandma into the room she referred to as "the Captain's Library." She turned around and motioned conspiratorially with her head for me to close the doors.

The room was completely lined with floor-to-ceiling bookcases, with the exception of a couple of tall windows that looked out onto the street. The dark wooden floors were covered with a variety of Oriental rugs in different patterns. There were several rectangular tables with stacks and stacks of books. There were paintings of ships on the walls and models of more ships on the tables. Two club chairs faced each other in front of a marble fireplace with a large portrait of "the captain," as Hattie called him, over the mantle. A fire burned brightly in the fireplace.

"What time is it?" Hattie asked me, motioning me to sit in one of the chairs.

"It's almost one."

"Let's see here, where to start? I have to go get my hair dipped at 1:30, so we don't have a lot of time right now," she mused to herself.

"Before you get going, I need to tell you something," I said.

"There's more?" Hattie asked.

"Well, yeah," I hesitated. "When Uncle Walter and I went to the Sheriff's Department to fill out the theft report, I went to the bathroom. I was in one of the stalls when Sheriff Lyman came in and started talking with someone else about Quicksilver and the pouch of gold."

"Wait a minute," Hattie interrupted, "who's Sheriff Lyman? What happened to Sheriff Billings?"

"Lyman's the new sheriff; Billings retired, but he was the one who told me to come see you."

"He did? That's interesting. I always thought he was about as smart as a box of hair. Go on."

I couldn't help but laugh: "a box of hair."

"Well, anyway, Sheriff Lyman had like this secret conversation in the bathroom and told this other guy — his name was Charlie — that it looked like it was another case for the Eagle's Nook file."

"Hmmmm," Hattie said. "Looks like you're in it now."

"In what?" I asked.

"Let me think for a minute, Nick."

I sat in my chair and watched Grandma Hattie start pacing in front of the fireplace with considerable determination.

She finally stopped and turned to me, asking, "What's your interest in this, Nick? What do you intend to do?"

"I'm not sure — except that, right now, it feels like I don't know enough to know where to start — like I don't have enough pieces of the puzzle to be able to put it together, you know what I mean? I know I should try and figure out how to get Quicksilver back, but I don't even know where to start, especially when it feels like the people who might know something about all of this are intentionally not telling me. It's really weird."

"Fair enough," Hattie said, sensing my frustration. Suddenly there was a knock at the door as it slid back and Katia stuck her face through the opening.

"Sorry to bother, Hattie, but Doyle asked that I remind you about your appointment. He's waiting with the car out front."

"Oh, of course, Katia. Thank you. Tell Doyle I'll be there in a minute."

With that, Katia slid the door closed and Hattie turned back to me: "There's a stepstool over there," Hattie said, motioning across the room. "Bring it here in front of the mantle. Come on. Chop chop, no time to lose," she said, clapping her hands.

I got the stepstool and put it in front of the fireplace. "Now move those candlesticks." Standing on the stepstool, I did as I was told. "Now kind of push the frame on the left bottom in with your left hand and jerk the bottom right side open with your right hand." I looked at Hattie to make sure I'd had heard her right. "Go ahead, do it." I put my hands in the positions she told me to and tugged

The wall safe in the library.

gently. "Don't be afraid. You can't hurt it." I pushed and pulled at the same time with a little more force and the entire picture swung open like a door, a little too fast, slamming my left hand against the wall.

"Sugar!" I said, shaking my hand in the air.

"Sugar?" Grandma asked. "Don't you know anything stronger than that?"

I turned and looked at Grandma directly and silently mouthed a word that rhymes with "hit."

"Yeah, that's what I thought," she said. "Are you all right?"

"I'll be okay," I said, massaging my hand. I guess I shouldn't have been surprised, but I was a little: Behind the portrait, recessed into the wall, was an old-fashioned safe.

"Now, let's get it open," Grandma said. "The combination's 32-33-34, right, left, right. Got it?"

"Yeah, hold on," I said, twirling the dial. I heard something click.

"Now, pull down on the handle."

I did, and the door opened.

"Let me see, let me see," Grandma said, impatiently. "I haven't looked in there for a long time."

"What am I looking for?" I asked.

"That's what I'm trying to remember. Oh yes, okay. There should be a fairly slim black leather book with a red spine. It says 'Ship's Log' on it. And 'Schooner Lindisfarne' underneath that. And there should be a green leather folded packet, tied with cotton string."

I knew there were other ships' logs on the library shelves that had belonged to Captain Niebaum, because I'd looked at them before. I wondered why this one was in the safe.

I dug through the assorted journals and envelopes. "Is this it?" I asked, handing the packet to Hattie.

"Yes, that's it," Grandma said, turning it over in her hands. "The log should be right there."

"I've got it," I said, holding it up, inspecting its cover.

"Okay, now hurry. Close the safe and put the candlesticks back just like they were. I've got to get going. No one knows that safe is there except for me. And now you."

I did as I was told. Grandma was pacing again. "There's one more thing you're going to need. It's a huge book called, let me see if I can remember... something like, oh, what was it? It has 'Masonic' in the title. But it's longer than that.

Oh, wait a minute, the author is Manley P. Hall. How did I ever remember that?"

"Where is it, Grandma?"

"If I'm remembering correctly, it's on the very top shelf to the right of the fireplace. You're going to need the ladder over there," she said pointing to a ladder attached to the bookcase on the other side of the room. It had wheels, top and bottom, so you could push it around the bookshelves. "And be careful. That book is heavier than all get out."

"Okay. Then what?"

Hattie was headed for the door. "Read the log. No, you don't have to read the whole thing. Just the entry where the red ribbon is. And the papers in the packet. Read those, too."

"What about the big book?"

"Oh, yes, that. Read the section on 'gnomes'."

"*Gnomes?*" I asked incredulously.

"Yes. Gnomes. That's what I said. We can talk about it tonight at dinner," Hattie said as she left the library. I heard the front door open and Hattie shout down the stairs "I'm coming, I'm coming."

I stood in the middle of the library and scratched my head. "This is starting to get weird," I said out loud. With some uncertainty, I pulled the library ladder around so that it was next to the fireplace. I started climbing and about midway up I noticed a German-to-English dictionary in front of my face. I remembered that Captain Niebaum spoke six languages fluently; German must have been one of them. I reminded myself I still had to look up *merkwürdiger*, and find out what it meant.

I reached the top shelf and saw a very large book, one of the biggest I had ever seen, lying on its side. Printed on the spine was its title: *The Secret Teachings of All Ages: An Encyclopedic Outline of Masonic, Hermetic, Qabbalistic and Rosicrucian Symbolical Philosophy*, by Manley P. Hall. More weirdness. I struggled to pull it off the shelf and quickly realized it was so heavy that I'd have to take it slow backing down the ladder. I finally settled on propping it against the ladder, holding it with one hand and the ladder rail with the other and letting gravity do the work of sliding it down.

Back on the ground, I put the massive book on one of the library tables and went back up the ladder to retrieve the German dictionary. Thumbing through the entries, I found *merkwürdiger*, which I found out meant "strange." *So Katia thinks I'm a strange boy? Because I like tomato soup and Tater-Tots?* The lunch wasn't even my idea. I decided not to spend any time thinking about

Katia. There were more important things to do.

I could have stayed in the library, but thought it better to take the book, the ship's log and the leather packet up to my room and read them where I could have some privacy. I gathered them up and slid the wooden doors open onto the entry hall. Without thinking about it, I looked left and right. For some reason I wanted to make sure no one was around — especially Katia. It hadn't taken long to feel like a spy in my own grandmother's house.

Nigel's base of operation — an Airstream trailer in Space 78 at Bothe State Park, halfway between St. Helena and Calistoga.

Chapter XI

The Badger Settles In

Friday, June 16, 1967
Bothe Napa Valley State Park, Space 78
Napa Valley, California

The one thing about working for someone as rich as Lord Higgenbotham, Nigel thought to himself, was that there was virtually nothing that couldn't be arranged. When Nigel accepted the assignment and told Higgenbotham what his requirements were, Higgenbotham put one of his personal assistants on the job. Nigel had explained to the assistant that his anonymity was of premiere importance. He needed a place to live where the comings and goings of a stranger in a small town wouldn't be noticed by neighbors or anyone else.

A couple of hours after he had landed in San Francisco, Nigel found himself arriving at the southern end of the Napa Valley. The rolling, dun-colored hills were studded with huge, dark-green oak trees. Here and there were stands of extremely tall, very stately eucalyptus trees. As he wound his way north up the small valley (which he had noted on the map was only thirty miles long and five miles wide at its widest part), more and more vineyards became apparent, spread across the valley floor and occasionally onto the low foothills, planted in geometric rows, this way and that, resembling a lush, very green quilt. The rather impressive hills, which framed the valley on both sides, were a dusky, cerulean blue, the likes of which he hadn't seen since he was in northern Italy. The combination of the classical music on his radio and the beautiful surroundings put Nigel in a good mood. *Maybe I'll actually enjoy this assignment,* he thought to himself. It certainly beat his last one, covering a violent political coup in South America.

It was in this frame of mind that he turned off of Highway 29, north of the small town called St. Helena, population 2,817, ready to find out just how efficient Lord Higgenbotham's operation really was. It was the Higgenbotham's assistant, Phillipa, who came up with the idea: Why not have a small, efficient trailer delivered to a local campground for Nigel to live in? Everybody's a stranger in a campground and everyone's constantly coming and going. Nigel had lived on a boat for a number of years, so the idea of living in cramped quarters didn't bother him. And the transient atmosphere of a campground was a big plus.

He pulled up to the ranger station of the Bothe Napa Valley State Park and explained to the ranger that he had a reservation and that his trailer had already been delivered to the site. The young ranger looked sharp in what had to be a very new forest green uniform. "Yes, here you are: Nigel Stayne, space 78. I see you'll be with us awhile."

"For a month, I think. Possibly longer," Nigel replied.

"Well, the valley may be relatively small, but there's plenty to see. You won't be bored."

"No, I'm not planning on being bored," Nigel replied, thinking the ranger was a little too familiar for his taste.

Nigel had told Phillipa to reserve the most secluded site possible. He'd see soon enough. The ranger marked the directions to the site on a map of the campground.

"Are you familiar with poison oak?" the ranger asked.

"Poison what?" Nigel asked, surprised.

"Poison oak. Hearing your accent, I thought you might not be. There's a lot of it around here and you really want to stay away from it. It causes a terrible rash. No fun at all."

"No fun at all. I'll remember that," Nigel said testily. Nigel was beginning not to like the ranger.

"Here. Here's a sheet that shows you how to identify it. 'Leaves of three, let it be.' That's what we always say."

"Leaves of three..." Nigel muttered to himself.

"And ticks?"

"Ticks?"

"Yes. Ticks. Unfortunately they've been rather bad lately. And you know they carry Lyme Disease, right?"

"Right. Lyme Disease. I suppose you have a sheet on that, too?"

"Yes, as a matter of fact. Here you go" he said, handing him the sheet on ticks with a smile. "Enjoy your stay, Mr. Stayne," he said, waving him off.

Nigel drove off muttering: "Enjoy your stay! Cheeky one, he is. Poison plants and disease-in-

"Leaves of three"
— poison oak.

fested insects! 'Enjoy your stay.'" Nigel said in a voice meant to mimic the ranger's. *Bloody hell,* he said to himself.

His mood picked up somewhat when he rounded the corner of the narrow dirt road that wound its way through the dense redwood, bay and fir forest and saw the shiny, aluminum-clad Airstream trailer in Space 78. He noticed there were several boxes of firewood stacked next to the trailer — a good sign, and he had to admit the site, owing to the dense foliage everywhere, was beautiful and very secluded. There was a creek babbling nearby and delicate ferns and grasses growing seemingly everywhere. Nigel got out of the Wagoneer and looked up at the majestic redwoods; a light wind moaned through the tops, making them sway back and forth in a gentle rhythm. With the exception of the warnings regarding the poison oak and the infected ticks, the overriding feeling he got from the valley was that it was a very peaceful, beautiful place. "Quite delightful, really," he thought to himself.

Nigel searched for the key to the trailer which Phillipa said would be wedged under the right tire and that's right where it was. He unlocked the door and looked around, opening drawers and closets, looking into cubbyholes and opening all the windows to let some fresh air into the small space. Pulling up the mattress, he found a pistol and a box of ammunition. *Well done, Phillipa.* Nigel thought to himself.

Nigel put away the few things he had brought with him and stretched out on the bed. He decided that he'd take today off and start in tomorrow. *But where to start?* he wondered. He didn't have much to go on. Nigel hadn't intended to take a nap, but within a couple minutes of listening to the whispering wind, he was fast asleep, repeating the words "leaves of three, let it be" in his sleep.

The winery Capt. Gustave Niebaum built in 1879.

Chapter XII

The Secrets of the Log

Saturday, June 17, 1967, continued
Grandma Hattie's house
San Francisco, California

I lugged the big book and the other items from the safe up the stairs to my room. I lowered the desk from the wall and wondered whether or not the brass chains would hold the weight of the *Secret Teachings* book. I put the book gently on the desk; so far, so good.

I crawled onto my bunk and decided to read the ship's log first. I carefully opened the log, fearful that the whole thing might fall apart, remembering that Grandma had said I only needed to read the part marked with the red ribbon. I didn't have any doubt the pages were written in Captain Niebaum's handwriting; I recognized it from the other logs I'd looked at in grandma's library a long time ago. The entry started on a left-hand page (for those who don't read cursive, a printed version of the entry in the ship's log can be found on page 311).

SHIP'S LOG

S.S. *Lindisfarne, Voyage #19*

From *Glasgow, Scotland*   Towards *Reykjavik, Iceland*

Date *28 February, 1879*

Major disturbance onboard just after eight bells this evening. Under full sail, heading SW in the Firth of Henry. First mate Nyquist at the helm. Cold night, good wind. Third mate Higgenbotham, in a very agitated state, summons me from my cabin to go belowdecks. We were met by Second mate Syrjälä standing next to one of the large crates we took on board in Glasgow. Syrjälä explained that he and Higgenbotham were in the hold inspecting the lashings on the cargo when he thought he heard faint voices inside the wooden crate. Fearing stowaways, he immediately dispatched Higgenbotham to bring me belowdecks. After some deliberation, it was decided to open the crate. There were indeed stowaways in the crate (and in other crates, as well). After several hours and considerable confusion (along with some minor injuries), the situation was brought under control. Higgenbotham produced a firearm but, thankfully, no shots were fired. A most unusual evening, indeed.

Signed,
Gustave Niebaum, Master
1st Mate: P. Nyquist
2nd Mate: L. Syrälä
3rd Mate: T. Higgenbotham

The page from the actual ship's log (see page 311 for a printed version).

Stowaways, I thought. Interesting, but it didn't help me in figuring out the mystery of who stole Quicksilver. I closed the log and then immediately re-opened it. What had I seen? I turned back to the page I had just read and then flipped through the rest of the log. The back side of the page that contained the account of the stowaways had been covered with what looked like smudged pencil — it was completely gray, from side to side and top to bottom. None of the other pages in the log were that way. What was that about, I wondered? Not coming up with an explanation, I reached for the green leather packet. It smelled musty and old. The papers inside crackled as I unfolded them. The top page was, again, written in the captain's distinctive handwriting. It said: "Private property of Captain Gustave Niebaum. To be viewed by my family heirs only."

I put down the packet. Technically I wasn't a blood relative of the captain's, but then neither was Hattie. But, as his adoptive daughter, Hattie had been the captain's sole heir. And since my family was dead, I figured I was Hattie's only heir. Satisfied that I had a right to read what the captain had written, I started in (for those who don't read cursive, a printed version of the contents of the captain's letter can be found on page 312).

CAPTAIN GUSTAVE NIEBAUM
EAGLE'S NOOK
RUTHERFORD, CALIFORNIA

Greetings to whomever is reading this. My only hope is that you have some connection with me and that you will hold the information I am about to pass on with the respect that it deserves — both for my reputation and legacy and the fate of the little ones.

First, a bit of my history: I was raised in Oulu, a Swedish-speaking community in Finland, from 1842 to 1858. Ours was a family who never doubted the existence of the little ones, even though they were encountered only on the rarest of occasions and certainly not by everyone in our community. I, myself, happened upon one only once in my childhood when I caught a little one helping himself to some of our eggs when I mistakenly wandered into the henhouse instead of the outhouse in the middle of the night. I'm sure the little one was more frightened than I; he was very surprised and humbled when I told him he could take however many eggs he needed, as we had more than enough for our family. Such generosity was commended in our family, but I must say that no one ever let me forget that I had confused the chicken house with the outhouse. My mother and father taught me to respect the little ones for their cooperation and willingness to share in bad times, which for those of us with very little, could mean the difference between survival and disaster.

My siblings and I grew up hearing of other families who were afraid of the little ones, spoke poorly of them, and sought every opportunity to stamp them out of our locale. My parents, who were in every way wise – wise with the accumulated wisdom of their parents and their grandparents behind them – taught us the greatest rule of all: To treat others as we would want to be treated. They explained to me and my sister and brother, Helli and Olavi, that if we could only remember this one rule, it would see us to live good and honorable lives. They taught us that just because someone's outward appearance might be different than our own was no reason to treat them differently from anyone else, for indeed, we also looked different in their eyes. And how was it that we wanted to be treated, they asked? We, their children, took their teachings to heart and lived by them as best we could, each in our own way.

I have provided you with this preamble to explain why I acted as I did aboard the Lindisfarne on the night of 28 February 1879, my second encounter with the little ones. I deliberately did not call them by their name because my ship's log is read by a variety of people, not all of whom, as I have already stated, share my beliefs and attitudes. In fact, it is my opinion that the vast majority of people no longer even believe in the existence of the little people, thinking instead that they are merely part of the imaginative minds of writers who create books for children.

When third mate Thom Higgenbotham hailed me in my cabin, he did not elaborate on the situation to me, only stating that my presence was needed immediately belowdecks. We arrived in the hold to a scene of considerable commotion. All of the stowaways had been taken from the crates where they had been hiding and it seemed everyone was talking at once at a very high level. I commanded their silence and inquired if there was a leader in their group. All the men — for there wasn't a female amongst them — turned toward one man, bowing their heads in the process. Their leader puffed up and announced, in a deep baritone, to the assembly: "I am known to all as King Gob, Lord of all Gob-sons Everywhere, Keeper of the Flame, Possessor of Mystical Knowledge, Inheritor of the Wind, and Grand Architect of the Hidden World. And whom, may I inquire, am I addressing?"

I replied as gravely as possible, informing him and his tribe that I was "Captain Gustave Niebaum, Master of the Schooner Lindisfarne," the vessel on which he and his men were now trespass-ing."

"Trespassing!" the king bellowed. "Trespassing! "No. No. Nothing of the sort. Nothing of the sort.

No, sir, you are mistaken. Wycoff! Where's Wycoff?"

Wycoff, who was apparently the equivalent of the king's purser, stepped forward. "Wycoff! Show the captain how we intend to pay for our passage!" Wycoff stammered that the payment was still in the "guld buxbom." The king ordered him to open it immediately. Once it was located, Wycoff did, indeed, open the large crate and, to the astonishment of my mates, revealed that it was full of all manner of gold. "There! You see? Our store of payment, captain," the king said. I explained to him that payment for passage was customarily handled prior to boarding the ship, to which King Gob replied that they hadn't passed anywhere yet and it was their custom to pay for goods and services after said goods and services were successfully rendered.

Sensing a rise in tension, I suggested to the king that we continue our discussion in private, in my cabin. The king agreed, but there was the question of what to do with the rest of his tribe in the meantime. Before I could silence him, third mate Higgenbotham suggested that they all be thrown overboard and a considerable skirmish then ensued. Higgenbotham foolishly brandished his firearm. I immediately reprimanded him and, with the help of the king, we quieted the group.

Some of the little ones suffered minor injuries, which second mate Syrjälä attended to. I ordered Higgenbotham to his quarters, informing him that I would deal with him later. Because Second Mate Syrjälä seemed to be the most cool-headed, I left him in charge of the king's subjects, and suggested that he contact the ship's cook and arrange food and drink for the stowaways. This action was favorably received by the men.

Reader, please forgive the fact that I have not yet described the physical appearance of the king and his men. I have deliberately withheld that information, so as not to prejudice the reader's response. For me (no doubt influenced by my upbringing), they were simply men of a different sort, but men nonetheless. But to other eyes, they were gnomes (those people my parents referred to as "little ones"), with all the superstitions and wrongful information contained in that designation. If the reader is living in a time far in the future, perhaps my reluctance will seem unnecessary, prejudice over such things having been left in the past. If that is the case, I congratulate you and your enlightened times. But for now, I cannot overstate how misunderstood the gnomes are in the minds of most men.

King Gob and I had our meeting, which lasted more than an hour. The king has a fondness for talking and pursued his points vehemently and in earnest. Over the course of the meeting, we reached an agreement, suitable to all parties. The king explained that he and his troop were on a mission of exploration. Conditions in his native country — he and his tribe were now living on the Åland Islands — had become increasingly difficult, with a hostile populace and an increase in the number of church bells, which, to the ears of all gnomes, was exceedingly painful. He had heard of America and wanted to see for himself if relocating his people was a possibility — hence their presence aboard the Lindisfarne. He offered to pay me for their passage then and there. I explained that there was no need for payment, as fortune had been very kind to me. He appeared to be confused by this, but I explained that I had just constructed a winery in a beautiful valley in California and that I was in desperate need of a series of caves dug into the hillside in which to age my wine (recalling my parents' stories regarding the gnomes' magical ability for mining and tunneling that I had been told as a child). I explained that I would happily grant him and his men passage to California if he, in exchange, would construct the caves and tunnels I required. "This is but a trifling," he responded. "Are you sure you wouldn't prefer gold?" I assured him the caves were more important to me than any gold, and we shook hands to seal the arrangement. I thus assured him that once he and his men had finished their labor, they would be free to go as they pleased.

He seemed particularly intrigued when I told him about Mt. St. Helena at the head of the Napa Valley and the fact it contained not only gold and silver, but quicksilver, as well, which again I remembered from old stories as a particular favorite of the gnome people.

Truth be told, I was less concerned with the party of gnomes on board than I was with the considerable gold they were transporting, having seen for myself in Alaska what gold can do to otherwise decent men. I convinced the king to have the "guld buxbom" moved to my cabin for safekeeping for the duration of the voyage. As a sign of his trust in me, he agreed. As you are probably aware, the gnome folk have a distaste for daylight and conduct their affairs only after dark, quite the reverse from us "Uplanders," as they refer to people such as myself. Even so, it was agreed that they would stay below decks at all times unless I gave them permission otherwise. They had brought with them all the provisions they required with regard to food and drink, so contact between them and the crew could be kept to a minimum. Given Higgenbotham's apparent distrust and dislike of the gnomes, it would not take much effort on his part to incite other like-minded crew members into a mutinous situation, which I was determined to avoid at all costs.

It pleases me to report that it was, in fact, a successful voyage, save for one unfortunate incident, although more to the distress of the king than to me. As you are probably aware, this was a particularly long voyage, from England, around Cape Horn, to Australia, Japan and finally the Hawaiian Islands as our last port of call before returning home to San Francisco. There were five gnomes out of the party of eighteen who never got used to the sea-faring life, plagued as they were with seasickness. The king had implored them to stay together as every one of them would be needed once they arrived to what he referred in as the "New World." But, alas, it finally proved too much for the sickly five. They jumped ship while we were tied up in Kauai. The king convinced me to stay in port an extra day as he sent search parties to find the runaways, but to no avail. The king was at first mightily disturbed for, as he told me, one of the missing men was the Wizard of the tribe, the one who possessed essential knowledge of all the gnomes' most amazing feats. The king explained to me that each of his men had their own special ability (what we would call "magic"), but each man had only one special ability. The Wizard alone possessed all the combined magic, making him a very powerful member of the tribe. For as con-sequential a loss as it was, I must report that the king was stoical in his manner and did not ask for any further delays in our departure.

Once in San Francisco, I arranged to have the gnomes transported by wagon (all of them safely in their stow-away crates) to St. Helena. I met them there and showed them the location where I desired the caves to be built, along with a plan of their design and specifications. I explained to the king that I would be embarking on another voyage in two days' time – destination Alaska – but I would check on his progress when I returned in two months.

The return trip from Alaska was a hellish one, and we arrived in San Francisco some three weeks late. I was most anxious to return to St. Helena and my love, Susan, and greatly curious as to the gnomes' progress with the caves. As my arrival at the winery was after dark, I was expecting to find the gnomes at work, but they were nowhere to be found. Surprised that the king might have gone back on his word, I began an inspection and was overwhelmed with pleasure at the discovery that the caves were completely excavated to the exact specifications of the plans. On the back wall of the furthest and deepest cave I found an envelope and a small leather pouch hanging from a nail. The envelope contained a letter from the king which read:

My Dear Captain: If you have made it thus far, you will have realized that your caves have been completed to your specifications. I sincerely hope that your dreams of making fine wine will become a reality in the not too distant future and that we might, some time, find the occasion to share in your efforts. Respectfully yours, G.

P.S. As a token of our gratitude and friendship, I offer this amulet. It is of royal provenance and will forever signify its bearer as a friend of our tribe.

I never saw the king again and know not his fate, nor that of his tribe. It pleases me, however, when I gaze upon the luminous lavender silhouette of Mt. St. Helena at sunset, to think that he and his men took my advice and are burrowed into the hillside, content in their new surroundings.

By my hand,
Capt. Gustave Niebaum
Eagle's Nook
St. Helena, California
29 June 1901

P.S. One last occurrence should be noted here, one which remained a mystery to me for some time. Several years ago a large barrel of Charbono wine was stolen from the aging caves here at Eagle's Nook. In its place was a leather pouch filled with gold nuggets, the worth of which far exceeded the value of the wine. I reported the theft to Sheriff Dunlap and turned the leather pouch and gold over to him for use in his investigation. After pondering the theft for some time, it finally occurred to me that, with their predilection for procuring what they desired without first obtaining an agreement of sale, the details of the disappearance of the wine were much aligned with the habits of the little ones. Shortly thereafter, I informed Sheriff Dunlap the case had been resolved to my satisfaction and he reluctantly returned the pouch of gold (I say "reluctantly" because I would not reveal the identity of the so-called "thieves," much to his consternation — so much so that he insisted on keeping the investigation open and, to my knowledge, it remains so as of this writing).

At one point I had to put the captain's letter down and think about what he had written. Here the captain was worrying that the reader might be prejudiced against the gnomes and I found myself thinking that they couldn't possibly be real — let alone that I could be prejudiced against them. I wondered if I was being suckered into some elaborate scam. Just an hour ago I thought things were strange; now I found myself in a whole new territory, unsure of what to think, one way or the other. I wondered if at any minute, Grandma Hattie would pop into my room, laughing hysterically that I'd been such a dupe. Even so, I decided to keep reading and try not to let my imagination run away with me for the time being.

After I finished the letter, I just sat on my bunk and stared off into space. While I was reading the captain's words, I'd fallen into another world — a world where gnomes lived as matter-of-factly as I did. I looked out of the open porthole to the city below — a city of streetcars, people on bicycles, sailboats on the bay, all of them real and touchable. Now that I had finished the captain's story, I decided that it couldn't be true. Or maybe, somehow, it could have been true when he'd written it, but it wasn't true now. It just couldn't be.

I knew I was supposed to read the section on "gnomes" in the big book, as Hattie had instructed, but I had the sudden urge to be out in the real world. I wanted to be outside and just walk. I'd read about gnomes when I got back. Maybe the fresh air would clear my brain. I certainly hoped so.

The library at Grandma Hattie's house. That's Capt. Niebaum over the fireplace. The safe, and all it contained, was behind the portrait.

Chapter XIII

Dinner with Hattie

Saturday, June 17, 1967, continued
Grandma Hattie's house
San Francisco, California

I returned from my walk to find a note on my bedroom door. It read, "Meet me in the library for dinner at six. xoxo, H." I knew my grandmother was probably taking a nap, as she did almost every afternoon. For as quirky as she was, she followed the same schedule nearly every day. From my previous visits I knew she always had dinner at seven, and that it was usually served in the kitchen. The change in the time and location told me something was up. It wasn't like Grandma to make changes to her daily routine.

Even though it was a typically cool summer day in San Francisco, I had worked up a sweat climbing up and down the hills in Pacific Heights. I decided to take a shower and then read about the gnomes.

After I'd showered, I sat at my desk and opened the big book. Truly, it was like nothing I'd ever seen. Not only was the book itself huge, but the writing was so complicated and dense that it was almost like it was written in a foreign language. At the beginning of each chapter were full-page illustrations of all kinds of mysterious things, like pyramids, strange animals, flying chariots, creatures from zodiac, ancient gods and goddesses, more detailed and finely drawn than any I had ever seen. From a quick flipping through the pages, I decided that the book was like an encyclopedia of ancient religions and mystical practices. Whatever it was, it was way over my head.

I turned to the back of the book and sure enough, "gnome" was listed in the index. As I turned to the page it occurred to me that there was a whole lot I didn't know anything about and that, maybe I didn't want to know about any of it anyway.

Gnomes were listed under the heading of "Elementals" (whatever they were) and included a drawing of what appeared to be a couple of particularly ancient ones. I read from the book: *A mischievous and grotesque little creature, usually dressed in many layers of russet brown or green clothing. Most of them appear very aged, often with long, white beards. Their figures are inclined to rotundity. They can be seen scampering out of holes, in the stumps of trees, and sometimes they vanish by actually dissolving into the tree itself.*

I shook my head in disbelief. There was no way this stuff could be true. I tried to read on, but didn't understand much more, other than the fact that gnomes and trolls were basically the same thing, it just depended on where they lived.

I stretched out on my bunk and stared at the ceiling. "Sometimes they vanish by actually dissolving into the tree itself." Now that was troubling. In fact this whole business about the captain and the gnomes was more than troubling. With that thought I must have dozed off, which wouldn't have come as a surprise to my friends at school. I found it so easy to fall asleep, any time or anywhere, my friends teased me for being a "recreational sleeper." The teasing didn't bother me because so much of the time I felt so intensely "on" that it was a relief to be able to turn everything "off," more or less at will. The next thing I knew, Doyle was shouting up the stairs that it was time for dinner. I yelled back "I'm coming," and looked at the clock, which read 7:10. Knowing Hattie's insistence on punctuality, I jumped up, tucked my shirt in, and ran down the stairs.

I knocked quietly on the doors to the library before letting myself in.

"Oh, there you are. I thought maybe I was being stood up."

"Sorry, grandma. I guess I accidentally dozed off."

"I thought naps were for the very young and the very old. Like me. Are you okay?"

"Oh, yeah. I'm okay. I'm fine," I replied, wondering if I really was "okay."

"Well then, first things first. I thought we'd have dinner in here tonight instead of the kitchen because I thought some privacy might be a good idea."

"Okay."

"So what did you think about what you read?"

"To tell you the truth, I don't know what to think. I did notice that the back side of the page in the ship's log describing finding the stowaways was covered in what looked like smudged pencil. Do you know why?"

"The only thing I can tell you — because I used to do the same thing when I was a child," Hattie said, "is that covering the backside of a piece of paper with graphite from a pencil basically turns it into a sheet of carbon paper."

"What do you mean?"

"Say there's something you want to trace from the front side of the piece of paper. You simply cover the back side with a more or less even layer of graphite and then lay it on top of a blank piece of paper and trace what's on the front and, *voila*, you've made an exact duplicate on the second sheet."

"So you think someone made a copy of that page?"

"I'd say yes. But I have no idea who might have done it, or when or why."

I sat thinking for a minute. Hattie broke the silence: "What did you think of the captain's other writings?"

"Like I said, I don't know what to think."

"Well, which way are you leaning?"

I hesitated and then said "I'm thinking that it's made up. That maybe the captain made it up to pull a joke on someone."

"Hmmmm," Hattie said pensively.

"What do you think, Grandma? You can't really believe all that stuff is true!"

"As a matter of fact, I do."

"Have you ever seen one?"

"What? A gnome?"

"Yeah."

"Well, no, I haven't. But I was old enough to remember the captain's stories of that barrel of wine that went missing from Eagle's Nook and the captain showing me the pouch filled with gold that was left behind. And the amulet was certainly real."

"But you've never actually seen a gnome. And how do you know the amulet still actually exists?"

"Because it's is right there in the safe."

That brought me up short. "No way," I said with disbelief.

"Yes way," she said. "The amulet and the pouch of gold are in there," she repeated, pointing at the wall safe. "Look for yourself."

I went through the same routine as I had earlier in the day, minus whacking my hand with the picture frame. When I had the safe open, Hattie told me to get the small cardboard box in the back. I grabbed it and, getting off the stepstool, put it on the table in between the two chairs where we were sitting. When I had the box in my hands, I could swear it was vibrating. I sat back down in my chair, staring at the box nervously.

"Well, what are you waiting for? Open it."

My hands were visibly shaking as I started opening it. Inside was something wrapped in paper and a small red velvet box. I picked up the paper-wrapped parcel and unwrapped it. To my astonishment, I was holding a leather pouch identical to the one I'd found in the trough at Twin Oaks just a couple of days ago. I carefully opened it and turned it over. Sure enough, a large handful of gold nuggets fell out on the table.

"Well? What do you think now?" asked Hattie.

"I think it's just like the one I found at Uncle Walter's."

"Open the other one."

I picked up the red velvet box and opened the lid. Inside was an elaborate piece of jewelry, obviously the one the captain referred to in his papers.

"Go ahead. Take it out," urged Hattie.

I took it out of its box and examined it. There was a faceted, dark blue, rectangular stone in the middle, surrounded by an intricate pattern of slender silver cords. I recognized the pattern as a Celtic knot from a report on Ireland I'd written in school.

I handed the amulet to Hattie and sat back in my chair. Hattie held the sparkling amulet up to firelight. After thinking for a minute I said, "I still think this is some kind of trick. I mean, couldn't someone — I mean some regular human — have made those leather pouches and filled them with gold nuggets? And couldn't that piece of jewelry just have come from some fancy jewelry store?"

"I don't think so on either count," said Hattie. "First, leaving leather pouches filled with gold as payment for items which have disappeared from their owners — and mind you, this has happened repeatedly over a very long time — is a pretty elaborate, not to mention expensive, trick — pulled off by whom? It doesn't make any sense, at least not by my logic. And the amulet? Years ago I took it to Shreve's and had it appraised. The jeweler was dumbfounded. The stone — a sapphire — as beautiful and large as it is, is something that can be more or less easily acquired. But the setting is something else. The jeweler determined that it's made of rhodium, the rarest metal on the planet — much rarer than platinum — and, to his knowledge, it's never been used to create a piece of jewelry. He told me whoever had made it had access to knowledge that was simply unknown to man."

"Are you telling me the truth, Grandma?"

"Of course I am. What reason would I have to lie about such a thing?"

I hesitated. "It's just that I know how much you like practical jokes — like the time you put those little plastic dinosaurs in my oatmeal when I was a kid and then said you had no idea how they got there."

Hattie laughed to herself. "Oh that. I'm surprised you even remember. You'll have to admit, it was pretty funny, if I do say so myself."

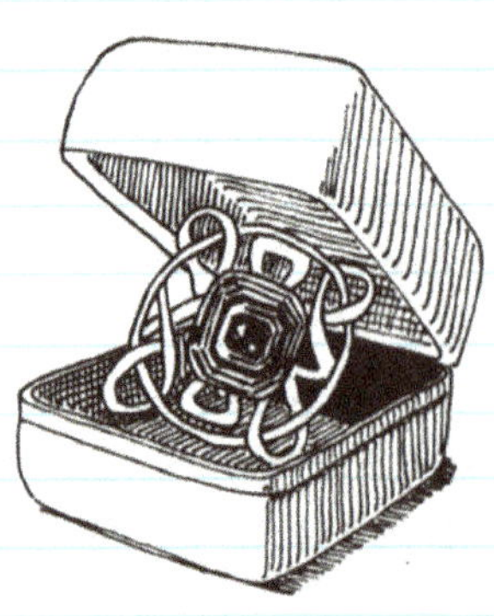

The sapphire amulet.

"Now, maybe. But not back then. In fact, I was kind of freaked out. Just like I am now," I said.

"Well, let me tell you what I know. Years ago I decided to do a study on gnomes, given their association with the captain and Eagle's Nook. I had in mind that I might write a story about them and the caves where we age our wines and use it as a way to get publicity for the winery. People could believe it or not, but like I said, I thought it would bring people to the winery. I never got around to writing it, but I did a great deal of research on them.

"People of the captain's generation — Europeans, mainly — took the existence of gnomes, trolls, fairies and the like, as a matter of fact. As you read, some enlightened folks, like the captain's parents, took a live-and-let-live approach to them, knowing that treating them well and with respect, there could come a time when the little ones might help the humans. I ran across many reports of just such behavior. But the majority of humans were afraid of them — afraid that the gnomes would steal their children, cause their crops to fail or cast a spell on them. People who were afraid did their best to get rid of the little people. And the church certainly went out of its way to make them out to be agents of the devil. Eventually their numbers dwindled or they disappeared deeper into their caves.

"You read the captain's account of why the gnome king and his men stowed away on his schooner — they were looking for a new place to live where they wouldn't be persecuted, not to mention some place far away from the sound of church bells. Basically, they just wanted to be left alone.

"Another thing I found out is that more than one authority thought it was possible that gnomes could still be living underground in caves. Considering that they only come out at night, I imagine if the caves were in the right place, it would be possible for them to avoid being detected unless, of course, they do silly things like steal horses and leave bags of gold as payment... " Hattie said, trailing off.

"Which brings me to another point," she continued. "Don't you think it makes sense that little people might want or need a little horse? I know they're valuable and all that, but would anyone else really want to steal a small horse?"

"I know. I thought about that," I said with resignation. "And the bag of gold pretty much seals the deal that it really was the gnomes who took Quicksilver."

"Exactly what I think. Are you hungry?"

"Starved."

"Ring for Doyle, will you?"

I got up and pushed the small black button in the wall next to the fireplace. Almost immediately there was a gentle knock at the library door and Doyle poked his head in, saying "yes, ma'am?"

"Doyle, will you be so kind as to tell Katia to get jiggy with dinner? Nick and I are famished."

Both Doyle and I stifled a laugh. Doyle bowed out with only a "yes, ma'am." Alone again, we both sat in silence in front of the fire for a minute or two.

"So what are you going to do now?" Hattie finally asked.

"I was just thinking about that. It feels like I don't have much of a choice — I mean, I can't just walk away from all this. I guess I've got to see what I can find on Mt. St. Helena."

"Well, at least you have this," Hattie said, holding up the amulet.

"What do you mean?"

"I think you may need it — and sooner rather than later."

"You'd let me use it?"

"I wouldn't let you leave here without it; it's the one bit of insurance that you won't be put into some trance for a hundred years or something."

"Grandma! Why would you say something like that?"

"Oh. Sorry. I didn't tell you about that part, did I?

Mt. St. Helena stands impressively at the northern end of the Napa Valley, some 4342 feet tall.

Chapter XIV

The Badger Method

Sunday, June 18, 1967
Bothe Napa Valley State Park, Space 78
Napa Valley, California

The following day, (as I would learn later) around the same time I was returning from San Francisco on the ferry, Nigel was sitting at the small dinette table in the Airstream trailer at the campground. A large newsprint drawing tablet nearly covered the table. The oversized tablet was one of the things Nigel requested, insisting that it be 18 inches by 24 inches, just like the ones he always used when he was on a challenging assignment. The tablets had become a critical part of Nigel's method of brainstorming.

Armed with a hot cup of tea and a sharp pencil, Nigel hunched over the tablet and wrote down "Known" in big letters at the top of the sheet of paper. That was another part of his method, namely separating the known from the unknown. Underneath "known," he wrote: *Thom Higgenbotham's evidence.* Nigel stopped and considered whether this belonged under the "Known" heading or not. Thom Higgenbotham was Lord Higgenbotham's great uncle on his father's side — his great-grandfather's brother. He was a sailor and, as near as Nigel could tell, a scoundrel and a drunk. His claim to fame was that he had sailed aboard Captain Gustave Niebaum's schooner when a band of gnomes was discovered as stowaways. Thom Higgenbotham had gone so far as to make an exact copy of the ship's log entry for the night it occurred, something he kept on his body his entire life. Not only did he claim to have seen the gnomes with his own eyes, he said so to anyone who would listen to him or buy him a drink. He also insisted that the gnomes had been put into crates and taken by wagon to Captain Niebaum's winery — Thom knew this, he said, because he followed them there on horseback. But the most important part of his tale was the fabulous treasure of gold that went with gnomes — again, something he claimed to have witnessed first-hand.

Somehow, Lord Higgenbotham had been the one to inherit the copy of the ship's log, a photocopy of which Nigel now had in his possession. Nigel read it several times and had decided that it didn't amount to much if you considered it on its own, without the stories Thom told were stripped away - stories for which he had no evidence other than his drunken ramblings. Lord Higgenbotham had also inherited a scrapbook of sorts, one Thom had put together, composed of newspaper and magazine clippings related to Captain Niebaum. The fact that Niebaum had become one of the richest men in America (which Thom was certain had something to do with the gnomes) meant plenty of press coverage over Niebaum's lengthy life. To say Thom Higgenbotham was obsessed with Niebaum and the gnome's treasure would be to put it mildly.

Nigel knew Lord Higgenbotham liked his money, sure enough, but he figured the gnomes' treasure wasn't the most important thing for him. Getting the scoop on a story with international appeal, that was the real prize. That, and proving to his detractors that a relative of his hadn't been crazy after all. Higgenbotham owned countless newspapers in countless countries, and exposing the existence of a tribe of gnomes would sell, literally, millions of newspapers. Lord Higgenbotham had grown up hearing his great uncle's stories repeated over and over again by one family member or another. It wasn't a surprise that Lord Higgenbotham found it easy to believe the gnomes were real.

So where was Thom Higgenbotham's story going to be — in the Known or Unknown column? After thinking about it for some time Nigel decided that, for the time being, he'd assume it was true. After all, if it wasn't true, the gig was up and he might as well pack up and go home.

With that settled, Nigel went back to the tablet. What else was known? From tales told to him when he was a kid, even Nigel knew that gnomes supposedly lived underground, usually in caves, and that they hoarded gold, silver and jewels. Since he was already playing fast-and-loose with the definition of "Known," he wrote down "gnomes live in caves; like gold, silver, etc." And although he didn't know what would be gained from it, Captain Niebaum certainly had been real and Eagle's Nook winery was still in existence, so he wrote both those down in the "Known" column, as well.

When he was on assignment in a new town for any length of time, one of the first things Nigel did was to go to the local library and get a library card. He found libraries to be great places for uncovering all kinds of information, all in one place, convenient and free. The other item he considered a necessity was a copy of the local newspaper. From one corner of the world to the other, most

Big newsprint tablet.

newspapers were pretty much the same, no matter what language they were in or what size the town was — births, marriages, city council goings-on, and the like — but every once in awhile he found tidbits of real value to his work. With that in mind, he decided to drive into town, find the library, get lunch and a newspaper and maybe check out Eagle's Nook winery.

His first stop was the library where he got a card, immediately checking out a book on the history of the Napa Valley, a couple of what looked like kids' books on the folklore of "little people," and one strange one, *The Secret Teachings of All Ages: An Encyclopedic Outline of Masonic, Hermetic, Qabbalistic and Rosicrucian Symbolical Philosophy*, which the reference librarian told Nigel contained information on gnomes.

Instead of going to a restaurant, Nigel picked up a sandwich and a local newspaper at a grocery store in town and decided to head back to the campground. He'd visit Eagle's Nook another day; right now he wanted to take a look at the books he had gotten at the library to see if he could add anything to the "Known" column.

Once back at the trailer, Nigel started with the Napa Valley history book. If it was gold and silver the gnomes were after, Nigel wondered if either of the precious metals was present in the valley. It didn't take him long to discover there had been several silver mines in the valley, up on Mt. St. Helena which, if there hadn't been so many trees in the way, Nigel could have seen from his campsite. The mine was active in the mid-1800s, but had long since been abandoned. In addition to silver and gold, quicksilver had also been found on the mountain. Of particular interest to Nigel, a fellow Scotsman — none other than Robert Louis Stevenson — had spent most of the summer living in an abandoned mining building on Mt. St. Helena in 1880 with his new wife. The site where they lived was now a state park; Nigel decided he'd check it out when and if he had time.

Nigel moved on to the folklore books, along with *The Secret Teachings of All Ages*, which turned out to be very interesting, even though it was nearly impossible to read. From the folklore books Nigel confirmed what he had been told as a child, namely that gnomes were mischievous, were not to be trusted, were excellent thieves, and were capable of putting all manner of spells on unsuspecting humans. It was in *The Secret Teachings* book, however, that something caught his eye; gnomes did, indeed, like gold and silver, but they had a special fondness for quicksilver.

"Now we're getting somewhere," Nigel said to himself as he added the new facts to the "Known" column. "Looks like I might be visiting Mt. St. Helena sooner than I thought."

Nigel took a bite out of his sandwich and stood back, looking at the big sheet of paper, pleased with his progress. He sat down at the dinette table and picked up the local newspaper — *The St. Helena Star*. The front page was the usual assortment of local concerns. "Typical," Nigel thought to himself, with the possible exception of a story on a pony that had gone missing from a local farm. *Now that's news,* he said out loud, chuckling to himself. He perused the rest of the paper without much interest, until he reached the weekly Police Blotter column. "This is rich," Nigel said, reading about complaints of barking dogs at 2 a.m., lost wallets, reckless driving and a couple of citations issued for public drunkenness. *Must be the wine,* he thought. One lost-and-found item caught his eye: "Found: Leather pouch on the premises of Twin Oaks Pony Farm. Describe contents to claim ownership." Nigel turned back to the front page; Twin Oaks Pony Farm was the same place where the pony had gone missing. Nigel ate the last of his sandwich deep in thought, wondering what the connection between the two might be.

•　　•　　•

I had read for a couple of hours in the living room when Grandpa came in and asked if I wanted lunch.

"Sure. But can I ask you a question first?"

"Shoot."

"Why has this been packed away in the attic for what? Like 40 years?"

"Actually it's 44 years; 45 next month."

"Okay. Büt why?"

"Because I made someone a solemn promise that I wouldn't publish the story or, for that matter, let anyone else see it for 45 years."

"Who'd you promise?"

"Where are you in the book?"

"You've had dinner with Grandma Hattie and it looks like Nigel is hot on your trail."

"That guy was such a butt. Keep reading. You'll figure out who I promised."

"Can I – sorry, *may* I ask another question?"

"Of course."

"If you're not supposed to, why are you letting me read it?"

"I've been thinking about that and I really don't have an answer. If I was being super honest, I guess I'd have to say there's some ego involved. I've always wanted someone to read it; hell, I wanted the whole world to read it – you know, best-seller and all that. But there was that promise I made. So I put the journals in that locker in the attic and tried not to think about 'em. I used to be like counting down the years, but 45 of them is a long time to wait. I gotta' admit, I kind of lost interest somewhere along the way. At least until I heard what you said about what happened at Darren's place the other night."

"Can I let Darren read them?"

Grandpa was silent for a minute and then said, "No, I don't think so. At least not now. Let me think about it. Come on, let's have some lunch."

Leaving San Francisco in the ferry boat, headed north to Vallejo.

Chapter XV

Crossed Paths

Sunday, June 18, 1967
Twin Oaks Pony Farm
St. Helena, California

I sat on the ferry as it crossed the San Francisco Bay, reading *Silverado Squatters*, more to keep my mind from replaying all the events at Grandma Hattie's, over and over, than anything else. It wasn't really working, so I gave in and put the book down.

When I was saying goodbye to Grandma, she hugged me and then made me take the amulet out of my pocket to show her I'd actually remembered to take it. Then she wanted to know where the *Secret Teachings* book was. I explained that it was too big to carry back to St. Helena and that I'd get a copy at the library.

"Promise me you'll read it," she said. "I know it's not easy reading, but you need to know what you're up against. Those gnomes are not all sweetness and light."

And they can vanish by dissolving into a tree I thought to myself. Right now, my protection against all this weird stuff was simply not to believe the gnomes were for real. I was okay with that — in fact it was a comfort to think this was all just some kind of a silly hoax. I couldn't help but wonder, though, what was going to happen if the day came that I might be forced to admit they actually existed. Would I be sorry I didn't take all of this more seriously?

.   .   .

I went back to reading *Silverado Squatters*. I'd just gotten to the part where Robert Louis Stevenson walked down the steep, forested hillside from the Silverado Mine, where he and his wife, Fanny, had taken up residence in an abandoned bunkhouse. Before they could go to sleep that first night, Stevenson had to fetch some hay to make into mattresses. He took a shortcut through the woods to his neighbors at the Toll House below. Along the way, he made note of what he observed: *Signs were not wanting of the ancient greatness of Silverado. The footpath was well-marked, and had been well-trodden by thirsty miners. And far down, buried in foliage, deep out of sight of Silverado, I came on a last outpost of the mine — a mound of gravel, some wreck of wooden aqueduct, and the mouth of a tunnel like a treasure grotto in a fairy story. A stream of water, fed by the invisible leakage from our shaft, and dyed red with cinnabar or iron, ran trippingly forth out of the bowels of the cave; and, looking far under the arch, I could see something like an iron lantern fastened on the rocky wall. It was a promising spot for the imagination. No boy could have left it unexplored.*

Now that's interesting, I thought to myself. Was what I just read information on where to find the cave where the gnomes lived? Had Robert Louis Stevenson deliberately left a clue buried in his story, a clue overlooked by generations of readers? The words describing the cave "like a treasure grotto in a fairy story," were enough to get my curiosity going. If the gnomes did, in fact, live on Mt. St. Helena, their cave couldn't be that hard to find, could it? I wondered if the Toll House Stevenson described was still there? *If it was, it should be possible to hike the trail in reverse and find the cave,* I thought to myself. I made the decision, right then and there, to get to Mt. St. Helena as soon as I could, whatever it took.

The ferry disembarked at Vallejo; I only had to wait ten minutes or so for the bus back to St. Helena. I'd called Ma-D before I left Hattie's to tell her what time to pick me up. Sure enough, when the bus stopped in St. Helena a little over an hour later, Ma-D was in the truck, waiting for me. She wanted to know all about Hattie and how my visit had been. There was no way I could have possibly explained all that had gone on, so I made some small talk and hoped it would satisfy her. I suddenly remembered the *Secret Teachings* book and asked Ma-D if we could stop at the library. A couple of minutes later, we pulled up in front of the library and I jumped out, telling Ma-D I'd just be a minute. I ran to the reference desk and asked the librarian if she had a copy of — and then knowing I'd never be able to remember the entire title by heart — I handed her a small piece of paper on which I'd written the name of the *Secret Teachings* book.

The librarian, someone I didn't know, looked at the piece of paper and said, "Yes we have a copy of it, but it's checked out right now. Someone came in yesterday and asked for it. That's very strange. That book hardly ever gets checked out."

I was disappointed and was about to fill out a request for the book when the librarian said, "Looks like it's your lucky day. Here it comes now."

"What?"

"The book."

I turned and looked in the direction of the front doors of the library. The reference librarian was motioning to a man wearing khaki pants and one of those safari jackets with all the pockets on the outside. The man walked over to the reference desk, looking slightly confused.

"Mr. Stayne," isn't it?" the librarian said.

"Yes."

"I remember you from yesterday — when you applied for your library card."

"You have an excellent memory."

"Thank you," she said, looking down at the desk.

"How can I be of assistance?"

"Oh, I'm sorry. But this young man here just came in asking for the book — the *Secret Teachings* book you have in your hand. I told him it was checked out and, now you're here and it looks like it's about to be checked back in again," she said with a slight giggle.

"Indeed," the man said, handing me the book.

"Thanks," I said. "It's so small."

"What is?" he asked.

"The book. The one my grandmother has is enormous."

"I read in the front matter that this is a facsimile edition, but it assures the reader that not a single word has been omitted. I gather the original edition was, indeed, enormous," the man said, and then, holding out his hand "Nigel Stayne."

"Nick Sinclair," I replied, shaking Nigel's hand.

"A pleasure meeting you. I wouldn't think that someone as young as you would be interested in such an esoteric work."

"Yeah... I mean, no... it's just that I ran across a copy at my grandmother's house and the illustrations really interested me," I said, thinking fast.

"Yes, they are amazing, indeed."

Nigel and I parted company with a wave. I hurried to the checkout counter and then out the doors of the library where I waved to Nigel again as he got into a dusty Jeep Bronco.

"Sorry, that took longer than I expected," I said, sliding into the cab of the truck.

"Who was that you waved to?" Ma-D asked.

"Some guy with a really thick accent — Irish or Scottish, I think. He just happened to be returning the book I wanted."

"Well, there's a coincidence for you," Ma-D said, starting the ignition. "Must be your lucky day."

"That's what the librarian said. Maybe it is." But didn't someone say that *there's no such thing as a coincidence?* I thought to myself, wondering if I was missing something important.

.   .   .

Nigel sat in the Wagoneer without starting it. "Now, that was odd," he thought to himself. Over the years, Nigel had accepted what the writer William Burroughs had said, namely that there was no such thing as a coincidence, and that if something struck him as "odd," it was usually more than that.

Getting out his notebook and pen, he wrote down Nick's name. He also wrote down "Twin Oaks Pony Farm," which he noted from the logo on the side of the truck he had just seen Nick get into, recalling it from the mentions in the newspaper. Nigel knew there was something important here; he just didn't have the facts to support it. *Yet,* he thought to himself. Thinking for a moment longer, he also made a note that he thought Nick was lying when he said he was only interested in the illustrations in the *Secret Teachings* book. Just a hunch, he thought, but he knew from experience his intuition was rarely wrong.

He started the truck and headed south on Highway 29. Eagle's Nook winery was only a few miles south of St. Helena. *Time to do some digging,* he thought to himself.

.   .   .

Walter and Ma-D's truck.

Once we got back to the farm, I jumped out of the truck, got my backpack out of the back, scratched a barking Snoops on the head and ran to the bunkhouse, shouting over my shoulder "Thanks, Ma-D. I'm going to change my clothes."

"You want some lunch?"

"Sure, that'd be great."

"I'll have it ready in a few minutes."

Once in my room, I changed into my jeans and t-shirt and flopped on the bed. I knew I had to get up to Mt. St. Helena sooner rather than later. Like tomorrow. I started thinking about how I'd go about getting there and what I'd need to take with me. A couple of years ago, Walter and Ma-D had taken me on a trip to visit Clear Lake. To get there, you had to go up and over Mt. St. Helena and I remembered Walter pointing out Robert Louis Stevenson State Park as we passed it, so I had a general idea of where it was; I knew I couldn't miss it because I remembered there was a sign for the park right on the road. I also knew it was about eight miles from the farm to Calistoga because Chuy and I had ridden there last summer. I guessed that from Calistoga to the state park was about the same distance, but all uphill and in some spots really steep. Getting back would be a cinch, as it was all basically downhill.

I wasn't worried about being able to ride my bike up Mt. St. Helena and back because I knew I could, but I couldn't just go without getting permission first and that might be iffy. I don't know why, but the "permission" part was always iffy. It's just the way adults are. Even so, I thought I could probably come up with something to convince Walter or Ma-D to let me go. But the more I thought about the trip, I wondered what exactly was I going to do once I got there? You know? Like, I get up there and just look around? For what?

I got off the bed and went into the living room of the bunkhouse and looked at a large map of the Napa Valley that was tacked to the wall. It had been there forever and basically just showed where the various wineries were located. The map triggered something in my memory and I instinctively walked back into my bedroom to the small bookcase next to the desk. What was it I was looking for? I scanned the books and there it was: *Mount St. Helena & R.L. Stevenson State Park: a History and Guide* by Ken Stanton — a book Ma-D had given me last Christmas. I had only thumbed through it at the time before putting it in the bookcase, meaning to read it later. I remembered it had been written by a hiker and a mountain climber who lived in St. Helena. Ma-D knew the author and thought that I would like the book. But I was remembering something else, what was it? I thumbed through the book until it flopped open to the last page. There,

The Toll House, before it burned down in 1883, as it looked when Robert Louis Stevenson lived on Mt. St. Helena during the summer of 1880.

in an envelope attached to the inside back cover, was a folded map. I pulled it out and opened it up. "Yes!" I said out loud. It was a detailed United States Geologic Survey map of Mt. St. Helena, with all the important sites marked in red — where the trail started, the location of the mine itself, where the old Toll House had been — everything. I pulled my copy of *Silverado Squatters* out of my backpack and reread the part about the "fairy treasure grotto:"

The footpath was well marked, and had been well-trodden by thirsty miners. And far down, buried in foliage, deep out of sight of Silverado, I came on a last outpost of the mine — a mound of gravel, some wreck of wooden aqueduct, and the mouth of a tunnel like a treasure grotto in a fairy story.

I guessed that the "thirsty" miners were probably going to the Toll House for a drink. So by knowing the location of the mine and the abandoned bunkhouse and where the Toll House had been, I should be able to walk the same route as Stevenson had, from one to the other fairly easily; the "well trodden" path might even still be there. What a find! I was thinking I'd have to thank Ma-D for the book all over again, when I heard her calling that lunch was ready.

.   .   .

Nigel pulled into the parking lot of the Eagle's Nook winery. Time to turn on the charm, he thought as he walked toward the winery — a very large, four-story, vine-covered stone building. Inside the tasting room it took a minute for his eyes to addjust. The cool room was dimly lit and smelled of wine. Nigel went over to what looked like an historical display hanging on the back wall. There, amidst the sepia-toned photographs of the early days of the winery, were three portraits: in the middle, a handsome bearded man identified as Captain Gustave Niebaum; on the right, his wife Susan and on the left, a beautiful young woman, identified only as Hattie Sinclair. "Sinclair!" Nigel said out loud — louder than he intended. That was the last name of the boy he met at the library! Nigel immediately went over to the wine-tasting counter where a young woman stood, waiting to pour wine to visitors. "Excuse me, but I was just admiring the portraits of Captain Niebaum and his wife over there, he said, nodding towards the portraits. "I was wondering who the other woman is, Hattie Sinclair?"

"That's Mrs. Niebaum's niece."

"Oh really? Were they close?" said Nigel, confused.

"You could say so. Captain and Mrs. Niebaum adopted her after Hattie's parents both died in the influenza epidemic of 1918."

"Oh my. How tragic," Nigel said with exaggerated sympathy.

"Yes, very," said the young woman behind the counter.

"Did she ever have a role in the winery?" Nigel asked, still trying to figure out how Hattie Sinclair fit into the picture.

"She's always had a role here," the woman said somewhat defensively. "She still does."

"In what way?" Nigel asked.

"She owns it."

"Really?" Nigel responded, genuinely surprised.

"She's in her sixties now and keeps a fairly low profile, but she's very much a hands-on owner."

"How interesting," Nigel mused. "I had no idea."

"No. Most people don't. I think most folks think Captain Niebaum is somehow still alive..."

"You don't say," Nigel said, with a polite chuckle. "Oh, just one more thing if you wouldn't mind. I met a very affable young man this morning at the library, of all places. He introduced himself as Nick Sinclair. He wouldn't be a relative, would he?" Nigel asked, knowing he was probably pushing his questions too far.

The young woman hesitated and then leaned forward over the counter and said in a low tone, "Yes. Nick is her grandson."

There were many more questions Nigel would have liked to ask, but he knew he'd reached the end of what could be called a polite line of questioning. Any more and he'd be seen as prying.

"Well, thank you so much. You've been very helpful," Nigel said, thinking to himself, *if you only knew.*

Nigel exited the winery parking lot. About a mile up the highway, he saw a gas station and pulled in. There was a telephone booth by the side of the station. Nigel went into the booth and looked up the address of Twin Oaks Pony Farm and then went into the office and asked the woman behind the counter if she could tell him how to get to Mee Lane. She looked out the window and pointed across the highway and said, "if you had a rock, you could probably hit it from here, mister. It's right there on the other side of the road."

Nigel thanked her and thought to himself, *this must be my lucky day.*

•   •   •

I walked into the kitchen and was surprised Walter and Henry weren't there.

"Where's Walter and Henry?"

"They went over to the big feed store in Santa Rosa. Don't know what they needed that they couldn't get here," Ma-D said, fixing a plate for me. She peppered me with some more questions about Hattie, which I was able to answer to her satisfaction. Sensing an opportunity, what with Walter gone, I started in:

"Do you remember that book you gave me last Christmas — the one about Mt. St. Helena?" I asked her, my mouth full of egg salad sandwich.

"Don't talk with your mouth full!" Ma-D said. "Of course I do. Ken Stanton's book. I just saw him the other day at the grocery store. Why?"

"I was looking at it and it's pretty interesting. Is it okay if I take my bike up there tomorrow and do some exploring?"

"You're going to ride your bike all the way to Mt. St. Helena?"

"Sure. Chuy and I rode up to Calistoga last summer. It wasn't so hard."

"Yeah, but you didn't try to make it up the mountain. It's practically straight up. And the traffic is horrible. All those people racing up to the lake."

"Ma-D, please?"

"I swear, Nick, sometimes I wish you wouldn't tell me where you're going."

"I promise that I'll be careful. Really, Ma-D."

"And that you'll be home before dinner. Promise."

"It's a deal. Promise."

I quickly finished my lunch and decided I needed to make a list of what I would need for tomorrow's trip. I was walking across the lawn to the bunkhouse when, hearing the sound of tires crunching gravel, I looked over to where Mee Lane ran on the north side of the farm. It was a white Jeep Wagoneer, travelling very slowly. By the time I figured out where I had seen it before, it had passed out of view. I was certain, however, that it was driven by the same man I'd met this morning at the library — Nigel? Yes. Nigel Stayne, that was it. Strange name, I thought. Even stranger was the sense of uneasiness that crept over me. *Something's going on,* I thought to myself.

A tall grove of native madrones provided shade for a planting of brightly colored fuchsias, the favorite flowers of hummingbirds.

Chapter XVI

The Old Man of the Mountain

Monday, June 19, 1967
Somewhere on Mt. St. Helena
Napa Valley, California

At about the same time as I was packing my backpack for the trip up Mt. St. Helena, Nigel Stayne was halfway through his first cup of tea, furiously writing on his big paper tablet in his trailer at the campground. It wasn't even six o'clock in the morning.

Nigel had started by writing down names and words. Then he started adding arrows indicating connections between the words. The first name he wrote down was Thom Higgenbotham, then Captain Niebaum, then the gnomes or trolls, or whatever they were. He started another column with Captain Niebaum at the top, then Hattie Sinclair and then Nick Sinclair. The third column started with the *Secret Teachings* book and how many times it had cropped up in the past few days. Under the book's name he put his own name, Hattie Sinclair (because Nick had mentioned the fact that his grandmother had a copy of the book when Nigel met him at the library), and Nick's name again. After looking at the chart intently and thinking for a minute or two, Nigel added a bunch of arrows all pointing to "gnomes." It was now clear to Nigel that they were the thread that connected all the other elements on his chart. *Now it gets interesting,* he thought to himself.

In the fourth column he wrote Twin Oaks Pony Farm and then Nick's name. He wasn't sure what the connection was there, but he had seen Nick get into a truck with the Twin Oaks name written on the door panel and he had definitely seen Nick on the property when he drove by yesterday afternoon to check it out. To the side he wrote that not only had something been stolen from Twin Oaks — a Shetland pony — but something had been found, namely a mysterious leather pouch. He began the fifth and final column with "Gnomes." Next, he wrote "like to live in caves," then "like gold, silver and quicksilver," and finally, "Mt. St. Helena," adding "the only place in the valley where there were likely to be abandoned caves where gold, silver, and quicksilver used to be mined." Next, he drew a heavy line connecting Captain Niebaum, the gnomes, and Mt. St. Helena. And then lines connecting Niebaum, Hattie, Nick and the gnomes. Finally he added links between Niebaum, Nick, and Twin Oaks Pony Farm. He stood up and looked at the diagram.

"Oh, this is grand," he said out loud, "it looks just like a spider's web, ready for catching prey."

.   .   .

Pedaling up Highway 29, I was glad I'd made an early start of it while it was still overcast and cool. It wouldn't be long before the cloud cover disappeared and it would begin to get hot. I turned east on Zinfandel Lane and then north on Silverado Trail, which would lead directly to the base of Mt. St. Helena. From there it would be a steep climb up the mountain.

It only took about a half hour to get to the end of Silverado Trail, on the outskirts of Calistoga. I took a long drink of water from my canteen and took off. The climb up the mountain started gradually enough, with wide, sweeping turns, but it soon turned much steeper, with tighter turns through the heavily-forested mountainside. I switched to the lowest gear; I seemed to be going so slowly, I wondered if I were going forward at all. After about 45 minutes of hard pedaling, I saw the familiar yellowish sign with brown lettering on the right-hand side of the road: Robert Louis Stevenson State Park, Elevation 2203 feet. I leaned my bike against a tree and then sat down in the shade with my canteen and caught my breath. I took a long drink from my canteen; the water was warm, but it still tasted good. The way I figured it, I'd just finished the hardest part of the day. According to the map, the old Silverado Mine, where Stevenson spent the summer of 1880, wasn't far from where I was now and it wasn't much of a climb. I'd see what luck I'd have finding the trail, if there was one, and from there, hopefully, to the "fairy treasure grotto," Robert Louis Stevenson had described.

.   .   .

Meanwhile, back on the valley floor, Nigel thought about what to do next. It wasn't even eight o'clock and he felt as though he'd already finished a day's work. *Maybe I'll treat myself,* Nigel thought. There were pay showers at the campground, but they were closed due to drought conditions in the valley. He pulled the neck of his t-shirt over his nose and, taking a whiff, decided it was time to go into Calistoga for a shower and a swim at one of the many hot springs resorts in town, seemingly on every corner. And then breakfast, he thought, a big American breakfast. He was in such a good mood that he found himself singing "We'll have pie in the sky, by and by," as he walked to his truck.

• • •

I locked my bike to a big bay tree and walked across the road to the entrance of the state park, which was little more than the start of a narrow trail through the dense forest. Luckily it was clearly marked and only took me a few minute's hike to arrive at a stone marker with a bronze plaque proclaiming the spot where Stevenson and his new wife had lived for that summer, some 87 years ago. I dug the topographical map out of my knapsack and looked at it carefully. If the map was correct, I was standing very close to the location of the old Silverado Mine. I couldn't see it from where I was standing because it was on the upside of the mountain, some 50 feet or so above where I was standing. *So, somewhere down there*, I thought to myself, looking in the opposite direction, *should be the opening to a mine shaft with a creek coming out of it. Or at least it had been when Stevenson described it nearly a hundred years ago. Not all that convincing of a theory*, I thought, but I started looking through the shrubby undergrowth for signs of a trail anyway.

• • •

At the same time, down at the bottom of the mountain, in a cafe on the main street of Calistoga, Nigel was sitting at the counter, staring at a big mug of steaming hot tea. He was thinking about the events of yesterday. He felt good about the connections he had made, but the one thing he hadn't figured out was the identity of the old lady driving the Twin Oaks Pony Farm truck. And, more importantly, what was her connection to Nick? Nigel thought it over: Was there any reason he couldn't just go there and find out? The waitress set a big platter of ham and eggs and hash browns in front of him. As he dug into it, he started to concoct a cover story for a visit to the Twin Oaks Pony Farm, something he was very good at doing.

• • •

I walked along the edge of the flat clearing in the forest that contained the stone monument and plaque. After three tries, back and forth, peering over the edge and down the mountain, I still

The Robert Louis Stevenson monument.

couldn't see anything that even looked like a trail.

"This isn't getting anywhere," I thought, so I headed down the side of the mountain, slipping and sliding most of the way, to another flat spot, where I could look up, checking for signs of a trail from below.

The forest was thick here, producing a dense, cool shade. The pine and fir trees were enormous — more than 150 feet tall, I guessed. The floor of the forest was, for the most part, covered with a thick mat of dried needles and leaves that crunched when I walked over them. A warm breeze whispered through the forest carrying with it a strong, pleasant smell of resin. There were clumps of undergrowth — manzanita mostly — here and there, but not much else. I was just standing there, wondering what I should do next when I noticed it off in the distance: a little bit of color lit up by a thin shaft of sunlight piercing through the trees overhead.

Hot pink.

I looked closer. Could there really be something hot pink in the middle of an old forest like this? Whatever it was, there was no question about it being bright pink and, even more unlikely, it looked like it was coming out of a tall thicket of madrone trees. As I approached it, the pink color disappeared. I crawled under and through the madrones and was surprised that once I was inside, it was more or less open space, with just the bare bronze-colored trunks of the madrones growing straight up, almost like someone had pruned all the small branches and leaves off the bottom of the trunks, leaving a dense leafy ceiling overhead. Straight ahead of me was what looked like a narrow path. I followed it for about fifty feet until I came to a small pond surrounded by the biggest fuchsia plants I had ever seen — maybe nine feet tall — in full bloom, with what must have been thousands of bright pink flowers hanging off their branches in the dappled sunlight under the madrones. Somewhat overcome by the sight, I stood very still, just taking in the scene. Then, one by one, they came in darting, flitting this way and that, some of them coming very close to me and then stopping in mid-air, as if someone had pressed the pause button on a television: dozens of metallic green and blue hummingbirds whirring by, descending on the fuchsia flowers, busily gathering nectar from the hanging flowers. I stood there for a minute or two in awe of all the activity. And then it hit me: Fuchsias! *The same plants that were taken from Black's Nursery. Now this is something,* I thought to myself.

I turned around and noticed that the path continued past the pond and the fuchsias. Could it lead to the "treasure grotto?" There was only one way to find

The entrance to Clyde's mine, with the cinnebar-stained water seeping out.

out. I took off down the path, which turned to the right and then made a long sweep to the left, all of it under the canopy of the madrones. *Someone's used this recently,* I thought. And then suddenly the path ended at the side of the mountain and, sure enough, there was the opening to a cave, framed with old wood timbers. Inside the rustic frame decrepit wooden doors on rusted hinges hung partially open, offering nothing more than a view of complete darkness inside.

"Wow," I said out loud. After inspecting it for a minute, my first thought was: *Great. It's here. I found it. Now I'm going home.* The more I thought about it, though, the more I realized that I had to go in, even though every muscle in my body disagreed. Remembering the words Stevenson had written about the cave, namely that "No boy could have left it unexplored," I pulled myself together, gently opened the wooden door and entered the cave. I expected the door to creak loudly when I pushed on it, but it didn't make any noise at all, like maybe it was still in use. The door closed slowly and silently on its own, leaving me in complete darkness. I took off my backpack and reached inside for my flashlight. I turned it on and the circle of light showed just about what you'd expect on the inside of an old mineshaft: roughly hewn rock walls, a dusty, dirt floor, and a lot of darkness ahead. I could hear my heart beating, along with water dripping somewhere. To make matters worse, I started shivering, not only from nerves but because it was surprisingly cold inside the mine. I pointed my shaking flashlight to the floor of the cave and noticed there was a thin stream of reddish-colored water running on one side of the cave and remembered what Stevenson had written in *Silverado Squatters* about the "stream of water... dyed red with cinnabar or iron, ran... out of the bowels of the cave." Even though I was more certain than ever that I'd found the right cave, I had to fight the urge to get back outside in the sunlight as fast as possible, if only to warm up again. For some reason my mind flashed on Chuy; if he were here, he'd be laughing all the way, egging me on to see what was around the next corner. "Okay, okay" I said to myself in a whisper.

I walked slowly, sweeping the beam of the flashlight from top to bottom and from left to right, like I had seen some detective do on t.v. The direction of the mineshaft seemed to lead directly into the side of the mountain and then started to head down. *I am not liking this one bit,* I thought. Just then I stepped on what must have been a small, particularly round rock, causing my foot to roll out from under me. In an instant I was down on my backpack, the flashlight rolling away from me further into the cave. I picked myself up in time to see the flashlight hit the side of the mineshaft and go out, leaving me in total darkness. "No!" I said under my breath. Trying not to panic, I told myself I'd seen where the flashlight had landed and that I could crawl over to where it was. Even though my mind was racing and my heart was pounding like a hammer, I told myself calmly that, even if the impact had ruined the light bulb, there was another one stored in a little foam compartment in the bottom of the handle of the flashlight. I could make it. I could find the flashlight and make it work. I could find the flashlight and make it work and get out of the cave. Even in complete darkness, I felt kind of ridiculous crawling on all fours, but I couldn't risk standing up and falling back down again. I'd been in the dark before, but this was darker than dark — it was pitch black. I inched my way over to the side of the cave and started feeling around. Hallelu-jah! I found it! I sat with my back against the rock wall and started unscrewing the bottom of the flashlight as fast as I could. I had just found the replacement light bulb when I thought I heard something. *What was that? Oh please, please, please… tell me I didn't just hear what I think I did.* I stopped what I was doing and listened carefully. No question about it, there was the sound of footsteps coming from somewhere deeper in the cave. Even though my hands were shak-ing like crazy, I knew I needed that flashlight, now more than ever. Somehow I managed to unscrew the top of the flashlight, take the old bulb out and put the new one in, all the while listening as carefully as I could. There was no sound. I stopped breathing. Suddenly, from somewhere in front of me, there was a scratch and a flash of light. I switched on my flashlight and two blood-curdling screams echoed in the cave. The light from my flashlight showed an old man with a white beard standing in front of me not twenty feet away, with a burning match in one hand and an unlit kerosene lantern in the other.

I have no idea why I said it, but I called out "who goes there?" in a very shaky voice.

"Who *goes* there?" came the reply.

"Yeah. Who goes there?" I said, more confidently this time.

"I go there," the old man replied. "And what are you doin' here trespassin' on my property and scarin' the livin' daylights outt'a me?" the old man said angrily.

"I… I…" I stammered, but couldn't think of anything to say.

"Ah, come on," the old man said walking over to me, extending a hand to help me up. "Let's get outta'

Clyde Charles Cates III

here." I got up on my feet and followed the old man out of the mine. In a few minutes, we were standing outside. I had never been so happy to see sunlight in my life.

"Let me take a look at ya'. Why you're nothin' but a punk kid. How old are ya?"

"Fourteen."

"Fourteen! I don't think I was ever fourteen. Least not that I can remember. You're not a claim jumper, are ya?"

"A claim jumper?"

"Yeah, that's what I said."

"No, no. I'm not a claim jumper."

"Then what in tarnation were ya doin' sitting in the dark in my mine? I damn near soiled myself."

"Tell me about it," I said under my breath.

"I just did. Now you tell me what ya were doin' in there."

"I was exploring."

"Exploring? You mean like you were lookin' fer somethin'?"

"Yeah, you could say that."

"Like gold?"

"No. I wasn't looking for gold."

"Well, it's a good thing because all the gold, not to mention silver, in that there mine is mine. What's your name?"

"Nick. Nick Sinclair."

"Well, mine's Clyde," he said sticking out his hand. "Clyde Charles Cates, the third," flashing a smile with a prominent gold front tooth. "Nice hat you got there. Kinda' looks like mine. So what are ya doin' up here — really?" Clyde asked, having obviously calmed down a little.

"Like I said, trying to find something."

"Really? Like what? I might know where it is, depending on what your *it* is."

"It's a little hard to explain," I said, not sure how much I should say.

"Wanna' come back to my camp and talk about it?"

"Sure," I said, not sure what I was getting myself into. All I knew was that after that cave incident, I felt like I could survive anything. That, and I really needed to sit down for a minute and calm down.

I followed Clyde around the mountain to its western side, walking behind him on a very narrow path. After about five minutes, we entered another stand of madrones, just like the one in front of the mine where we just were. Once through the madrones, we were in a small rock canyon, maybe 15 feet wide and

Clyde's place.

about 30 feet deep. The walls of the canyon were about 20 feet tall on both sides. At the back end someone — I assumed it was Clyde — had built a lean-to roof that covered the width of the small canyon. It was like a big three-sided room, with solid rock for the walls. The front of the structure was open, but I saw that panels of canvas had been pushed to both sides. I guessed that they could be pulled across the front in bad weather. There was a fire ring in front of the lean-to with a couple of sawed-off logs that served as a place to sit and an old wooden table with a couple of battered chairs.

"Be it ever so humble..." Clyde said to me, making a sweeping motion with his hand. "Welcome to my abode."

"Wow," I said. "It's kind of a like an open air cave."

"It ain't much, but it's fine by me. You hungry?"

"I am."

"I got some hash left over from last night."

"Thanks. But my aunt packed me a lunch. I've got it in my backpack."

"Well, have a seat. I'll go an' put a plate together for myself. Won't be a minute. You want some water?"

"No thanks. I've got some."

I sat on one of the logs in front of the empty fire ring. I heard Clyde whistling while he made his lunch. A few minutes later he returned with a tin plate full of something — I wasn't quite sure what it was, but Clyde appeared to enjoy it.

"So you live here?" I asked.

"Yup."

"For how long?"

"Forever. Nah, not really. But it feels like it. My grand-daddy used to own most of the south side of the mountain, including the Silverado Mine. He built hisself a big house on the other side of the road. That's where my old man was raised. And me too. Burnt to the ground in the fire of '45."

"Do you still own it?"

"The house?"

"No. The side of the mountain."

"Not much of it. My old man didn't have much of a head for business. Whenever he ran up a debt, he gave whoever he owed an acre or two of the mountain. Alls that's left is a few acres 'round my mine where we met up and this here canyon."

"Have you found much gold?"

"Not enough to make me rich – yet – but enough to keep me in pork and beans and a little whiskey now and then. And this," he said with a big grin."

"Your tooth?" I asked.

"Yep. That's my own gold. Doc in town made it for me. Not many people can say that."

"That's for sure." I said. "Just out of curiosity, why were you walking in the dark back in the mine?"

"Because I can. I know that whole mine by heart. To tell ya' the truth, though, it's a kinda' game I play, jes' to see if I can still do it. And I don't like wastin' kerosene. Stuff's gotten expensive. Waste not, want not, that's what I always say."

"Do you like it up here, living by yourself?"

"I was born dumb and I've had a couple of setbacks since," Clyde said laughing. "Every time I go into town, it reminds me why I do what I do. Had a dog once. Damn fool got hisself into a fight with a bear. Bear won. I jes' never known no other life. And it suits me just fine, most of the time. Winter gets a little grim, but I handle it. What about you?"

"Me?"

"Yeah. Ain't nobody else here."

I thought for a minute. I decided that if I was ever going to find Quicksilver, I was probably going to need some help. And maybe Clyde knew something. He didn't seem like the kind of guy that would be surprised by much, so I decided to just tell the truth.

"I live down in St. Helena on the Twin Oaks Pony Farm. My aunt and uncle own it. The other night one of my uncle's best ponies was stolen."

"A pony?"

"Yeah."

"You're pullin' my leg."

"No. A Shetland pony."

"Who'd wanna' steal a pony?"

"That's what I'm trying to figure out," I said and then hesitated. It seemed weird to say out loud something I hardly believed was true, but I said it anyway. "I think... I think maybe gnomes stole him."

"Why those thievin' little varmits!" Clyde said, standing up. "Nipped stuff from me, too — tools and the like. Left me some gold payment, I'll say that for 'em. But makin' me go into town for replacements all the time — oh, I hate that. A man's time is worth somethin' too, you know!" he said, all worked up.

I couldn't believe my ears. "So you've seen them?"

"No. And I don't want to. But I've heard 'em playing that weird fairy music of theirs. No sir, I steer clear of those no-gooders. This mountain's big enough for them and me without me knowing any more than I already do — those robbin' sneaks give me the willies."

So they are up here, I thought to myself. For the first time since this whole thing had started, I was excited instead of confused. "Do you know where they live?"

"I can take ya' a ways and then point you in the general direction, but I don't want to meet my neighbors, no thank you," Clyde said and then paused. "And if I were you, I wouldn't want to meet them neither. They can be powerful nasty, those little ones, and they 'specially don't like outsiders poking their noses in their business."

"They poked their noses into my uncle's business and took what they wanted — and I'm going to get it back." I said angrily.

"Whoa there, young one. If yer smart, you'll take my advice: Let cooler heads prevail. Tell your uncle to use the gold — I'm assumin' they left some gold, right?

"Yeah, they did. A leather pouch full of it," I said.

"Thought so. They always do. Tell that uncle of yours to use the gold to get hisself another horse, just like I had buy new tools to replace the ones they took. Don't meddle where you're not wanted."

I sat and thought for a minute. I knew what Clyde was saying was probably right. But I also knew there was no way I wasn't at least going to try and get Quicksilver back. I was too close now.

"Will you at least show me where you think they live?"

"So you're one of those, eh?"

"One of what?" I asked.

"A stubborn son-of-a-gun."

"I guess you could say that," I replied.

"All right. But let's get going. I've got gold in that mine that's waitin' to be found. And it ain't gonna' get found on its own."

We left Clyde's hide-away and continued around the west side of the mountain on the same narrow path. We walked for about a quarter mile before coming on a slight rise. From our position, most of the western side of the mountain was visible. Clyde pointed to something: "See that scar on the side of the mountain — the one that almost looks like a teardrop?"

"Yeah, I see it."

"Well, there's a cave underneath it; you just can't see it from here because there's kind of a rock basin underneath it. It's the old Great Western Quicksilver Mine from way back when. That's where I think they live. No, I take that back: I know they live there."

"How do you know?"

"Let's just say I've done some explorin' of my own. Nighttime explorin'. Not too much, mind you, and not too close, but I seen some weird lights up there. Weird music, too. That's where they are, all right."

"How do you get there?"

"You just follow this path. Eventually it peters out, but by then you'll butt up against the side of that basin in front of the mine.

"Thanks for showing me the way, Clyde."

"Don't be thankin' me, Ned. I think the only thing I jes' showed you is the way to a whole peck a trouble."

"It's Nick not Ned," I said.

"It's what?" Clyde asked with a confused look on his face.

"My name. It's Nick not Ned."

"Sorry. Nick-Not-Ned. Got it." Clyde said.

I wasn't sure if he thought my name was Nick-Not-Ned or Nick, but it was getting too confusing to try and explain any further right then.

We walked back to where the path had a fork in it: to the right led to Clyde's mine, the left to the Silverado Mine, where I had entered the park.

"Well, it was nice meeting you, Clyde," I said, holding out my hand.

"Nice meetin' you too — even though you probably took a couple of years off my life," Clyde said, chuckling.

"Well, I guess we're even then. Oh, I almost forgot. Did you plant those fuchsias in the front of your mine?"

"The whatchyas?"

"The fuchsias — those plants with the pink flowers."

"No, they jes' showed up one day. Long time ago."

"That's what I thought. See ya' later, Clyde," I said, waving over my shoulder as I headed off on the upper path.

"So long, Nick-Not-Ned. See ya' next time," Clyde said, raising his hat.

•   •   •

For the second time in a week, I hardly remembered anything about the ride home, other than it was a whole lot easier — and faster — than the ride up. My brain was going a hundred miles an hour but, for some reason, I felt better about what I was doing. At least everything seemed a little more real now. And just for the record, I wasn't sure if that was a good thing or not.

I pulled into the Twin Oaks driveway and put my bike on the front porch of the bunkhouse. Snoops woke up from his favorite place on the porch and barked like crazy. I was down on my knees letting him lick my face when Ma-D appeared on the back porch of the house.

"Look who's home. I didn't expect you for another hour or so."

"Yeah, I took off a little early. Didn't want you worrying."

"Well, aren't you Mister Considerate?"

"That's me, Ma-D."

"We had a visitor today. You should have been here."

"Oh yeah? Who?" I asked.

"A Mr. Stayne. Nigel Stayne. Said he met you at the library yesterday."

I did a double-take and looked at Ma-D in disbelief.

"Nigel Stayne? What the..."

Here are a few of the very strange illustrations in *The Secret Teachings of All Ages.* The ink
drawings on the left and right are how the
book depicts gnomes. I wondered if they really
looked like that. Pictured directly below is the
cover of the *Secret Teachings* book – it's huge –
about 12 by 18 inches.

<h1>Chapter XVII</h1>

Dinner with Nigel

Monday, June 19, 1967, continued
Twin Oaks Pony Farm
St. Helena, California

"He was here? At the farm?" I couldn't believe it.

"He showed up just after lunch. What a charming man. Of course, I've always been a fool for anyone with an accent."

"Did he say what he wanted?"

"As a matter of fact, he did. Said he'd read the story about Quicksilver in the *Star*. He's a photojournalist, you know. He wants to write about our horses. When he told me some of the stories he's covered, I realized I'd read one of them just last month in *National Geographic*. It was about that horrible earthquake in China. I invited him for dinner."

"Tonight?"

"Yes. I'm making lasagna. What's wrong? You look like someone just stepped on your toe."

"No, I'm all right," I replied. Truth was I didn't know why I'd taken a dislike to the man. There was just something about him that made me uncomfortable.

"Well go get cleaned up. He's coming at six. And wear one of your white shirts. It isn't often we have famous guests here."

"Famous?" I asked.

"Yes, famous. He's met Queen Elizabeth."

"Oh really?"

"Really. We were talking about breeding ponies and he told me he'd done a story on the queen and her dorgies."

"Dorgies?"

"It's a cross between a Pembroke Welsh Corgi and a miniature dachshund. Seems that the queen's sister, Princess Margaret, has a mini dachshund and he, well you know... got together with one of the queen's corgis. And now she has dorgies."

"Fascinating," I said, not meaning it.

"Well, go on. Get ready for dinner."

Snoops followed me into the mercifully cool bunkhouse. I sat on my bed for a minute, trying to sort through my feelings and realized I should call Grandma Hattie and let her know what I'd found on the mountain.

I dialed her number from the telephone in the bunkhouse living room. Katia answered and put Hattie on.

"Hi Grandma."

"How's it going, Nick?"

"Okay. I just wanted to let you know I went up on Mt. St. Helena today."

"Oh really?"

"Yeah. I found out quite a bit. It's kind of a long story, but I'm about 100 percent sure the you-know-whos are there."

"Really? But I can't say I'm surprised. What did you find?"

"A whole bunch of fuchsias, stolen from Black's Nursery a few years back."

"Fuchsias?"

"Yes."

"My word. I can't even imagine..."

"Neither can I, but they're there. Planted all together on the side of the mountain. Did I tell you Mr. Black found a pouch filled with gold nuggets after the fuchsias disappeared?"

"No, but it makes sense. What are you going to do next?"

I paused. "That's the problem. I'm not sure what to do. What in the world do fuchsias have to do with gnomes?"

"Your guess is as good as mine, but you're a smart boy, Nick. You'll figure it out."

"I hope so. Listen, Grandma, I've got to run. Ma-D invited some reporter from England to dinner and I've got to clean up."

"That sounds interesting."

"Yeah, I guess so. I'll call you later, okay?"

"Yes, yes, that's fine. Just be careful, Nick. And let me know what you're going to do before you do it, okay?"

"I will, Grandma."

•　　•　　•

I changed into a clean pair of jeans and a white shirt, which seemed strange to be wearing at the farm. As I was putting on my shoes, Henry walked into the bunkhouse.

"Hey Nick. You here?"

"Yeah, I'm here."

"Guess someone special's comin' to dinner," Henry said, poking his head into my bedroom.

"So I hear."

"Ma-D told me I had to look 'presentable.' I thought I always looked presentable."

"I don't know what to say, Henry. Probably best to just do as you're told."

"I know that's right," Henry said, lumbering off to his bedroom.

I looked at my watch: it was five o'clock. I decided to take the opportunity to read what the *Secret Teachings* book had to say about gnomes — something I'd been avoiding. I took the book out to the front porch of the bunkhouse. Snoops followed me out and found his favorite spot. The old canvas porch swing creaked loudly when I sat on it. Swinging gently back and forth, I found the section on gnomes and started reading:

The type of gnome most frequently seen is the brownie or elf. They are mischievous and grotesque little creatures; their figures are inclined to rotundity.

I wondered how much of this information could be trusted. I also wondered if the illustrations could be trusted — if so, these guys were really creepy looking. I was no expert on gnomes, but from the fairy tales I'd read as a kid, I thought elves were much smaller than gnomes. Of course, those were fairy tales and this was... what?

I read on:

Many authorities state that they are of a tricky and malicious nature, difficult to manage, and treacherous. Writers agree, however, that when their confidence is won they are faithful and true. The philosophers and initiates of the ancient world were instructed concerning these mysterious little people and were taught how to communicate with them and gain their cooperation in undertak-

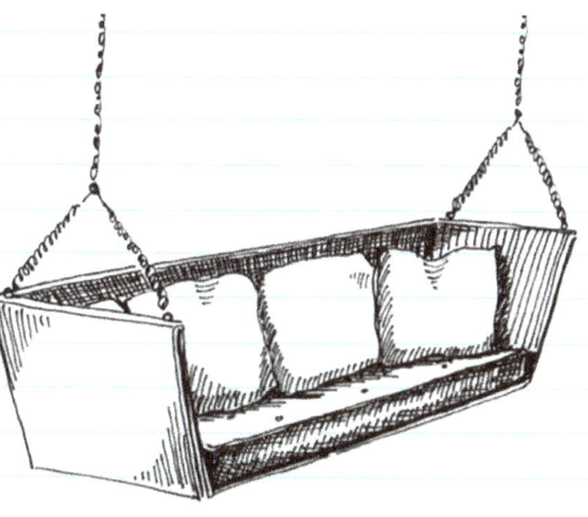

The old porch swing.

ings of importance. The same philosophers were always warned, however, never to betray the trust of the elementals, for if they did, the creatures, working through the subjective nature of man, could cause them endless sorrow and probably ultimate destruction. So long as the mystic served others, the gnomes would serve him, but if he sought to use their aid selfishly to gain temporal power they would turn upon him with unrelenting fury. The same was true if he sought to deceive them.

The writing was all pretty dense, but I learned that part of their "malicious" nature included stealing things from their human neighbors — *that part's true* I thought to myself — and that their mystical music could attract humans and put them in a spell that would last for a hundred years. "I hope *that* part isn't true," I said quietly, closing the book. I just sat there for a while, thinking. I didn't like that part about "endless sorrow" and "ultimate destruction." Did I want to have anything to do with any of this stuff? It wouldn't take much to convince me to leave it all behind and let the sheriff do his job — even though I knew he probably wouldn't be able get Quicksilver back. No way. He'd already said as much about not being able to solve the case. But right now nobody, except for Grandma Hattie, knew what I suspected and she probably wouldn't give me a hard time if I decided to back out. At least I hoped she wouldn't. I never knew what Grandma Hattie would do, one way or another. The more I thought about it, though, the more I realized it wasn't about Grandma Hattie or anyone else — it was about me. If I didn't do anything, it would bug me, big time. If I copped out, I'd always be a cop-out. It was beginning to feel like I didn't have much of a choice. I was already knee-deep in this thing. No matter where it led, there was only one way out, which was to keep on going whether I found Quicksilver or not. Feeling more than a little trapped, I decided I'd better go to the library tomorrow and see if there was anything else I might be able to learn about the gnomes. Even if only parts were true, if I was going to confront them at some point, the more I knew about them the better off I'd be.

Ma-D interrupted my thoughts by calling from the back porch.

"Give me a hand, will you Nick? It's too hot to eat inside. Help me set the table in the grape arbor, will you?"

"Sure Ma-D." I said, walking over to the back porch, kind of relieved to be back in the real world.

Between the back lawn and the vegetable garden there was a grape arbor with an old picnic table under it. The grape vines were thick, their branches arching over the sides. Once you were inside the arbor, it was cool, green, and shady.

Ma-D loaded me up with a tablecloth, plates, napkins and silverware. I spread the yellow-and-white-checked tablecloth over the wooden table, and placed the plates, napkins and silverware in their spots. Ma-D called from the back porch again, this time with a load of small candles in jelly jars and a bouquet of nasturtiums. *Boy, she's going all out,* I thought to myself.

At a few minutes after six, Nigel arrived. Ma-D greeted him on the front porch. Once inside the house, there were handshakes all around between Nigel and Walter, Henry and me. I noticed that Walter, Henry and I all had white shirts on. Apparently we'd all gotten the same message from Ma-D. I thought that we looked like we were members of a singing group or something.

Ma-D had me drag some wicker chairs from the porch of the bunkhouse in the shade on the back lawn. Walter poured iced tea mixed with lemonade for everyone. There was polite conversation, peppered with Nigel's stories of adventures from one far-away place or another. Ma-D had her hospitality turned on high and had Nigel repeat the story about Queen Elizabeth's dorgies so everyone could hear it firsthand.

We all moved to the picnic table under the arbor and Ma-D served her lasagna and a big salad and garlic bread. When he was finished, Nigel announced it was the best lasagna he'd had since he was in Tuscany, which made Ma-D blush. I helped clear the table and as I was walking away, I heard Nigel ask Walter if there had been any news on Quicksilver. By the time I returned with the dessert plates, Walter was still rambling on about the sheriff's department and how he didn't think they'd ever find Quicksilver, let alone who took him. My thoughts exactly.

"Have you thought about starting your own investigation?" Nigel asked Walter.

"Nah. Wouldn't know where to start," Walter replied.

"Well, did anything unusual occur around the time of the theft?" Nigel asked.

There was a silence and then I saw Henry open his mouth and say "What about the gol...?" It was the first thing Henry had said during the entire dinner, which got Nigel's attention. Henry stopped in mid-sentence when I coughed and shot him a look that could have stopped a train.

"What about the what?" Nigel calmly asked Henry.

"Ah, nothin'. I don't know what I was thinkin'" Henry said, looking down at the table.

Right then Ma-D returned to the table, carrying a blueberry pie and a bowl of vanilla ice cream. It was so good, no one said much while they ate it, just a lot of "umms" and "ahhhs." Everyone complimented Ma-D on the meal, which she deflected with a wave of her napkin. Then Nigel turned to me and, out of the blue, asked,

"So what do you think of the *Secret Teachings* book?"

I wasn't prepared for this. I hesitated, finally saying, "Honestly, not much. It doesn't make much sense to me."

"What book is that, Nick?" Walter asked.

"Oh, just a book I got at the library. Mr. Stayne had taken it out before me. That's how we met — at the library."

"Nick always has his nose stuck in one book or another," Walter said.

In an effort to turn the attention away from me, I asked Nigel "So are you on assignment here?"

"Yes. The *London Sun* wants an 'insider' piece on the Napa Valley. A lot of Europeans are becoming interested in what your winemakers are up to. And I must say, it's a beautiful valley you have here."

"Where are you staying?" I asked.

"I have a place between here and Calistoga. Nice spot," Nigel answered. I was hoping for something a little more specific, but let it drop.

The conversation started to peter out and Nigel announced that it was time for him to go, blaming his early departure on "still being a little jet-lagged." As we were saying our goodbyes, Nigel asked again if it was all right to write a story on Walter and Ma-D and their horses. Ma-D agreed enthusiastically while Walter just stood there as Nigel made an appointment with them for ten o'clock tomorrow morning to take some pictures and do an interview.

.　　.　　.

Nigel drove off thinking to himself how easy it was to deceive people and knowing for certain that the kid was hiding something. Or, more likely, a number of things.

When Nigel got to his trailer, it was still hot inside. He opened all the windows to let the cool night air in. He had been surprised that no matter how hot the days were in the valley, the evenings cooled off dramatically. He found he liked making a fire in the fire pit after dark and just sitting there, thinking and watching the flames. It reminded him of his youth, when he had been in the Boys Brigade back in Scotland. He built a fire and reminded himself to get some more firewood tomorrow.

There was some magic in fire, he thought, the way the flames put people into a kind of meditative state, one thought leading to another. He was bothered that he still didn't know the relationship between Nick and Ma-D and Walter. Nick had called Walter "uncle;" were they really his aunt and uncle? If so, where were his parents? He'd have to look into that. The more he thought about it, the more he was convinced that he and Nick were on the same path. It pained him to think that Nick might be several steps ahead of him. He wondered what it would take to get Nick to work with him. There had to be a way. "There's always a way," he said out loud. "They don't call me 'The Badger' for nothing."

Bothe campground was heavily forested with a dense variety of native trees. Inset: *The swimming pool at Bothe, filled with ice-cold spring water.*

Chapter XVIII

Caught!

Tuesday, June 20, 1967
Bothe Napa Valley State Park
Napa Valley, California

I got up early again the next day. It was going to be another scorcher and I had a lot do. I figured I'd get the nastiest job out of the way first. I walked over to the corral and started mucking it out with a big metal rake. I was slowed down by Snoops who kept wanting roll in the manure. I tried to explain to him how disgusting it was, but he was having nothing of it and I had to keep shooing him out of the corral. He finally went over and sacked out in the shade of the barn, leaving me to think about last night and Nigel Stayne. Although I didn't have much to go on, I got the distinct feeling that Nigel was fishing for information. I was glad I had stopped Henry from saying anything about the gold. "The less this guy knows, the better," I thought to myself.

After I finished taking the manure to the compost pile, I sat on the corral fence and watched the ponies. They all looked okay, but it was odd not seeing Quicksilver among them. I wondered if they'd ever all be together again? Deep down, I doubted it. I had the feeling of being too far out on a shaky limb with no net below. Truth be told, everything about this, this... whatever it was, was making me uncomfortable. Having some help would have made a difference, but that didn't seem likely and Chuy wasn't supposed to get back for another couple of months or more, so it really was up to just me. Did I have what it was going to take to figure this whole thing out and get Quicksilver back? I wasn't sure. At all.

I gave the vegetable garden a good watering and then walked over to the house and into the kitchen.

"Morning Walter. Morning Ma-D."

Walter grunted over the top of his newspaper. Ma-D was still in a good mood from her successful dinner party last night.

"And good morning to you. Sleep well?"

"Yeah. I slept just fine. Where's Henry?"

"He's moving the irrigation lines in the pasture. Going to be a hot one today – newspaper says over 100," Walter said.

"Wash your hands and sit down, Nick," Ma-D said. "Eggs over medium?"

"Please," I said, walking over to the sink, where the already hot morning sun was streaming in through the open window and the sweet potato leaves turning them a glowing green. "I already cleaned the stalls and watered the vegetables. Anything else you need me to do?"

"You can take the trash out to the incinerator," Ma-D said.

"And bring those two bottles of spring water in from the front porch," Walter chimed in. "I can't even lift 'em any more."

"Okay," I said. "After that, I'd like to go to the library before it gets hot."

"Do you need a ride?" Ma-D asked, setting a plate of eggs, bacon and fried potatoes in front of me.

"No, I'll take my bike."

"Are you sure?"

"Yeah. I like riding. Just not when it's over 100 degrees."

We all ate in silence for a minute or two. Ma-D was the first to speak.

"He certainly is an interesting man," she said.

"Who?" Walter asked.

"Who do you think? Nigel!"

"Oh, him. Actually, I thought he was a little pompous — all Tuscany this and Queen Elizabeth that..."

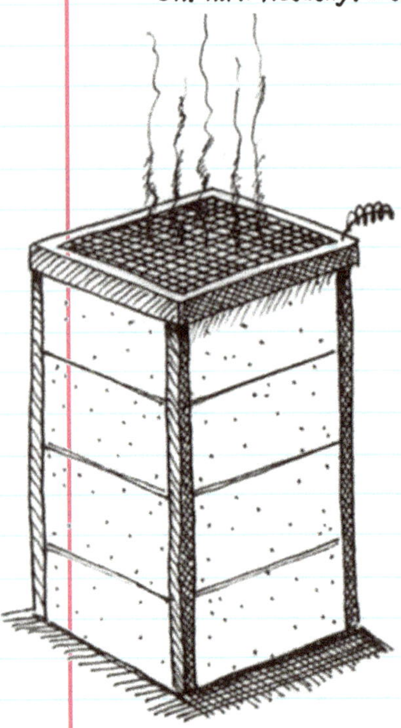

The incinerator.

"He can't help it if he's led a fascinating life," Ma-D said.

"Fascinating?" Walter asked dismissively.

"Yes, *fascinating*. We think it's a big deal to go the state fair in Sacramento."

"Which we won't be doing if we don't get Quicksilver back," Walter pointed out quickly.

"Oh, that's right, isn't it?" Ma-D said with honest concern. She added a thoughtful "hmmmmmm" to his Walter's observation.

"Yeah. That's right," Walter said with a touch of anger.

"Well, don't forget that Nigel is coming over this morning at ten to interview us and take pictures. It's too bad you didn't get your hair cut, Walter."

"Hair cut! How was I supposed to know I was going to get my picture taken?"

I finished my breakfast and decided to get going

before the conversation took a turn for the worse. I excused myself and took the trash bin out to the incinerator behind the barn. I stuffed the paper and other burnable stuff inside and lit a match. Walter had instructed me never to leave it alone while it was burning, so I stood there watching the flames licking through the wire grate on top. I was glad I wasn't going to be here when Nigel came. I figured the fewer of his questions I had to answer, the better.

I waited until the fire had burned itself out, brought the bottles of spring water in, and said goodbye to Ma-D and Walter and headed into St. Helena on my bicycle. I took the shortcut to the library, through the parking lot of the big grocery store off of Main Street. I brought my bike to a screeching stop when I spied Nigel Stayne loading a big box into the back of his Wagoneer. I quickly hid myself behind a parked car and watched. Nigel proceeded to load three more identical boxes into his truck, which I recognized as the boxed firewood kept near the store's entrance. *Why in the world would anyone want firewood in the middle of a heat wave?* I thought to myself. I crouched down behind the car as Nigel drove out of the parking lot. "Now that was odd," I said out loud.

The library was only a couple of blocks from the grocery store. I put my bike in the rack and hurried into the library, which was pleasantly cool and quiet. I walked over to the card catalog but then changed my mind and went over to where the encyclopedias were. I thought maybe it was best to start with something I trusted — like the *Encyclopedia Britannica*. I pulled down the "G" volume and quickly found "Gnome:"

In European folklore, dwarfish, subterranean goblin or earth spirit who guards mines of precious treasures hidden in the earth. He is represented in medieval mythologies as a small, physically deformed (usually hunchbacked) creature resembling a dry, gnarled old man. Gob, king of the gnome race, ruled with a magic sword and is said to have influenced the melancholic temperament of man.

The term was popularized through the works of the 16th century Swiss alchemist Paracelsus in which gnomes were described as capable of moving through solid earth as fish move through water.

That, of course, led me to look up "Paracelsus" and "alchemist," but neither shed any light on how to deal with a band of gnomes I suspected of stealing a Shetland pony. I went over to the card catalog and looked up "gnomes" in the subject index. There were plenty of titles, but they were all books in the children's section which, I decided, wouldn't be any help.

I sat down in a chair next to the card catalog, disappointed in what I had been able to turn up. I closed my eyes for a minute and let my mind wander. Why was I thinking about those big boxes of firewood I saw Nigel putting in his truck? Where had I seen them before? I sat bolt upright, my eyes wide open now: *Of course!* I thought. A couple of weeks before school ended, a bunch of my friends from the dorm had gone on an overnight camping trip to the coast with Mr. Hayes. I remembered Mr. Hayes stopping at the store before we reached the campground, saying he'd forgotten the most important thing for any camping trip. When he returned, I saw him put one of those boxes of firewood into his van, along with a grocery bag. When he got back in the van, I asked him what was in the bag. Mr. Hayes looked at me and asked "well, it wouldn't be camping trip, would it, without a campfire and s'mores, would it?"

The more I thought about it, there was no other reason for someone to buy firewood in the middle of summer other than for a campfire, was there? Did that mean Nigel was camping? It seemed like kind of a long shot, but if I was right, where was the campground? I remembered that Nigel said he was staying "between St. Helena and Calistoga." And he said he was in a nice "spot;" he didn't say a nice house or hotel. I tried to picture what was between St. Helena and Calistoga. All I could recall was last summer, during a similar hot spell, Ma-D had driven me and Chuy to a public swimming pool with water that was freezing cold and that you could see the pool from the highway about halfway between St. Helena and Calistoga. *Wait a minute,* I thought to myself. I remembered that Ma-D had to pay a "day use" fee for us to use the pool and that she had paid it to someone in a uniform. I figured I must not have been paying very close attention, because it was all pretty vague, but the more I thought about it the more I was convinced that the public pool was part of a campground.

Because I had spent so little time at the library, I had some time to burn. I didn't think the place that had the swimming pool could be more than three or four miles up the highway, so I decided to check it out. Once outside the library, the hot air took me by surprise. *It's gonna' be a hot ride,* I thought to myself.

Twenty minutes of hard pedaling later, the sign was right there in front of me: Bothe State Park, one-quarter mile ahead. Now that I'd discovered the place, how was I was going to tell if Nigel was staying there? I looked at my watch; it was a few minutes before ten. Nigel was supposed to be at the farm, interviewing Ma-D and Walter, so his Wagoneer wouldn't be around for me to identify. I found myself wondering how big the campground was and how was I going to be able to tell Nigel's spot from anybody else's if, in fact, he was actually staying there? From out of the blue I had an idea, just as I was approaching the ranger station.

"Hi," I said to the ranger.

"Hi. You here for the pool?" he asked, adding "you look like you could use it."

"Actually not. I'm here to see my uncle, only he didn't tell me what campsite he was in. His name is Nigel. Nigel Stayne."

"Or sure. Only he's not here. I saw him leave about ten minutes ago."

"Is that right? Would it be all right if I waited for him? I'm a little early."

"You're not trying to sneak in and use the pool for free, are you?" he asked with a smile.

"No, I wasn't, but maybe I will go swimming. Is the water still as cold as it was last year?," I said, trying to make normal conversation.

"You bet'ya," he said. "It's spring-fed, cold as ice. That'll be two dollars."

I couldn't very well tell him why I was really there — heck, I didn't really know myself. It was easier to just go ahead and gave him the money even though I was pretty sure I wasn't going to make it to the pool for a leisurely swim.

"Oh, and what space is my uncle in?"

"Sorry. He's in space 78. Just follow the road to the right. You'll find it."

"Thanks again," I said, riding off.

It was a little cooler in the dappled shade of the forested campground, but not much. There were plenty of families camping and lots of little kids on bikes, riding this way and that, shouting and laughing. In the distance, I could hear the sounds of people at the pool. I rode slowly around the campground and saw space 78 a little off to one side of the road, with an aluminum trailer parked in it. I noticed the four boxes of firewood next to the door of the trailer, so there was no question I was in the right spot. I wondered how much time I had before Nigel came back — *at least an hour*, I thought. *More than enough to do... what?* I wasn't quite sure. I leaned my bicycle against the trailer and walked around to the other side where I couldn't be seen by other campers. There was a fairly good-sized window on that side and the drapes weren't completely drawn. I went around to the front of the trailer again and grabbed one of the boxes of firewood to stand on to get a better view inside. I stood on top of the box, my hands cupped around my eyes to cut out the reflection. Everything was about what you'd expect, except that Nigel apparently wasn't much on housekeeping: the bed was unmade, there were dirty dishes in the sink, and open books, maps, and papers everywhere. I scanned the inside of the trailer once more and noticed a large piece of paper, taped to a cabinet, with a lot of messy writing and arrows and lines going here and there. Immediately, my own name, Grandma Hattie's and Twin Oaks Pony Farm jumped out at me. *Oh man!* I said to myself. I

Nigel's chart.

started reading it across, in order.

Two headings, written larger than the other words, were printed across the top of the page: "Known" and "Unknown."

Jeez, I thought to myself, *he does the same thing I do to figure something out.* I saw Captain Niebaum connected to Eagle's Nook, connected to the gnomes, connected to gold, silver, and quicksilver, connected to caves and Mt. St. Helena, all with an arrow pointing to my name, which was circled at the bottom of the page, along with Twin Oaks Pony Farm. Although it was over 100 degrees by now, I felt a shiver go through my entire body. At the same moment, someone gripped my right shoulder tightly. I froze, my heart practically pounding out of my chest.

"Looking for something?" the voice behind me said.

"What are you doing here?" I stammered, as I slowly turned around.

"Don't you think that's a question I should be asking you?" Nigel said, pointing something that looked like it might be a gun in his jacket pocket at me. "For the record, I forgot my tape recorder. Lucky me."

"What's in your pocket?" I said, my voice shaking.

"What do you think? A man has the right to protect his property, doesn't he? And it looks to me like you were about to break into my trailer."

"I wasn't going to break in, believe me. I just wanted to see what you were up to. That's all."

"I'd say we both know what we're up to now. Inside," he said, motioning with the hand that was in his pocket.

Nigel walked around to the front of the trailer and unlocked the door. I thought about making a break for it, but decided against it. I didn't think Nigel was stupid enough to use the gun, but I didn't want to test him.

I went in first and Nigel, who had taken the gun out of his pocket, motioned with it for me to sit down at a small, built-in table. Nigel leaned against the counter, directly in front of me.

"Could you put that thing away?" I said. "You're not going to need it."

"That's what I like," Nigel said, putting the gun on the counter next to him, "a prisoner who cooperates from the beginning."

"I'm not your prisoner," I said defiantly.

"Oh yeah. Why don't you try walking out the door?"

"You could keep this tough talk going all morning, Mr. Stayne. "I've dealt with bullies before. Why don't you just tell me what you want?"

"So you think I'm a bully?"

"I'd say so."

"Well, I think you're in a bit of a sticky wicket, kid. I caught you trying to break into my trailer here, and I believe I'd be within my rights to call the sheriff and have you arrested. And I'm also guessing that you'd rather not have me do that."

"Like I said, why don't you just tell me what you want?"

"Listen. We both know you're way over your head in this deal. I'm guessing you want to play the hero and get your uncle's little horsey back and I want my story."

"He's not my uncle."

"You called him that last night at dinner."

"Ma-D and Walter are my foster parents."

Nigel paused. "I see. What happened to your... ?"

Before he could say anything more, I interrupted him: "Don't. Please," I said, looking straight at Nigel.

Nigel paused again. "So, am I right about the half-baked plan?"

"Actually, it's not even half-baked yet."

"That's what I'm saying, kid. You need my help."

I instinctively knew I needed to buy some time, without Nigel breathing down my neck, to figure out what to do next. I figured the only way I could do that was to convince Nigel I'd cooperate with him. Or something like that.

I was silent for a bit. "Yeah, I guess I do."

"Now you're being reasonable."

"I still don't know what you want from me," I said as earnestly as possible.

"Like I said, I want my story."

"What story?" I said, throwing up my hands.

"Those damn gnomes. Are they for real?"

"To tell you the truth, I'm not sure."

"So you haven't seen them?"

"No."

"Do you know where they live?"

"Possibly."

"Possibly?" Nigel said angrily.

"I haven't had a chance to check it out yet."

"Well, that's good enough for me. Why don't we go together to this 'possible' spot and we'll both see if they're there or not?"

"What's in it for me?"

"Did anyone ever tell you you're a real smartass, kid? I'll help you get that horse back — that's what's in it for you."

"Can we back up here for a minute? I'm not sure I understand where you're coming from."

"What do you mean, 'coming from' ?"

"I mean, why are you doing this?"

"Because someone hired me to."

"Who?"

"Lord Higgenbotham. He's one of the richest men in the world — not some pissant kid like you — and you better believe he'll go to any lengths to get this story and so will I."

"Sorry for being so dense, but why?"

"Why?" Nigel said incredulously.

"Yeah. Why's it such a big deal to him?"

"Good god, kid, you *are* dense. Because he owns most of the biggest news-papers and magazines around the world. Let's just say a story like this would be good for business."

"Okay," I said with exasperation, "now I understand." I realized I had to think fast now. At least one thing was clear now: Nigel needed me more than I needed him. And, for some reason, I didn't think that he'd call the sheriff, and even if he did, I'd probably be able to talk myself out of any real trouble with Sheriff Lyman. I decided to risk Nigel's anger.

"There's still a couple of things I don't understand," I said, as nicely as I could.

"Jeez, you're a pain. Like what?"

"Well, how do you know about the gnomes?"

"From Higgenbotham. Some great uncle of his sailed with Captain Niebaum. He was on board ship when the gnomes were found. He claimed he saw them being carted off to Niebaum's winery — which I gather your grandmother now owns."

"What of it?"

"Well, it puts you in a position of knowing a lot more than I do."

"Okay," I said to myself. Nigel had just admitted what I suspected. "Does

Lord Higgenbotham have any proof of any of this?"

"What's with the third degree, kid? I'm the one with all the cards in this game. Are we going to work together or not?"

"I'm just trying to figure out why Higgenbotham is so sure the gnomes really exist because, to tell you the truth, I'm not certain they do."

"Oh, that's just dandy."

"Well, it's the truth. Does Higgenbotham have any proof?"

"Not much. Just a page copied out of the ship's log from the night the gnomes were discovered as stowaways."

"Have you seen it?"

"Of course. I have a copy of it."

"Can I see it?"

"What's with you, kid? I think I'd be better off if I just called the sheriff."

I ignored the threat. "I'm just trying to figure out if any of this is worth it. Can I see the copy?"

"You're the cockiest s.o.b. I've ever run across," Nigel said, rummaging through his briefcase. "Here," he practically shouted, shoving the copy at me.

I looked it over; sure enough, it was an exact copy of what was written in the log Hattie had in her safe — the result of graphite being spread over the back of the page from the log. I pretended to read every word carefully; I needed to think about what to do next.

"It's not much," I said, "it doesn't even mention they're gnomes."

"Yeah, but this great uncle, or whatever he was, claimed he'd seen them."

"I don't know Mr. Stayne. This could all be a wild goose chase. I need to think about it," I said, wanting to see how far I could push him.

"Think about it!" Nigel said, turning bright red, veins bulging on the sides of his neck. "What the hell is there to think about?"

"If you ask me, quite a bit," I said, standing up. "You know where I live," I said calmly, opening the door to leave.

"Why you little sh... !"

I closed the door to the trailer quietly. I heard things being thrown around inside and a whole lot of cussing. I was already on my bike, riding away when Nigel ran out of the trailer yelling "I'm calling the sheriff!"

"Go ahead," I called back over my shoulder. And then proceeded to ride as fast as I could out of the campground.

I admit that it was a little strange, but the water in the horse trough felt really good after that very hot bike ride home.

Chapter XIX

The Plan Comes to Life

Tuesday, June 20, 1967, continued
Twin Oaks Pony Farm
St. Helena, California

Nigel walked back into his trailer. He couldn't remember being so frustrated and angry. *Even so,* he thought to himself, *I shouldn't have yelled at him. It was a stupid thing to do. I know better than to draw attention to myself.* He sat at the dinette table, his head in his hands. "I've been played," he said to himself. "How did I let that happen?"

Nigel struggled to pull himself together. "I refuse to let some teenager get the better of me," he said out loud. He walked down towards the swimming pool where there was a public telephone. He fished the business card Walter had given him yesterday out of his wallet and called the Twin Oaks Pony Farm. He was in no mood to do a fake interview. And in no mood to deal with Nick again without punching him in the nose.

.   .   .

I was pretty shook up when I left the campground, and it was hotter than blazes, but I rode as fast as I could. I wanted to put as much distance between me and Nigel as quickly as possible. If I hadn't been furiously pedaling my bike, I would have noticed how much my legs were shaking. *Nigel's an idiot,* I thought to myself, *and probably a dangerous idiot. What was he doing with a gun, anyway?*

I was glad when I finally pulled into the driveway at the farm. I walked my bike up onto the porch of the bunkhouse and leaned it against the wall. Snoops barely raised his head, acknowledging my presence with a lift of his eyebrows. It was too hot for him to do much more. I realized my t-shirt was soaked with sweat. I walked over to the corral and topped off the water trough with the hose. I took off my shirt and shoes and climbed in, submerging myself up to my nose. The horses looked over at me, not sure what to make of a human being sitting in their water trough.

"Lord above! What are you doing?" came Ma-D's disembodied voice from the kitchen window.

"Cooling off."

"Are you okay?"

"I will be in a few minutes."

"Sakes alive," she said with mock exasperation, and went back to what she was doing in the kitchen.

I held my breath and put my head underwater again, my cowboy hat floating to the surface. The cool water felt great, not to mention the fact that being completely submerged I felt safe — like no one could see me. *What a morning*, I thought to myself, air bubbles coming from my nose and mouth.

Once I'd cooled off, helped by my wet hat, I gathered up my shoes and shirt, went to the porch swing and settled in. As I rocked back and forth, the rusted springs creaked rhythmically and my mind started to wander. As tough as the morning was, I felt like I had stood up to Nigel. I was pretty sure that whatever problem Nigel presented in the future could be dealt with then. Right now, I had to come up with an excuse to spend the night on Mt. St. Helena, which I didn't think was going to be easy. I considered abandoning the overnight stay, but figured it would be a whole lot easier confronting the gnomes when they were up — at night — than going into their cave during the day when I assumed they were sleeping. Once again, I wished Chuy was around; he was great at figuring out stuff like this.

Through the kitchen screen door, I could hear Ma-D's quick steps on the wooden floor and the clanking of pots and pans. In the background I could also hear the radio blaring the news station she always listened to. She kept it up loud so she wouldn't miss a word while she had the fan, the Mixmaster, or some other appliance going full blast. I closed my eyes and continued to rock back and forth. The broadcaster on the radio introduced their science correspondent who, in turn, said something about the upcoming summer solstice. The science guy explained that the summer solstice was going to occur Thursday night, June 22nd, the day after tomorrow, marking the longest day of the year, and that this year there was going to be a full moon on the same night. According to the reporter, the moon was only full on the summer solstice once every twenty-eight years and that ancient pagan cultures attached considerable importance to the combination of events, often staging elaborate celebrations to mark the occasion.

I continued to swing back and forth — creak, creak, creak — when suddenly I sat upright and said, out loud, "that's it!" I must have said it louder than I thought, because Ma-D called across the lawn from the screen door "that's what?"

"Oh, nothing... I was just thinking out loud," I yelled back. Inside the kitchen, Ma-D shook her head and went back to cutting out dough for dinner biscuits.

I made myself comfortable in the swing and began to formulate a plan. I could use the full moon appearing on the summer solstice as an excuse to spend the night on the mountain. I'd say that I was doing a report for school and wanted to see the event as clearly as possible from a high elevation, away from the lights of town. No sooner had I thought of it, I had to admit it was a lame plan. I didn't think Walter or Ma-D would go for it, but it was all I had right then and there wasn't a whole lot of time to think of something better.

•　　•　　•

"You want to do what?" Walter asked incredulously. I had just proposed the idea of spending Thursday night on Mt. St. Helena, to witness, close-up, so to speak, the full moon on the summer solstice. We were all seated around the kitchen table, finishing some peach cobbler. Henry looked at me like something fishy was going on, but kept his mouth shut. I kept my eyes on what was left of my peach cobbler until Walter had finished talking.

"I gotta' say, Nick, you come up with some good ones. You know and I know that you could see it just as well from right here at the farm. We'll just turn out all the lights and walk out into the field. What's so special to see anyway?" Walter asked.

Ma-D interrupted, saying "seems to me I did hear something about that on the news today — how it only happens once every... "

"Twenty-eight years," I jumped in. "I'll be 43 years old the next time it happens Uncle Walter," I pleaded. "It's a real astronomical event!"

"I just don't think it's safe for a boy to go camping by himself up on that mountain. It's rattlesnake heaven on those rocks. And just last month, Judge Bergen said he had a black bear tearing up his fences up there. I think it's best if you just stay right here. If it's altitude you want, you can watch your 'astronomical event' from the top of the water tower."

Disappointed, I took my plate to the sink. I had to admit that I wasn't surprised at Walter's

Rattlesnake!

response. It was what I expected. There was an awkward silence around the table when I returned. I felt like I had to say something to make it go away.

"I understand what you're saying, Uncle Walter. But this is important to me. Promise that you won't get mad if I keep trying to convince you."

Walter looked surprised. "You can try, but I doubt I'm going to change my mind."

"It's worth a try. To me," I said. I excused myself and said I was going out to the bunkhouse to read. It was Henry's turn to do the dishes, so I knew I'd have a few minutes alone to make the telephone call I didn't want to make.

It had always been a delicate and somewhat confusing balance as to who had authority over me: Walter and Ma-D or Grandma Hattie? On important stuff — like the decision to go to boarding school — Hattie made the decisions. But for day-to-day things, Hattie left it to Walter and Ma-D to decide what I could or couldn't do. I knew what I wanted to do was important, it just didn't sound like it the way I'd described it to Uncle Walter and Ma-D. I had no idea how things would have turned out if I'd told the truth, like *I want to go spend the night on Mt. St. Helena because that's when the gnomes who stole Quicksilver are awake. Oh, and by the way, I'm going to get Quicksilver back.* It may have been the truth, but it would never fly, not in a million years.

Although it made me uncomfortable, I figured the only way I was going to get to spend Saturday night on the mountain was to get Grandma Hattie to tell Walter and Ma-D it was all right with her. I was probably upsetting a balance of power that had worked okay for a long time, but it was a risk I had to take.

Once I had Hattie on the phone, I told her I had to make it quick, because I didn't know how long it would be before Henry came in. I explained my real plan to her and then the alternate version I told Walter and Ma-D. And Walter's reaction to it. I also told her that I wouldn't really be alone, because Clyde would be there, which required an explanation of who Clyde was and why he lived on the mountain, conveniently leaving out the part about Clyde wanting to have nothing to do with the gnomes. I asked Hattie to call Walter and explain that I wouldn't actually be alone and tell him that she thought it was okay if I made the trip.

"Why didn't you just tell Walter about Clyde yourself?" Hattie asked.

Napa County black bear.

"Because it wouldn't come out right, Grandma. He'd ask too many questions about Clyde and then he'd still say no. If you tell him it's okay, he'll believe you."

"I need to give this some thought. Let's talk in the morning."

"Sure, grandma," I said, disappointed. Maybe I was being unrealistic, but I was hoping she'd agree with my plan right away — like *now*. "Thanks for your help," I said halfheartedly.

I hung up the phone just as Henry came into the bunkhouse.

"Ma-D forgot to tell you about that newspaper guy, what's his name?"

"Nigel?"

"Yeah. Anyway, he called this morning and said he couldn't make it for the interview. He's coming tomorrow instead. Ma-D wanted you to know in case you wanted to be here for it."

"I think I better pass on that one, Henry."

Main Street in St. Helena. The tan building at the end of the block
is Steve's Hardware – if they don't have it, you probably don't need it.

Chapter XX

Hattie Comes Through

Wednesday, June 21, 1967
Twin Oaks Pony Farm
St. Helena, California

The next morning, before breakfast, I was mucking out the corral, deep in thought. I didn't notice that Walter had walked over from the house and was standing practically right behind me until he said "morning." I jumped about a foot straight in the air and spun around at the same time.

"Oh, man. You scared me half to death," I said.

"I never seen someone jump straight up like that and spin around at the same time. Think you could do it again?"

"I doubt it."

"Well, it's a good trick," Walter said, suppressing a smile. "Listen, I, I just got off the phone with Hattie. Why didn't you tell me about that miner up on the mountain? What's his name? Clyde?"

"Yeah, it's Clyde." The question had taken me by surprise. I paused and then said "I don't know. I didn't think it would make any difference. You seemed like you already had your mind made up."

"Well, do you trust this guy?"

"What do you mean?"

"You know, can this guy handle things if something goes wrong? He's not some kind of creep, is he?"

"No, he's not a creep. He's a great guy. He's been living up there by himself for I don't know how long. I'd say he's pretty capable."

"Well, your grandmother seems to think that it's okay for you to go."

"What do you think?" I asked, knowing it was important to show Walter I respected his opinion.

"I think Clyde changes the picture. I'm inclined to agree with Hattie."

"So that means I can go?"

"Yes. It means you can go," Walter said with some reluctance, puffing on his pipe. "But so help me, you'd better be back here by noon on Friday or else the Sheriff's Department and I are coming after you, with Ma-D right behind... and I don't think you want that."

"No sir. I don't want that. I'll be home by noon on Friday."

"All right then, that's settled. Ma-D told me to tell you that breakfast is ready."

"I'll be right there," I said, trying not to let my excitement show.

•　　•　　•

Over breakfast, I learned that Nigel was coming to do the interview with Ma-D and Walter at 9:30. There was no way I wanted to be around Nigel, so I asked if it was okay if I went into town to get some supplies for my trip.

"Are you sure you don't want to be here for the interview?" Ma-D asked.

"I'm sure. It's you guys he really wants to talk to."

"Oh, all right, be that way," Ma-D said.

"I'm going to mow the lawn and water the garden and then take off. Is that okay?"

"Fine by me," Walter said.

"I'll see you after noon," I said, waving goodbye. I wanted to make sure I stayed away long enough to avoid Nigel.

"Wait just a minute," Ma-D called out, "are you going to want take some lunch with you?"

"No, I'll grab something in town. Thanks anyway," I said through the screen door. "See ya."

•　　•　　•

Once I got into town, I decided to go to the library first. I sat at one of the tables and got a pencil and paper pad out of my backpack. I made a list of what I'd need on the mountain: sleeping bag, flashlight, extra batteries, rope, canteen, knife, jacket, and maybe a sandwich or two. The only things I needed to buy were the extra batteries; I had everything else back at the farm. On my way home I'd stop in at the gas station and check the air in my tires.

I sat thinking for a bit and decided to make a list of what I knew about the gnomes:

1. They're small, probably between two and three feet tall.
2. Most of them are old and fat and have white beards.

3. They're smart, crafty, and wily.

4. They like precious metals, especially gold, silver, and quicksilver.

5. They only come out at night.

6. They live in caves.

7. Their clothes are usually green or brown.

8. They probably couldn't be trusted any further than you could throw them. *I wonder how far I could throw one if I had to,* I thought to myself.

9. The king of the gnomes was named Gob.

10. Their music can cast a spell on humans, making them fall asleep for one hundred years.

11. They can dissolve into trees and swim through the earth like a fish in water.

I decided to leave off the parts about them causing "endless sorrow" and "ultimate destruction." I looked over the list and wondered if even half of it was true. There was no telling. At least not yet. It was both comforting and scary that, one way or another, by tomorrow night I'd know a whole lot more or, quite possibly, nothing at all. *Or maybe I'd be stuck in a 100-year trance,* I thought with an involuntary shudder. But one thing didn't make sense to me: If they could do all this magic stuff, what did they want with a horse? I puzzled over it for awhile and couldn't come up with an answer. I wondered if I'd missed something and there was some other, more sane explanation for who stole Quicksilver? What was it I'd learned last year in science class? Occam's Razor? I thought that was it. It was basically a scientific law that said *the simplest explanation is usually the correct one.* My explanation for the theft of Quicksilver was anything but simple.

Since I had time to kill I walked my bike over to Steve's Hardware store and bought an extra set of batteries for my flashlight, along with another extra bulb. There was no way I was going to get caught in the dark.

I went across the street to Guigni's Delicatessen. It was a little before noon so it wasn't very crowded. I ordered a tuna sandwich and sat at the table in the front window, watching people walking up and down Main Street. Everyone looked so normal, I thought to myself, and they're probably doing normal, everyday things. And what am I doing? I shook my head. And I've got to tell you, normal had started looking pretty good to me about then, but I was committed to the plan, which, in that moment made me want to jump out of my skin. A wave of panic washed over me, but I managed to take some deep breaths and it went away, taking my appetite with it. I looked at my tuna sandwich. I definitely wasn't hungry anymore.

.   .   .

As promised, Nigel showed up promptly at nine-thirty and apologized for having to reschedule their meeting from yesterday. He looked every bit the photojournalist, with his camera around his neck and little tape recorder at the ready. He interviewed Ma-D and Walter together, sitting at the table under the grape arbor. Then they toured the farm and he took what seemed to Ma-D like a couple of hundred pictures. Towards the end, Walter was losing his patience and started muttering complaints in Ma-D's ear. The last time he did it, she elbowed him in the ribs and managed to hiss "cut it out, Walter!" while maintaining a big smile for the camera.

"Well, that should do it," Nigel said, putting his camera back in its case.

"Finally!" Walter said under his breath. Ma-D glared at him.

"By the way, where's young Nick?" Nigel asked, nonchalantly. "I thought he might be here."

"He had to go into town. 'For supplies.' From the sound of it, you'd think he was going to Timbuktu," Ma-D said, chuckling and looking over at Walter.

"Oh really? Where's he going?"

"Just to Mt. St. Helena. Tomorrow night is the Summer Solstice — plus a full moon. He wants to observe it up close, I guess. Or at least closer than here on the valley floor."

"Interesting," Nigel said, barely containing his excitement.

With that, Nigel said his goodbyes and told Walter and Ma-D he'd send them copies of the pictures he had taken after he got back to Scotland. And hopefully, there would be an article he could send to them as well, if he was able to get it published.

Walter and Ma-D stood next to each other, waving goodbye. Ma-D flushed from the compliment of someone taking such an interest in her and Walter and their pony farm. As usual, Walter was skeptical and had the feeling that Nigel was somehow using them. *Proof is in the pudding,* he thought to himself. *We'll see if an article comes out of this.* He doubted it.

.   .   .

"Bingo!" Nigel said aloud as he closed the door to his truck. "I knew there was more than one way to skin this cat."

.   .   .

Later that night, I was in the bunkhouse, going over the stuff in my backpack, making sure I had everything I needed. Henry walked in carrying a small package and handed it to me.

"What's this?" I asked.

"A snake bite kit I happened to have. You better take it with you."

"Thanks Henry."

"Yeah, whatever. Jes' hope you don't have to use it."

"You and me both."

"Don't have nothin' for them bears. You're on your own on that one."

.   .   .

At the time Nick was checking his supplies, Nigel was doing the same thing in his trailer at the campground. After he left Walter and Ma-D's place, he drove up to the Robert Louis Stevenson State Park to check it out. There was a perfect spot for a lookout, up a densely wooded hill overlooking the entrance to the park. He decided to be at the entrance of the park right at the break of dawn tomorrow. There was no way he was going to miss Nick going in.

I'm glad I brought this, he thought to himself, unpacking a camouflage outfit, complete with hat and paint for his face.

.   .   .

After lunch, I went back to the living room and kept reading. Saturdays were my day to mow all the lawns, but I figured I'd mow them later. I was getting into the story and wanted to find out what happened. Grandpa had a meeting with someone at the winery, so he wasn't around to answer my questions. And I was starting to have plenty of them. I decided I'd write them down so I wouldn't forget any.

I went into the kitchen where Grandpa kept a silver cup filled with yellow Ticonderoga pencils (all of them always sharp) and several different-sized bright orange Rhodia writing tablets on the long kitchen table. Having just read it, I figured that he must have gotten that habit from Grandma Hattie which, for some reason, amused me. I took a pencil and a tablet and sat at the game table in the living room and started writing:

1. What happened to Grandma Hattie's big house in San Francisco?
2. What happened to Walter and Ma-D?
3. What happened to Clyde?
4. Was Clarence the tortoise in the story the same Clarence the tortoise that lived in our pond?

I looked at my watch: Only 1:30. Considering how late it stayed light out, I figured I could spend the afternoon reading and still have time to mow the lawns. Thinking about it, I guessed that Grandpa would probably want me to mow them before dinner rather than after, but that still gave me a plenty of time to read – maybe even enough to finish the journal.

Clyde and I played dominoes at his place while I waited for it to get dark.
I tried not to think about what I had to do in just a couple of hours.

Chapter XXI

On Mt. St. Helena

Thursday, June 22, 1967
Somewhere on Mt. St. Helena
Napa Valley, California

On the morning of the solstice, I couldn't decide whether it was better to leave early and beat the heat, or to take off later in the afternoon. I didn't necessarily want to cool my heels all day on the mountain, but I didn't want to ride up there in 100 plus degrees either. I finally couldn't stand waiting around any longer and left the farm at 10:30, with Walter, Ma-D and Henry standing in the driveway, waving me off. You'd have thought I was taking an expedition to outer Mongolia. The ride to Calistoga wasn't so bad, but once I started up the mountain, I congratulated myself on making the right decision to leave earlier rather than later. It was already so hot that I had to get off and walk my bike a couple of times. I finally got to the parking area of the state park and locked my bicycle to the same tree as I had a few days before.

.   .   .

From his hiding spot on the opposite side of the road, Nigel said "Gotcha!" under his breath, as he watched Nick cross the road.

.   .   .

Witbeck wasn't used to being up at this time of the day, but there was so much to attend to — Midsummer's Night was the gnomes' biggest celebration of the year — and this year, with it coinciding with a full moon, was extra special. So many details! The tuning of the instruments, the gathering together of the quicksilver, firewood for the bonfires, the preparation of all the special dishes, not to mention making sure the king was able to make a magnificent entrance on his new pony. So many details, indeed. It was almost too much for Witbeck.

.   .   .

The hammock at Clyde's place.

Once I was on the mountain, I wasn't sure what to do next, but finally decided to see if Clyde was at the mine. I scrambled down through the forest of madrones and fuchsias, just in time to catch Clyde coming out of the mine.

"Well, if isn't Nick-Not-Ned." Clyde said. "Figured I'd see you agin."

"Yep. Tonight's the night. How you doing, Clyde?"

"I was jes' takin' a break for lunch. "Come on."

I followed Clyde around the hill to his place. Clyde offered me lunch, but I told him I'd packed a couple of sandwiches and asked if he wanted one.

"Don't mind if I do." Clyde said, "I'm ready for a break from those beans."

After lunch, Clyde said he was going back to the mine. He told me I was welcome to hang out at his place, adding, "You gotta' long night ahead ya'. Why don't you sack out in that hammock over there?" he said motioning to an old canvas hammock stretched between two big pine trees overlooking the valley below.

"I don't feel much like sleeping right now." I said.

"Then don't sleep. Jes' take a load off your feet. I take a little siesta there almost every afternoon. If you fall asleep, I'll wake you up when I come back from the mine."

Seeing as how there weren't a lot of options, I walked over to the hammock and climbed in. It rocked back and forth slowly and finally stopped. I folded my arms behind my head and stared up through the pine needles to the blue sky beyond. I had to admit, it felt good to put my feet up. I started to imagine what might happen tonight and got a queasy feeling in my stomach. *Must have eaten too fast, or something,* I thought to myself. A light breeze came off the valley floor and gently whispered through the tops of the pines. I inhaled deeply. The air was hot and dry, spiced with the scent of bay leaves and pines. I was probably asleep in three minutes.

•　　•　　•

"Some stake-out, watching the kid sleep," Nigel said under his breath, putting his binoculars down. He had followed the voices of Nick and the old guy, trailing them from the downside of the mountain. Once he saw where they stopped, he doubled back and was now on the hill above the old guy's camp. "Should have brought a book," he said to himself.

•　　•　　•

When I woke up, it was quite a bit cooler and the light was altogether different in the branches overhead. For a minute, I didn't know where I was or what I was doing. I looked at my watch: 4:47. "Oh, man!" I said out loud, surprised I had slept so long.

I tumbled out of the hammock and tried to straighten myself up. I could hear Clyde at the back of his canyon hideaway making noise in what I supposed was his kitchen. I walked over to check it out.

"I was wondering if you were gonna' wake up or not. Thought maybe those fairy folk already had ya' in a spell," Clyde said with a grin.

I cringed. "I thought you said you'd wake me up."

"Don't worry about it. Figured it was better if you were bright-eyed and bushy-tailed tonight. You still got plenty of time before dark."

"Ah, where do you, you know, take a leak around here?"

"Against any tree trunk down the mountain. Take your choice."

I did my business and walked back up to Clyde's kitchen. "You don't really believe that stuff about the gnomes being able to put people under a spell, do you?"

"All I know is what my granddaddy told me. And I believe everything he said. The best thing to do is keep as much real estate as possible between you and the little people. That's what he told me and that's what I done." Clyde was frying some bacon in a cast iron pan on a small camp stove. I didn't know how I could be hungry again when all I'd done was sleep all afternoon, but it sure did smell good.

•　　•　　•

"What are they trying to do?" Nigel thought to himself, *"drive me crazy with that bacon?"* He rustled through his backpack and found a candy bar he had hastily bought at the gas station in Calistoga. *This is going to be a very long*

night, he thought. Luckily, for him, he had no idea how long.

.   .   .

I watched as Clyde pulled the bacon strips out of the pan, one by one.

"You hungry?"

"Yeah, I am."

"Well it's not much. Jes' some bacon and some of Mr. Van Camp's beans."

"I've got a couple of Ma-D's biscuits in my pack."

"Well, go get 'em. Who's Ma-D?"

"She's my fos..." I hesitated, "she's my aunt."

I got the biscuits out of my pack and took them to Clyde. He sliced them in half and put them in the frying pan, toasting them in the bacon grease. When everything was hot, Clyde portioned the meal onto a couple of chipped enamel plates and we sat at the old table and ate in silence.

"What's a matter? Cat got your tongue?" Clyde asked, using his last half biscuit to clean every last bit off his plate.

"I guess."

"You scared?"

"Kinda'. It's just that I don't know what to expect."

"The worst, if I were you. Want some coffee?"

"Maybe so."

Clyde came back in a few minutes with a couple of metal mugs filled with steaming coffee.

"Thanks," I said and then continued. "Clyde, there's something I haven't told you."

"Oh yeah? Like what?"

I told him the story of Captain Niebaum and the stowaway gnomes, the bargain he made with them, and the amulet the king had given Niebaum: "a symbol of friendship between our families for all time," I said, quoting the king.

I reached into my pocket and pulled out the amulet which I'd wrapped in Kleenex. I unwrapped it and handed it to Clyde.

"Well now, that's quite the story," Clyde said, looking at the back and front of the amulet, "and this here's quite the piece of work. There's no magic dust on this or nothin' is there?" Clyde asked.

"Not that I know of."

"What's it made of?" Clyde asked, holding it up to his mouth and biting the metal.

"My grandmother said a jeweler told her it was made of rhodium."

"Rhoda-what?"

"Rhodium."

"Never heard of it."

"It's the rarest metal on earth — more rare than platinum."

"Do tell? You got any reason to believe it ain't the real deal?"

"My grandmother doesn't think so."

Clyde thought for a minute and handed the amulet back to me. "Well then, I'm guessin' you got no cause for frettin'. You got that there amulet and if it works the way it's supposed to, maybe you'll be okay with them gnome folks, seein' as how that captain guy did them a good turn."

"You think so?"

"I'm thinkin' that's the way they operate. Jes' don't go losing it. That's your ticket outta' there."

"No, I'm not losing it," I said, putting it back in my pocket. "You can bet on that."

.   .   .

Nigel was too far up the hill to hear the conversation but, with his binoculars, he saw Nick handing what looked like a piece of jewelry to the old guy and the old guy biting it. "Wonder what that's all about?" Nigel asked himself.

.   .   .

"You play dominoes?" Clyde asked.

"Yeah, I play with Ma-D sometimes."

"I ain't had nobody to play bones with for a long time. Never could teach that dog to play," Clyde said with a chuckle. He walked into the lean-to and came back with what looked like a cereal bowl full of dominoes, which he spilled onto the table. We both started turning them over so only the blank sides showed. Then I stopped suddenly.

"Whoa," I said, "what are these?"

"Whaddaya' mean 'what are these?' They're dominoes. I thought you said you knew how to play."

"I do, but how come they have so many dots?"

"Don't tell me you never seen double-nines before?"

"No. I've only played double sixes."

"Double sixes is for wussies. I can see you've got a lot to learn, boy."

I started to pull my dominoes from the pile in the middle of the table.

"You can't do that!" Clyde said.

"Whaddaya' mean?"

"Can't choose your bones without first laying your hands on the pile and mixin' them up real good. Gotta' get your own juju on the tiles. Where you been hidin' anyway?"

It didn't take me long to get used to the double nines, or the special game Clyde played, called "Racehorse." It was just like regular dominoes, but if you made a score or put down a double, you got to play again. I held my own, but Clyde won the first two games. "He may have been born dumb and had a couple of setbacks since," I thought to myself, "but he knows his dominoes."

.   .   .

"I hate that kid," Nigel said to himself. "First he makes me watch him sleep for three hours and now he and that old coot are playing dominoes? I can't believe it!"

.   .   .

"My daddy used to say the worst vice of all was 'advice'," Clyde said, lighting an oil lamp on the table, "but here goes anyway. I think we oughta' play until it's completely dark. It'll be safer that way."

"Safer to play dominoes?" I asked, not understanding.

"No. Safer for you and this trip you're about to take."

"I brought a flashlight."

"I don't want you usin' it. No tellin' what them gnome folks can see. The full moon gonna' be risin' soon. Once it gets up high enough, you'll be able to see jes' fine. Did you bring somethin' to cover up that white t-shirt?

"I've got a blue windbreaker in my pack."

"That oughta' work. You can't take no chances with bein' seen. Now let's play another game. You're losin' bad."

We played another couple of rounds. I was beginning to catch on and was almost even with Clyde when I looked through the trees on top of the canyon wall.

"Holy sh..."

"What?" Clyde asked with alarm.

"I've never seen it so big!"

Clyde turned around. "Right on time, ya' big cheese ball."

Biggest full moon
I've ever seen.

"Why's it look so big?" I asked.

"Cause it's the longest day of the year. Whadda' they teachin' in school these days?"

"Nothing about full moons."

"Too bad for you. Go get your jacket. It's time to get going."

My stomach felt like an elevator and it had just fallen about ten floors. I walked over to my backpack and pulled out the windbreaker. I looked through the almost black outlines of the trees to the dark, dusky hills on the west side of the valley, a few twinkling lights here and there. People probably sitting on their couches watching television or reading a book, or eating ice cream. I had the sudden desire to just disappear and have everything go back to the way it was before Quicksilver disappeared.

"Ya' comin' or not?" Clyde said, standing up from the table. "I'll walk with you down to the path. From there, you're on your own."

My heart sank, but there was no turning back now. Clyde started walking down the mountain with me following close behind. Clyde was right about one thing: once my eyes adjusted, there was plenty of light from the moon to see where I was going.

"Okay, here we are," Clyde said. "You remember what I said the other day about just following this trail until it peters out. After that, head for that tall rock wall — it'll be right in front of you. Then it's up to you. You'll just have to follow your nose and figure out a way up the wall."

"Thanks Clyde. Hopefully I'll see you before sun-up."

"Don't dilly-dally around, boy. Get in, do what you gotta' do, and get back" Clyde said sternly. "By the way, waddaya' want me to do if you don't get back?" he asked matter-of-factly.

"Oh, I'll make it back," I said with mock confidence, not knowing what else to say. I hadn't even thought about what it meant to 'not get back.' Just thinking about it made me feel sick.

"Well, good luck then. I'll be waitin' for ya."

"Thanks, Clyde. See you later."

We shook hands and I took off up the trail.

.   .   .

Somewhere up the hill, Nigel followed Nick's every move.

If it were daylight and I could actually see what I was doing,
there's probably no way I'd be trying to climb that rock wall.

Chapter XXII

Midsummer Night's Madness

Thursday, June 22, 1967, continued
Somewhere on Mt. St. Helena
Napa Valley, California

It didn't take long for the sound of my footfall and the crickets singing in the dry weeds to realize how alone I was. And the queasiness in the pit of my stomach meant only one thing: I was now officially scared. But I couldn't think about that. In fact, I tried to keep my mind blank: *Just keep putting one foot in front of the other and get to that rock wall,* I told myself. That's what I had to do.

The moon was at my back, casting my shadow far ahead of me. There wasn't a breath of wind and, now and then, when the crickets stopped their singing, it was completely silent. Or was it? I stood still for a minute, straining to hear what I thought I had. Nothing. Just the crickets. I set off again and after a few minutes, it was there again. I stopped in my tracks. It was very faint, and not like anything I'd ever heard before, but it was definitely music. I stood there thinking. *It couldn't be coming from a radio or a television because no one, except for Clyde, lived on this side of the mountain.* I knew that noise traveled up; could it be coming from the valley floor? *It's possible,* I thought to myself. But the shiver that went through my entire body told me otherwise.

A better explanation was that my mind was playing tricks on me, so I decided to whistle quietly to myself — at least the sounds I was hearing would be my own. I started to whistle and then stopped almost immediately. My whistling was so shaky it did nothing but remind me of how scared I was. I kept walking and thinking. *Maybe,* I thought, *it would be best if I just stopped right where I was and hung out for a few hours, and then went back to Clyde's place claiming, truthfully, that I hadn't found anything. Maybe I should just leave it at that and sit right where I was until morning.*

I kept walking while I considered my options, my heart pounding much faster than normal. I was on a downslope now and the rhythm of my steps carried me along, closer to where the music seemed to be coming from. Yep. There was no denying it now: it was faint, but it was there — a kind of dreamlike music, high-pitched, at once strange, but becoming more familiar. I wondered if I was falling under its spell? I quickly pinched my arm hard. It hurt. *Good,* I thought. *I'm still here and sane. At least I think I am.* All of sudden I no longer thought about turning back: I had to know where the music was coming from and who was making it.

I walked faster now, on an upslope through a dense stand of towering pine trees. Once through the pines, I found myself on a rise, covered with dry grass up to my waist. I turned around to get my bearings and looked across the valley. The landscape was completely black now, with a barely distinguishable band of deep, deep blue sky along the ridge tops of the western hills, where the sun had set hours earlier. I looked up at the moon. It didn't seem so big now, but it was very bright. I'd read something once about the moon "sailing across the night sky." It definitely looked like it was sailing, something I'd never sensed before. As I stood there taking it all in, a slight breeze picked up and made whispering sounds through the tops of the trees. I could hear my heart beating and there, once again, the strange music, carried on the breeze. I turned and looked up the mountain. I could see the outcropping of rocks Clyde told me about, the ones that looked almost like the walls of some old stone fortress. I could see the rock walls clearly, because they seemed to be outlined by a cool, bluish light. It re-minded me of the light from an acetylene torch — the kind that you weren't sup-posed to look at — cool and blue to the eye but hot enough to cut metal.

I looked again at the top of the rock wall and wondered what could be causing the blue light. As I studied the scene, the moon moved just enough to illuminate what looked like a narrow path between some big boulders and the undergrowth — a path that looked like it might lead to the rock wall.

I set off up the narrow, overgrown path, having to crouch down to get through some of the spots, but there was clearly a trail, even though it was only a few inches wide. The manzanita and small scrub oaks scratched my face and arms as I made my way through. Gradually the brush disappeared and I was able to stand up straight. The clearing where I stood was covered with gravel. I stood there and looked up at the craggy, nearly vertical rock wall. I could no longer see the weird blue light. And it was silent now — no music. Even so, I knew this had to be the place where it had been coming from. *Now,* I thought to myself, *how do I get up the rock wall?* Luckily, I was wearing the right kind of boots and the rocks were craggy and uneven enough to provide plenty of toe- and hand-holds to make it up without any climbing equipment. At least that's what I told myself, which was a good thing because the only thing I had in my backpack that resembled climbing gear was a length of rope.

I patted my front shirt pocket to make sure the amulet was still there which, thankfully, it was. I stepped closer to the rock wall and looked for somewhere to start my ascent. *Good thing it's dark,* I thought to myself. *If I could see what's actually here, I probably wouldn't even try this.*

I started feeling around the rocks for something to hang on to with my hands, my foot trying to find a secure step up at the same time. I was deep in concentration when I froze, hanging off the rocks, a couple of feet off the ground. What was it? A sound. Like a twig breaking. Deer? Maybe. Bear? Could be. I started to tremble.

"Hello Nick," a familiar voice said quietly.

I fell to the ground, landing on my backpack, and spun around to see the whites of someone's eyes, presumably Nigel Stayne's judging by the accent. As surprised and shaken as I was, I couldn't help but notice how ridiculous Nigel looked, covered from head to toe in camouflage clothes and face paint.

"What the hell?" I whispered.

"Surprised?"

"You could say that. What are you doing here?"

"Same thing you are."

"What? You've come to help me get Quicksilver back?" I said sarcastically.

"No. It's just like I told you. I've come to get my story. And my share of the gold."

"How'd you know...?"

"Your Ma-D is a chatty one, isn't she?" Nigel interrupted.

"Oh man. Ma-D!" I couldn't believe it.

"So are we going to climb these rocks or not? Looks like you could use some help," Nigel said sarcastically.

I thought for a minute. "No. I don't need any help. Especially not from you," I said, still whispering. "What do you say to you going your way, and I'll go mine?"

"Fine by me, old boy. Considering that you've already served my purposes in getting me this far."

With that, Nigel walked along the upside of the rock wall and disappeared around the corner.

"Unbelievable," I said to myself, standing up and brushing myself off, my heart still pounding. I wondered what other surprises were ahead of me.

I decided it was so weird that Nigel was here on the mountain that it was probably best to just put him out of my mind. I couldn't process it: it was far more important to concentrate on what was in front of me, like that rock wall.

There was nothing I could do about him anyway. "Jerk!" I said under my breath and then tried to find the same handholds I had used before I fell. Eventually I did and started my way back up the rock face. It was slow going. After about twenty difficult, scary minutes, I reached the top and caught my breath.

I snaked my way along the top of the stone wall, stomach down, reaching a spot that was kind of comfortable. I peeked over the edge. I couldn't make out much, as the area I was looking at was in the shadows of the neighboring pine trees. One thing was clear though: a single blue flame burning in the darkness. I wondered what it was for and how it got there.

The music was more distinct now, but I still couldn't identify its source. As soon as the moon was a little higher in the sky, it cast more light on the scene below. I decided it was some kind of colosseum — whether it was natural, man-made, or gnome-made, I had no way of knowing. It was basically a big oval space, about a hundred feet long and fifty feet wide, with the arched entrance to a cave at one end. A wide stone step led down from the cave opening to the colosseum. The floor looked level and the rock walls rose about fifty feet, slightly angled outward. As the moon continued to provide more light, I could pick out what looked like piles of twigs and branches stacked up teepee-style, arranged in a big circle on the floor. In between the stone step to the cave and the circle of twigs, the blue flame continued to burn. In an effort to calm myself, I counted them twice: there were twelve perfectly arranged piles. Something clicked in my brain. I remembered what Ma-D had been listening to on the radio, something about midsummer's night being an important night for celebrations in ancient cultures. I wondered if that was why the piles of brush were laid out like they were. I also wondered where that ratbag Nigel was, but decided I didn't care, as long as he was nowhere near me and didn't do anything that got us both caught.

I looked at my watch: 11:15. Every now and then the strange music would start up again and then die away, almost like an orchestra warming up for a performance. After another twenty minutes or so, my left leg started to go to sleep and I wished I'd taken a pee before I'd climbed up the wall. This was getting very uncomfortable. I repositioned myself slowly, trying to get some blood flowing in my leg. I was able to turn over and lie on my side, propping my head up with my hand. That wasn't going to work either, so I turned over on my stomach again. Nothing happened for what seemed like forever. "I hope my whole body doesn't fall asleep," I thought to myself as I felt my leg start to tingle again. No sooner had the thought crossed my mind than I heard deep, resonant vibrations coming from inside the cave, like from a gong or something. I looked at my watch again:

twelve midnight on the dot. The gong — or whatever it was — sounded twelve times. Each time, it seemed to reverber-ate deeper in my chest. I carefully pulled myself a little closer to the edge using my elbows; I wasn't about to miss any of this.

Moments after the last strike of the gong, the music started in again, only this time faster, higher, and loud-er. From the mouth of the cave came a procession of four small men, each less

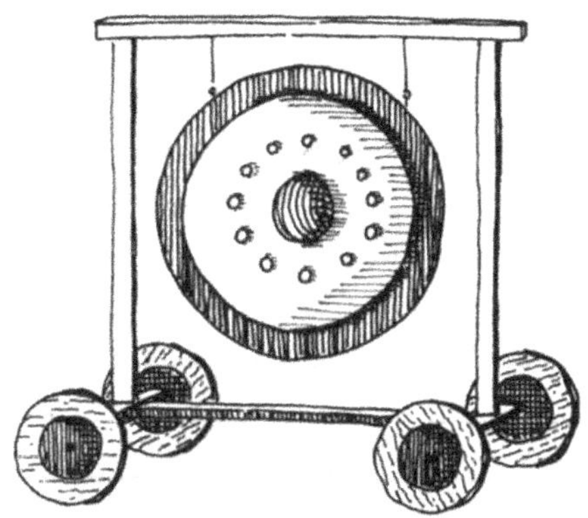

The golden gong.

than three feet tall, each playing an instrument the likes of which I'd never seen — neither the instruments nor the musicians. I couldn't help but notice that all the gnomes (because that's what they had to be, right?) looked as if they were wearing layers and layers of clothing, of all different colors and patterns, just like I had read. I pinched myself again to make sure I wasn't in a trance and could actually believe what I was seeing. No, I wasn't in a trance, but I was defi-nitely having difficulty believing that what was in front of me was real.

The musicians moved to one side of the colosseum. With that, two more gnomes appeared from the cave pushing a giant metallic gold gong, easily three times as tall as any one of them. The gong was mounted on a stand with small wooden wheels. The two gnomes pushed it to the other side of the colosseum, opposite the musicians. One gnome trailed behind carrying what looked like a big croquet mallet. Everything was quiet for a minute or two and then the gnome with the mallet started hitting the gong — another twelve times, only this time the noise it made wasn't particularly loud, but it was so low that it not only made my body vibrate, but it felt like the whole mountain was shaking.

After the twelfth strike of the gong, one of the musicians — the one who played a big curved horn — brought the instrument to his lips and played it with great flourish, like he was announcing something. As he finished, four more gnomes ran out of the cave opening, carrying thick, short sticks. As they ran out, they dipped the ends of the sticks into the blue flame, causing them to burst into flames. They then positioned themselves around the outside of the circle of brush piles. The gong was struck again, only once this time, and the torch-carrying gnomes quickly lit three piles each until all twelve were blaz-ing. Flickering orange light filled the amphitheater and bounced off its walls. I

scrunched down, hoping that the fires didn't light my face.

Along with the sound of fire crackling, I heard another sound, one I recognized: the faint clopping sound of a horse's hooves. In an instant, a beardless gnome appeared in the opening of the cave pulling a rope. My heart jumped — at the end of the rope was Quicksilver! He was being ridden by what looked like a very old, very fat gnome, with a very long, white beard and wearing a gold crown that looked like it might fall off at any moment. *Quicksilver,* I thought wildly. I'd found him! The musician with the horn played a longer flourish this time while the fire-starting gnomes quick-stepped into the cave and reappeared carrying an ornate wooden chair. They placed the chair in the middle of one side of the colosseum and then went over to Quicksilver and helped the old gnome — who I figured had to be the king — off the horse, an operation performed with considerable difficulty. The four attendants then helped the presumed king onto his throne, again with a great deal of pushing and pulling. After he was finally seated, two of the attendants stood on either side of his throne. The king straightened his crown, clapped his hands four times and said with great authority, "Let the celebration begin!"

The musicians started off playing softly and slowly. There was some movement at the mouth of the cave, but I couldn't tell what it was. Gradually, as it made its way through the arched opening, I could see it was a very large, mirror-like sphere, maybe seven feet tall. The sphere quivered as it rolled, like a big ball of silver Jell-O, making a squishing sound as it passed over the floor of the colosseum. I could now see that it was pushed from the back by two more gnomes. With its reflective surface, it reminded me of one of those mirror globes people put on pedestals in their gardens.

The gnomes continued pushing the mirrored sphere, which, by now, I suspected was quicksilver, into the middle of the circle of bonfires. The surface of the big globe reflecting the fires was mesmerizing. The walls of the colosseum were ablaze with gold and silver light, dancing across the rock surfaces, all warm light and black shadows. All the gnomes, save for the king, formed a circle around the fires and the music quickly became louder and faster. The gnomes danced around the mirrored globe jumping, twisting, and turning in what looked like some kind of organized frenzy. Some were dancing by themselves, some dancing together. Some had musical instruments which they played with abandon. I looked up to where the king was sitting and saw him rocking back and forth, slapping his thighs and swinging his feet (which didn't reach the floor) back and forth, laughing uproariously.

The more the gnomes danced and twisted and turned, the more the sphere began to quiver and shake, splintering the reflections of the flames, the moon and the stars, into a shimmering mosaic of thousands of glints of gold- and silver-colored light. I was so dazzled by what I saw, I failed to notice that I was leaning dangerously over the edge of the rock wall. As I scrunched my way back to a more secure position, a few small pebbles tumbled down to the floor of the colosseum. They had barely hit bottom when the king yelled something and, in an instant, the music stopped, the fires were extinguished and a smoky, silent darkness replaced the light and music-filled magic that had been there just a moment before. The gravelly voice of the king rang out in the darkness, "There's an outsider in our midst! Seize the interloper!"

I panicked. Without thinking about it, I started down the outside of the rock wall as fast as I could, half sliding and then falling, completely out of control. I landed on a small manzanita bush and was immediately surrounded by a group of gnomes, all of them pointing long, sharp, wooden poles menacingly in my direction. In the next instant, I was airborne, hoisted up by the hands of the gnomes and carried quickly off around the base of the rock wall. This time, however, instead of going over the rock face, the little men carried me, kicking and squirming, through a concealed opening at its base.

It wasn't long before I was being propped up in front of the king. Next to him, one of his attendants held a single torch. For all my imagination, I never thought I'd be in a situation like this. I was scratched, bruised, and bleeding. My clothes were torn and I was surrounded by a bunch of gnomes pointing sharp sticks at me. Not to mention standing before the king of some ancient race of little people! My heart was in my throat, about to experience... what? Maybe I would wake up and it would be 100 years from now?

Before I could catch my breath the king commanded "State your name, interloper!"

"My name is Nick Sinclair. I am a friend of yours and the entire tribe of gnomes — a friend for life, Your Highness," I managed to say as strongly as possible. I'd decided to say that last part, "Your Highness," even though the king was, of course, very short, thinking it was the proper thing to do. Apparently it didn't impress the king: he immediately started laughing so hard he had a terrible coughing fit. Two gnomes ran over and began hitting him furiously on his back. When he finally recovered, he shouted at me: "You! A friend? For life? Hah! I've never laid eyes on you. You are both an interloper and a liar!"

"I am not!" I said angrily. "And I have proof. My distant relative, Captain

Gustav Niebaum, brought you to this country. I read in his ship's log about your journey. I have the amulet you gave him — the one that you said would signify friendship between his heirs and your people for all time," I said as I fished in my shirt pocket for the amulet.

"'For all time' is a long time, my boy, and all that was a long time ago. But you're right about Captain Niebaum. He *was* my friend. Show me the amulet," the king said, sticking his hand out.

I dug frantically in my shirt pocket, and then in all my other pockets. "It was right here a minute ago, I swear!" I stammered. "It, it must have fallen out of my pocket when I fell off the wall."

"A likely story," the king snarled, turning to one of his men. "Put him in a trance. Immediately."

Oh sh... I thought to myself, closing my eyes. *Here it comes — the 100-year nap.*

With that, one of the gnomes who had pounded the king's back leaned over and whispered something in his ear. "Speak up! What's that you're mumbling?" the king shouted. This time in a voice so loud I could hear it, the gnome said, leaning in to the king's ear, "Your Highness, do you not recall? The Wizard is no longer amongst us. There can be no trance."

"Of course. Of course," the king sputtered, embarrassed. "Well, then tie him up, you incompetents! What are you waiting for?"

I struggled as the gnomes began wrapping a thick rope around me. "King Gob! If you just let me find the amulet, I can prove to you that I am Captain Niebaum's heir and friend of the gnomes!" I felt like there were a thousand small hands winding the rope around me, from my shoulders to my feet.

"If that amulet is anywhere on this mountain, my men will find it. If they don't find it by dawn, however, yours will be a sorry fate," King Gob said as he struggled to get off his chair. Once he was on his feet, he started off in the direction of the cave. I yelled at him (by now figuring out King Gob was hard of hearing), "Your Highness!" King Gob turned around, startled.

"I have said all I am going to say concerning this matter," the King said curtly.

"But Your Highness, the amulet is wrapped in Kleenex."

"Kleenex? What is this Kleenex?" the king asked.

"It's, it's soft white paper. I, I didn't want anything to happen to it," I tried to explain.

"How nice," the king said gruffly. "I doubt if it will present a problem to my men. Kleenex! Hah!" he said, turning on his heels a little unsteadily and walked through the opening of the cave and disappeared into the mountain.

I felt like I had been wrapped in a cocoon of rope. I was hoisted into the air, this time carried into the cave. The inside of the old mine was lit with torches attached to the walls every twenty feet or so. Once inside, the tunnel immediately split, one arm of it going left and the other right. The gnomes carried me to the left and then, with a lot of huffing and grunting, stood me upright. One of the gnomes undid the knot that was holding the rope in place and then all six of them lined up, facing away from me, and held onto the rope like they were a team on one side of a tug-of-war contest. I began to spin around and then fell on my side. The gnomes kept pulling the rope, as I spun around on the floor, just like someone pulling thread off a spool. They finally got to the end where the rope was tied under my arms and around my chest. One of the gnomes ordered me to stand up, which I tried to do, but fell a couple of times because I was so dizzy. When I finally steadied myself on my feet I saw that I was standing in front of a hole in the floor, maybe ten feet in diameter. The same gnome who'd told me to stand up, now ordered me to sit down at the edge of the hole. I did as I was told. I turned my head around to see the six gnomes lined up behind me, holding onto the rope in close formation. The gnome in charge told me to lower myself over the edge, which I did, and then they slowly lowered me into the darkness of the hole. I hoped they had enough strength to keep me from falling. My feet hit the bottom of the hole at what I guessed was about fifteen feet below the floor of the cave. The rope went limp and I immediately untied it from my chest and looked up.

"Hey! Anyone still there?"

After a minute or so, a small head appeared over the edge of the hole. It was the beardless gnome, the one who led Quicksilver into the colosseum.

"Yes?"

"Can someone tell me what's happening?"

"You're being held until we can determine if you are who you say you are," said the pleasantest voice I'd heard so far this evening. "If what you say is true, and you really did drop the amulet when you fell, you have nothing to worry about, except to explain why you are here."

"Well, I *am* Nick Sinclair and I *did* have the amulet in my pocket when I started out tonight."

"Then there's no need to worry."

"No reason to worry? Really?" I said with some desperation.

"Like my father said, we have a knack for finding things — wrapped or un-wrapped," the voice said with a slight chuckle.

"You're King Gob's son?"

"Yes, I'm G. Prince G. And by the way, if you feel around you'll find a candle with some matches next to it. You'll see there's a cot for you to sleep on, a container of water, and there's a hole in the floor for you to take care of your bodily functions. We may be strange to you, but we're not barbarians."

"Thanks, I guess," I said not knowing what to say.

"Well, good night then," Prince G said.

"I'm not so sure about that... just one more thing, if you would. Can you tell me what's going to happen next? No hundred-year naps, please."

The prince chuckled and said, "No. No hundred-year naps. I can say that for sure. As far everything else, I can't be positive, but I suspect we'll get back to you tomorrow night with news of whether the amulet has been found or not. And then you'll have a chance to explain your side of the story. Of course it all depends on what kind of mood my father is in."

"Tomorrow night!" I said, panicking. "I'm supposed to be home by noon to-morrow."

"You're in our world now."

"I'm toast," I said under my breath.

"Well, good night again," Prince G said and then disappeared.

I felt around for the candle and the matches. I lit the candle and sat down on the cot, realizing I was in a pile of trouble. A big pile. As I considered my options — which were slim to none — I heard shouts and scuffling from up above.

"Let me go, you little bastards, let me go!" I immediately recognized Nigel's voice.

So they caught you, too? I thought to myself. I couldn't help but to smile just a little.

.   .   .

A little after 4 o'clock, Grandpa came back from the winery, and walked into the living room.

"I'm complimented that you're finding the story so interesting that you've spent all day reading, but don't forget it's your day to mow the lawns."

"I know. I know. I'm going to do it. But first, will you answer some questions? I've got them written down."

"Okay."

"What happened to Grandma Hattie's big house in San Francisco?"

"I sold it after she died. She loved the place but I never much cared for it – it was just *too* big. Believe it or not, it's the Finnish Embassy now, which I think Hattie would have gotten a kick out of."

"And what about Ma-D and Walter? Are they still alive?"

"No. They were quite the pair. Ma-D was a few years older than Walter and she died first, some twenty-five years ago. They both lived into their nineties. They left me the farm. I rent it to Dr. Barker, the veterinarian."

"On Mee Lane?"

"Yep."

"What about Clyde? What happened to him?"

"For years I visited him every midsummer's night. He was a good guy. He kept mining right up until the end. Never struck it rich, but he seemed to enjoy his life. He had to go to an old folks home for the last few of months of his life. I made sure he was okay."

"What happened to his place on Mt. St. Helena?"

"You'll find out if you keep reading. Kind of ironic, actually."

"So you're not going to tell me?"

"No. You'll find out soon enough. I think it's in the second journal. What else?"

"Is our Clarence the same Clarence that Grandma Hattie had in San Francisco?"

Grandpa laughed. "If you can believe it, yes. After Hattie died and I sold the house, I brought him back up here. You know tortoises live practically forever – at least a hundred years."

"How old is he now?"

"I have no idea, but he's had quite the life. Speaking of Clarence, take some lettuce out to him, will you? While you're out there mowing."

"Okay, okay. I can take a hint."

The gnome prison cell was like a giant bored hole in the floor of the cave, just big enough to go stir crazy in. Inset: That's about how deep it was.

Chapter XXIII

Appointment at Midnight

Friday, June 23, 1967
On Mt. St. Helena, in the gnome's cave
Napa Valley, California

I could hear Nigel's threats and swearing tirades echoing off the walls of the cave. *The gnomes must have more than one of these hole-in-the-ground jail cells,* I thought to myself. I thought about yelling out to him, but realized I didn't want to have a conversation with him or hear what he had to say. I had enough problems of my own. First and foremost was the trouble I'd be in for not getting back to the farm by noon tomorrow. What bothered me, was knowing how worried Ma-D and Walter would be, and for that matter, probably Hattie, too. The more I thought about it the more I realized there was nothing I could do about it. Or was there? There had to be something I could use to bargain with the king. The simple fact was that I had to get off the mountain as soon as possible and take Quicksilver with me. Period. End of sentence. I'd be in so much trouble if I didn't, I just couldn't accept any other option. But bargaining chips? Did I have any? I lay down on the cot and fell asleep without intending to, thinking that at that moment it looked like the king held all the cards.

I awoke in the gloom of my subterranean cell to the sound of someone quietly calling my name. I looked up and saw Prince G's face peering down at me.

"Are you awake?" the prince asked. "I've got news."

"What is it?" I said, sitting up, looking at my watch: 6:10 a.m.

"Our men found the amulet. You're in luck."

"That *is* good news," I said and noticed that the prince was lowering something with a rope into my cell.

"My father has agreed to meet with you, now that he knows who you are. At midnight."

"Midnight?"

"Yes. For us, midnight is like your noon."

"He can't see me before then?"

"He's not what you call a 'morning person'. You're lucky he's seeing you then and not even later."

"Somehow I'm not feeling all that lucky right now," I said as the package from above reached me. "What's this?"

"It's something to eat and a book. I know it's going to be a long day for you."

"Thanks," I said.

"It's *White Fang* by Jack London. It's one of my favorite books. I have to go. I'll see you tonight — friend of the gnomes."

"Wait a minute," I said.

"What is it?" the prince's head reappeared at the top of the hole.

"What do you want me to call you?"

The prince thought about it for a moment and then said "When you're in front of my father, Prince G, but when he's not around, you can just call me 'G.'"

"Okay. Just G it is. Is there any way I can get another candle? I fell asleep last night and forgot to blow it out."

"I'll have one of the guards bring you one. Goodbye."

"Goodbye."

I untied the rope from the cloth satchel. In it was a hunk of dark bread, a bunch of blackberries and the book. I tore off a piece of the bread and sat on my cot. It was covered in a reddish, very soft wool blanket — *not bad for a prison cell,* I thought to myself. *He was right about one thing,* I thought to myself, looking at my watch again, *it is going to be a long day,* calculating that I had almost eighteen hours to go before my meeting with the king. *But at least they found the amulet,* I thought to myself with relief.

•   •   •

I spent the long hours walking around my cell, literally in circles, thinking what I could possibly say to the king that would get me and Quicksilver released. About an hour after G's visit, one of the guards did, indeed, lower a candle into the cell, without so much as a word. At noon, the same guard lowered another satchel, this one filled with another hunk of bread, a hardboiled egg and a piece of cheese. It wasn't Ma-D's cooking, but it was welcome. I cringed at the thought of how worried Ma-D must be, but reminded myself that if I returned home with Quicksilver, things would probably be okay. Maybe. Probably not. Every time I felt like I was going stir-crazy, I'd force myself to read *White Fang.* G was right — it was a good book. At one point, though, — around 5 o'clock — I got so anxious and jumpy I thought about yelling over to that weasel, Nigel, if only to have someone to share complaints with; it didn't take long for me to decide not to. *Just breathe,* I told myself, *you'll get through it.* Around 8 o'clock in the evening, I lay down on the cot. I wasn't particularly tired but within a few minutes I mercifully fell asleep again, thinking just before I dozed off that being a recreational sleeper had its advantages.

.   .   .

"I knew I shouldn't have let him go!" Walter said, pacing around the kitchen.

"Look, Walter, all of us, including Hattie, decided it was okay. The only thing for us to do now is figure out how to find him and get him home," Ma-D said, her hands wringing a dishtowel which hung from her apron.

"I'm calling the sheriff," Walter said in exasperation.

"No, Walter. Let's wait one more hour. If he hasn't shown up by nine, you can call the sheriff. This is so unlike Nick, I can't believe he won't show up before dark."

"Whatever you say, Ma-D," Walter said angrily, slamming the screen door to the front porch. "Whatever you say."

.   .   .

Once again, I awoke to the sound of G calling down to me. I shook myself awake, looked at my watch and saw that it was ten minutes to midnight. "Thank goodness," I said out loud and then looked up.

"My father will see you now," G said. "I thought you'd like a minute or so to prepare yourself."

"Prepare myself?," I said, "that's what I've been trying to do for the last eighteen hours."

"So, are you ready?"

"As much as I'm ever going to be," I said, running my hands through my hair. "How do I get out of here?"

"The men will be here shortly. They'll pull you out with the rope."

I paced around, waiting for the rope to appear. I tucked in my shirt, but there wasn't much I could do about the dirt all over it or the rips in my pants. I heard a noise and looked up and saw the rope being lowered. It had a big knot at the bottom, which I assumed was for my feet. I pulled on the rope and felt resistance. I was ready to be pulled up when I suddenly let go, and ran over to my cot and picked up my backpack, hoping I'd have reason to need it soon. I didn't want to even think about spending any more time in the cell. I threw the backpack over my shoulder and grabbed the rope, pulling on it twice. They pulled me up slowly. When I reached the top, I scrambled over the edge and stood up. There were six gnomes standing around me. The one in charge told me to sit down, which I did. I was surprised when one of the gnomes came up behind me and placed a black blindfold over my eyes, tying it tightly in the back.

"What the..."

"There's no need to worry, sir," said the gnome in charge, "it's just that no Uplander can know the route to the king's chambers. Stand up now and we'll guide you there."

The noise of our conversation must have woken Nigel; his shouts, swearing and threats could be heard from somewhere deeper in the cave, echoing off the rock walls.

"That's one angry guy," I said to myself.

"Ay, he's a feisty one," one of the gnomes said. "This way, sir."

I was led through a maze of tunnels, this way and that, and up and down stairs. We finally stopped and one of the gnomes knocked three times on what sounded like a wooden door. From the other side of the doors, a familiar voice boomed, "Bring him in."

The doors groaned open and I was led into the room.

"Take his blindfold off."

I leaned over and one of the gnomes untied the blindfold. I stood upright and looked around. I couldn't believe my eyes.

The room wasn't that big — maybe twenty-five feet square. And definitely not high-ceilinged; I was almost five feet, eight inches tall and the ceiling was only a couple of feet over my head, but what a room! The walls and ceiling were completely covered in gold that looked like it had been beaten into place, completely covering the rock walls. There were candles and torches of all sizes everywhere, reflected over and over in the gold luster. The whole room seemed to glitter, an effect enhanced by the shiny black, glasslike floor. I looked down at my feet and could see myself darkly reflected, upside down. It was an eerie sensation, almost like my upright self was standing on an upside-down down version of myself, suspended in a black void. I began to feel a little lightheaded.

"Impressed?"

I turned in the direction of the voice and saw the king sitting at the head of a very long rectangular table, filled with all manner of food and dozens and dozens of candles. The entire tribe, all thirteen of them, were seated around the table, all eyes on me. I hoped I wasn't going to faint.

"That's putting it mildly," I managed to say.

"Come, sit down, friend of the gnomes. Share in our midnight feast."

I walked a little unsteadily to the table and sat in the small empty chair to the left of the king. The chair was so small my knees pressed against the underside of the table. I scooted myself in so it wouldn't be noticeable. Prince G was seated to his father's right; we acknowledged each other with nods across the table. Seated very closely on either side of the king, but slightly behind him, were two gnomes, obviously of some importance. In front of me was an empty gold dinner plate and a gold goblet.

"What will you have to drink, young Nick?" the king asked. "We have everything you could wish for."

"Water would be fine, thank you."

"Are you sure?"

"Yessir," I stammered. "Water is fine."

"Pass young Nick the water."

Many small hands passed what appeared to be a solid gold pitcher down the table.

"Please, please, help yourself," the king said, making a sweeping gesture at all the food on the table.

"Thank you, Your Highness."

"As I'm sure you've been told, my men have found the amulet, wrapped in, what was it? Kleex?"

"Kleenex, Your Highness."

"Yes, that's right, kleexie. You're a lucky young man."

"So I've been told," I said, still not feeling the slightest bit lucky.

"And my men also found this," the king said, reaching under the table. "I assume it's yours," handing me my hat.

"My lucky hat," I exclaimed. With everything that was going on I hadn't even realized it was gone.

"It's an unusual example of headgear," the king said, "was it originally a crow's nest?"

"No, it's always been a cowboy hat; it's just seen better days," I said as I put it on the floor next to my chair, thinking perhaps my luck *was* changing.

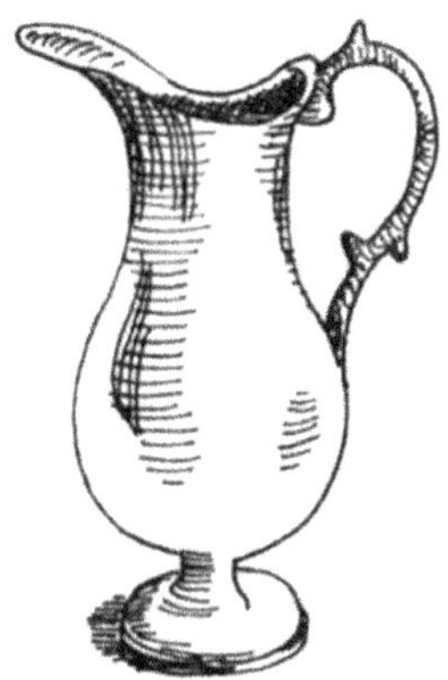

The solid gold water pitcher.

"Now, explain to me, young Nick, exactly how is it that you are related to my friend, Captain Niebaum?" the king asked, popping what looked like a walnut half into his mouth.

"Well... ah... I'm not. Not exactly."

"Ah hah!" the king shouted, looking first at the gnome on his left and then to Prince G on his right, raising his eyebrows.

"It's a little complicated. You see, Captain Niebaum and his wife didn't have children. The captain's wife, Susan, had a sister who lived in San Francisco with her husband and small daughter, named Hattie. Susan's sister and her husband both died, leaving Hattie an orphan. Captain Niebaum and his wife adopted Hattie as their own. And Hattie is my grandmother. She was the captain's sole heir, as I am hers."

"I see," said the king, scratching his long beard. "Forgive me for asking, but what of your grandmother's husband and your mother and father? Are they not heirs?" the king asked, clearing his throat. "You see I am just trying to assess how many 'friends for all time' I might have."

"I'm afraid they're all dead," I said, looking straight at the king.

"My, my. That's a lot of death in one family. I'm truly sorry," the king said, returning my gaze solemnly.

"Thank you," I said.

"So, your grandmother gave you the amulet?"

"Yes."

"Why?"

"Because she knew I was coming to see you."

"Hmmm. So now to the crux of the story... why are... " the king said, trailing off, as the gnome who had been in charge of bringing me to the king's chambers entered the hall and walked over to the gnome seated at the king's left and whispered something in his ear. In turn, that gnome stood up and whispered in the king's ear.

"He can scream all he wants! Put the lid on his cell." the king said angrily. "Uplanders!" he declared dismissively, taking a long drink from his goblet. He then motioned to the prince to pour him more.

"I apologize for the interruption, young Nick. Are you aware we apprehended another intruder last night?"

"Yes."

"Do you know him?" the king asked, arching one eyebrow.

Something clicked in my brain. It was finally there — the bargaining chip I was looking for. I had been so intent on not having anything to do with Nigel, I'd neglected to see that Nigel could be of use after all.

"Ah, yes I do," I said, adding "but he's no friend of mine and definitely no friend of yours and your men."

"Oh really," the king said. "Tell me more," he said, leaning his face in towards mine.

"His name is Nigel Stayne and he's been sent here from London by a very rich man named Lord Higgenbotham. Lord Higgenbotham owns many newspapers all over the world and Nigel Stayne is what is called a 'photojournalist,' someone who takes pictures and writes stories about things that sell those newspapers. He's been sent here to expose you and your men to the world," I said with some drama, looking around the table at all the gnomes.

The men around the table made grunting noises and started banging their knives against their goblets.

"Silence!" the king shouted. He sat without saying anything for a bit and then asked me "and how did this Lord Biggenbottom know of our existence?"

"Higgenbotham. Lord Higgenbotham," I said, correcting the king. "A distant relative of his was on the sailing ship *Lindisfarne* when you were discovered. The relative's name was Thom Higgenbotham and he copied a page from the Lindesfarne's log book that described you and your men being found aboard the schooner. Lord Higgenbotham inherited that copied page and grew up hearing the family stories that this relative had seen you and your men being transported to Eagle's Nook in crates on a horse drawn wagon. Nigel Stayne pieced the story together from there and, without my knowing it, followed me here."

The king sat silent again, rubbing his chin. "I think I remember this sailor. Tim... Tad..."

"That's Thom," I said. "Thom Higgenbotham."

"Yes, that's it, Thom Higgenbotham. A third class wharf rat if there ever was one. Captain Niebaum went to some lengths to keep us apart. Strange, after all these years... " the king stopped in mid-sentence, lost in his thoughts. After a minute or two, he continued: "So all of this brings us to you, young Nick, and the reason for your coming to see me."

"I was getting to that," I said, trying to hide my nervousness. I decided to just be as direct as possible. "I came to convince you to give my uncle's horse back."

"Give your uncle's horse back?" the king asked irritably.

"Yes, Your Highness, the horse your men took from the Twin Oaks Pony Farm belongs to my uncle."

"You don't say?" the king said, genuinely surprised. And then in an abrupt change of mood said, practically yelling: "But I'm certain my men paid for that horse! We always do."

"I realize that, but my uncle would be willing to give you the payment back in exchange for the return of his horse," I said, thinking quickly.

"But I like that horse," the king said despondently. "What's his name?"

"Quicksilver."

"No wonder I like him so much."

"I have no doubt that you do, Your Highness. And there might be a way for you to work out a deal with my uncle — to purchase him legitimately this time," I said, making things up as I went along. "But Quicksilver must return with me to my uncle's farm first, before any deal can be made," I said adamantly.

"The horse has been bought and paid for," the king said, his voice rising. "The horse belongs to me."

"I beg to differ, Your Highness. According to the rules of your world, Quicksilver has been, as you say, 'bought and paid for.' In our world — the world in which my uncle and Quicksilver live — Quicksilver has been 'stolen and paid for.'"

"Stolen!" the king shouted, slamming his fist on the table.

"Yes, stolen," I said. "Remember that night you and your men were discovered on the *Lindisfarne*?" I said, my voice softening. "How Captain Niebaum explained to you the human practice of paying for goods or services first, before you could take the goods or use the service?"

"Hmmmmm... yes, yes. You make a point."

"That's all I'm saying, Your Highness. I think there's a way to approach this where both you and my uncle will be satisfied. But as I said, I must leave here with Quicksilver tonight, or there will be no deal of any kind."

"But..." the king interjected.

"If I may, Your Highness," I continued. "I have an idea that may interest you."

"Continue," the king said, cocking his head to one side.

"If you allow me to take Quicksilver with me tonight, I'll arrange to have Nigel Stayne removed from your midst. I have to imagine having a screaming lunatic in your residence could be quite an inconvenience."

"Oh, don't worry about him. We'll just put him in a trance. That'll take care of..." Again, the gnome on the left jumped up and started whispering in the king's ear. I glanced over to Prince G and saw him rolling his eyes and shaking his head.

"Oh, yes, yes. I keep forgetting..." the king said to the gnome.

The king sat, an unhappy expression on his face, pondering his choices.

"So you say you can rid us of that nuisance... that Mr. Snits, or whatever his name is?"

"Stayne, Your Highness. Yes, I can get rid of him for you."

"How soon?"

"Within 24 hours," I said, pulling the number out of thin air.

"And this promise would be in the form of a solemn oath between the two of us?"

"Yes."

"Hmmmm," the king muttered under his beard. "I need to think about this turn of events." All of the gnomes around the table nodded their heads in agreement.

•   •   •

While the king and his men were doing their thinking, in the valley below Walter sat at the kitchen table, his hands wrapped around a mug of coffee. The only light on was the little one over the clock that was part of stove; the hum of the refrigerator was the only noise in the room. Walter looked at the clock. 1:30 a.m. Ma-D had gone to bed at midnight. Henry had some harebrained idea and drove up to Mt. St. Helena to be there in case Nick showed up in the middle of the night. *He was probably asleep in his truck,* Walter thought to himself. Snoops pretended to be asleep on his rug under the stove, opening one eye or the other every so often to make sure Walter was all right.

Walter felt like he had done everything possible. The last time he'd met with Sheriff Lyman, the sheriff had given him his home telephone number. Even though it was the middle of the night, Walter decided he had to take action and dialed the number. After he explained the situation, Sheriff Lyman (who didn't sound like he'd been asleep) said he'd contact the Calistoga Police Department immediately and instruct them to organize the local Search and Rescue Unit at first light tomorrow. After they'd done a preliminary search, he would decide whether or not to call out the Mounted Posse and the Aero Squadron. Sheriff Lyman told Walter they'd meet up at on Mt. St. Helena, at the parking area which led to Robert Louis Stevenson State Park, at 5 o'clock the next morning and invited Walter to be there. The sheriff also asked Walter to bring Snoops along, as it wasn't unusual, he explained, for a family dog to be the one that found a missing family member.

He and Ma-D had talked earlier in the evening and decided to wait until there was something definite to report before they called Hattie. They didn't want to worry her needlessly; he hoped they had made the right decision.

Walter looked at Snoops absentmindedly. He wondered whether he should go to bed and try to sleep, or just have another cup of coffee and stay up. He got up and walked over to the stove. Snoops moved to a spot under the kitchen table. "Go to sleep," Walter told Snoops. "You need to be at the top of your game tomorrow." Snoops looked up at Walter and cocked his head; he knew something important was going on. Walter turned the heat on under the coffee pot. There was no way he was going to sleep tonight.

G showed me the back way out of the gnome's cave, leading to the corral.

Chapter XXIV

A Deal is Struck

Friday, June 23 through Saturday, June 24, 1967
On Mt. St. Helena
Napa Valley, California

Not long after the king made the proclamation that he had to "think about this turn of events" his head rolled forward, chin on his chest, and I could hear soft snoring sounds. I looked around the table and all the gnomes were eating, drinking, and talking quietly amongst themselves, treating the king's nap as a kind of intermission. Puzzled, I looked across the table at G. He motioned me with his finger to lean across the table. I cupped one hand to the side of my mouth and asked "What's going on? Is he sleeping?"

"He claims he's not. It happens all the time. He says he's looking at the inside of his eyelids so he can think more deeply. Don't worry, it usually doesn't last very long."

I decided to use the opportunity to help myself to some cheese and an apple. The prince raised his goblet to me, as if to say "cheers," and I lifted mine in a salute back to him. Sure enough, after about five minutes, the king sputtered and coughed back to life and turned to me and said, "As I was saying... ." The table quieted and the conversation resumed.

"Let us assume," the king began, "that I let you take the horse with you tonight and that you will intercede on my behalf with your uncle to find a way to, as you put it, make sure both your uncle and I are satisfied."

"Yes," I said, trying to suppress a grin. Had I convinced him? It was beginning to sound like it.

"And that you will remain true to your word and have Mr. Snits removed from his cell and taken away from here."

"Stayne. Mr Stayne. Yes, you can count on me to do that."

"Then we are in agreement, except for one detail."

"What detail is that, Your Highness?"

"Let us back up a moment. Are you aware of the fact that I lost five of my tribe when Captain Niebaum called on the island of Kauai?"

"Yes. I read that in the captain's personal papers."

"Then you know that amongst the five is Dagywn, our Wizard. Each of us

is born with, what shall I say, our own particular skills, but Dagywn alone pos-
sesses them all, along with the secrets of our strongest magic. It is of utmost
importance that he return — along with the others if at all possible. But Dagywn
is the most important — he must return to the tribe!" the king reiterated, raising his voice.

"I understand, Your Highness, but what does that have to do with me?"

"Do with it? Why, I want you to bring him, and the others, back to me," he
said, pointing his finger first at me and then at his chest.

My heart sank. I had allowed myself to think that the deal was done. And now
this. I had to think fast. From out of nowhere something I had read came into my
head, namely *When in doubt, tell the truth.*

"I can't."

"What do you mean, 'you can't'?" the king bellowed.

"Well... that's not exactly what I meant to say. I may be able to do as you
desire, but I can't do it by myself."

"Then take someone from your own tribe with you. I don't care." the king
said, exasperated.

"That's not the point, either, Your Highness. It's that I can't make that decision myself. I'm not old enough to decide these kinds of things."

"Why not?"

"Our laws say that someone must be 18 years or older to enter into this kind
of agreement."

"How old are you?"

"14. Almost 15."

"Well, I'm not waiting four of your years to get Dagywn back," the king said
and then sat silent for a moment. "So, if you can't make these agreements on
your own, who can?"

"Grandma Hattie. My guardian."

"Ah, we're back to Grandma Hattie."

"Yes, we are."

The king sat, contemplating the situation. "Is she a reasonable woman?"

"I would say so, yes."

"Then you will set up a meeting between me and Grandma Hattie and we will
come to an agreement."

Even imagining a meeting between the two of them made my mind reel; I
quickly responded nonetheless.

"I can do that, Your Highness."

"Good. Then it's settled. Once Grandma Hattie agrees to have you bring Dagywn back, you may have your horse back."

"No, Your Highness."

"No? No one says *no* to me," he said visibly shaking.

I saw the prince make a face across the table, like he was expecting something to blow up any minute. But I wasn't having any of it. I knew the king was pushing his luck, trying to get as much out of the deal as possible.

"I mean you no disrespect, Your Highness. But what you propose is not fair. If I agree to rid you of Mr. Stayne and you agree to let me take Quicksilver home tonight, we are more or less even in our commitments to one another. As a show of good will, I have additionally agreed to represent your interest in buying Quicksilver from my uncle and do my best to arrange a deal where you both are satisfied. So, I have more at stake in this deal than you, but I'm willing to let this stand as our agreement. Now you have added another condition — one that I will willingly perform if I'm allowed to by my guardian — but it cannot be part of our original deal. You strike me as a very fair man, Your Highness, just as Captain Niebaum described you. But what you are suggesting is simply not fair. To make such a demand of me would do harm to your reputation as a great man," I said, laying it on thick.

"You have a brazen tongue, young Nick, but I have to admit what you say makes sense. I'll not tarnish my sterling reputation over the likes of this. But, I assume correctly, do I not, that you will take responsibility for setting up a meeting between me and your grandmother with the seriousness it deserves?"

"You have my word, Your Highness."

"Very well then, we have a deal," the king said, raising his goblet. Everyone around the table raised their glasses and shouted "Hear, hear!"

I waited for the commotion to die down. I wasn't sure I should ask, but I did anyway.

"Your Highness, now that we have an agreement, may I have the amulet back? I'd like to return it to my grandmother."

"Actually, no. I will return it in person when your grandmother and I meet and I am satisfied with the outcome of our discussion."

I thought about it for a minute and then nodded as graciously as I could to the king.

Now that the deal had been agreed to, I wanted nothing more than to get Quicksilver and start making my way back to the farm. I had no idea how I was going to do it — I just wanted to be out of the cave, *now*. But it was not to be.

Now that we were through negotiating, it was clearly time to socialize. And eat. And eat some more.

Platters of food were passed around again and again. As anxious as I was to get going, I knew I had to take some and pretend to enjoy it. I definitely didn't want to offend the king and risk any part of our new agreement. I couldn't help but notice that for such a small being, the king had an enormous appetite and an even bigger thirst. Over time he grew more talkative, explaining that Prince G loved books, and it was from a book the prince had shared with him, on the royal palaces of Russia, that he got the idea for the solid gold chamber we now sitting in. It seems that the Empress Catherine I of Russia had a room entirely covered in amber at her summer palace near St. Petersburg. The king was so taken with it that he wanted a similar room of his own, only instead of being covered with what he called a "semi-precious material," he wanted his chamber to be completely covered with solid hammered gold. I couldn't help but be impressed with the opulence of the room — who wouldn't be in awe of such an achievement? Sensing my interest, the king continued, explaining that the black floor was made of thousands of small pieces of obsidian the gnomes had gathered from Glass Mountain, just a few miles south of Mt. St. Helena. I was familiar with the mountain — Chuy and I had hiked it last summer, looking for arrowheads chipped from the black, glasslike rock by the native Indian tribes that used to inhabit the valley. According to the king, the hardest part of it was polishing it to a smooth surface. "It was 'all hands on deck,'" the king said, chuckling. "That's something I picked up from your Captain Niebaum."

"If I may, Your Highness, there's one thing I'd like to know."

"Certainly. What is it?"

"I was just wondering why you're here — I mean, you haven't always lived here, have you?."

"To tell you the truth, we've been moving from place to place for some time now. We started out in Sweden, moved to Finland, and then to the Åland Islands, which are between Sweden and Finland, in the Baltic Sea. We kept thinking things would get better, but they didn't."

"Better?"

"Well, the church bells for one. And what they represented. For some reason the church made our people — our tribe — out to be in ca-

A chunk of obsidian.

hoots with the devil, which we certainly are not. We don't even believe in a devil. But it was more than that. The worst was when we started to be forgotten by the Uplanders. Very few of them believed in us any more. And when you're forgotten, it becomes easier and easier to disappear, which is something we wanted to make certain never happened. So I decided to take a group of my men — and my son, of course — to explore other lands where we might live. I had it in my mind that we might have better luck in the New World. And here we are. Now I just have to figure out how to get us all together again. And for that, I need that damned Dagywn."

With that the king then pitched forward for one of his spontaneous naps.

Even though I wanted — needed — to go, there was a part of me that would have liked to stick around until the king woke up so I could ask him more questions. I looked at my watch and saw that it was already a few minutes before 5 o'clock in the morning. I had to get going. I leaned across the table and, in a low voice, asked G if there was any chance of leaving. "I've got to get home. Like right now," I said desperately.

"Actually, I think this could be a serious nap. Let's go now. I'll take you to Quicksilver."

I practically jumped out of my chair and nodded thanks to everyone around the table. I grabbed my backpack from under the table, put my hat on and followed G out of the chamber and into a tunnel.

"This way," the prince summoned with his hand. "My father had a pen constructed for Quicksilver below the colosseum. I'll show you the shortcut."

I followed the prince and in a couple of minutes we were outside in the colosseum. The prince motioned again and led me to a small opening in the rocks, which led to a steep set of stairs leading down.

"Follow those to the bottom. You can't miss the pen; it'll be on your right."

"Thanks, Just G," I said, "you're a... a... prince."

"Don't I know it," G said with a smile. "I wish I knew where Quicksilver's bit and lead are, but I don't."

"Don't worry, I have some rope in my backpack. We'll be okay." I was just about to shake hands with prince when I stopped, saying "Listen G, will you tell your father two things? They're important."

"Sure. What is it?"

"First, I'm not sure how I'm going to do it, but I'll have someone here in the next 24 hours to get Stayne out of your cave. Hopefully sooner rather than later. Tell your father to make sure your guards know to expect whoever it is and to let him do his business — without interference, okay?"

"Okay. What else?"

"Stayne is a very persistent guy. I'll do my best to have him stay away for as long as possible, but I'm guessing he'll be back — maybe not for a long time, but he'll probably show up one day, out of the blue. So have your guards keep their eyes open for him. Believe me, you don't want him anywhere near here."

"Got it," said the prince. "Thanks for the warning."

"I left the copy of *White Fang* in the cell. Thanks for loaning it to me. It's a good book, just like you said."

"Did you finish it?"

"No. I had a few other things on my mind."

"Maybe I'll bring it to your place sometime."

"You know where I live?"

"Witbeck, he's the one who stole Quicksilver, told me," the prince said. "I know the way."

"Well, all right then. Maybe I'll see you," I said, somewhat surprised.

"Maybe so," G said, shaking my hand. "See you," he said, waving, as I took off down the stone stairway.

•　　•　　•

I practically flew down the steps. I got to the bottom of the stairs and outside. I looked up at the sky. It was just beginning to lighten. For as interesting as the gnome's cave seemed to be, it was wonderful to be free and in the fresh air. I ran to the right, expecting to find a wooden corral, but found instead a low rock enclosure with Quicksilver whinnying over the wall. I threw my arms around his neck. "Man, am I glad to see you!" I said scratching Quicksilver's ears. "Let's get you home."

•　　•　　•

Walter arrived at the parking area right at 5 o'clock, just as he was told. He parked next to Henry's truck and could see that the windows of the cab were fogged up. Walter knocked on the window. Henry slowly rolled down the window, looking a little rough around the edges.

"Time to get up, Henry."

"You find him?" Henry said rubbing his hands over his face.

"No. We're about to go lookin.'"

"All right, let me get straightened out here," he said as he unfolded himself from the truck, making a lot of grunts and groans as he did.

Just then a couple of sheriff's department cruisers showed up, along with a big white van. The van held a dozen volunteers from the Search and Rescue Unit. Everyone shook hands and introduced themselves. Walter got Snoops out of the truck and put him on a leash and told him "Let's go find Nick." Snoops looked at Walter and barked a couple of times, then started straining on the leash to get going. The sheriff addressed the group saying that, for now, they'd take the trail to the monument and then start up the fire trail and fan out from there. With that, the group walked across the road and started up the side of the mountain.

•   •   •

I got the rope out of my backpack and made a lead with a double half-hitch and slipped it over Quicksilver's neck. "Come on. Let's get outta' here," I said, leading Quicksilver out of the stone corral. I walked around the base of the rock wall that formed the colosseum, on the opposite side of where I was last night — or was it the night before last? I'd lost all track of time. I picked up the trail and headed back to Clyde's place, the sky a pale grayish-blue, with wisps of fog swirling up and over the mountain. We had been walking for about fifteen minutes when I thought I saw something up ahead, but then the fog obscured whatever it was. I looked harder as the fog lifted a little. I couldn't be sure, but it looked like Clyde and it looked like he was jumping from one foot to the other.

After a few more minutes of walking, I was close enough to see that it was, in fact, Clyde, who began waving his hands over his head like I couldn't see him. I began to jog and was soon face-to-face with him. He gave me a bear hug and then started talking really fast.

"Damn, boy, I thought you were a goner. Ya' got the horse! I knew ya' could do it. You all right? What took ya so long? Did they put ya' in a spell?"

"I'm okay, Clyde. I'm okay. And no, they didn't put me in a spell."

"Well, thank your lucky stars for that, and you got the horse back."

"Yeah, but it took me... I don't even know how long it took me. And I had to make a lot of promises I'm not sure I can keep."

"Come on back to my place. We can have some coffee or somethin'."

"How long you been standing there, Clyde?"

"A while. I sure 'nuf thought you was a goner," he said, shaking his head, leading the way back.

It wasn't long before we were back at Clyde's. I tied Quicksilver to a tree and Clyde asked if I wanted anything.

"Do you have something I could use for some water for Quicksilver?"

"Sure. I got a bucket. I'll go get it. You want somethin'?"

"No, I gotta' get back to the farm. Pronto."

"How you gonna do that, now that you got the horse with ya'?"

"I don't know. I'll figure something out."

Clyde came back sloshing a wooden bucket of water and put it down in front of Quicksilver. We both watched as Quicksilver drank.

"I don't mean to be rude, Clyde, but I better be going."

"Nah, that's all right. We'll have time to talk later. I'll walk with ya' a ways."

We started off in the direction of Clyde's mine, but then I remembered my bicycle was locked to the tree in the parking area.

"I need to get back to the main trail, Clyde. My bicycle is in the parking area."

"How you gonna' manage a horse and a bicycle?"

"I don't know," I said and then heard a dog barking. I stopped and listened.

"Snoops?" I said, not believing it could be him.

Next thing I knew, Snoops had his paws on my chest, trying to lick my face.

"Snoops! What in the world are you doing here?" I wondered if it was possible that he'd followed me from the farm somehow. Snoops kept barking and in the next instant it seemed like about a dozen or more people just appeared in front of me, with Walter in the lead and Sheriff Lyman and Henry right behind him.

"Nick!"

"Uncle Walter! Henry!"

"Thank goodness you're all right," Walter said, holding me by the shoulders. "And you've got Quicksilver! How'd you do that?"

"It's kind of a long story."

"Who's this with you?"

"Oh, I'm sorry. Uncle Walter, this is Clyde. Clyde Charles Cates the third."

Uncle Walter held out his hand to Clyde.

"Pleased to meet you, Clyde. You find the boy?"

I jumped in, saying "Yeah, you could say that." Clyde looked confused.

"Well, we're going to have to do something for you. Many, many thanks, Clyde!" He shook Clyde's hand again.

"Ah, it wasn't nothin'," Clyde said, shooting me a confused look.

Sheriff Lyman was on his walkie-talkie, presumably letting someone know that I'd been found. Walter turned to the sheriff and asked if it was possible to have someone from the sheriff's office call Ma-D and tell her I was okay. The sheriff said it wouldn't be a problem. Suddenly it seemed like everyone was talking at once and people I didn't know were asking a lot of questions. I felt uncomfortable being the center of so much attention. I was grateful when Walter finally said "let's get the boy and this horse back to the farm."

On the way back to the road, Henry took the lead with Quicksilver. Next on the trail was Sheriff Lyman with Walter and me following behind him. A couple of the sheriff's men stayed back to talk to Clyde. The rest of the search and rescue team were scattered here and there. An idea popped into my head and I called out ahead.

"Sheriff Lyman. May I talk to you a minute?"

The sheriff turned around and said "Sure."

I turned to Walter and said "I'm not trying to be all secretive or anything, Uncle Walter. It's just that I've got something I've got to tell the sheriff." Walter looked a little confused, but I motioned to the sheriff to follow me to where we could talk in private.

"What is it, Nick?"

"Well... I was wondering if you could do something for me. It's kind of import-ant. In fact, it's really important."

"Like what?"

"I made a deal with the folks that had Quicksilver. A promise, really."

"Okay. Go on."

"Do you know where the old Great Western Quicksilver Mine is?"

"Yeah, I think I know where it is."

"Well, if you have any problems finding it, Clyde can point it out for you."

"And... ?"

"And... oh boy... how do I put this? You gotta' climb up this rock wall at the base of the opening to the mine, go inside the cave, and take the first tunnel on the left. Keep walking a ways and you'll see at least a couple of big — like ten-feet around — holes in the ground. In the second one — which might have a cover over it — you'll find this guy, Nigel Stayne, inside. You need to get him out of there. I made a promise."

Sheriff Lyman thought for a minute. "This has to do with the horse, doesn't it?"

"Yeah. You could say so."

"Let me be more specific. It has to do with the folks who put the pouch of gold in the trough?"

"You got it."

The sheriff was silent again. "Are they going to be around?"

"Assuming we're both talking about the same 'they,' no. At least not to bother you. Their guards will be off duty for the next 24 hours."

"You're sure about all this, Nick?"

"Oh, yeah. I'm sure."

"We better get on this now."

"I think that's a good idea."

"So who is this Nigel Stayne guy anyway?"

"He's been sent here from England by some big-time publisher. He's a photo-journalist. His assignment was to expose 'them'."

"Has he done anything wrong?"

"Other than be a royal pain in the butt, no. Couldn't you just consider it a rescue?"

"I suppose. I just need to know what I'm getting myself into."

"Well, I can tell you one thing."

"What's that?"

"He's going to be hoppin' mad."

"We can handle that."

"And you're going to need a rope to get him out of the hole."

"We've got it."

"And sheriff... "

"Yes?"

"He probably has a gun."

The smell of just-cut grass wafted into my room in the bunkhouse
and made me feel that all was okay with the world.

Chapter XXV

Back at the Farm

Saturday, June 24, 1967
Twin Oaks Pony Farm
St. Helena, California

Once we all got back to the parking area there were a lot of handshakes, hugs, and thank-yous. The Search and Rescue van took off, leaving Walter, Henry, Snoops, Quicksilver and me by ourselves. Walter told Henry to take Snoops back to the farm and come back with the pony trailer. He and I would stay behind with Quicksilver and wait for Henry come back.

After Henry took off, I tied Quicksilver to a tree trunk and got in the cab of Walter's truck, where Walter sat, puffing on his pipe, his window, thankfully, open.

"You all right?" he asked me as I closed the door.

"I think so," I said a little hesitantly.

"Want to talk about it?"

"Well, I got Quicksilver back."

"So I see," Walter said with a touch of sarcasm and a chuckle. "How'd you know where to find him?"

I hadn't thought through what my story was going to be and wasn't sure how much to tell Walter. *I could just tell him the truth,* I thought, *but I'm not sure he'd believe me.* I finally decided on basically telling the truth, just modifying it a bit.

"There's a group of foreigners who are kind of camped out on the side of Mt. St. Helena. Their leader took an interest in Quicksilver and wanted him for himself. Apparently, in their way of thinking, it's okay to take things that aren't theirs as long as they leave payment behind, usually overpayment."

"How'd you figure out it was them?"

"The pouch of gold. I found out from the Police Blotter in the *Star* that there'd been other times when the same thing has happened. These "foreigners" have been around here for a long time."

"What are they, like gypsies?"

"Kind of."

"So how'd you find out where they were — where Quicksilver was?"

"The first time I was hiking on Mt. St. Helena I ran into Clyde. We started talking about one thing and another and he told me he thought he knew where they lived. So that's where I looked."

"What did you do, just go in there and take him?"

"No. I had to do a lot negotiating. That's why I didn't get home on time."

"Negotiating?"

"Yeah, that's something we have to talk about."

"Like what?"

"Well, I told the leader of the group that maybe we could start the deal over — if I got Quicksilver back, we'd return the gold to him and then start over again."

Walter sat thinking for a while, puffing on his pipe, and then said "I don't have a problem giving this guy, whoever he is, his gold back, but I'm not sure about starting any deal over again."

"All I promised him is that you'd consider it. I didn't promise that you'd agree to anything, one way or the other."

"Fair enough," Walter said. "Are you hungry?"

"Starved," I said.

"Why don't you stay here with Quicksilver and I'll go into Calistoga and get something. I'm starved, too, and it's going to be a while before Henry gets back. Whaddaya' want?"

"I'm not too particular right now. You choose."

•   •   •

I sat down on a big rock next to Quicksilver. All at once I realized how tired I was. More tired than I could remember. Had I been up all night? I tried to piece together the events of the last couple of days. It hurt my brain. Day was night and night was day. All I was sure of was that I'd gotten Quicksilver back. And the only way I knew that for sure was that Quicksilver was breathing his warm breath into my right ear right now. Quicksilver was real and touchable. I couldn't think about anything else.

Walter came back in about a half an hour with a couple of cheeseburgers, fries and chocolate malt milkshakes. Just the smell of the French fries was nearly too much for me.

"Where'd you get these?" I asked Walter.

"At the Sarafornia. Felt a little funny ordering hamburgers and shakes when everyone else was eatin' breakfast, but I figured these would travel better," he said with a chuckle.

"I think you made a good call," I said.

We sat on the tailgate of the truck, neither of us saying a word, and practically inhaled the food.

I finished and burped loudly. "Excuse me," I said, a little embarrassed.

"You're excused," Walter said, letting go with, not a burp, but a full-fledged belch. I started to laugh. "Whoa, Uncle Walter. What would Ma-D think?"

"Best not to think about that."

We continued to sit on the tailgate, not saying anything, just content and full. All I could think about now was a hot shower and some sleep.

Just then there was a commotion across the road. I peered up the mountain and saw the sheriff and his men escorting someone down the trail, hands behind his back, shouting insults and swearing all the way.

"Well, I'll be," Walter said, squinting.

My stomach sinking, I feigned ignorance. "What is it?"

"Not what. Who. I believe that's Nigel Stayne coming down the trail in handcuffs."

"Hmmmm," I said, wishing I could disappear. "This isn't going to be pretty."

"What's that?" Walter asked.

"I don't think Mr. Stayne is going to be too happy with me."

"Why not?"

"We'll see."

We watched as Nigel was marched down the trail and across the road. He still wore his camouflage outfit, but it looked like he'd tried to rub the face paint off. There were red blotches on his face and neck. "Where's he been hiding out?" Walter asked me.

"He had it in his mind to expose the people who took Quicksilver — to reveal them to the world. Not because they took Quicksilver. He just wanted to expose them. Let's just say they didn't take too kindly to the idea."

Once the officers and Stayne made it to the parking area, Stayne took one look at me and started in: "There's the little bastard that ratted me out," he said, practically snarling.

"Keep your mouth shut, Mr. Stayne," the sheriff said, handing him over to his men. "You don't need any more trouble than you're already in. Put him in the car, Charlie."

The sheriff walked over to us. "Thanks, Nick. You were right. He did have a gun on him. And no permit."

"Really?"

"Yeah. And didn't you tell me he was working on a story or something?"

"Yes."

"Hell, yeah," Walter chimed in. "Even told me and Ma-D he was here on as-signment, like it was some kind of a big deal."

"Well, he's in hot water now."

"How's that?" Walter asked.

"Packin' a gun without a permit is bad enough, but he's got a visitor's visa, not a work visa. The I.N.S. isn't going to like that."

"What's going to happen to him?"

"Oh, he'll be deported all right."

"How soon?" I asked.

"Not long. Although they might cut him some slack and let him stay — in jail, mind you — until his poison oak clears up."

"Poison oak?" I said.

"Yeah, he's covered in it. He's not a happy camper."

•   •   •

Just as the sheriff and his men were pulling out, Henry showed up with the pony trailer. We got Quicksilver in the trailer and headed back to the farm, me riding with Walter. Within five minutes of getting in his truck, I was sound asleep.

I shook myself awake when I felt the truck come to a stop. I looked around at the house, bunkhouse, corral, and the garden. It felt like I'd been away for a month. Ma-D came rushing out of the house and practically pulled me out of the truck and gave me a huge hug. When she finally pulled away, I saw that she was crying, which embarrassed me.

"Boy, you look a fright. What happened to you?"

"I kinda' slipped down a rock wall."

"It's lucky you're alive," she said, shaking her head.

Just then Henry drove in, towing the horse trailer. Henry had already told Ma-D, when he came to pick up the trailer, that I'd found Quicksilver.

Henry's truck and the pony trailer.

"Well, if this isn't some kind of a

homecoming," she said, waving to Henry. "Nick and Quicksilver, back on the farm." Turning back to me she said "Good work, Nick. I don't know how you did it — and to tell you the truth, I'm not sure I want to know — but I'm glad you did whatever you did. Maybe Walter will stop being such a grouch now," she said, shooting Walter the stink eye look.

"Thanks, Ma-D."

"Now why don't you get cleaned up. You hungry?"

"No, Uncle Walter and I had cheeseburgers up on Mt. St. Helena, waiting for Henry to get back with the trailer."

"Cheeseburgers? At this hour of the morning?"

"Yeah, and boy, were they good."

"That's crazy."

"Maybe," I said, "but what I really need right now is a hot shower and some sleep. You don't mind if I sack out for a while, do you? I didn't get much sleep last night."

"Go on. Git. Do what you have to do. I'm just happy to have you back."

As I walked over to the bunkhouse, I turned around and saw Ma-D hugging Quicksilver. I hadn't had time to think about everything that had happened, start to finish; for the time being, I was just happy it had turned out the way it did. And all I cared about right now was making a beeline to the shower and my bed.

.   .   .

I didn't wake up until almost 2:30 in the afternoon. I lay in bed for a while, staring up at the ceiling. I could hear the lawnmower through the open window. Someone, most likely Henry, was doing my job. The green smell of freshly cut grass washed into the room. A slight breeze blew the white curtains back and forth, like the air itself was breathing in and out. Little pools of sunlight and shadow danced across the ceiling and walls. I was glad to be back. Back to normal. I thought about what I had to do next. Calling Grandma Hattie was at the top of the list.

I pulled on my clothes and walked barefoot over to the telephone and dialed her number. Katia answered and was her usual abrupt self. I could hear her calling Hattie to the phone.

"Is that you, Nick?"

"Sure is, Grandma."

"Do you have news to report?"

"I do."

"Well, give me the headlines!"

I gave her a shorthand version of the events. When I was finished, Hattie whistled in amazement.

"That's quite a story," she said. "You believe me now?"

"Believe what?"

"About the gnomes."

"Oh yeah. I believe. Kind of hard not to," I said.

"I almost wish I could have been there to see them," Hattie said.

"Well, you may have a chance yet. There's more to the story."

"Like what?"

"The king wants to have a meeting with you."

"With *me*?"

"Yeah. I had to bargain with him to let me take Quicksilver."

"What kind of bargain?"

"Do you remember the part in Captain Niebaum's papers about the gnomes that jumped ship in Kauai?"

"Yes, vaguely."

"Well, one of the five who jumped was Dagywn, the tribe's Wizard. All gnomes are born with their own particular magic, but the Wizard is the only one who can do it all, and more. Like the serious stuff, apparently. And the king wants him back — and he wants me to help get him."

"What did you tell him?"

"I told him flat out that I couldn't make that decision on my own. I told him that I was too young and that you were the only person who could say yes or no."

"Do you know what he wants, specifically?"

"No, not really. I think that's what he wants to talk to you about."

"Interesting," Hattie said, pausing.

"Will you do it?"

"Why not?" Hattie said. "When does he want to meet?"

"He didn't say, but I'd say the sooner the better."

"Well, you know I'm due to come up to Eagle's Nook on the first of July. Hold on, let me get my calendar."

I heard her put the phone down and the sound of her walking across the wooden floor in the kitchen.

"Okay, are you there?"

"I'm here."

"Hold on, let me get my glasses on. Why don't we make it for Monday the 3rd of July? That'll give me a couple of days to get settled."

"All right. I'll let him know."

"Where do you think we should meet?"

"He's going to want you to come to him, but I don't think that's a good idea — for a lot of reasons. Do you think Doyle would be willing to pick him up on Mt. St. Helena?"

"If I ask him, he will."

"Then I think you should meet at Eagle's Nook. But it'll probably be late."

"Like how late?"

"Let's just say the king isn't a morning person. And remember their day is our night, so I'm guessing he'll want to meet around midnight."

"I haven't stayed up past eleven since I can remember, but I'm game. I've wanted to meet them for a long time."

"Okay Grandma. I'll set it up."

"Let me know how it goes and if there's anything I need to do before the meeting, okay?"

"Okay."

"And I... "

"Yes."

"Congratulations. That was a job well done."

"Thanks, Grandma. But I couldn't have done it without your help."

"Of course you couldn't have. That's why I'm here."

"Good-bye, Grandma."

"Ciao bambino."

• • •

I lazed around for the rest of the afternoon. I checked on Quicksilver to make sure he was okay. I knew horses don't smile, but I could swear Quicksilver was smiling.

I decided to go back to the bunkhouse to write in my journal, something I'd been avoiding. I was a little intimidated by just how much had gone on, but once I sat down and got started, the words started to fly onto the pages. When I got to the end I looked at my watch: almost 5 o'clock. I couldn't believe I'd been writing for over two hours; it felt more like a thirty minutes. It was a good feeling to get it down on paper.

Ma-D went all out on dinner that night with pan-fried chicken, mashed potatoes and country gravy with lots of pepper, and string beans from the garden, cooked with bits of bacon. As usual, I stuffed myself. Everyone was so full after dinner that we decided to postpone dessert — cherry pie — and go sit on the front porch for a while.

We all took our positions and settled in. Walter lit his pipe and was momentarily lost in a cloud of blue smoke. Snoops walked around in a circle about five times and finally laid down. Henry put his feet up on the porch rail and groaned. "Ma-D you're killing me with that food of yours. But it's gonna' be a happy death, I can tell ya' that."

"Oh, I think you've got a few good years left, Henry. I wouldn't worry too much," Ma-D said.

"If it weren't so good, I wouldn't eat so much, Ma-D."

"What? You want me to start cooking lousy food, Henry?"

"No I wouldn't want you to do that. Maybe just not so good."

"Not gonna' happen, Henry. Maybe you oughta' think about getting a smaller nose bag."

"All right, you two. Knock it off. You sound like a couple of kids," Walter said. "Besides, I think this would be a good time for all of us to say thanks to Nick for doing what he did. I have a feeling it was a lot more difficult than he's letting on."

Ma-D was the first one to start singing *For He's a Jolly Good Fellow*. Walter and Henry soon joined in and the volume went up a couple of notches. I could feel myself blushing. They finished with a spirited "hip-hip-hoorah!" and a lot of pats on the back and hugs for me.

"Now who wants pie?" Ma-D said.

I raised my hand, as did Walter and Henry.

"Get in here, Henry and give me a hand. Besides you need the exercise."

I looked around at all of them there on the front porch. As far as tribes go, I thought to myself, this was a pretty good one.

Miniature donkeys were new to me — I didn't even know such a breed existed.

Chapter XXVI

What a Difference a Day Makes

Sunday, June 25, 1967
Multiple locations
St. Helena, Napa, and El Verano, California

The next morning I woke up early to the sound of Henry clomping in and out of the bunkhouse. I looked at my watch. 6:30. I guessed he wanted to get an early start on his yearly trip to visit his sister up north, in Eureka. I was still a little blurry-eyed, but I got dressed anyway and went out to see him off.

"You're up early, Henry."

"Yeah, trying to beat the heat. The old gal runs great but there's no AC. That trip up 101 can get a mite toasty late in the day."

"How long you gonna' be gone?"

"Depends on how much stuff my sister has for me to do around her place. Two or three weeks, probably. Mr. D. told me not to sweat it. Probably 'cause you're here to pick up the slack. To tell you the truth, I probably work harder up there than I do down here."

"Well, safe travels, Henry, and don't work too hard."

"Thanks Nick. See ya' when I get back. Oh, and Nick …"

"Yeah."

"I didn't get to movin' the irrigation lines in the pasture yesterday. Would you mind…"

"No problem, Henry. Snoops and I will take care of it."

Henry pulled off down the driveway in a cloud of dust. I thought about going back to bed and then decided to stay up and get going on the day. The memory of the time I spent in the hole was still fresh enough that I could clearly compare that experience with everything that I was free to do and see right now. *What a difference a day makes,* I thought to myself.

Moving the long aluminum irrigation lines by hand was a lot easier to do with two people, but I could handle it on my own. There was a row of five Rainbird sprinklers on top of the pipe. I always liked the sound they made when I turned on the water — kind of a slow, clicking, chiiit-chiiit-chiiit and then a faster chit-chit-chit as the sprinkler reversed its direction. It, and the crickets and

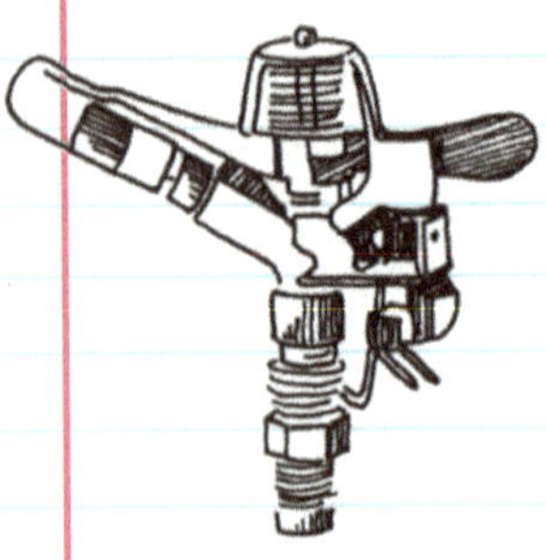

Rainbird sprinkler.

the cricket-noise they made, were the sounds of summer for me. I watched the long arcs of water, each one making a bunch of mini rainbows in the low early morning sunlight. Snoops was busy trying to bite the spray of water from one of the sprinklers, until he got tired and totally soaked. I whistled for him. He came loping up to me and shook himself hard, covering me with water.

"Thanks, Snoops. I'm not sure I needed that."

I decided to water the vegetable garden while I was up and at it. It always amazed me how quickly everything grew. The cucumbers I'd planted just over a week ago had doubled in size and were already twirling their way up the bamboo teepees. Snoops was lying on his back, feet in the air, scratching himself on the gravel path. "Silly dog," I said, "Let's go see if there's any breakfast."

I went over to the house and walked into the kitchen, leaving Snoops to dry out on the sunny back porch. Ma-D was standing at the kitchen counter, whisking a bowlful of batter.

"You're up early," Ma-D said, "I thought you'd sleep in after all the ruckus yesterday."

"No. Henry woke me up. He left early this morning."

"I thought I heard his truck."

"Yeah. He wanted to take off before it got too hot. Anyway, once I was up, I just decided to stay up. It's really beautiful out there this morning."

Ma-D looked at me with a puzzled expression, but didn't say anything right away. "Well, take a seat, nature boy; blueberry waffles are on the way. Where's Walter?" she asked to no one in particular. She walked over to the stairwell and shouted up "Walter! Breakfast! Step lively!" She walked back to the kitchen, muttering "someone decided to sleep in this morning."

I was already half-way through my first waffle when Walter showed up. "Well, look who's here. Sleeping Beauty," Ma-D said. Walter just scowled at her as he poured himself a cup of coffee.

"What's got into her?" Walter asked me.

"I don't know. She's acting kind of frisky."

"Speaking of frisky, now that Quicksilver is back and we're going to the State Fair, someone better get frisky with making sure the Winnebago is up for the trip," Ma-D said, looking at Walter.

Walter surprised me by saying "You're right, Ma-D. I'll take it in for a service next week." Ma-D was surprised too. From the look on her face, I could tell she was wondering if she'd actually heard Walter agreeing with her.

"Well, I'll be," she said under her breath. "What's the world coming to?"

*   *   *

When we'd had all finished breakfast, I asked Walter what he had planned for the day.

"Considering it's Sunday, not that much. I was thinking about driving the tractor into town and getting the hydraulics checked out. Something's not right with the system. You need something?"

"Nothing, really. I was just thinking about what I agreed to up on the mountain. It was my idea to return the gold to them if they let me take the horse back. It only seemed fair."

"I agree," Walter said. Ma-D looked at him in disbelief and shook her head again.

I continued, "I'd just like to make sure I hold up my end of the bargain, as soon as possible. I don't want any problems with them."

"I don't think the sheriff will be in today, but I can give him a call at home and see if he'll okay the release of the gold. Shouldn't be a problem, considering it's a closed case now."

"Thanks, Walter."

Walter went over to the telephone on the wall and dialed the sheriff's number. Ma-D told me to just sit. She was going to clear the table and do the dishes. *Whatever it was that was going around, it was also affecting her,* I thought to myself.

Walter came back to the table. "The sheriff said no problem. We can go down any time we want and pick it up."

"Could we go now?" I asked.

"Sure. Let's get it over with," Walter said. He turned to Ma-D and asked "Anything you need in Napa, Ma-D?"

"Since you're being so agreeable, I'd like a new car, a million dollars and a big swimming pool."

"Ma-D!"

"Oh, Walter. Lighten up. I was just funnin' with you," Ma-D said, walking over to him and giving him a kiss on the cheek, making Walter clearly uncomfortable.

I looked away so as not to make things worse for him, thinking, like Ma-D, "What *is* the world coming to?"

. . .

On the way down to the sheriff's department, Walter asked me what I thought we should get for Clyde as a way of thanking him for his help. I thought about it for a while and then said, "I'm not sure. He's not the kind of guy that needs a lot 'things'. Something, maybe, that would make it a little easier for him getting supplies from the road to his place. It's a pretty long hike. Like some sort of cart or something."

"Let me think about it," Walter said.

We both went into the sheriff's department and asked for Captain Wykowski, as Sheriff Lyman had told Walter to do. The captain walked out to the reception area carrying the leather pouch. We made introductions and shook hands. As the captain was shaking my hand he said, "Charlie Wykowski. I understand you're quite the hero."

"Hardly," I said.

"That's not the way I heard it. Congratulations. I'll bet that took some doing."

"Well," I said, "you're right about that." A light bulb went on in my head: Charlie was the name the sheriff used when I overheard the conversation in the bathroom — a scene from what seemed a very long time ago. If it was the same "Charlie," then he knew about the gnomes.

I looked Charlie in the eyes. In an instant exchange, we both realized that each of us knew the real story. Leaning into me, Captain Wykowski said, "I may want to take you out for a hamburger some time. I'd like to hear the whole story."

"Sure. Any time," I said.

"If he tells you the whole story," Walter said to the captain, "will you tell me? I feel like I'm getting the *Reader's Digest* condensed version, if you know what I mean."

"I'll leave that up to Nick, Mr. Dobson. Glad things worked out like they did. Frankly, we didn't have much hope for this one," he said, handing Walter the pouch.

"Ah... do you have a paper bag or something to put that in? I'd feel a little less conspicuous walking out of here."

"I should have thought of that. Let me go see what I can find."

The captain walked off, leaving Walter fidgeting with the pouch.

"'Local hero,'" he said, punching me in the arm. The captain returned with a grocery sack and handed it Walter.

"Will that do?"

"Just fine," Walter said, putting the pouch in the bag. "Thanks for your help."

"I think it's us that should be thanking Nick for his help," the captain said, waving us off.

"See, I told you I was right," Walter said to me as we were leaving the building: 'local hero'."

·   ·   ·

When we got to the truck, Walter gave the bag to me and told me to stuff it under my seat. He started the truck and turned to me: "I may have an idea."

"An idea for Clyde?"

"Yeah. I've got a friend over in Sonoma that might have just what we're looking for. Wanna' go take a look?"

"Sure," I said, thinking to myself that I liked this new, non-grouchy Walter.

We didn't talk much on the drive over to Sonoma. Occasionally Walter would point out something to me, but mostly it was just fine to ride in silence, through the vineyard-covered rolling hills.

Once we reached the town of Sonoma, Walter kept on driving. "Where we going?" I asked.

"Just outside of town. Little place called El Verano."

El Verano wasn't much more than a bend in the road, with hayfields, prune orchards and big eucalyptus trees lining both sides of the road. Walter slowed the truck and turned down a nondescript gravel driveway with prune orchards on both sides. We arrived at a small, two-story farm house with a big white barn to one side.

Walter got out of truck and then, not seeing anyone, leaned back in and honked the horn a couple of times. "Jack doesn't hear so well," Walter said.

In a minute or so, a tall, white-haired man in overalls stepped around the barn and yelled "Walter! Good to see you." I got out of the truck and walked over to where they were standing.

"Jack, I'd like you to meet Nick. You've heard me talk about him. Jack, this is Nick."

"Nice to meet you, sir," I said, shaking his hand.

"And nice to meet you, son." Jack turned to Walter and said, "To what do I owe the pleasure?"

"Nick and I are on a mission to find just the right thing for someone who did a good turn for us. We were wondering if you were still raising those little asses?"

I looked at Walter in disbelief. What in the world was he talking about?

"Sure 'nuf. Never going to give them up. They're about the only fun I have any more."

"Can we take a look?"

"Sure. I was just giving them some feed."

Jack led the way behind the barn. A large corral was attached to the back side, containing a dozen small donkeys, about the same size as Quicksilver. I didn't even know such an animal existed.

"Whaddaya' think?" Walter asked me.

"I think they're great."

"No, whaddaya' think about getting one of these for Clyde?"

"Oh, I get it." I said and then thought for a minute. "I think you might be right."

"Jack, is it all right if I show Nick inside the barn?"

"Sure, help yourself."

Walter and I walked around to the front of the barn and went in. Inside there were six different small wooden carts lined up, all different. Some had seats that you could sit on; others were just box carts without seats.

"When you said 'a cart or something,'" Walter said, "I thought of my friend Jack here. He makes these carts himself. But I'm thinkin' that a donkey and a cart is even better. What do you think?"

"I think it makes sense. Besides, I think Clyde could use a little company up there."

"Let's go talk to Jack," Walter said.

When we got back to the corral, Jack was sitting on the corral fence, surrounded by the donkeys, talking to each one of them.

"So, Jack, can you bear to part with one?" Walter asked.

"Nope."

"Nope? You mean you can't sell me one?"

"No, but I can sell you two."

"Two?"

"Yeah, two. Donkeys don't like to be by themselves. They get lonely and out-of-sorts. Gotta' have at least two. They can get sick from being lonely. Just like anybody else."

"I didn't know that," Walter said.

"Yep. Scientifically proven."

Walter looked at me. I pushed my shoulders up, thinking it was up to Walter.

"What about a cart, Jack? Could you build us one?"

"Sure I can. But if you want the donkeys to pull a cart, you gotta' get the bigger ones — at least 34 inches tall."

"Do you breed them to be that big?" Walter asked.

"Not really. They just all come out different. You know these donkeys are just the way God made 'em. They're not the product of breeding. They're a naturally dwarf breed. They're found on just two islands — Sicily and Sardinia — off the coast of Italy."

"I didn't know that either," Walter said.

I wondered to myself if that's what the gnomes were — what Jack just said — a naturally dwarf breed: "Just as God made 'em."

"So, to answer your question, I can build you a cart and I can sell you two donkeys," Jack said.

"It's a deal," Walter said, smiling at me. "Can we show you which cart we want?"

"Sure," Jack said.

We walked back to the barn and I picked out the smallest box cart, thinking it made the most sense, considering how narrow the paths were around Clyde's place. I had no idea how Clyde was going to react to a couple of donkeys, but somehow the idea seemed like it might work. Jack said he could have the cart done in a couple of weeks. Walter told Jack to give him a call when it was done and we'd come back over with the horse trailer and pick out which of the donkeys we wanted then. I'd never seen Walter act quite so impulsively. Normally it took him forever and a day to make a decision. I thought about Ma-D's question that morning at breakfast: *What is the world coming to?* I didn't know, but it was kind of fun.

•   •   •

As if the donkeys and cart weren't enough, on the way home, Walter spied a vegetable stand next to the road just outside Sonoma, with a bunch of plastic pails out front, filled with flowers. Walter pulled to a stop and went into the stand, emerging a couple of minutes later with a big bouquet of sweet peas and a large honeydew melon. He held the melon up in front of me, saying, "It may not be a swimming pool, but honeydew's her favorite."

Portrait of Robert Louis Stevenson painted
by John Singer Sargent in 1887.

Chapter XXVII

A Night Visitor

Monday, June 26 1967
Twin Oaks Pony Farm
St. Helena, California

The next day after breakfast, Ma-D got it into her head to clean the Winnebago, inside and out. If Walter was going to take it in to be serviced, she didn't want anyone at the garage to think we were a slovenly bunch. Ma-D enlisted my help and told me to go get my old red wagon from the barn so I could take all the cleaning supplies out to the Winnebago in one trip. Meanwhile, Walter said he was going to make the last repairs to the rail fence around the property so I could start painting it later in the week.

I decided to start by washing the outside of the Winnebago, which involved getting a ladder, an old wash tub, and a long-handled brush. It was a bigger job than I'd imagined, but after I was done, the Winnebago looked almost new. Ma-D was going all out on the inside — curtains, cushions, everything. We all broke for a quick lunch and then went right back to work. Ma-D and I finished up around 3 o'clock, leaving all the windows and doors of the Winnebago open so it could air out.

As usual, the day had heated up — to over 90 degrees. I called for Snoops and started walking down to the river so we could both go for a swim. On our way there, we passed Chuy's house. Mrs. Martinez, Chuy's mom, was out watering the garden. I stopped to say hello and she said Chuy was doing okay but he was homesick. I wondered, as I continued walking to the river, whether Chuy would believe me about everything that had happened so far this summer. *Probably not,* I decided. If the situation were reversed, and Chuy told me the same story, I probably wouldn't have believed him either. As stories go, it was out there — *way* out there.

Snoops and I stayed at the river for a while, flopping around in the water, skipping rocks — which caused Snoops to bark like crazy — and exploring along the banks. I didn't find anything but a big brownish salamander under a rotten log. After about an hour, we walked back to the farm. I took a shower, put on clean clothes, and then went out and sat on the porch swing with a pen and my journal. After everything that had happened over the last couple of weeks, my most recent entries seemed tame — boring, almost.

I finished writing and then sat and daydreamed about how the meeting be-tween Grandma Hattie and King Gob might go. Somehow, the whole thing was a little hard to imagine. And how exactly was I supposed to help the king get a gnome back from Kauai? My train of thought was interrupted by Ma-D calling me for dinner. *Just as well,* I thought, *because — just like trying to imagine the meeting between Hattie and the king — I was having an even harder time imagining how I was supposed to find a gnome on some island in the middle of the Pacific Ocean and bring him back to California. Although, I gotta' say, it sounded like it could be fun. Maybe.*

.   .   .

Walter was standing on the back porch, tending the barbecue. I saw a platter full of t-bone steaks on the table next to grill.

"Those look good," I said.

"The best the butcher had," Walter said.

"What's the occasion?" I asked.

"Just a small reward for all of us for working so hard today."

I walked into the kitchen. Ma-D was tossing a salad in a big wooden bowl. In a few minutes, Walter came in with the platter of grilled steaks. Ma-D took three big baked potatoes out of the oven and put one on each plate. Walter did the same with the steaks and then Ma-D came back and added a big spoonful of creamed spinach.

"Man, that looks good," I said.

"Well, dig in," Walter said.

Which is exactly what we all did. The bouquet of sweet peas on the table reminded me of just how much the mood had changed at the farm over the past few days.

"Nick and I will do the dishes, Ma-D. You go in the living room and warm up the t.v." Walter said.

Walter and I made quick work of the dishes and joined Ma-D in the living room, Snoops following behind. I sat on the couch and put my feet up on the ottoman and kind of slid down, making myself seriously comfortable. We watched *Gun-smoke* and *The Lucy Show*, both of which were okay, but I was glad to see them come to an end as I was practically falling asleep on the couch. I looked at Ma-D and Walter and they looked like they were half-asleep, too. We said our good-nights and Snoops and I walked across to the bunkhouse. There were no lights on, which was strange, until I remembered Henry wasn't there. "Looks like we've got the place to ourselves," I said to Snoops, as we went inside. I brushed my teeth and got in bed. I thought about reading but decided I was too tired. I turned out the light and immediately fell asleep.

.   .   .

I had only been asleep for a couple of hours when Snoops started barking the kind of bark he made when something was really wrong. I got him to stop and was getting out of bed when I heard a light knocking at the front door of the bunkhouse. I looked at my watch: a little after midnight. Who in the world would be knocking at this time of night, I wondered? I lifted the curtain on the front door and didn't see anyone. I opened the door a little and Snoops started barking even louder. I looked down. G was standing there, looking absolutely terrified. I held Snoops by the collar and told him to stop barking. Walter yelled out the second story bedroom window from the main house.

"What's going on, Nick?"

"Nothing," I said, ushering G into the bunkhouse, trying to act like there was nothing unusual about someone showing up at your door in the middle of the night. "Snoops just caught wind of a skunk, I think."

"Make him quiet down will you."

"I will."

I closed the door to the bunkhouse. G just stood there shaking while Snoops smelled him all over.

"Hold on G. Let me put Snoops in my bedroom." I said, leading him away. I closed the bedroom door and went back to the living room to a visibly relieved G. I closed the curtains in the living room and turned on one of the lamps.

"Sorry about that, G. Sit down." G had to jump up onto the couch. When he scooched himself back, his feet stuck out straight in front of him.

"I'm not too crazy about dogs," G said.

"I can see why."

"He'll be okay there in your room?" G asked, warily.

"Yeah, he'll be fine."

"Well, that's over," G said, still shaking a little, "kind of."

"Are you okay?"

"I will be in a minute or two."

I felt badly for him, saying "I'm glad you're here."

"I brought you *White Fang*, so you could finish it," G. said, holding up the book. I hadn't even noticed he was carrying it.

"Thanks. I've been looking for something good to read."

"I'm always looking for something good to read," G said, a little sadly.

I wasn't quite sure why I asked, but I did. "Does your father know you're out?"

"Probably not, but it's not a big deal. He was kind of out of it when I left."

Sensing he might be lonely, I asked if the prince had anyone to pal around with up on the mountain.

"Not really. A couple of the guys are okay, but most of them are getting old. And old-fashioned. My best friend, Sulo, was one of the guys who jumped ship in Kauai."

"That's too bad," I said. "My best friend — he lives just down the lane — is away in Mexico this summer. I know how it is."

"I know where Mexico is," G said, brightening a little. "It was in one of the books I found — a road atlas. It's south of here, right?"

"Yeah," I said, "Mexico starts south of the California border. I was silent for a moment and then asked "How do you find the books you read?"

"Any way I can," G said. "I found the atlas in a garbage can next to a gas station in Calistoga. And there used to be a bookstore on Lincoln Avenue that put books out in front of the store. Every so often, they'd forget and leave them out all night. That's where I got most of the ones I have. I'd leave some gold, of course, to pay for them. But that hasn't happened in a long time." This time it was G's turn to be silent. "What I'd really like to do is go to school," he finally said.

"Really?" I said.

"Yeah. Really."

"Your tribe doesn't have any school?"

"Not really. We're supposed to learn what we need to know by listening to stories told by the old ones. We're not much for writing things down. It's okay, but ever since we came to the mountain, I've had the feeling that there's a whole lot more to learn than what I've been told. But that's the rub."

"What do you mean?" I asked.

"What makes us special is that we haven't changed like you Uplanders have. Over the centuries, you've grown, learned new things and, just as importantly, forgotten things. We're just the opposite of you in so many ways. We still remember things from our beginnings, thousands of years ago. We haven't changed. The world changed around us."

"Like what?"

"Well, everyone used to live in caves. We still do, but you don't. And our magic — it's natural magic — earth magic. It's part of us and we're part of it. You Uplanders have progressed in so many ways, and yet most of you left your magic behind, so far behind you can't even remember what it's like. For us, it's just like I said, a natural part of the natural world. And we're part of that world — just like the birds and the bees and the bears and the trees — you name it — we're all con-nected. It's an unusual Uplander who understands that connection. I'd be lying if I didn't say there are some things you have that I'd like to have — sometimes it feels like I'm stuck between two worlds."

"What is it that you'd like from, from," I hesitated, "our world? "

"Knowledge, I suppose. Knowledge of the modern world. You have your own magic and mysteries I know almost nothing about."

I thought for a minute. "Would your father let you go to school?"

"I doubt it. I wouldn't even know how to ask him. Besides, he sees it as his duty that we never change and forget our ways."

"We have to go to school whether we want to or not," I said.

"Who wouldn't want to go to school?"

"Oh, there are some people who just don't like it."

"I can't even imagine..." G said, trailing off.

"Speaking of your father," I said, "would you deliver a message to him?"

"Sure."

"Will you tell him that I've set up the meeting with my grandmother for next Monday. It has to be at her place because she's too old to be hiking around your mountain in the dark. She's agreed to send her car and driver to pick him up. I'll be there, too, so tell him not to worry. He should be in that parking area next to the road, at the entrance of the trail, at 11:30. Do you know where I'm talking about?"

"Yeah. I sometimes find things to read there."

"Do you think he'll do it?"

"Probably. I've never known him to leave the mountain, but I think he'd do just about anything if he thought it would get Dagywn back."

"Good," I said. "Oh, and I have the gold to return to him. Would you take it with you and give it to him?"

"Sure."

"Wait here for just a minute. I have to go over to the house to get it."

"Your dog won't get out?"

"No, he can't get out. Don't worry."

I walked across the lawn in the dark. The other day, when we got home with the gold, Walter didn't know where to put it, so he hid it in the freezer. Ma-D got mad at him because, she said, "We don't know where it's been," and made him wrap it in a plastic bag first. I entered the kitchen as quietly as I could and retrieved the plastic-wrapped leather pouch from the freezer.

I walked back over to the bunkhouse and handed the pouch to G.

"It's freezing," G said, laying it down on the couch. "Why's it so cold?"

"It's kind of a long story. It won't stay frozen for long."

"Do you mind if I ask you a question?"

"Like what?"

"I was just wondering what it was I witnessed the other night on the mountain? The ceremony, or whatever it was — with all the bonfires and music."

"It was our annual celebration of the longest day of the year. It's the day we celebrate the year that's just passed, and look forward to the year that's to come."

"The summer solstice."

"Is that what your people call it?"

"Yeah."

"Well, this year there was also a full moon that night, so it was very special."

"Like how?"

"We usually don't roll out the ball of liquid silver — it's our prize possession."

"We call it quicksilver, or mercury."

"Yeah, we've heard that. That ball is all that we've mined over the years on the mountain. It started as a little ball my father brought with him from the Old Country. Now it's bigger than any tribe has ever been able to gather together. It's one of the reasons my father thinks this is where we belong. Usually the celebration goes on all night long and ends with the silver ball being shattered into little rolling bits and then gathered back together again into one big ball. Your presence put a quick end to all that. The men were very disappointed."

"I didn't mean to break up the party."

"Everyone knows that. The men have no intention of getting even with you."

"That's a relief," I said, and then added, "how would they get even — if they wanted to?"

Prince G paused for a minute. "Maybe it's best if you don't know."

"Okay," I said, disappointed. I wanted to know if some of the stuff I'd read was true. "One other question — were your people always so... were they always the size they are now?"

"In the beginning we were a little bigger than we are now, but we've always been naturally small. Over the eons, we've become smaller."

"And each of you has a unique ability, right?"

"Right."

"What's yours?"

G laughed softly. "I can levitate things."

"Levitate?"

"Yeah. To tell you the truth, it doesn't come in all that handy. Except for the time a huge rock rolled onto Tuomo's foot — I was a hero for a couple of days after that."

"Can you levitate anything?"

"Just about," G said as the copy of *White Fang* sprang off the couch where he was sitting and sailed across the room. I caught it in mid-air.

"Wow," I said, not quite believing what I'd seen.

Turning serious, G said, "There was one other time..."

"One other time, what?" I asked.

"One other time my ability to levitate actually did some good."

"When was that?"

"Ten years ago. I saved a little Uplander boy's life."

"Really?"

"Yeah. Witbeck and I were exploring the east side of the mountain when we heard a loud crash. A car had run into a tree; it was really awful. There was a man and a woman and two young boys. Everyone in the car, except for the youngest boy, was dead. The youngest boy was breathing, but not conscious. I levitated him out of the car and laid him down on the side of the road just as the car exploded into flames. It wasn't long before another car with flashing red lights came over the mountain and stopped. Witbeck and I hid behind a tree trunk and watched over the boy until he was taken away. I don't know why, but I've always felt certain he survived."

"He did," I said seriously.

"Why do you say that?" G asked, his head to one side.

I had my head down and was silent for a minute. When I looked up my eyes were welling with tears. "Because that little boy was me."

G was silent for a minute and then said "actually, I knew that, but I didn't want to just come right out and say it. I didn't want to you to think the situation was any weirder than it already is."

"What do you mean?" I asked.

"Well, I probably shouldn't be telling you this, but my father's been aware of just about everything you've done since the accident. He's been watching you."

"Watching me? Like how?"

"Not him, actually. He has the crows do most of his watching."

"Crows?" I said. *This* is *getting weird*, I thought to myself.

"Yeah. They're naturally nosy and have quite the vocabulary. Plus they can get just about anywhere they want, and they're easy to understand."

"I don't believe this. Why?" I said as much to myself as to G.

"Let's just say it has everything to do with getting Dagywn back. It always has been, going all the way back to Captain Niebaum and the guys jumping ship. After the car accident, it came down to just you and your grandma. And he never thought your grandmother was the one for the job. No offense, but you said yourself that she's old. So it's been down to just you for some time now. You should know he knew all about your visit to your grandma in San Francisco, the fact that you had the amulet — the whole thing."

"So why did we go through that... whatever it was the other night — him pretending that he didn't know who I was?"

"From what he was told by Whitbeck and the crows, he knew who you were, but he had never met you in person — he had never seen you. In order to be certain you were who you said you were, he needed to see that amulet as proof. And then, well, you dropped it, which complicated things."

We both sat quietly for a bit, me completely lost in thought with this new information. I snapped out of it, saying "well, I guess I owe you my life — thanks for what you did, G" I said earnestly, giving him a hug. G was clearly uncomfortable. He was right about one thing, though — the situation *was* weird. So weird, in fact, I'd have to figure out what it all really meant later, when I had time to think it through. As if he were reading my mind, G asked "Can we talk about something else?" I was happy to oblige and from out of nowhere I said, "Have you ever read any books by Robert Louis Stevenson?"

"No."

"Well, he's a writer who was originally from Scotland, but he came to California, almost a hundred years ago, to marry a woman who lived here. He didn't have any money for a honeymoon, so he and his new wife spent their first summer together in an abandoned mine building on Mt. St. Helena."

"Yeah, I've read that plaque the Uplanders put there a long time ago."

"Anyway, a while after his stay there, he wrote a book called *Treasure Island*. I have a copy. It's really good. Do you want to read it?"

"Sure," G said enthusiastically.

"Let me get it," I said, walking to my room, "don't worry, I won't let Snoops out."

I returned with the book and handed it to G. "You know that little cave on the side of the mountain where all the fuchsias are?"

"Sure. I helped plant them there."

"Well, Stevenson knew about it, too, and there are a lot of people who think he got the idea for the treasure cave in *Treasure Island* from that cave on Mt. St. Helena."

"Really?"

"Yeah."

"Do you know what year he was on the mountain?"

"It was 1880."

"I was pretty young and don't remember that much, but we were already on the mountain then. I didn't know his name but it must the same man some of the old guys still laugh about — they claim he was the only Uplander they didn't take anything from because he didn't have anything to take."

"Really?" Now it was my turn to be surprised. "How old were you?"

"I've been trying to figure out how our years compare to yours. I think it's about 10 years to 1, so in your years, I would have been around five years old."

I did some quick calculating in my head and said "so you and I are about the same age."

"Yeah. That's one of the reasons I wanted to come see you. Just to be able to talk with someone my own age. Don't get me wrong, I have a lot of respect for my people and the old ones, but sometimes... sometimes it's just kind of a pain."

"I know what you mean. I don't know why, but I seem to spend a lot of time around my 'elders', too. They're all pretty cool, but sometimes if I see an old person coming my way, I feel like running in the opposite direction."

G laughed. It was the first time I'd heard him laugh.

"I should get going," G said.

"Okay. But I'm glad you came, G. I hope you like the book."

"I'm sure I will. Thanks. And I hope it doesn't bother you too much that my

father's been watching you."

"I'll get over it, I guess," I said honestly. "Oh, there's one thing I haven't been able to figure out."

"What's that?"

"What's the deal with those fuchsia plants, anyway?"

G laughed again. "Oh, those. It was one of Witbeck's more elaborate schemes. Without Dagywn, none of us can appear and disappear at will, like we can when he's around — except Witbeck, that is — that's his one special power. So he was trying to come up with a way for my father to get around without having to walk — he hates walking. Like I said, we're adept at communicating with all living things. So Witbeck made a deal with the hummingbirds that if we planted and maintained a whole bunch of fuchsias — which is their favorite flower to get nectar from — they'd be responsible for transporting my father around."

"Like how?" I said, confused.

"Witbeck had Tuomo, who's our main inventor and handyman, make a kind of sling for him."

"A sling?"

"Yeah. Tuomo knit and tied a bunch of vines together, kind of like a fishing net, with a bunch of long leads. The idea was for my father to sit in the sling part and for the hummingbirds to pull him through the air by holding onto the leads. He was all excited, because you know how fast hummingbirds fly, right?"

"Yeah, I do. Did it work?

"No."

"Why not?"

"You've seen my father. It seems like every year he gets heavier. The hummingbirds couldn't even get him off the ground."

I laughed. "Sorry, I shouldn't laugh, but that must have been something."

"Everyone who was there had to scatter, they were laughing so hard. It was bad. Witbeck caught all hell from my father for humiliating him. You want to see

how it works?"

"What do you mean?"

"It may not have worked for him, but it does for me. That's how I got here tonight."

"Really?".

"Yeah. Come on. Take a look."

I followed G out of the bunkhouse and over to the pasture behind the barn. The moon was beginning to wane, so there wasn't much light, but the closer I got to the wire fence, I could make out hundreds of small, shimmering shapes sitting on the top wire and the sling laid out on the pasture, just as G had described it.

G crawled under the fence and positioned himself in the middle of the sling, pulling it up under his backside. "See you later," G said, and then made a kind of clicking noise. The hummingbirds rose up in unison, wings fluttering so fast they hummed, and then grabbed onto the leads. In a second, G was aloft, straight up in the air, and then, in the next second he disappeared with a whooshing sound into the dark, starry night.

"Now that was very cool," I said under my breath.

Grandma Hattie's house in Rutherford was on the same property
as the winery and not that far from Walter and Ma'D's pony farm.

Chapter XXVIII

Advance Planning

Tuesday, June 27 through July 2, 1967
Twin Oaks Pony Farm and Grandma Hattie's house at Eagle's Nook
St. Helena and Rutherford, California

First thing Tuesday morning, right after breakfast, Walter and I went to get paint at Steve's Hardware store. On the way there, I told Walter that I'd had a visitor the night before.

"I didn't think it was a skunk," Walter said. "So who was it and what did they want?"

"Actually, it was the son of the person who had Quicksilver. He's a good guy. We're both about the same age. He was going back to his father's, so I gave him the gold to return."

"You trust him to get it back to his dad?"

"Definitely."

"Any particular reason he showed up in the middle of the night?"

I hesitated. I decided it was easiest to just go with the truth again. "It's the custom of his people to reverse day and night. For him, it was like showing up at noon."

Walter shook his head. "I used to think I wanted to know the whole story, but I'm not so sure," he said, adding "you and Quicksilver are back and that's all that's really important."

"Right," I said, relieved that he was willing to leave it at that.

We pulled into the parking lot at the back of Steve's and went in through the back door. Walter bought a five-gallon bucket of white paint for the rail fence that enclosed the entire farm. I carried the heavy bucket out to the parking lot and slid it into the back of the truck, thinking it contained five gallons of hard work. Once back at the farm, Walter simply handed me two new packages of sandpaper and told me to "have at it." I went into the bunkhouse and to get my hat, then started in on the job.

Sanding the fence took the better part of two full days. For the rest of the week, I followed the same routine. Up early, paint until around 3 or 4 o'clock, and then knock off and go to the river for a swim. Luckily, it wasn't as hot as usual, but not even Snoops wanted to stick around and watch me paint when it started to warm up after lunch.

I was happy with the mindless work. It allowed me to think about other things, most of which led back to the gnomes, being watched (which, I had to admit, really did creep me out) and what it would be like to be one of them. I thought that G, even though he was a prince, probably didn't have such a great life. I wondered whether he would ever have a chance to go to school. I doubted it. That led to thinking about my own school and whether or not I'd be able to share what had happened this summer with anyone there. The more I thought about it, the more I was sure the only person who might believe me was Mr. Hayes — and even he was iffy. Oh, and I should mention that I was looking at Sammy, Ma-D's pet crow, with whole new eyes these days. Seemed to me there was every possibility he was a spy. How weird is that? Kind of made me want to chase him off the farm, but I didn't think Ma-D would approve.

I finished painting the fence on Sunday, just before lunch. It looked good and Walter seemed happy, only finding a couple of "holidays," as he called the spots I missed. I waited until 4 o'clock before riding my bicycle over to see Grandma Hattie at Eagle's Nook. It was a short ride down the highway to her house, which was tucked up against Mt. St. John, the highest peak on the western side of the valley. I was there in less than fifteen minutes.

Grandma Hattie's house was a big Victorian mansion, three stories tall and built out of wood, but nowhere near as big as her house in San Francisco. I walked my bicycle up the front steps, onto the big porch that wrapped around the entire house. I knocked on the front door and then let myself in. Compared to the bright heat outdoors, it was dim and cool inside. Most of the rooms had shiny wood floors and dark wood paneling, giving the place a comfortable feeling, even with its high ceilings. From open windows here and there, the saturated green of the vineyards surrounding the house came peeking in. I had always liked that house.

"Anybody home?" I yelled.

"In the kitchen," Hattie hollered. Come on in."

I found them all there — Hattie, Doyle, and Katia — making tall glasses of iced tea. There were hugs, kisses, and handshakes all around. Hattie stood back and said "what's that on your head?" I'd forgotten to take my hat off when I came in the house.

"It's my lucky hat," I said, taking it off.

"Lucky hat?" Grandma Hattie said. "That's a little like naming a one-eyed, three-legged dog 'Lucky'. You ought to let me buy you a new one."

"Maybe someday, Grandma, but I think there's still some luck left in this one," I said.

"If you say so," Hattie said, shaking her head, "let's go out to the front porch and take a load off."

I followed Hattie out to the porch, carrying the glasses of iced tea. We sat down in two identical white wicker rocking chairs, with a table in between.

"Isn't this lovely," Hattie said, raising her iced tea in a salute to the view across the vineyards and the very blue eastern hills.

"Sure is," I said.

"The heat always takes me a couple of days to get used to. It's so different from the city. What was it Mark Twain said? 'The coldest winter I ever spent was a summer in San Francisco?' I must admit, though, I think the heat does these old bones good. I don't even need that stupid cane when I'm here. But enough about me. We have things to discuss, don't we?"

"Yes, ma'am, we do."

"What are you thinking?"

What I was thinking was how much I should tell grandma about the king. Since Prince G told me about my being watched, I'd given the situation some thought. It wasn't that I disliked the king — for some reason he was hard not to like — but I definitely didn't trust him. And I didn't want to turn grandma against him before she had a chance to judge him for herself. After all, his watching me was my problem, not hers. I decided to leave the watching part out, at least for the time being.

"I'm thinking... how should I say this? I'm thinking that this meeting tomorrow is going to be interesting."

"'Interesting? Oh dear," Hattie said.

"What's wrong?"

"Nothing really, but that was the second to worst thing we could say about a date, back when I was in college."

"What was the first worst thing?" I asked.

"*Nice*," Hattie said laughing. "I'm sorry. I'm getting us off the subject. What exactly do you mean by 'interesting'?"

"Well, the king is... why am I having such a hard time describing him?"

"Autocratic?" Hattie asked.

"If that means he hogs the stage, then yes."

"Most kings do hog the stage," Hattie said. "It seems to go with the territory."

"And I have no idea what he has in mind about getting that wizard back from Kauai. Oh, and another thing. He kept the amulet."

"Really?" Hattie said, turning to look across the vineyards.

"He said he'll give it back if he gets what he wants."

"Well, he's got a helluva' crust, doesn't he? This *is* going to be interesting."

"Have you asked Doyle about picking up the king?"

"Yes. He fine with it."

"So I guess you told him what to expect — I mean the whole gnome thing?"

"Oh yes. He's a funny one, that Doyle. He didn't bat an eye. In fact, he seemed amused."

"Oh, he'll be amused all right," I said. "I'm thinking it's best if I go with him. I know the spot where they're supposed to meet up."

"Okay."

I hestitated for a moment and then said, "There's one more thing."

"What's that?" Grandma Hattie asked.

I explained the connection between G and me, and how G had almost certainly saved my life after the accident. Hattie was rarely surprised, but the news came as a shock and I could tell it saddened her. After a minute, she stood up and composed herself and then hugged me, saying, "Well, we owe him a debt of gratitude then, don't we?"

"I just thought you needed to know. I'll be here around 11 o'clock tomorrow night."

Hattie thought for a minute. "No, I don't think so. Why don't we invite Ma-D and Walter to dinner tomorrow? And then you can spend the night. I'll tell Ma-D and Walter that you and I have 'things' to talk about. Which, of course, we do."

"Okay. Do you want me to ask them or will you?"

"I'll call them after you leave."

I looked at my watch. "Speaking of which, I should probably go. Ma-D likes to serve dinner early on Sundays. She likes the kitchen to be cleaned up before we watch *The Ed Sullivan Show* and *Bonanza*."

"Does she watch *Bonanza* too? Oh, I just love that Little Joe. What a dish!"

I didn't really know what to say, so I just stood there for a second and finally said, "Well, okay then. I'll talk with you tomorrow."

"Ciao, bambino," she said waving. "See you tomorrow."

I was halfway down the steps, carrying my bicycle, when I turned around. "I almost forgot, Grandma. The king's a big eater. You might want to have something on hand for him to snack on."

"No, we wouldn't want him peckish, would we? Bad for negotiations. I'll have Katia see to it," Hattie said with a slight smile. "Good lord, if she knew who she was cooking for, she'd come undone."

"I think you're right about that Grandma. See you tomorrow."

The winding road up to Robert Louis Stevenson State Park on the top of Mt. St. Helena was a bit of a challenge for Grandma Hattie's huge limousine.

Chapter XXIX

Summit at Eagle's Nook

Monday, July 3, 1967
Grandma Hattie's house at Eagle's Nook
Rutherford, California

The next day I decided to go over to Hattie's a little early, just in case there was something she needed done before the night's big event. When I got there at around 4:30, there was a white panel truck in front of the house, with the name of the local appliance store painted on its side. The front door of the house was wide open and I could hear commotion in the kitchen.

When I entered the kitchen, sure enough everyone was in there — Hattie, Doyle, Katia and two guys from the appliance store.

"Hey everyone. What's going on?"

"You're just in time, I. Space age technology has arrived at Eagle's Nook," Hattie said.

"What is it?" I said, watching the guys from the appliance store pull something out of a big box.

"A microwave oven," Hattie said.

"Cool," I said. "I've heard about them." I looked in Katia's direction and noticed she was rolling her eyes.

"Heats up a cup of coffee in a minute and pops popcorn in three. No muss, no fuss," Hattie said, clearly pleased with herself.

The appliance guys struggled to get the oven up on the kitchen counter. They finally got it where Hattie wanted it and removed all the plastic and cardboard packing pieces and plugged it in.

"Now remember," one of the appliance guys said, "no metal or aluminum foil in there. Glass and plastic are all right."

"It won't melt the plastic?" Hattie asked.

"Nope. It just heats the food inside."

"Isn't that amazing?" Hattie said, looking around at all of us.

"As far as I know, you're the first person in St. Helena to have one, Mrs. Sinclair."

"That's me," Hattie said, "a real trailblazer."

The guys put all the packing stuff into the empty box and took off.

We all stood in the kitchen, staring at the new oven.

"It's going to make Katia's job much easier, don't you think?" Hattie said, looking at Katia.

"Yes, ma'am," Katia said flatly, not convinced in the slightest.

"Speaking of which, I've decided we're going to have take-out Chinese tonight. Doesn't that sound good?"

"Yeah, that's a good idea," I said.

"Come out on the porch, Doyle. You too, Nick."

Doyle and I followed Hattie out to the porch. "I decided not to ask Katia to cook something for our 'after hours' meeting tonight. She'd know something was up. So order a lot," she said, pulling a hundred dollar bill out of her pocket, "so there's plenty of leftovers".

"What do you want us to get?"

"You and Doyle choose. But be sure and get plenty of fried won-tons. I love those things."

"Okay," I said, putting the hundred dollar bill in my wallet. "Should we go now?"

"I think so. What time are Ma-D and Walter coming?"

"Six."

"Perfect. Go now, and then we won't have to worry about it."

Doyle and I drove to the Chinese restaurant in the truck Hattie kept at the winery. Once inside the restaurant, Doyle and I both took a menu and started ordering. The man behind the counter repeated the order and then looked at us: "That sounds like big party."

"More like two parties," I said, smiling.

Doyle and I sat down at one of the tables and discussed the details of the night's activities, although, in truth, there wasn't much to discuss, other than what time we should leave to pick up the king. I wondered if Doyle was as excited as I was, but didn't ask. We both agreed that 11:15 would give us plenty of time to meet the king at midnight up on Mt. St. Helena.

One of the cooks brought out two big

The Chinese restaurant in St. Helena.

cardboard boxes filled with little white boxes of food and set them on the counter. "She did say 'a lot'," I said, looking at all the food. Doyle and I each carried a box and put them in the back of the truck.

By the time we got back to Hattie's, Walter and Ma-D were already there, just getting out of their truck.

We exchanged greetings and then Doyle and I each took a box out of the truck and carried them into the house.

"What in the world is that?" Ma-D asked.

"Dinner," I said.

"Dinner?" Ma-D said in disbelief.

"Yeah, Chinese take-out."

"You didn't tell me the football team was coming," Ma-D said.

"Grandma just wanted to be sure that we had some leftovers," I replied.

"Your grandmother!" Ma-D said, shaking her head.

*   *   *

We had dinner out on the screened porch. It was a warm evening with a slight breeze. We rarely went out to dinner, so the Chinese food tasted both different and delicious. Everyone had seconds, except for Hattie, who said she had to watch her "girlish figure." The sun was casting long shadows across the vineyards when Katia had finished clearing the table and brought out the fortune cookies. I thought back to the last time I had Chinese food at the end of the school year, at the place Mr. Hayes had taken us in Santa Cruz. I remembered my fortune cookie — what had it said? "A legacy, however obscure, will soon be yours." That was it, I thought. "A legacy, however obscure... ". It was true. Captain Niebaum's log was a fairly obscure legacy, but it had certainly led to something pretty fantastic. "With more to come," I thought to myself.

"Oh my," Hattie said, holding the paper fortune in her hands.

"What is it, Hattie?" Ma-D asked.

"Let me put my glasses on," she said, "I've got to be sure I'm reading this right. 'You would look better in a butch haircut,'" she said, laughing. "There you have it. What do you think?"

"I think you got Walter's fortune," Ma-D said.

"Mine says, 'Expect a trip to an exotic locale in the near future,'" I said.

"Sacramento. The fair," Walter said.

"I don't know if I'd call Sacramento 'exotic,'" I said.

"It's exotic enough for me," Walter said, defensively.

"All right, Sacramento it is," I said, secretly hoping that it might be Kauai.

. . .

Walter and Ma-D stayed a while longer and then took off back to the farm, saying they didn't like leaving Snoops alone for too long, especially when Henry wasn't around. Hattie and I went into the kitchen. Katia had her hands on her hips, looking perplexed.

"What do you want me to do with all these leftovers?" she asked Hattie.

"Just put all the little boxes into one box and put them in the refrigerator," Hattie said.

"We'll never eat them all," Katia complained.

"Oh, I don't know. I love Chinese food for breakfast."

"Are you going to be here for breakfast?" Katia asked me.

"Oh, I'm sorry, Katia. I forgot to tell you. Nick's spending the night. Is the blue room made up?" Hattie said.

"No. I didn't know we were expecting guests," Katia said, obviously perturbed.

"Nick's hardly a guest, Katia. Would you mind making it up, please?"

Katia said something in German I couldn't understand and clumped off up the stairs.

Hattie, Doyle and I all looked at each other. We didn't have to say anything because we were all in agreement: Katia was a pill.

"I think I'm going to take a rest," Hattie announced. "I have a feeling we have a long night ahead of us. What are you men going to do?"

I looked at Doyle. "Oh, I don't know. Watch t.v. or something. You don't have a set of dominoes around here, do you?" I asked Grandma.

"Of course we do. They're in the living room. In the drawer of the game table."

"Are they double nines?"

"Dear Nick," Hattie said. "Double nines? What else would they be? Double sixes are for..."

"Wussies?"

"Precisely," Hattie said, and then, under her breath, "'wussies,' that's a good one. I'll have to remember that." She started up the stairs and then stopped. "What time are you two going to take off?"

"11:15," we both said in unison.

"Well, I see you have that worked out. Wake me up before you go, would you? Takes me longer and longer to recreate the legend these days, if you know what I mean."

"I'll wake you, ma'am," Doyle said with a grin.

"Yes, well, I think we're going to need all the 'legend' we can get tonight," grandma said.

.   .   .

Doyle knew how to play dominoes, but I had to teach him the "Racehorse" variation Clyde had taught me. By 10:30, when we had each won a game, Doyle made coffee for us. We were going to play another game, but decided we didn't have enough time and watched the news instead. I didn't pay much attention, but at least it helped pass the time.

At 11:10, Doyle went upstairs and woke Hattie. He came back downstairs and said "are you ready?" to me.

"As ready as I'll ever be."

"What should we take? The truck or the limousine? Doyle asked.

"The king's a pretty wide fellow," I said. "We'd better take the limousine."

We got into the black Cadillac and took off down the lane to the highway. Doyle tuned in the local radio station. Neither of us said much on the way up to Calistoga; each of us was pretty much lost in our own thoughts. We drove down Lincoln Avenue, the main street of Calistoga. Not much was going on, just a few people on the sidewalk here and there. Nothing like tomorrow when the street would be teaming with people watching the annual 4th of July parade.

Lincoln Avenue, the main drag in Calistoga.

Doyle took it slow up the mountain. The long car wasn't exactly built to take hairpin turns at high speed. When we finally reached the parking area for the state park, I instructed Doyle to turn into the one on the west side of the road. It took some backing-and-forthing to get the limousine positioned in the small turnout. Once Doyle finally had the whale of a car parked, I jumped out, peering around in the darkness. Nothing. I walked over to where the trail started and heard someone quietly calling my name. It was G.

"G! What are you doing here?" I asked with surprise.

"My father wanted me to come."

"Where is he?"

"They're not too far behind. He wanted me to come ahead so you'd know they were coming. He's not much of a hiker."

"Did you say 'they'?"

"Yes. Witbeck and Wycoff are with him."

"Oh boy," I said under my breath, thinking it was a good thing we'd brought the limousine.

"Here they come now," G said, turning and walking back up the trail.

I could just make out a tangle of small, dark shapes, jostling each other, swearing, half-walking, half-slipping down the trail. They finally made their way to the parking area. I turned around and could see Doyle standing next to the back of car, taking in the scene. G seemed in good shape, but the three older gnomes were huffing and puffing. They stood in a group, trying to pull themselves together, the king straightening his crown, pulling it down to his ears.

"Your Highness," I said, "It's good to see you," bowing slightly.

"Likewise, young Nick," the king said, after a long session of clearing his throat.

"I haven't been formally introduced to your advisors, Your Highness."

"Oh my, how rude of me," the king sputtered. "This is Witbeck, my chamberlain, and Wycoff, my master of the exchequer. Men, this is young Nick."

The two gnomes bowed their heads. I did the same saying, "Pleased to meet you both. Now then, shall we go?"

"Yes, yes. Let's be off," said the king. "We have business to attend to."

The king led the charge, with me beside him. When we reached the limousine, I introduced Doyle to the group and explained that he would be doing the driving. Doyle shot me a very wide-eyed expression, communicating his surprise at the number of passengers. I just shook my head in response.

Doyle opened the back door and the king merely stuck his head in.

"This is quite a conveyance," he said. "Very commodious."

"Please, Your Highness," Doyle said, "get in and make yourself comfortable," offering him a hand.

The king managed, with Doyle's help, to climb in and get himself situated on the back seat.

"Oh, yes," he said, "this is very good. Come on, men. Nothing to it." The rest of the group climbed in, crawled around the king, and found spots to sit.

"All in?" Doyle asked, before closing the door. There was lots of head nodding, but they were clearly out of their element and a little confused.

Doyle and I got in the front seat. Doyle started the car and took off slowly. I lowered the privacy window between the front seat and the back and turned around. It hadn't occurred to me until then that none of them had been in a car before. The look on their faces said it all: they were petrified. Trying to put them at ease, I said, "It's a short trip to my grandmother's house. And Doyle is an excellent driver. You don't have to do anything. You can just sit and relax. We'll be there in no time."

My words seemed to calm them a little. I then asked if the king would like to hear some music.

"Is there a band in here, too?"

"No, Your Highness, no band. But we have a device called a radio. It plays music." With that I found a station playing classical music. I turned around and saw the king swaying his head to the rhythm of the music.

"Can you make it louder?" the king asked.

"Of course," I said, turning the radio up.

"Yes, yes. This is very fine," the king said. Turning to Wycoff, he commented, "Remember this, Wycoff. Radio. We must get one." Wycoff nodded his head in agreement. I turned around and wondered how this was all going to turn out.

•　　•　　•

To my relief, everything went smoothly for the rest of the ride to Hattie's and the king and his men found it much easier getting out of the limousine than getting in. Doyle walked ahead of the group and opened the front door. The group passed into the foyer. Once they were all inside, Doyle walked over the stairwell and called up.

"Madam?"

"Yes, Doyle."

"Your guests have arrived."

"I'll be right down."

Whatever "recreating the legend" meant, Hattie had certainly gone to some effort to make an impression on the king. She was wearing a long, black satin kimono and a gold turtleneck that sparkled. She was also wearing large gold and diamond earrings I'd never seen before. She looked great. Standing next to the king, I heard an audible "hmmmmm" come from him as he watched Hattie descend the stairs.

"Oh, my goodness," Hattie said, surveying the group. "It's a party."

"Let me introduce you, Grandma," I said. "His Highness, King Gob; his son, Prince G, the king's chamberlain, Wycoff, and chancellor of the exchequer, Witbeck."

"Pleased, I'm sure," Hattie said, holding out her hand and bowing her head to the king. The king took Hattie's hand and kissed it. I might have been wrong, but I could swear I saw Hattie flutter her eyelashes at the king.

"Please," Hattie said, motioning to the living room, "Let's make ourselves comfortable."

I stayed in the entry hall and surveyed the living room; someone had lit all the candles and there was a fire burning brightly in the fireplace. Soft music was playing in the background and I noticed a small footstool in front of one of the armchairs in front of fireplace, placed there, I thought, to make it easier for the king to get into the chair. This was a side of my grandmother I hadn't seen before.

"Your Highness, if you would sit there," Hattie said, indicating the chair with her hand. For as stout and short as he was, the king, with the aid of the footstool, got into the chair rather nimbly.

Having gotten the king seated, Hattie turned to the others, "please, all of you, make yourselves comfortable anywhere you'd like. The prince, Witbeck and Wycoff looked around and scrambled onto the couch. Hattie sat in the chair next to the king and said "Nick has explained to me the basics of what you'd like to discuss, your highness. Considering the complexity of your request, I thought it best to limit the refreshments to some of our world famous mineral water. Doyle, will you see that everyone has some?"

"Yes ma'am."

The look on the king's face said he would have preferred something stronger, but he genially accepted the bubbly mineral water from Doyle. When everyone had been served, Hattie raised her glass to her visitors and said: "Here's to my esteemed guests," she said, "a pleasure to have you all here."

"The pleasure is all ours," said the king, raising his glass to Hattie. "Lovely place you have here."

"Thank you, Your Highness. The captain, as you know, and his wife designed it themselves."

"The last time we were here, which was some time ago, the captain was away on a trip. I've never been inside the house before."

"Well, it looks pretty much the same as it always has, which is fine by me." In an effort to include him in the conversation, Hattie turned to the prince. "And Prince G. That's an unusual name. Does it stand for something?"

"Goblet," the king said, answering for his son.

"Goblet?" Hattie asked, not sure she had heard correctly, looking at the prince, who merely shook his head up and down slightly.

With that Hattie let out a very loud laugh, tilting her head back toward the ceiling. Once she had recovered, she put her hand over her mouth and said, "Please forgive me, I mean no offense," she said, bowing her head in the prince's direction. She turned to the king, who had a horrified expression on his face, and said, "Did I ever tell you about the time I was in Finland? No, of course I haven't. Well, I went to Finland many years ago to see if I could drum up some business — the captain was Finnish, you recall — so I thought there might be a business opportunity there. Practically everywhere I went, people wanted to know where I was from and I told them, 'I'm from the Napa Valley in California.' To a one, they would start to laugh — and some quite heartily, I might add. It happened so many times, I finally had to ask someone what was so funny about what I said. One kind gentleman finally explained to me that in Finnish, 'Napa' meant 'bellybutton'. So I was Hattie Sinclair of Bellybutton Valley, California."

This time it was the king's turn to laugh. And once he started laughing, we all did too. As the laughter faded, Hattie turned to G and said, "Before we begin our business, Nick has told me of your bravery, Prince G. As you might imagine, both Nick and I are very much in your debt and are truly thankful for your actions. If there's anything I can ever do for you, please don't hesitate to ask."

In ways G couldn't have possibly imagined, that was exactly what was going to happen in the not-so-distant future. For the time being, however, Prince G simply lowered his head in acknowledgement to Hattie. With that, Hattie turned to the King, saying "Your Highness. I understand you have a business proposition for me, and by extension, Nick."

"Indeed, indeed," the king said. "Your grandson here is a very competent and honorable, not to mention persuasive, young man. He convinced me to return the horse to him, as you know. He held up his side of the bargain and returned the payment I had left for taking the horse. He also agreed to intercede on my behalf to come to an agreement with his uncle allowing me to, perhaps, purchase the horse. Not to mention arranging this meeting with you and having a very nasty intruder removed from our midst. Like I said, a very competent young man," the king said, nodding in my direction.

"If you don't mind my saying, Your Highness, it appears that you got the better end of the bargain. Nick has done rather a lot for you in exchange for one smallish horse," Hattie said in an even tone.

The king raised his eyebrows. "Perhaps. But I can be persuasive, too. Young Nick seemed very intent for me to return the horse to him. I was just taking advantage of the situation."

"Yes, I'd say you were," Hattie said.

"So that's how we arrived at this meeting — to see if you would grant him permission to perform a very special mission in my behalf."

"Hold it right there, Your Highness," Hattie said, holding up her hand. "Let's get this straight from the get-go. As Nick explained to me — and as you yourself have just said — Nick's obligation to you was simply to arrange this meeting, not to determine its outcome one way or another. I know he'll do his best to arrange for you to buy Quicksilver from Walter, legitimately this time, won't you Nick?"

"I will," I said.

Hattie continued. "But this 'special mission' as you put it, is outside the original agreement. Am I being reasonable in my thinking?" Witbeck and Wycoff whispered to each other and then looked at the king, nodding their heads in unison.

"I suppose it could be considered that way," the king said.

"All right, then," Hattie said, smiling. "Now that we have that clear, what is it you propose, Your Highness?"

The king cleared his throat and thought for a minute. "I propose that Nick help me find Dagywn, our Wizard, and the other men who jumped from Captain Niebaum's ship in Kauai, many years ago."

"I apologize for interrupting again, Your Highness," Hattie said, "but I need to make sure I understand this. You're asking for Nick's help, right?"

"That's correct," the king said.

"Are you also proposing to pay him for his services?"

"Er... of course there would be payment," the king said, stammering a bit.

"And how exactly is he to perform this task for you?"

"That's one of the reasons I'm thinking of, ah, hiring Nick. I am not current with all that goes on in your world and the Uplander way of doing things. But I assume since we once sailed from Kauai to here, he could do the same thing in reverse."

"Interesting," Hattie said. "Doyle? His Highness's glass appears to be empty. As do Witbeck's and Wycoff's."

"Of course, ma'am."

While Doyle refreshed the men's drinks, I could tell Hattie was thinking of something. As soon as Doyle was done, Hattie continued.

"Now, Your Highness, I have a proposal for you," she said bowing her head in his direction. "But first, I have some questions for Nick." She turned to me. "Is this a task you'd be interested in undertaking for the king, Nick?"

"Yes."

"Did you tell me that you took a class in sailing last year at school?"

"Yes. It was one of my electives."

"And did you also tell me that it was Mr. Hayes who taught the class?"

"That's right."

Hattie turned to the king again. "So here is what I propose. Understand that we may not get all the details worked out tonight, but we may agree to agree, as it were."

"Go on," the king said, interested.

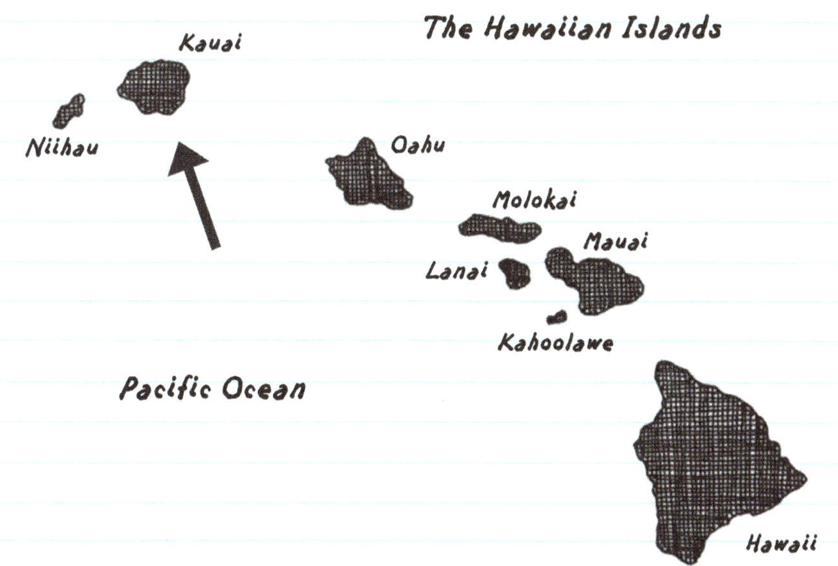

"I have my late husband's — Nick's grandfather's — sailboat berthed at the St. Francis Yacht Club in San Francisco. I had it built for his thirtieth birthday, many years ago. That sailboat gave us many happy hours, and it was always my hope that someday Nick would take an interest in it and that it would give him the same joy it gave us."

"I see," said the king.

I had forgotten all about the sailboat — *Bluebird*, I thought it was called. Now that Hattie had mentioned it, I had dim recollections of an old black-and-white photograph of it hanging somewhere. Where? In Hattie's house in San Francisco? I couldn't remember.

Grandma continued: "the *Bluebird*, that's the boat's name, is in need of some repairs and updating, Your Highness. But if I assume correctly, that you intend for Nick to perform this task for you next summer, when he's on vacation, there will be time to make the repairs, and whatever else we'll need to do to make the yacht seaworthy. Am I correct in assuming that you'll pay for these improvements?

The king looked a little taken aback, but simply said, "Of course."

"Then if Nick agrees to continue to take sailing classes next year in school and — and this is a big one — he can convince Mr. Hayes to accompany him and whoever else we will need to hire as a crew, we have an agreement, Your Highness. We can work out the details as we go along. Does that meet with your approval?" Hattie said, looking directly at the king.

"Yes, yes. Yes, indeed," the king said, a little flummoxed. "My goodness," he continued, "I certainly see where the boy gets his persuasive powers."

"Oh, you haven't seen anything yet, Your Highness," Hattie said, winking at the king.

"I believe you," he said.

"Now, what do you say to a little repast to celebrate?"

"We'd be delighted, wouldn't we, men?"

"Doyle," Hattie said, motioning to him. Doyle came over to her and she indicated for him to lean over. She whispered something in his ear. He looked a little perplexed and whispered something back in her ear, to which she responded out loud, "That's what the microwave oven is for!" Doyle stood up, smiling, and walked off to the kitchen, shaking his head.

Hattie stood up and walked over to the king. "The food will be ready shortly," she said. "In the meantime, Your Highness, I believe you have something of mine."

"I do?" he said, looking confused.

"Yes. You do. The amulet."

"Oh, oh that. Yes, of course. I was just about to get it."

"Of course you were," Hattie said as she watched him fumble around the many layers and folds of his outfit. Turning to look at the prince and Witbeck and Wycoff on the couch, Hattie said, "do you fellows make it a habit to wear all the clothes you own at the same time?"

Witbeck and Wycoff looked down at what they were wearing and then started to laugh. The prince looked uncomfortable, like he had made a mistake or something and the king was too busy looking for the amulet to have heard Hattie's question, which was probably a good thing, I thought.

The king finally found the amulet and handed it to Hattie. She bowed her head and then leaned over and gave him a peck on the cheek. The king blushed. My mouth fell open, and the prince's eyes got as big as saucers. "Now, let's eat," Hattie said. "Follow me, boys," she said as she walked towards the kitchen.

With some difficulty, the king managed to get out of the chair and Witbeck and Wycoff off the couch. The three of them fell in behind Hattie, following her dutifully. As they left the living room, I saw the king turn around and look at Witbeck and Wycoff, raising and lowering his eyebrows several times and forming his mouth into a small "o." I looked at the prince and nodded with my head for him to hold back and not go with the others. I felt badly for him. Hattie had not only made fun of his name, but his clothes, as well. I knew his feelings had been hurt. Once everyone was out of the room, I turned to the prince and said, "Well, all things considered, I think that went pretty well."

"Yes, I agree, but your grandmother... "

"I know, I know," I broke in. "she can be a little... "

"Rude?" the prince said.

"Yes, you're right. And I apologize for her."

"And I want to go on that trip to Kauai," the prince said, plaintively.

"I'm glad to hear you say that, because that's just what I was thinking. There's no way I can find Dagywn and the others without your help."

"Really?"

"Really."

"But my father would never let me go."

I thought for a minute and then said "Maybe if my grandmother told him it was a good idea..."

"Oh, now that *is* a good idea," the prince said smiling. "If anyone could convince him, she could."

"Let me see what I can do," I said. "Let's get something to eat while there's still something left."

•   •   •

G and I entered the kitchen to find a great deal of activity. Hattie was leaning against the counter, holding court. All the lights were on low and there were candles here, there and everywhere. Doyle had put all the little boxes of left-over Chinese food in the middle of the big harvest table, signaling to the king to take a look at the offering. After peering inside several of the boxes, he asked "What is it?"

"Chinese food," Hattie said.

"How'd you get it here?" the king asked.

"In the truck," Hattie said, amused.

"All the way from China?" the king asked in disbelief.

"No, you big silly. From the Chinese restaurant in town," Hattie said with a laugh.

The king just looked at Hattie, clearly not understanding the concept of a restaurant.

"Here, do you want me to show you how to do it?" Hattie asked.

"That would be wonderful, Hattie. May I call you Hattie?"

"If I can call you Gobbie," Hattie said.

G and I looked on in disbelief. G actually put his hand over his eyes. Hattie got a plate from the stack on the table and started piling on chow mein, egg fu yung, General Tso's chicken, and a small mountain of rice.

"Now, gentlemen, let me introduce you to space-age technology," Hattie said, holding up the plate. "You put your plate of food in this microwave oven here, close the door, and set the timer for oh, say two minutes. When the buzzer rings, open the door and you'll have a nice hot meal."

"No!" said the king. "That's not possible."

"Oh yes it is," Hattie said, "just watch."

She stuck the plate in the microwave, set the timer and stood back. The room was silent except for the humming noise of the microwave. The king, Witbeck and Wycoff moved in for a closer look, their noses practically pressed against the glass door of the microwave. The buzzer went off and all three of them jumped back at the same time. G and I had to hold back from laughing.

"Make way, make way," Hattie said, going over to the oven. "Now, I believe this is yours," she said looking at the king and holding up the plate of steaming food. "Sit down, sit down, make yourself comfortable," she said. "Who's next?"

Eventually everyone had their hot food. Hattie sat at the head of the table, taking it all in. It looked like a scene from some medieval banquet, Hattie thought to herself. Somewhere, she hoped, the captain is smiling. She felt sure he'd approve. Just then the room went silent and everyone around the table was looking in Hattie's direction, but past her. Hattie turned around and saw Katia standing in the doorway in her nightdress, her mouth wide open. She let out a small shriek and then fainted, falling in a heap on the floor. Hattie ran over to her, motioning for me to help her. "She always could bust up a good party," Hattie said, holding Katia's head in her hands.

"Doyle, you and Nick carry her up to her room and get her in bed. I'll get her a sedative from my room. She'll wake up tomorrow and think she's had a dream."

•　　•　　•

Hattie was right about one thing: Katia knew how to bust up a party. By the time Doyle and I got back to the kitchen, the king and his men were just sitting quietly, looking sheepish.

"Perhaps we should go now," Witbeck said, looking pleadingly at Doyle. I looked up at the clock on the kitchen wall. It was a little past 3 o'clock.

"Of course," Doyle said.

"Will she be all right?" Witbeck asked.

"Yes, she'll be fine. Nothing a good night's sleep won't take care of."

"Well, then, I think we should go before we cause any more mayhem," Witbeck said, standing up.

"I'll go with you," I said to Doyle.

"No, you don't have to. Go on to bed. It's late."

"No, I started this and I want to see it through to the end," I said.

•　　•　　•

About halfway to Calistoga, I turned around to see if everyone was okay. No one had spoken for several minutes. I wasn't surprised to see that all of them, including G, were sound asleep. I put the window up between the front seat and the back, so Doyle and I could talk.

"That was quite the evening," I said.

"Yeah, you could say that," Doyle replied. "Trouble is, you can't ever tell anyone about it, because who'd believe you?"

"I don't think anybody would," I said.

"That was some performance your grandmother put on," Doyle said.

"Do you think it was a performance? I'm not so sure. I think maybe that's who she really is. She just doesn't get the opportunity to be on center stage very often," I said.

"Maybe you're right. But performance or not, she's quite the lady."

"She certainly is," I said.

.   .   .

We finally reached the parking area where we'd picked up the group just four or so hours ago. Doyle and I got out of the front seat, each of us opening one of the back doors of the limousine. The overhead light went on and the gnomes shook themselves awake, squinting in the light, trying to figure out where they were. Except for G, they all looked a little worse for wear.

Both Doyle and I helped the gnomes out. They stood in a group, trying to pull themselves together. The king was the first to speak.

"Many thanks to you, young Nick and to you, Doyle, for providing us transportation. It has been a memorable evening. Very memorable."

"Glad to be of service, Your Highness," Doyle said.

"Likewise," I said, "I'm sure we'll be talking again soon."

"I look forward to it," the king said, "and now it's back up the mountain with us. Come on, men."

I caught G's eyes and waved goodbye. G waved back and I knew I'd be seeing him back at the bunkhouse, probably sooner rather than later. The king was leading the group across the parking area when he suddenly stopped and turned around. He walked back to me and leaned in, practically touching his forehead to mine. He patted me on the back and said, "That grandmother of yours — marvelous woman. Just marvelous."

"Ah, thank you, Your Highness. And good night," I said.

The king waved, then turned around and rejoined his group.

I stood there looking at them all and shouted out "Are you sure you'll be all right?"

"We'll be all right," the king said with a backwards wave over his shoulder.

I walked over to the limousine, got into the front seat and let out a large sigh.

"You okay?" Doyle asked.

"Yeah, I'm okay," I said, hesitating.

"But?" Doyle said.

"But the king just told me he thinks Hattie is a 'marvelous woman – just marvelous.'"

Doyle whistled.

"Yeah. My thoughts exactly," I said.

Sailing Grandma Hattie's sailboat to Kauai to find Dagywn the Wizard and the other missing gnomes seemed like a complete fantasy to me.

Chapter XXX

Endings and Beginnings

August 30, 1967
Multiple locations

The rest of the summer was fairly routine, especially when compared with the first part. Chuy got home from Mexico the first week of August. He and I picked up where we'd left off. It was good to have someone to pal around with again. Chuy said that Mexico was okay, but kind of boring. I decided not to tell him about the gnomes, at least not right away. Instead, I told Chuy the same version I'd told Walter, which was a pretty good story on its own.

Chuy's parents let him go with me and Walter and Ma-D to the State Fair in Sacramento. We had a great time and, best of all, Quicksilver won first prize in the Shetland pony division, which made everyone very proud and happy. I think all of us were secretly holding our breath while he was being judged, hoping he wouldn't fart or sneeze in the judge's face. For whatever reason, he behaved and won the day and came home with a blue ribbon. Even Hattie was there; she had Doyle drive her to the fair for the day and took everyone out to a steakhouse afterwards to celebrate.

After we got back to the valley, Walter enlisted Chuy and I to help in getting the miniature donkeys from his friend's place in El Verano up to Clyde's spot on Mt. St. Helena. We even brought materials to build a corral for the donkeys, which Clyde named Sam and Sally. Although he was a little confused and overwhelmed by the gesture, when Clyde saw the donkey cart, he immediately understood how useful it would be. And it made me feel good, knowing that Clyde would have the donkeys to talk to, even though he had said he was okay with being alone.

Ultimately, I was glad I hadn't told Chuy about the gnomes because, as it turned out, I didn't have to. Chuy spent the night with me one night in August. He and I were in the bunkhouse playing a new board game called *Feudal*, which was kind of like chess, but better. Since there was no one around to tell us not to, we stayed up late playing the game. Right around midnight, I heard the familiar knocking at the door. I opened the door and simply said "Hi, G How's it going?" Chuy looked like he had plotzed in his pants, but it didn't take long for G and I to explain the story. We wound up talking all night long and even taught G how to play *Feudal*. G left just before it started to get light and Chuy got to see him take off in the hummingbird-powered sling, which, if he hadn't seen it for himself, he would have never believed. I was glad that now someone else knew and, more importantly, believed my story.

After he won his blue ribbon, there was no way Walter was going to sell Quicksilver to the king. I thought this might be a problem, but luckily it wasn't. I'm guessing the king had his scouts roaming all over Mt. St. Helena on a regular basis, because it wasn't long after Walter and I had delivered the miniature donkeys to Clyde, that I received word, via G, that the king wanted a donkey, too. G told me that his father thought a donkey, being a sturdier animal, could handle his weight better than a horse could. It made sense to me, but I had to explain to G that the donkeys were sold only in pairs, so if the king wanted one, he had to take two. This was acceptable to Gob and in a surprise move he actually offered to pay for them in advance. Within a week, Walter and I were delivering two more donkeys to Mt. St. Helena. I left Walter to have a chat with Clyde while I delivered the donkeys to the old Great Western Mine. G instructed me to leave the donkeys in the corral they had built for Quicksilver, which is what I did. Everything was fine until few days later when the king became aware of Henry's cart and, of course, he wanted one of those, too, only he wanted one with a seat so he could ride sitting in the cart. Arrangements were made with Jack in El Verano, and a couple of weeks later Walter and I made the trip up Mt. St. Helena one more time to deliver the cart. It was a good thing that the king paid so well for our services; otherwise I'm sure Walter would have groused about all the extra work he was doing.

"What kind of people pay this much to have stuff done for them and who the heck pays in gold nuggets any more?" Walter asked me one day.

"Do you really want to know?" I asked. Walter thought about it for a minute and then said "I guess not. But it sure is strange."

"You're right about that, " I said. Thinking to myself, *If you only knew how strange....*

Toward the end of August Chuy and I picked prunes at a neighbor's orchard. It was hot, hard work, but all the kids in the valley did it — if you didn't pick prunes, you picked walnuts. It didn't pay much, but it

Judging Quicksilver at the State Fair.

The hamburgers at Taylor's Refresher are the best.

added up. After we got paid, Chuy and I felt rich and went to see the new James Bond movie, *You Only Live Twice* at the theater in town and treated ourselves to cheeseburgers at Taylor's Refresher afterwards

Sheriff Lyman called Walter and told him that Nigel had, indeed, been deported, but not before he spent two weeks in the jail's infirmary, getting over his poison oak rash which, apparently, was really bad. He told Walter that he doubted Nigel would ever be allowed into the country again, adding "It would take someone with an awful lot of clout to pull those kinds of strings." When I heard that, I immediately thought of Lord Higgenbothem and seriously doubted I'd seen the last of Nigel.

I went over to visit Hattie one day and learned that she and the king had been communicating about G coming on the trip to Kauai and that she felt certain she was going to convince the king to allow G to come along. "I was on the front porch having coffee and from out of nowhere this swarm of hummingbirds was hovering right in front of me. They were carrying a letter tied up in these little bits of vine and they dropped it right on my table. Can you even imagine such a thing?" she asked me.

I'd told Chuy about the possibility of sailing to Kauai the next summer that Hattie had, in fact, convinced the king to let G come too. The more we talked about it, the more we were convinced that Chuy should come too, but Chuy was certain his parents would say no. I thought about it for a while and then decided that if Hattie could get her way with the king, maybe she could do the same with Chuy's parents. I explained the situation to Hattie and she agreed to give it a try. She invited Chuy's parents to dinner at her house, along with me and Chuy. She explained the proposition to Chuy's parents, describing the trip as a "scientific expedition, along with some important anthropologic field work." In the end, Chuy's parents agreed, but only if Chuy kept a 3.75 grade point average during his next school year. To say Chuy instantly became an inspired student would be an understatement. When it was all said and done, Hattie had one more fan: Chuy.

I had to be back at school on September 3rd. Hattie had already gone back to San Francisco and wanted me to spend a few days with her before I went back. I crated my bicycle and Walter and I took it to the bus station in Napa to send back to Pebble Beach. The next day, Walter and Ma-D drove me to Hattie's and we all went out to lunch at the Garden Court restaurant in the Palace Hotel. It was one of the best rooms in the city — basically like a huge conservatory with towering potted palms and big marble columns and crystal chandeliers everywhere. The food was only so-so, but we were all in good spirits and impressed by the beautiful surroundings. We all agreed it had been a good — a very good — summer.

The next day Hattie took me shopping for the things I needed for the school. She had Katia pack a picnic lunch which we took to the St. Francis Yacht Club. Doyle, Hattie and I ate it aboard the *Bluebird*. It was a beautiful 78-foot sailboat, all built of wood. As I stood on the dock, admiring the boat, I noticed a large crow, perched on the forward hatch of the cabin. "Nice try," I said to it, clapping my hands and telling it to get lost. It flew off across the water, cawing angrily the whole way. After lunch, we explored every inch of the *Bluebird*, entertained by Hattie's memories of sailing with my grandfather. I took a lot of photographs. I couldn't wait to share them with Mr. Hayes when I got back to school.

That night we had a quiet dinner at Hattie's. Katia had made split pea soup with big chunks of ham in it, and cornbread right out of the oven. It tasted good, considering how cold and foggy it was outside. After saying goodnight to everyone, I went upstairs to my room and started packing. I had to be at the bus station a little before eight the next morning and I wanted to be ready to go. As I moved around my small room, I looked up and noticed a small, framed photograph leaning up on the bookshelf. I took it down and immediately recognized the *Bluebird* on San Francisco bay. Angel Island was in the background and a much younger Hattie and my grandfather were waving to whomever took the picture. Hattie must have put the photograph there. For some reason it made me a little sad, but also excited. The *Bluebird* had a long past and, just maybe, it was part of my future. *We'll see*, I thought to myself. I decided to take the photograph to school with me and put it in my suitcase.

• • •

The next morning, I got up early, packed the last of my things and went downstairs. Doyle and Katia were already in the kitchen. I knew not to expect Grandma, as she usually didn't come downstairs until 10 o'clock.

"Top of the morning," Doyle said.

"Same to you, Doyle," I said.

"There's a cup of cocoa and some toast for you," Katia said, turning around from the sink. "And an envelope from your grandmother."

"Thanks, Katia."

"Do you want anything else?"

"No, I think I'm fine."

I sat down at the kitchen table and drank some of the cocoa, and then dunked a piece of the buttered sourdough toast in it. I'd always liked the combination of the salty butter, the sourdough and the sweet cocoa. I opened the envelope. Inside were ten ten-dollar bills and a note from Hattie:

"Nick, I'd say that was a summer to remember, wouldn't you? I know I don't have to tell you to do your best in school, so I won't. But here's a little walking around money for you to have some FUN.   xoxoxox, H."

I put the envelope in my pocket and finished the cocoa and toast. I took my plate to the sink and said, "Thanks for everything, Katia. See you in a couple of months."

"Safe travels," Katia said brusquely.

Stiff as a board, I thought to myself.

"Ready?" Doyle said.

"Ready," I said.

"I've already put your suitcase in the car."

"Thanks, Doyle."

I sat in the front of the limousine with Doyle. It was a short drive from Hattie's to the bus station, where I would catch the bus over to Oakland, across the bay. Once we reached the station, I stuck out my hand to Doyle and shook it. "Thanks for being so... so steady, Doyle."

"Yes, well, I'd say you're pretty steady yourself," Doyle said.

"See you at Thanksgiving," I said.

"See you then. Take care of yourself," Doyle said.

I picked up my suitcase and walked over to where the Oakland bus was idling and got on. It would be just a thirty-minute trip — over the Bay Bridge to Jack London Square in Oakland where, in turn, the Amtrak train would depart for Salinas. The trip down the coast took about three hours. There was no one sitting next to me on the train, so I alternately dozed, wrote in my journal, or daydreamed, looking out the window. Once in Salinas it was another short bus trip to Monterey, and then a cab to Pebble Beach, and back to school.

I stepped out of the cab and looked at my watch. I'd left San Francisco a little after eight and it was now a little before one o'clock. *Should still be able to grab something at the cafeteria for lunch,* I thought. I picked up my suitcase in one hand and my journal in the other and took off across the campus. Its familiarity was comforting, as was the light overcast sky, the briny smell of the ocean in the air, and the sound of the sea gulls cawing overhead. It was good to be back.

"Nick!" a voice came across the campus.

"Mr. Hayes. Good to see you. How are you?"

"Just fine. How was your summer?"

"I'm not sure you'd believe me if I told you," I said, smiling.

"Well, you could always give me a try," Mr. Hayes said.

"Oh, don't worry. I will."

"Where are you living this year?" Mr. Hayes asked.

"Same as last," I said.

"Good," Mr. Hayes said, "Come see me a little later. I'm in the same place, too. We'll get caught up," and started to walk off. He halted and yelled back to me, "Hey, did you ever figure out what that fortune cookie meant?"

"It's all right here," I said, holding up my journal. "I wrote the whole thing down."

•   •   •

Tuesday, July 23, 1967
Headquarters of the International News Agency
London, England

Once again, Nigel Stayne found himself sitting in one of the black leather club chairs outside Lord Higgenbothem's office. Only this time, Nigel knew why he was being summoned. Even the thought of the meeting made his stomach turn. Same as before, the receptionist received a call, looked over to Nigel and announced "Lord Higgenbothem will see you now." Was that a look of pity Nigel noticed behind her glasses?

Nigel entered Higgenbothem's office. Just as before, he was seated at his enormous desk. Higgenbothem looked up from the papers on his desk and motioned for Nigel to sit down.

"Well, well, well. If it isn't the famous Badger. Make yourself comfortable."

Nigel had already written him a letter, explaining the details of what had happened on his assignment. The letter was posted from jail in California, no less. Nigel took a seat in front of the desk and didn't say anything.

"So you found them?" Lord Higgenbothem said softly.

"Ah, yessir, I did."

"And you actually photographed them?"

"Yessir."

"And you were a prisoner in their cave?"

"That too."

"And you've returned without any evidence that they exist? Which is, if you'll recall, why I sent you there in the first place."

"No sir, they destroyed my camera."

"You know something, Badger. I'm not nterested in your excuses in the slightest. I like results. And you've provided me with a handful of jack squat," Higgenbothem said, his voice rising. He sat silently for a minute, pinching the bridge of his nose, his eyes closed. Suddenly he looked up at Nigel and practically shouted "And what, exactly, do you intend to do next?"

"I, I'm not certain, Lord Higgenbothem. It's your call, sir," stammered Nigel.

"You're damn right, it's my call," Higgenbothem shouted, struggling to rise from his chair. "You know the gnomes exist. And you know where they live. You're going to go back and get the bloody story, you stupid twit! And more importantly, the damn photographs!" With that, he picked up a glass paperweight on his desk and hurled it directly at Nigel. Nigel ducked as it sailed by, landing on a very large Chinese vase next to the window, breaking it into a thousand pieces.

Unfazed, Lord Higgenbothem continued in a low voice. "I'm sure you heard about the fire at the kennel where you board your dogs."

"Yes, yes I did," Nigel responded, puzzled.

"Yes, well, we were able to get your dogs out in time. The others weren't so lucky."

"Sir?"

"Fail again, Badger, and those terriers will be toast."

"Sir!"

"This meeting is over, Badger. Go!"

•   •   •

I walked into the kitchen and held up the journal. "Done!" I said. I'd finished it in bed last night, some time past 2. And then proceeded to have very strange dreams.

Grandpa and Doyle have a tradition of making sourdough pancakes on Sunday mornings. Grandpa was mixing the batter while Doyle was frying up some bacon.

"What do you think?"

"'What do I think?'" I said. "I'm not sure what I think. I know it's a good story."

"So what's bothering you?"

"Well, if what you wrote is true, then it's okay to talk in front of Doyle, right?"

Doyle turned around from the stove and said, "Oh yes. I was there. Quite memorable, I'd say."

"One thing I can't figure out is, if the gnomes are for real, how come no one knows about them?"

"I do. And Doyle does. Grandma Hattie did. But to answer your question, for the time being, they don't want be known."

"Why not?"

"It's a little complicated. But the last time I had contact with them, they were in the middle of trying to figure out what their role was going to be in the 20th century world."

"When was that?"

"What? The 20th century?"

"No. When was the last time you had contact with them?"

"1968."

"You haven't seen them since then?

"Nope."

"Why not?"

"To paraphrase Greta Garbo, 'they want to be alone.'"

"Greta who?"

"Greta Garbo. She was an actress, a long time ago."

"So they're like hiding?"

"Basically, yes."

"Was it Prince G who made you promise not to share the story?"

"Yes."

"Were you disappointed?"

"You could say that. To tell you the truth, it's still a disappointment to me."

Grandpa paused a minute and then continued, "while we're in the 'major truth' mode here, I should say that it pleases me that at least you read it, although I can't say what good it's going to do you, because you can't share it with anybody either."

"I thought you said you'd think about it – about my letting Darren read it."

"I have thought about it. I think it's better if you kept it to yourself."

"Bummer."

"I know, but things could get complicated really quickly. And I'm trying to keep things simple these days."

"Would you let me do what you did – go up on Mt. St. Helena and look for the gnomes?"

"To tell you the truth, probably not."

"Why not?"

"Because it's really dangerous."

"You made it, didn't you?"

"Yeah, but it could have just as easily ended in disaster. I was just lucky."

"I could be lucky, too.

"Luck is not a good thing to bet on, Joaquin."

I decided to leave it alone for now and change the subject.

"Did you get Dagwyn the Wizard back?"

"You'll have to read the second journal to find that out."

"Can I?

"It's '*may* I,' and yes, you may."

With that and a trip to the attic, I was set to take off on another voyage into the past. But this time with the conviction that if the gnomes really were real, I wanted to meet them. After all, if Grandpa had figured out a way to find them, I could, too.

The End

And now a sneak peek at the first chapter of *The Voyage of the Silverado*, Part II of The Silverado Journals.

Chapter I

Party Interrupted

December 23, 1967
Grandma Hattie's house
San Francisco, California

"Sinclair residence, Doyle speaking."

"Hi Doyle, it's Mr... it's Tim Hayes, Nick's English teacher."

"Oh yes, Mr. Hayes, how are you?"

"I'm fine, thank you. I was wondering if Nick was available; it's rather important."

"Yes, I'm sure he's here somewhere — if you'll hold the line, I'll find him for you."

"Thanks Doyle."

Doyle put the telephone down on the kitchen counter and went off in search of Nick. The house was absolutely crawling with people for Hattie's annual Christmas party. Doyle found Nick in the library talking with Cyril Magnin, who everyone simply called 'Mr. San Franciso.'

"Mr. Magnin, Nick, sorry to disturb you, but you have a call Nick. It's Mr. Hayes. He says it's important."

Nick excused himself from Mr. Magnin and quickly walked to the kitchen. He couldn't imagine why Mr. Hayes would be calling him — especially during Christmas vacation and at this time of night.

"Hi Mr. Hayes,"

"I'm glad I got you, Nick. Sounds like I'm interrupting a party so I'll get right to the point. You need to know that someone was in your dorm room tonight and they got away with something."

"What?!"

"Like I said. One of the guys from campus security noticed a light in your room and decided to take a look. By the time he got to the second floor, some guy dressed in black was just coming out of your room carrying a book. When he saw the security guard he ran down the hall and disappeared."

"Aw shi... "

"Yeah, I know. Are you thinking what I'm thinking?"

"Probably. The only thing I have that anyone could possibly be interested in is my journal from last summer... and the only person who'd be interested in it is Nigel Stayne."

"That's what I figured. Do you think it was him?"

"No, I doubt it. He's still too hot to risk coming back into the country. He must have hired someone to steal it for him."

"Do you have a copy?"

"Yeah, I made a copy for Grandma Hattie to keep. Not that it matters now, darn it."

"This means Nigel is going to know about our plans for next summer."

"I know. I just didn't see this coming," I said. "Guess I should have kept it with me all the time. I never thought he'd steal it, but I don't know why not — he's such a low life."

"Don't beat yourself up, Nick. We'll deal with it."

"Thanks, but I don't think this is the last of it — no way."

"You're probably right, but right now we can't do much about it. Go back to your party. We'll talk after Christmas."

"Okay. Thanks for calling... I guess. Oh, and Merry Christmas."

"Yeah, Merry Christmas to you, too."

As we wished each other Merry Christmas, we were both shaking our heads in disbelief over what had just happened.

•　　•　　•

A couple of days after Christmas, I received a postcard from Scotland with a photograph of the River Tweed on the front. On the other side the message read:

Nice job on the journal, although I feel I've been portrayed rather badly. I'm not such a bad chap, as you would have found out if we'd teamed up together — things would have gone rather better for us both. Ah well, there's always next summer (by the way, thanks for all the details). See you in Kauai. Yours faithfully, Nigel

"What a shmuck!" I thought when I'd finished reading the postcard.

I'd been looking forward to this summer's voyage to Kauai, even though I had no idea how we were going to find Dagwyn once we got there. Now I figured

I needed to let everyone know it was going to be like a team stepping onto a baseball field with two strikes already against it. *A lousy way to start what was already going to be challenge,* I thought to myself, *really lousy.* And I couldn't help but to think that I was at least partly responsible for making it way more difficult.

.   .   .

Ship's Log
(printed, from cursive version on page 112)

S. S. Lindisfarne, Voyage #19
From: Glasgow, Scotland
Towards: Reykjavik, Iceland
Date: 28 February, 1879

Major disturbance onboard just after eight bells this evening. Under full sail, heading SW in the Firth of Henry. First mate Nyquist at the helm. Cold night, good wind. Third mate Higgenbotham, in a very agitated state, summons me from my cabin to go below decks. We were met by Second mate Syrjälä standing next to one of the large crates we took on board in Glasgow. Syrjälä explained that he and Higgenbotham were in the hold inspecting the lashings on the cargo when he thought he heard faint voices inside the wooden crate. Fearing stowaways, he immediately dispatched Higgenbotham to bring me belowdecks. After some deliberation, it was decided to open the crate. There were indeed stowaways in the crate (and in other crates, as well). After several hours and considerable confusion (along with some minor injuries), the situation was resolved. Higgenbotham produced a firearm but, thankfully, no shots were fired. A most unusual evening, indeed.

Signed,
Gustave Niebaum
Master
1st Mate: P. Nyquist
2nd Mate: L. Syrjälä
3rd Mate: T. Higgenbotham

Captain Niebaum's Letter
(printed, from cursive version on page 114)

CAPTAIN GUSTAVE NIEBAUM
EAGLE'S NOOK
RUTHERFORD, CALIFORNIA

Greetings to whomever is reading this. My only hope is that you have some connection with me and that you will hold the information I am about to pass on with the respect that it deserves – both for my reputation and legacy and the fate of the little ones.

First, a bit of my history: I was raised in Oulu, a Swedish-speaking community in Finland, and lived there from 1842 to 1858. Ours was a family who never doubted the existence of the little ones, even though they were encountered only on the rarest of occasions and certainly not by everyone in our community. I, myself, happened upon one only once in my childhood when I caught him helping himself to some of our eggs when I mistakenly wandered into the henhouse instead of the outhouse in the middle of the night. I'm sure the little one was more frightened than I; he was very surprised and humbled when I told him he could take however many eggs he needed, as we had more than enough for our family. Such generosity was encouraged in our family, but I must say that no one in my family ever let me forget that I had confused the chicken house with the outhouse. My mother and father taught me to respect the little ones for their cooperation and willingness to share in bad times, which for those of us with very little, could mean the difference between survival and death.

My siblings and I grew up hearing of other families who were afraid of the little ones, spoke poorly of them, and sought every opportunity to stamp them out of our locale. My parents, who were in every way wise – wise with the accumulated wisdom of their parents and their grandparents before them – taught us the greatest rule of all: To treat others as we would want to be treated. They explained to me and my sister and brother, Helli and Olavi, that if we could only remember this one rule, it would see us to live good and honorable lives. They taught us that just because someone's outward appearance might be different than our own was no reason to treat them differently from anyone else, for indeed, we also looked different in their eyes. And how was it that we wanted to be treated, they asked? We, their children, took their teachings to heart and lived by them as best we could, each in our own way.

I have provided you with this preamble to explain why I acted as I did aboard the *Lindisfarne* on the night of 28 February 1867, my second encounter with the little ones. I deliberately did not call them by their name because my ship's log is read by a variety of people, not all of whom, as I have already stated, share my beliefs and attitudes. In fact, it is my opinion that the vast majority of people no longer even believe in the existence of the little people, thinking instead that they are merely part of the imaginative minds of writers who create books for children.

When third mate Thom Higgenbotham hailed me in my cabin, he did not elaborate on the situation to me, only stating that my presence was needed immediately belowdecks. We arrived in the hold to a scene of considerable commotion. All of the stowaways had been taken from the crates where they had been hiding and it seemed everyone was talking at once at a very high level. I commanded their silence and inquired if there was a leader in their group. All the men – for there wasn't a female amongst them – turned toward one man, bowing their heads in the process. Their leader puffed up and announced, in a deep baritone, to the assembly: "I am known to all as King Gob, Lord of all Gobsons Everywhere, Keeper of the Flame, Possessor of All Mystical Knowledge, Inheritor of the Wind, and Grand Architect of the Hidden World. And whom, may I inquire, am I addressing?"

I replied, matching his grave tone, informing him and his tribe that I was "Captain Gustave Niebaum, Master of the Schooner *Lindisfarne*," the vessel on which he and his men were now trespassing.

"Trespassing!" the king bellowed. "Trespassing! No. No. Nothing of the sort. Nothing of the sort. No, sir, you are mistaken. Wycoff! Where's Wycoff?"

Wycoff, who was apparently the equivalent of the king's purser, stepped forward. "Wycoff! Show the captain how we intend to pay for our passage!" Wycoff stammered that the payment was still in the "guld buxbom." The king ordered him to open it immediately. Once it was located, Wycoff did, indeed, open the large crate and, to the astonishment of my mates, revealed that it was full of all manner of gold. "There! You see? Our store of payment, captain," the king said.

I explained to him that payment for passage was something customarily handled prior to boarding the ship, to which King Gob replied that they hadn't passed anywhere yet and it was their custom to pay for goods and services after said goods and services were successfully rendered.

Sensing a rise in tension, I suggested to the king that we continue our discussion in private, in my cabin. The king agreed, but there was the question of what to do with the rest of his tribe in the meantime. Before I could silence him, third mate Higgenbotham suggested that they all be thrown overboard and a considerable skirmish then ensued. Higgenbotham foolishly brandished his firearm. I immediately relieved him of his gun, reprimanded him in no uncertain terms, and with the help of the king, we quieted the group. Some of the little ones suffered minor injuries, which second mate Syrjälä attended to. I ordered Higgenbotham to his quarters, informing him that I would deal with him later. Because Second Mate Syrjälä seemed to be the most cool-headed, I left him in charge of the king's subjects, and suggested that he contact the ship's cook and arrange food and drink for the stowaways. This action was favorably received by the men.

Reader, please forgive the fact that I have not yet described the physical appearance of the king and his men. I have deliberately withheld that information, so as not to prejudice the reader's response. For me (no doubt influenced by my upbringing), they were simply men of a different sort, but men nonetheless. But to other eyes, they were gnomes (those people my parents referred to as "little ones"), with all the superstitions and wrongful information contained in that designation. If the reader is living in a time far in the future, perhaps my reluctance will seem unnecessary, prejudice over such things having been left in the past. If that is the case, I congratulate you and your enlightened times. But for now, I cannot overstate how misunderstood the gnomes are in the minds of most men.

King Gob and I had our meeting, which lasted more than an hour. The king has a fondness for talking and pursued his points vehemently and in earnest. Over the course of the meeting, we reached an agreement, suitable to all parties. The king explained that he and his troop were on a mission of exploration. Conditions in his native country – he and his tribe were now living on the Åland Islands – had become increasingly difficult, with a hostile populace and an increase in the number of church bells, which, to the ears of all gnomes, was exceedingly painful. He had heard of America and wanted to see for himself if relocating his people there was a possibility. Hence, their presence aboard the *Lindisfarne*. He offered to pay me for their passage then and there. I explained that there was no need for payment, as fortune had been very kind to me. He appeared to be confused by this, but I explained that I had just constructed a winery in a beautiful valley in California and that I was in desperate need of a series of caves dug into the hillside in which to age my wine (recalling my parents' stories regarding the gnomes' magical ability for mining and tunneling that I had been told as a child). I explained that I would happily grant him and his men passage to California if he, in exchange, would construct the caves and tunnels I required. "This is but a trifling," he responded. "Are you sure you wouldn't prefer gold?" I assured him the caves were more important to me than any gold, and we shook hands and had one more dram of whiskey to seal the arrangement. I thus assured him that once he and his men had finished their labor, they would be free to go as they pleased. He seemed particularly intrigued when I told him about Mt. St. Helena at the head of the Napa Valley and the fact it contained not only gold and silver, but quicksilver, as well, which again I remembered from old stories as a particular favorite of the gnome people.

Truth be told, I was less concerned with the party of gnomes on board than I was with the considerable gold they were transporting, having seen for myself in Alaska what gold can do to otherwise decent men. I convinced the king to have the "guld buxbom" moved to my cabin for safekeeping for the duration of the voyage. As a sign of his trust in me, he agreed. As you are probably aware, the gnome folk have a distaste for daylight and conduct their affairs only after dark, quite the reverse from us "Uplanders," as they refer to people such as myself. Even so, it was agreed that they would stay below decks at all times unless I gave them permission otherwise. They had brought with them all the provisions they required with regard to food and drink, so contact between them and the crew could be kept to a minimum. Given Higgenbotham's apparent distrust and dislike of the gnomes, it would not take much effort on his part to incite other like-minded crew members into a mutinous situation, which I was determined to avoid at all costs.

It pleases me to report that it was, in fact, a successful voyage, save for one unfortunate incident, although more to the distress of the king than to me. As you are probably aware, this was a particularly long voyage, from England, around Cape Horn, to Australia, Japan and finally the Hawaiian Islands as our last port of call before returning home to San Francisco. There were five gnomes out of the party of eighteen who never got used to the sea-faring life, plagued as they were with seasickness. The king had implored them to stay together as every one of them would be needed once they arrived to what he referred in as the "New World." But, alas, it finally proved too much for the sickly five. They jumped ship while we were tied up in Kauai. The king convinced me to stay in port an extra day as he sent search parties in all directions to find the runaways, but to no avail. The king was at first mightily disturbed for, as he told me, one of the missing men was the Wizard of the tribe, the one who possessed essential knowledge for some of the gnomes most amazing feats. For as consequential a loss as it was, I must report that the king was stoical in his manner and did not ask for any further delays in our departure.

Once in San Francisco, I arranged to have the gnomes transported by wagon (all of them safely in their stow-away crates) to St. Helena. I met them there and showed them the location where I desired the caves to be built, along with a plan of their design and specifications. I explained to the king that I would be embarking on another voyage in two days' time – destination Alaska – but I would check on his progress when I returned in two months.

The return trip from Alaska was a hellish one, inclement weather adding an additional three weeks to our trip. When we finally arrived in San Francisco I was most anxious to return to St. Helena and my love, Susan, and greatly curious as to the gnomes' progress with the caves. As my arrival at the winery was after dark, I was expecting to find the gnomes at work, but they were nowhere to be found. Surprised that the king might have gone back on his word, I began an inspection and was overwhelmed with pleasure at the discovery that the caves were completely excavated to the exact specifications of the plans. On the back wall of the furthest and deepest cave I found an envelope and a small leather pouch hanging from a nail. The envelope contained a letter from the king which read:

My Dear Captain: If you have made it thus far, you will have realized that your caves have been completed to your specifications. I sincerely hope that your dreams of making fine wine will become a reality in the not too distant future and that we might, some time, find the occasion to share in a bottle or two. Respectfully yours, G.

P.S. As a token of our gratitude and friendship, I offer this amulet. It is of royal provenance and will forever signify its bearer as a friend of our tribe.

I never saw the king again and know not his fate, nor that of his tribe. It pleases
me, however, when I gaze upon the luminous lavender silhouette of Mt. St. Helena at sunset, to think that he and his men took my advice and are burrowed into
the hillside, content in their new surroundings.

By my hand,
Capt. Gustave Niebaum
Eagle's Nook
St. Helena, California
29 June 1901

P. S. One last occurrence should be noted here, one which remained a mystery to
me for some time. Several years ago a large barrel of Charbono wine was stolen from the aging caves here at Eagle's Nook. In its place was a leather pouch
filled with gold nuggets, the worth of which far exceeded the value of the wine. I
reported the theft to Sheriff Dunlap and turned the leather pouch and gold over
to him for use in his investigation. After pondering the theft for some time,
it finally occurred to me that, with their predilection for procuring what
they desired without first obtaining an agreement of sale, the details of the
disappearance of the wine were much aligned with the habits of the little
ones. Shortly thereafter, I informed Sheriff Dunlap the case had been resolved to
my satisfaction and he reluctantly returned the pouch of gold (I say "reluctantly"
because I would not reveal the identity of the so-called "thieves," much to his
consternation – so much so that he insisted on keeping the investigation open
and, to my knowledge, it remains so as of this writing).

Afterword

As I mentioned in the preface to this book, this story contains many things that actually happened, some of them quite strange. I've already written that Gustave Niebaum (1842 - 1908) was a real person – a Finnish sea captain who founded one of the most famous wineries in the Napa Valley in 1880. What I didn't tell you was that my own grandfather, Nels Sinnes (1894 -1975), was also a Finnish sea captain. When I was a pre-teen in the early 1960s, I was often parked at my grandparent's house in San Francisco while my parents were away. It was a typical San Francisco house with a garage on the ground floor and the house built above it. When I was at their house, I loved exploring my grandfather's dimly lit, dusty, workbench which ran the entire length of one side of the garage. It was much more than a mere, utilitarian workbench: it was a record of my grandfather's seafaring life. Among the hand tools, with carved monograms on their wooden handles, there were sepia-toned postcards of far-away places, calendars from decades I knew nothing about, business cards with foreign names and addresses, all layered and arranged just so. I used to pull up stool and just sit there, absorbing the dense collage in front of me.

One day when I was sitting at the workbench, my grandfather came down to the basement and wanted to know what I was doing. I started asking him questions about this postcard or that wooden box with the Chinese writing on it when, from out of nowhere, he produced a falling-apart notebook and handed it to me.

"Here. You can have this, but don't tell anyone you have it. I was supposed to have burned it after the war."

"What is it?"

"It's the log of the *S. S. Samoa* from when I was its master. I've torn out the pages that could get you in trouble."

Well that was something – the log of a ship that my grandfather was captain of, that was supposed to have been burned, with missing pages that could have gotten me in trouble!

I immediately took it upstairs to try and figure out what was so important about it that it should have been burned. Page after page of my grandfather's meticulous, beautiful handwriting citing the date, latitude and longitude of the ships location, and instructions for avoiding this submerged sandbar and that perilous current. But no clue to what might have been on the missing pages.

With the advent of the computer and the web, some 50 years later I was finally able to solve the mystery – namely, that the *S. S. Samoa* had been torpedoed by a Japanese submarine off the coast of Northern California shortly after the attack on Pearl Harbor in December 1941. As luck would have it (and there was a great deal of luck involved) both the ship, it's crew, including my grandfather, survived. It's quite a story, one which I'll save for another day. Although it's not directly related, I can't help feel that the experience of being given that mysterious ship's log somehow fed into the next one, which was truly weird.

The ship's log my grandfather gave me.

It was May of 1980 and we were on a family vacation in Kauai – my then wife and I, and our one-year-old daughter, who was teething, not napping and very grumpy. So grumpy, in fact, we almost packed it in and returned home. Quite accidentally we discovered that as soon as she was put in her car seat in the rental car she would fall asleep and, more importantly, stay asleep as long as the car was in motion. So we devised a schedule, taking turns driving our grumpy daughter around Kauai so she would sleep and allow the other parent a little free time to enjoy the sun and some swimming.

One day, when it was my turn, I found myself driving without any destination in mind, daughter asleep in the back seat. Without knowing where I was, I came upon a turnabout with one of those historical markers at the side of the pavement. The historical market explained that what I was looking at below me was the 'Alekoko (Menehune) Fishpond. Basically it looked like a large pond with rock walls. The marker went on to explain that legend says "the Menehune Fishpond was built by the Menehune who passed the rocks hand to hand. They were said to have completed this task in a single night." While I was standing there taking in the sight, the entire story contained in The Silverado Journals – beginning, middle and end – in great detail, was deposited in my brain. Bang! One minute it was not there and the next, it was there, fully formed. And if you're reading this after reading the book, the story you've read is just as it was received by my brain. I'd love to know where it came from but I'm guessing I'll never know.

I was working on this story on my 34th birthday, back in 1986. I opened the *San Francisco Chronicle* and saw this story:

To say I was surprised is to put it mildly. I took it as a sign that I might – or

27-Inch-Tall Horse Stolen in Sonoma

By Birney Jarvis

Sonoma County sheriff's deputies are searching for a thief who was low enough to snatch a 27-inch-tall horse.

The victim, a year-old black filly named Sweet & Fancy, was apparently snatched from a barn at the Li'l Horse Ranch near Petaluma early Tuesday morning.

"She's such a sweet little horse," lamented Sami Scheuring, who with her veterinarian husband owns a herd of 50 pedigreed miniature horses. "Why, her legs are just the size of broom handles. She's a little doll."

Sweet & Fancy weighs 75 pounds and stands 27 inches tall at the shoulders. Her feet, which were unshod, are 1½ inches in diameter, and she was last seen wearing a red horse blanket.

Mrs. Scheuring speculated that the thieves took Sweet & Fancy because she had just had a haircut and looked especially nice compared with the other tiny horses with their long, shaggy winter coats. The missing horse is valued at $5000.

The Scheurings' dog, Lacey, a miniature poodle, failed to foil the abduction, which apparently happened while the family slept.

The Scheurings' 45-acre ranch is on Old Lakeville Highway near state Highway 37.

Ron Scheuring, who has a small-animals veterinary practice in Mill Valley, said the horse thief did not need a trailer to transport his prey. Miniature horses are easy to pick up and tuck in the back seat of a car, and travel well in dog cages of the type used on airplanes.

The couple used just such transportation to fly one of their herd to Rome last fall for a television appearance, "and he seemed to enjoy it quite a bit," the veterinarian said.

The animals are used as pets and for show purposes. Like all horses, they trace their ancestry back to Eohippus, a small animal that lived 55 million years ago and was 10 to 20 inches tall.

The Scheurings' horses come from a line of miniature horses bred in Argentina 200 years ago. The little beasts were also bred in Europe in the 16th or 17th century as pets for royalty. Later, they hauled coal in mines.

Miniature horses grow as tall as 33 inches at the shoulder. At birth, they weigh as little as 15 pounds. Although they are too small for a person to ride, they are sometimes used in surrey races, Scheuring said. They have a life span of about 30 years.

A $500 reward has been offered for information leading to the return of Sweet & Fancy. Breeders and horse clubs also have been alerted to keep an eye out for her.

"These horses will be watched closely from now on," said Sami Scheuring. "I'm not vindictive at all, I just want Sweet & Fancy back."

Sami Scheuring trained Lady Natasha, half-sister of kidnap victim

might not – be on the right path, but at least I was on a path that was rooted in the real world. A few days later, the newspaper reported that the horse had been returned just as mysteriously as it had been stolen. That said, I felt sure I knew where it had been.

And, many years ago, I actually got a fortune cookie with the message "A legacy, no matter how obscure, will soon be yours." It was so mysterious that I kept it and, in fact, still have it in a drawer of my roll-top desk. Like Nick, I figured my "obscure legacy" had something to do with my grandfather's ship's log with the missing pages. I still think that. Or it could have had something to do with the fact that my father (also a sea captain, like my grandfather) once discovered stowaways aboard his ship when he docked in Hawaii. Instead of gnomes, they were two teenage brothers who had crawled into a crate when my dad's ship left San Francisco. As a kid, that story left an impression on me – is that what echoed back to me when I stood there looking at the Menehune Fishpond? I have no idea. The world works in mysterious ways.

Acknowledgements

For some of us, it takes a village to write a book like this. I'd like to thank my advance readers – my daughter Brooke, Tim Wolfe, Gene Lyerla, Kelly O'Hara, Gail Kenna, Anne Carey, and Jane Dornbush – for their time and valuable observations. Extra helpings of thanks go to Patty Langer for her dogged insistence on keeping it real and Amy Troutner whose sharp eyes found those last remaining, elusive typos. Real friends, all.

This book was so long in the making, it had a cast of editors. Many thanks to Robyn Brode Orsini, Jesse Wood, and especially Michele Amendola, for their important input and for making me look better as a writer.

Thank you Sandy Cooper for your technical expertise and experience. What a fortuitous meeting! And to Dorothy Smith and her valuable advice on pushing this project over the finish line.

Special thanks to Sean Behrens – an early reader of the manuscript – for his keen input and good ideas for how to make the story better. Your advice was very much appreciated, as is your friendship.

Over the years several people were incredibly important in seeing this story come to light. Don Mathews, Mike Bergin, Bob Kaufman, I couldn't have done this without your support. Thank you from the bottom of my heart.

Last, but in no way least, to Alan Freeland – gentleman, scholar, and forever the Prince of the City – I can't thank you enough for your long-time support and advice. Your encouraging words went a long way in keeping this project afloat.

acorts@me.com

About This Book

The body text of this book is set in Baskerville Regular. The typeface in the journal entries and illustration captions is my own printing, transformed into a digital typeface using Calligraphr (Calligraphr.com). The color illustrations are watercolors with ink accents. The pen-and-ink illustrations within the journal were created with a black Staedtler 0.5 pigment liner. *The Silverado Trail* was designed and composed on a Macintosh, using InDesign software.